SINNERS ANONYMOUS · BOOK ONE

SINNERS
anonymous

SOMME SKETCHER

Sinners Anonymous

Copyright © 2021 by Somme Sketcher

All rights reserved.

No portion of this book may be reproduced in any form without written permission from the publisher or author, except as permitted by U.S. copyright law.

This novel is entirely a work of fiction. The names, characters and incidents portrayed in it are the work of the author's imagination. Any resemblance to actual persons, living or dead, events or localities is entirely coincidental.

Cover Designer: The Pretty Little Design Co.

Editor: Light Hand Editing

A NOTE FROM
Somme

Dear reader,

Thank you for picking up a copy of Sinners Anonymous! I hope you love reading it as much as I loved writing it.

Before you dive in, you should know that this book is a **dark romance.** There are several triggers, including talk of suicide and sexual assault. Please read at your own risk.

Love,
Somme x

TABLE OF CONTENTS

Title Page
Copyright
A Note from Somme
Prologue
Chapter One

Chapter Two
Chapter Three
Chapter Four
Chapter Five
Chapter Six
Chapter Seven
Chapter Eight
Chapter Nine
Chapter Ten
Chapter Eleven
Chapter Twelve
Chapter Thirteen
Chapter Fourteen
Chapter Fifteen
Chapter Sixteen
Chapter Seventeen
Chapter Eighteen
Chapter Nineteen
Chapter Twenty
Chapter Twenty-One
Chapter Twenty-Two
Chapter Twenty-Three
Chapter Twenty-Four
Chapter Twenty-Five
Chapter Twenty-Six

Chapter Twenty-Seven
Chapter Twenty-Eight
Chapter Twenty-Nine
Chapter Thirty
Chapter Thirty-One
Chapter Thirty-Two
Chapter Thirty-Three
Chapter Thirty-Four
Chapter Thirty-Five
Chapter Thirty-Six
Chapter Thirty-Seven

"Every saint has a past; every sinner has a future."
- *Oscar Wilde*

NINE YEARS
Earlier

Angelo

Visconti women love a pissing match at funerals. It doesn't matter whether the deceased is their mama or their twelfth aunt twice-removed, it's always a fucking competition to see who can mourn the hardest.

Whimpers, sobs, sniffles. The ones muffled by a borrowed handkerchief or dabbed away with a crumbling Kleenex, I can almost tolerate. It's the cries on the other end of the scale that make me want to dive in the dirt with the dead. The shrieks, the wails, the screams.

I drag my gaze away from Bishop Francis and pin my Great Aunt Esme with a blistering glare.

The fucking gurgles.

"*Gesù Cristo,*" my cousin, Tor, mutters from the pew behind me. "I slit a bastard's throat last week. He made the exact same noise."

There's a ripple down my row, and I glance left to my brother, Rafe. He's biting down on his bottom lip to suppress a snigger. He catches my eye and cocks a brow as if to say, *what? It was funny.* Next to him, my other brother, Gabe, stares straight ahead, jaw steeled.

Bishop Francis drones on, chipping away at the liturgy. As Aunt Esme's gurgles get louder, a second cousin who's come over from Sicily especially for the occasion decides she won't be outdone. She lets out a screech before squeezing her way out of her pew, click-clacking down the aisle toward the altar, and letting out a wail that sounds like a deflating balloon as she sinks to her knees in front of the coffins.

I can't even remember her name.

Apologies muttered in clipped Italian. Feverish glances in my direction. A male cousin is on her heels and drags her back to her seat, lifting the hem of her lace veil to half scold, half comfort her.

But Bishop Francis has lost his train of thought. Now he's stammering over his words and shuffling papers, and behind me, I can feel the mood shift.

I get it. Roman Catholic funerals are excruciatingly long. Longer when there are two bodies to bury, and one of them is a deacon. The wooden pews are getting harder by the second, and minds are drifting away from grief and towards the Grand Visconti Hotel over in Devil's Cove, where the wake will take place.

Nobody throws a party like a recently deceased Visconti, let alone two of them.

The Bishop glances down to the front pew, meeting my eye. I give him a small nod as permission to wrap it up. No one in this church wants to get out of here faster than I do. He clears his throat and turns his attention back to the clergy.

"Dearly beloved, the family requests that you join them in the courtyard for the committal."

Eyes filled with pity and unspent tears land on me. My brothers and I stand, and with one last lingering look towards the coffins, I swallow the knot in my throat, roll my shoulders, and lead the way to the back of the church.

I stride through the sea of whispers, eyes fixed on the wrought iron doors ahead.

Nearly there. Nearly over.

My cell buzzes in my breast pocket. I hope it's my assistant letting me know the jet is refueled and ready to take me back to London.

An altar boy heaves open the doors, and for a moment, I stand on the steps and close my eyes, feeling the icy wind slap my cheeks, the frost nipping my nose. The weather has always been more extreme up here on the cliff than it is down in the town below; the winds harsher and the rain heavier. Mama, ever the optimist, would remind us that while it was colder in the wintertime, it was always warmer in the summer, too.

Life is all about balance, Angelo. The good always cancels out the bad.

When I open my eyes, Rafe is standing on one side of me, Gabe on the other. They both follow my gaze up to the low-hanging clouds, their bellies pregnant with the incoming storm.

Rafe lets out a hiss. "What a beautiful day to bury our parents."

Gabe says nothing.

We take the gravel path that snakes through the tombstones, until we are standing just yards from the edge of the cliff. There are two rectangular holes cut out of the muddy grass.

My fists clench.

Side by side. Together for eternity. There will be a sanitized version of their love story etched onto a joint headstone. I think of all the mid-morning joggers and wayward tourists that will stop to read it and believe it's their daily reminder that love exists.

Meanwhile, the sinful truth is buried six feet underneath them.

No matter what romantic prose is chiseled into a marble headstone, true love doesn't exist. It's nothing but hope in a different form. A concept for the poor and the powerless to latch onto when there's nothing else.

My eyes turn to the tide of suits and lace filtering through the graveyard toward us. Made men know love doesn't exist. Uncles and cousins grip their wives' and girlfriends' wrists instead of holding their hands. They offer clipped comfort in the hope they'll shut up, all while checking their watches, calculating when they'll be able to slip away to their whores, loosen their ties, and forget about their duties to the Cosa Nostra.

Visconti men in particular don't fall in love. Because falling suggests it was accidental, and everything this family does is cold and calculated.

A shaky hand grips my shoulder.

"Alonso would love this resting place," Uncle Alfredo says, voice choked with emotion. "Now, he can look up at his church and down at his town. He built both of them from nothing, you know?"

Staring down at the pile of dirt that is about to weigh down my mother, I offer him a curt nod. He pats me on the back and takes a step back. I'll give Uncle Alfredo one thing, he knows how to take a hint.

Mama is lowered first and I find myself sinking with her; the only woman I'll ever get on my knees for. My balled fists disappear into the mud. Another hand rests on my shoulder, and by the glint of the citrine ring, I know it's Rafe's.

"Heavenly Father, because you have chosen to call our sister Maria Visconti from this life to yourself, we commit her body to the earth where it will take its final resting place," Bishop Francis booms, his words quickly snatched away by the wind.

White heat seeps through my blood, and there's that bitterness again, burning the back of my throat. It tastes of secret and sin, and no matter how much whiskey I sink on the plane ride home or thereafter, I know I'll never get rid of it.

"...Ashes to ashes, dust to dust..." the Bishop drones on.

Incense burns, wisps of smoke merging with the morning fog. Then come the roses. Blood red and full of thorns, landing with a dull thud on the mahogany lid. Rafe crouches next to me, brings his fist up to his mouth, and blows. With a flick of his wrist, a pair of dice scatters across the lid, rolling off the curve and falling into the gap between the coffin and the soil.

"For my Lady Luck," he rasps, running a hand through his hair. "Good luck up there, Mama."

Gabe sinks to his knees too. Instead of throwing in the rose in his hand, he leans over, plants his lips to the wood and mutters something long and heartfelt.

It's the most I've seen him speak in years.

The flowers and the cards stop falling, and eyes turn to me, expectantly.

Slowly, I dig something out of my pocket. The wrapper crinkles in my hand, and I place it carefully on the coffin so it doesn't break.

There's a small laugh next to me.

"A fortune cookie," Rafe says weakly, a sad smile stretching his lips. "Why didn't I think of that?"

Mama believed in fate as much as she believed in God. But while she was content having never seen or heard the big man in the sky, she constantly sought out proof that fate existed. She searched for it everywhere. Five-dollar tarot readings by fortune tellers at the fair, the little eight-ball key ring attached to her house keys.

And goddamn fortune cookies. Mama lived by them; she'd crack one open after dinner every night, gently peeling out the little strip of paper like it was a treasured artifact. She'd find meaning in whatever vague prophecy it contained, then work on tweaking and molding her life around it.

It was a fortune cookie that had brought her from New York to Devil's Dip, Washington, in the first place.
Seek hope where the air is salty and the cliffs are steep.
She loved this damn town because she thought it was her destiny to start a life here. I wonder, whether hunched over in a fortune teller's wagon or with the shake of her eight-ball, she ever saw that this town would be the death of her, too.

My father is lowered next. There's a purple veil draped over his coffin and his green and gold robes are folded on top. The sobs start again, louder than they were for my mama. I rise to my feet and turn to the sea, feeling every pair of Visconti eyes burning into my back.

I know what they are all thinking. The death of my father marks a new era for the Cosa Nostra, and it starts with me.

The new capo of Devil's Dip.

As I stare out to the fishing boats and the cargo ships bobbing over the waves below, I realize I can feel other eyes on me, too. I turn my head right, my gaze stretching across the graveyard and to the other side of the small public road, where a crowd huddles under the bus shelter.

My jaw locks.

Fucking locals. Some are sitting on the bench, others are leaning against the phone booth with their arms crossed. All are watching my parents be lowered into the ground, and judging by their glares and brightly-colored clothes, none of them are here to pay their respects.

I lock eyes with an old man. His face is leathery and weather-worn, just like all the workers who have spent a lifetime fighting the elements down in the port below. He's wearing a brick-red coat and a yellow scarf, and after a few moments, he pulls his lips back to form a shit-eating grin.

My father always said my temper was different from my brothers. Their anger burns slow like a candle and is easy to extinguish, whereas mine is like a firework. Light my fuse and I explode mere seconds later, with no thought to the irreparable damage I will cause. *You're vicious, son.*

A great trait for a capo to have.

Not.

"Angelo, put the damn gun away," Uncle Alberto hisses in my ear, suddenly appearing beside me.

I don't even remember pulling it out of my waistband, let alone pointing it at the smug bastard across the road. But now the crowd is scattering like a shaken flock of pigeons, mouthing panicky words that are lost in the sound of the crashing waves and wind.

I glance behind me. Bishop Francis has stopped talking, the Visconti women have stopped sobbing, and everyone is staring at me in either sympathy, anger, or confusion. Everyone except for Rafe and Gabe, who have their hands hovering over the guns in their waistbands. Rafe catches my eye and gives a slight shake of his head.

Not a good idea, bro.

Despite standing a few feet from my dead parents with a damn gun in my hand, I huff out a laugh.

If Angelo jumped off the cliff, would you do it too?

Mama used to ask my brothers that every time I'd lure them into some stupid shit when we were younger. Burning down the old barn down the road, or cutting the brakes on our bikes to see who could get from our house on top of the hill to the lake at the bottom the fastest.

Their answer hasn't changed. Yes.

"They're here to make sure he's really dead," I growl.

"No, they are here to catch a glimpse of the man who will replace him." Uncle Alberto steps in front of me, blocking my view of the locals piling into trucks and cars, and grips my jaw. His eyes are a cocktail of pride and sorrow. "I can't wait to see what you do, Vicious. You're going to make your father proud."

My jaw muscle flexes against his thumb pad, and eventually, he lets go. With a strong hand on my shoulder, he guides me back to the graveside, and Bishop Francis takes this as his sign to carry on.

More flowers in the grave. Uncle Alfredo slides in a bottle of special-edition *Smugglers Club* whiskey, and, next to me, Uncle Alberto takes the Rolex off his wrist and tosses it in. "I won it off the old bastard years ago. Your old man was never good at poker." He cranes his neck to look at Rafe. "I don't know where you got your talent from, kid."

It's my turn. I don't sink to my knees like I did with my mama; instead, I lean over the coffin, his black rosary in my hand. The beaded chain is wrapped around my wrist twice, the cross swaying in the wind like a pendulum.

He never took it off.

Until I took it off for him.

I pause, curl the cross into the palm of my hand and slip it back into the pocket of my slacks. When I look up, my cousin Dante is glaring at me from the other side of the grave.

With the committal over, earth falls down on my mama with heavy thuds, each *slap* sounding more final than the last. I turn back to the sea, just as the first drops of rain start to fall.

I bring the rosary back out of my pocket and to my lips. "Forgive me Father," I mutter into the cold metal as a raindrop lands on my cheek, "for I have sinned."

Rafe appears beside me. Gabe strides over soon after. Behind us, everyone is hurrying to the row of waiting cars, shielding themselves from the rain under umbrellas and hymn books.

A strike of lightning flashes across the horizon.

God trying to smite me down.

"It's like that scene in *The Lion King*," Rafe murmurs into the collar of his shirt, tucking his hands into his pockets. "Whatever the light touches is your kingdom now, or something like that. It's all yours, bro."

I look down at my supposed kingdom. The creaky port on the left and the small town nestled into the dip of the cliff to the right. Then I turn to look further down the coast, to the darkness of Devil's Hollow and then to Devil's Cove, which, even through the mist and rain, is lit up like a fucking Christmas tree.

"I don't want it."

The words slip from my tongue like I knew they would.

Rafe slaps my back, hard, like we're not standing on the edge of a cliff on a very windy morning. "Big shoes to fill, my brother. But if anyone is up for the job, it's Vicious Visconti."

"My flight to London is in twenty minutes and I'm not coming back."

The silence pierces through the wind. It's deafening. Eventually, I meet the hard gaze of my brother, squaring my jaw under his scrutiny. He cocks a brow, eyes searching for a trace of amusement on my features, but, unlike him, I don't joke.

Gabe, as always, says nothing.

"You're not coming back to Devil's Dip?"

I'm not coming back to this life.

I don't explain. Instead, I nod toward the lone car still on the side of the road. Rafe's driver rolls down the window and stares at us impatiently. Next to it, Gabe's Harley is parked under a tree.

"Go to the wake. I'll catch up with you another time."

The vein in Rafe's temple pounds, his glare burning with all of the questions he won't ask. Turning back to the sea, I slip the rosary back into my pocket and drag a knuckle through my wet beard. A few moments later, the soggy crunch of gravel underfoot tells me my brothers have left. Only when the roar of Gabe's motorcycle fades out of earshot do I turn back to my parents' graves.

One of the gravediggers stops piling soil on top of my mother. He leans his weight against the handle of his shovel and stares up at me, warily.

As I pass, I slap a brick of notes against his muddy chest.

"Dig her up," I growl. "My mama doesn't belong here."

CHAPTER
One

Rory

"My name is Rory Carter and I do bad things."

The wind snatches the words from my lips, carrying them away from the cliff edge and over the choppy sea.

I like to do that sometimes. Say it aloud when I'm alone just to see how the truth tastes.

I'm not a criminal. I just do *bad things*. Morally questionable things. Spiteful, revengeful things. I didn't used to be like this, but now there's a stain on my soul so dark and stubborn that there's nothing I can do to scrub it away. So, I don't bother trying anymore. Instead, I *confess*.

I take a step closer to the edge, holding my breath when pebbles scatter under my sneakers and disappear into the raging Pacific below. The wind howls like a wolf, as if warning me of the incoming storm. From up here, I can see it looming in the distance, the black and gray smudges hanging low above the sea.

A bitter laugh escapes me. It was always going to come to this. Me, standing on the edge of Devil's Dip's highest cliff and thinking bad thoughts. Which is ironic, because, for the first time in three years, I'm doing a *good thing*. A completely selfless, self-sacrificing act that nobody in their right darn mind would do if they weren't desperate.

I twist the ring around my finger and swallow the knot in my throat.

If I was to...*jump*. What would it feel like? Would it hurt? Would everything go black? I don't believe in God, or heaven and hell, but I wonder—would I still scream a confession as I broke the surface of the water, in a last-bid attempt to save my soul?

Balling my fists and stuffing them into the pockets of my hoodie, I lift my toe and inch it farther toward the edge, until there's nothing underneath my foot but air.

Adrenaline zaps down my spine, and for a moment, I close my eyes and stick out my tongue, tasting the salt and moisture and danger. I let the wind take control of my body.

Is this the closest I'll ever get to being free?

Then I taste something else. Something thick and bitter.

"You hoping to fall, or fly?"

Oh, sparrow.

My eyes snap open and I scurry away from the edge, feeling like a naughty schoolgirl caught doing something she shouldn't.

Heart hammering, I twist my head to follow the voice, and my eyes lock on a man.

He stands less than a foot away. Sharp suit and an even sharper cheekbone, from what I can see of his profile. It becomes even more defined when he slips a cigarette between his lips and inhales deeply.

Smoke. That's what I could taste.

He's staring out to the sea as if he never said anything at all. Maybe he didn't. Jesus, how long has he been here? And where did he come from? Licking my weather-beaten lips, I glance to the road behind me, which runs parallel to the graveyard. A black sports car is parked haphazardly, the front wheels mounting the edge of an old tombstone.

The initial shock loses its grip on my shoulders, leaving room for another feeling. Panic. The last person I should be standing on an edge of a cliff with is a man who parks like *that*. Because if he has no respect for the dead, then he certainly doesn't respect the living.

Maybe he's the grim reaper?

I can't help but huff out a laugh at the stupid thought.

My eyes drag back to him. Well, he *is* dressed all in black. Just an expensive-looking coat instead of a cloak, and he holds a cigarette instead of a scythe. The cherry glows red against the gloomy sky as he takes another deep drag.

I tuck a wayward curl back under the hood of my sweater and draw the cord tighter under my chin. I should go. Not just because this man gives me the creeps, but because Alberto has eyes and ears everywhere. Max, my escort, isn't a snitch, but he'll be back any minute and—

"Because if you're hoping to fall..." He takes a deliberate step toward the edge and my heart leaps into my throat. He has the confidence of someone simply peering over the side of a swimming pool and not into the raging sea a hundred and fifty feet below. "You've got a long way to go."

Push him.

The thought rattles around my head, unwanted and unsavory, and I wish I could pour acid over it. *What is wrong with me?* Instead of thinking poisonous thoughts, I should tell him to step back, or grab his arm, because that's what my fingers are twitching to do. But I don't. Maybe it's the fear freezing the blood in my veins, or maybe it's the morbid curiosity haunting my soul, but I stay still and silent.

I stare in sick fascination at his leather wingtips teetering on the edge. Not only does this man not respect the dead, he doesn't respect *death*. Because if he takes half a step forward, or a sudden gust of wind blows the wrong way, he'll...*disappear*.

My fists clench. My pulse thumps in my temples so loud it drowns out the roar of the wind.

What would I do if he fell?

The question leaves my head as quickly as it arrives. Of course, I already know what I'd do. I'd cross the graveyard, round the church, and slip into my favorite phone box across the road. Then, instead of calling the Coast Guard, I'd dial the number I know better than my own, and I'd confess that I'd done nothing to help.

Because that's what compulsive sinners do.

Only when he finally takes a step back, do I realize I've been holding my breath. I let out a stale lungful of air, relieved that I *feel* relieved and not disappointed. It means my poisonous thoughts didn't win this time.

I glance up at his profile, just as he takes a final drag on his cigarette and flicks it into the sea. And then he turns and gazes right into my eyes, as if he knew exactly where to find them.

My heart hitches.

Whew, falcon. He's handsome.

Piercing green eyes and a squared-off jaw as sharp as his cheekbones. That's all my muddy brain has time to register before he turns beside me, his back now facing the gloomy horizon.

My breathing shallows. He's too close. Dangerously close, and now I feel like I have one foot over the edge again. I stand next to him, shoulder to shoulder, trying to remain still. Trying not to breathe too hard or fidget too much. Trying to ignore how the pressure of his arm burns through my raincoat, or how the ghost of his cigarette entwined with the oaky notes in his aftershave make my nipples tighten.

He stoops low to meet my ear and I brace for impact.

"Suicide is a sin," he rasps, his stubble grazing my cheek. "But Devil's Dip has a way of making you want to throw yourself over the edge, doesn't it?"

And then he's gone, those wingtips crunching over the gravel toward his car.

My chest rises and falls as my heart fights to remember its natural rhythm.

I stand there, stupefied and staring out to sea, until I hear the purr of an engine and the screeching of tires. Then with a shaky exhale I sink to my knees into the mud.

Who on earth is he, and what on earth was...that?

Once my heartbeat slows and the adrenaline loses its sharpness, my brain makes room for other observations. Like, the time. Oh, and the fact that it's *freezing* up here. I glance at my watch and mutter a bird-word. Max is picking me up from the front of the old church in less than three minutes, so if I want to make my usual phone call, then I better get it together.

I turn my back to the cliff edge, and the dangerous allure it holds, and trudge through the overgrown path that cuts through the graveyard. I pass the church and cross the road, tutting at the black tire marks on the asphalt, and slip into the phone booth next to the bus stop.

Tucking the receiver between my shoulder and cheek, I dial the number.

The line rings three times, then it clicks into the voicemail service.

"You have reached Sinners Anonymous," a woman's robotic voice says. "Please leave your sin after the tone."

After the long beep, I take a deep breath and let my soul bleed.

CHAPTER
Two

Rory

I F THESE DINING ROOM walls could talk, I bet they'd beg Alberto Visconti to shut up.

Just like every Friday night, he sits next to me at the head of the table, one hand curled around his whiskey glass the other weighing down my thigh like an anchor.

I once overheard a pool boy refer to him as *Anecdote Alberto*. As the head of the Devil's Cove *Cosa Nostra*, I've heard him called a lot of things—capo, boss, Big Al—but Anecdote Alberto definitely seems to be the most fitting. It didn't take me long to learn how to drown out his stories, but still, the baritone of his voice vibrates against my eardrums.

A server casts a shadow over my place setting. "The Merlot, *signorina*?"

"She'll have just the one tonight," Alberto growls, cutting his story short. "I won't have a repeat of last week."

Silence. The type that stretches over hills and canyons, not just across the long dining table. I can feel Tor's amused grin heating one of my cheeks and Dante's blistering glare scorching the other.

At last Friday's dinner, I figured out that if my wine ever dipped below the curve of the glass, a server would top it up in under thirty seconds. The conversation was so darn boring that I tested this theory a few too many times, and after dessert, I stood up, buckled on my stilettos, and pulled down the velvet curtain I'd grabbed onto to stop myself from falling. As if the copper curtain rail bouncing off my head wasn't punishment enough, Alberto is limiting my alcohol intake like I'm a child.

Squirming under the attention, I force a smile and nod to the server, like I totally agree with my fiance's decision. When he's gone, I stifle a sigh. The first—and last—time I sighed in front of Alberto, he yanked on my ponytail so hard my eyes watered.

I learned quickly it's better to vent my frustrations silently, usually by balling my fists until my fingernails carve half-moons into my palms.

Oh, and spitting in his mouthwash.

Alberto continues to regale us with the story about the time he challenged Al Capone's son to a sword fight, and I turn to gaze down the length of the table, deliberately avoiding eye contact with everyone sitting around it.

Tonight, it's just immediate family, but the table is decorated like there's a chance the Queen of England might swing by for an appetizer. Silky black table cloth, more silverware than I know the use for, and ornate flower displays that sit nail-bitingly close to dancing candle flames. In front of the French doors leading out to the beach, a pianist sits quietly behind the grand piano, waiting for Alberto to click his fingers, which signals the start of dinner service.

How the hell did I end up here?

Two-and-a-half months ago, I sank to my knees on the doorstep of Alberto's white colonial mansion and begged for mercy. Now, I'm living a life I don't recognize; playing a side character in a story I don't understand.

Everyone on the Devil's Coast knows the Visconti family because they own almost everything on it. Every bar, hotel, restaurant, and casino in Devil's Cove. The *Smugglers Club* whiskey factory in Devil's Hollow. The one corner of this coast their reach hasn't touched is my humble hometown of Devil's Dip.

And if Alberto keeps his side of the deal, it never will.

Taking a sip of water, I glance up and lock eyes with Dante Visconti. He's Alberto's oldest son, his underboss, and the coast's bigger jerk. He's tall, dark, and as much as I hate to admit it, very handsome. Everything about him is chiseled, including that scowl permanently carved into his forehead. His gaze darkens, and I know exactly what he's about to say, because he says it aloud at every Friday night dinner without fail.

"The head of the table is for the underboss and the *consigliere*," he growls quietly, ignoring Alberto's monologue. He squeezes the napkin next to his plate. "Not my father's plaything."

And there it is.

"Aw, come off it, bro," His brother Tor drawls beside him, shooting me a wink. "Aurora's not a teenager, she's twenty-one. Old enough to drink, just not old enough to handle it."

On cue, my Merlot arrives in a glass barely bigger than a thimble. Embarrassment creeps across my chest, and instinctively, my eyes drop to the steak knife laid out neatly in front of me.

Tempting.

But instead of using the Viscontis' silverware as a weapon, I do what I've become accustomed to: plastering on a fake smile and biting down my bitterness.

"Big Al keeping you on a tight leash tonight, hmm?" Tor says, lips twitching. Without waiting for an answer, he yanks a pack of cigarettes out of his jacket, pulls one out, and tucks it into the crook of his mouth. Slapping the thigh of the blond next to him, he grunts, "Come on doll, let's go for a smoke."

He saunters across the dining room and throws open the French doors, letting in an icy chill that rattles the window panes and raises goosebumps along my arms. His date trots after him like a lost puppy.

I knew of Tor Visconti long before his father put a rock on my finger. Every girl on the Devil's Coast knows Tor, some more intimately than others. Plump lips, tousled hair, and a smile that could melt the Arctic. And then there's that stupid nose stud that glints every time he tips his head back to sneer at me. He'd look almost feminine if it weren't for all the ink and the fact that his shoulders are the width of a football field.

I take a sip of wine and watch him through the window. I recognize his date as a fellow Devil's Dip girl. She's putting on a polished accent and clinging onto her designer purse like it's a lifeline, but I can see right through her act. I watch as she coils her long blond hair around her finger, giggling at whatever he's saying.

I get it. From the way he smokes his cigarette to the way he wears his suit—unbuttoned collar and a loosened tie—there's an air of rebellion about him that makes girls want to drop their panties. Of course, it helps that he runs the nightlife in Devil's Cove, so even in the unlikely event you don't want to be in his bed, you at least want to be in his clubs. Plus, I see the way he looks at his dates. Gazing at them from underneath those dark, thick lashes as he rakes his teeth over his bottom lip. It's like a silent promise that he'll give them the world. But that's all these girls ever are: dates. They come to dinner once, maybe twice, and then disappear off the face of the planet.

"May I get you anything, *Signor* Visconti?" a server mutters to Alberto, taking advantage of a break in his newest anecdote.

"Smugglers Club. On the rock."

Yes, *rock*. As in, one ice cube. In the short time I've personally known the Viscontis, I've learned two things about them.

The first, is that they aren't just a powerful family, they are in fact, the mafia. Cold-hearted, hot-blooded Sicilian-Americans who live and die by the Glocks tucked into the waistbands of their Armani suits.

The second, is that whatever they want, they get. Including one ice cube in their lowball glass.

"They'll be calling you *Signora* soon."

I turn to Amelia, who's sitting to my left. "I'm sorry?"

Her broad smile softens her sharp features. "*Signora*. See, *Signorina* is the title of an unmarried woman, like "Miss" in English. In just a month, you'll be married, and then you'll become *Signora*." She tucks a silky brown strand behind her ear and grins. "*Signora* Aurora Visconti. It's got quite the ring to it, don't you think?"

The name curdles like milk in my stomach, and if anyone else around this darn table had uttered it, I'd have known they were just trying to get a rise out of me.

But Amelia Visconti: she's different. She's softly spoken and kind and now that I come to think of it, really damn delusional. She's sitting around this table by choice—she married Donatello Visconti, Alberto's second son and *consigliere*. He sits on the other side of her, sifting through paperwork, and, unlike Dante, he couldn't care less that I took my seat at the table.

Donatello is clean in every sense of the word. Sharp suit, short, black hair, and he's probably the only blood-related Visconti that doesn't have a one-way ticket to hell. He and Amelia met at the Devil's Coast Academy when they were tweens, got married the moment they turned eighteen, and have apparently been glued to each other's side for the ten years since. I get the feeling he doesn't really care for the sleeping-with-the-fishes persona Alberto and Dante put out. He has a business degree from Harvard and Amelia is an accountant by trade. Together, they run the legitimate businesses in Devil's Cove. After one too many whiskeys, Alberto once told me he lets Amelia get away with having his son's balls in a vice because she makes the family a bucket-load of money.

I believe it. The *Lonely Planet Guide* calls the Visconti Grand Hotel "the *Burj Al Arab* Of the Pacific Northwest," and there are more Michelin Star restaurants in Devil's Cove per square mile than there are anywhere else in the world.

"Not long to go until the Big Day," Amelia whispers excitedly, nudging me with her elbow.

Unease sinks into the pit of my stomach like a lead balloon.

Amelia may have married a Visconti for love, but I'm sure that's a hell of a lot easier when your husband looks like an Italian Ryan Reynolds. It only takes one look at my fiance to realize that I'm not doing the same.

Alberto Visconti. Sure, he would have been handsome in his hey-day, and if your imagination can't stretch past the leathery skin, shock of white hair, and the enormous gut, then all you have to do is glance at his sons to get an idea of what he would have looked like. I'm sure his first wife married him for love—hell, maybe even his second and third wives, too. But pushing seventy, having unrelenting wealth, and living a life with a target on his back have ruined him.

Oh, and the fact that he's the cruelest man on the Coast.

I settle my eyes on the quilted wallpaper above Dante's head, another sigh brewing quietly under my rib cage.

My life wasn't meant to be like this. The night before my eighteenth birthday, I sat on the dock at the end of our cabin and created a mood board for my five-year-plan, using clippings from my mom's old magazines. I cut out a graduation cap and gown, and next to it stuck a photocopy of my acceptance letter to the Northwestern Aviation Academy. That girl...she was full of hope and had a pure heart. She didn't have bad thoughts and do bad things. She didn't have to call the Sinners Anonymous hotline every week.

What would she think if she saw me now? Dining with monsters.

A monster herself.

I guess I can't even blame Alberto for my sins; I turned nasty years before I met him.

I take a slug of wine and glance back out the French doors, following Tor's date's tinkling laugh. The breeze is still snaking through the gap in the doors, bringing in the smell of cigarette smoke with it. Suddenly, I'm back on the edge of the cliff overlooking Devil's Dip. My body at the mercy of the wind, my right sneaker hovering over nothing but air.

You hoping to fall, or fly?

"Oh, sparrow!" A sharp pain slices across my thigh. I look down and see Alberto has turned his hand over and dragged the faceted gem of his ring across my skin. "What the—"

"Aurora, Dante asked you a question," Alberto says through gritted teeth. His eyes flash like warning signs. "It's rude to ignore somebody when they are talking to you."

I blink, dropping my gaze back to my thigh. Blood seeps to the surface and trickles into a small rivulet toward the hemline of my dress.

This time, I do more than look at the steak knife. My fingers twitch toward it.

No. Not like this. Remember why you're here, Rory.

Forcing the anger deep down in my chest, I grab a napkin, dab it on my fresh wound, then turn my attention to Dante. His amusement is smeared all over his face and my goose, how I hate the way his lip curls into a sneer every time he's forced to look at me.

He throws his arm over the back of Tor's empty chair and cocks a brow.

"We're building a spa retreat on the north headland."

"Uninterrupted views of the sea and nothing else around for miles. The Russian tourists love that shit, especially in winter," Alberto adds, before draining his glass and snapping his fingers for another.

Dante ignores him. "It's a mess up there. Thick forest that'll take months to clear before we can even think about laying down the foundations." He takes a long sip of whiskey, eyes glittering at me over the rim. "But the main issue is these birds. They squawk at all hours, which doesn't fit in with the peaceful vibe we're going for. Hopefully, once we obliterate their habitat and their nests, they'll fuck off on their own accord, but if they don't..."

He trails off, letting his insinuation dangle over the table setting. "Then we'll need a more...*certain* way to get rid of them. Smoke them out or put poison on the forest floor, maybe. Since you're so *passionate* about wildlife, Aurora, I thought perhaps you might have some other suggestions?"

White heat burns through my veins, despite the chill coming in.

I suck in a lungful of air through my nostrils. Dab my bloodied thigh again.

"What bird is it?" I ask as calmly as I can manage.

He thrusts his cell under my nose. "I don't know. One of my men sent me a photo of it. Perhaps you'll recognize it."

I squint at the grainy picture on his phone and feel the blood rush out of my face.

"Dante," I croak. "That's a fruit dove."

"Sounds exotic."

"Exotic? They are near extinction! A protected species—you can't cut down the forest up there! In fact, you'll need to call the Fish and Wildlife Service immediately."

He leans back in his chair, a triumphant grin curling his lips. He's gotten exactly what he wanted out of me—a reaction. But I don't care; my mind is racing, trying to figure out how there could possibly be fruit doves in Devil's Cove. The particular breed in the photo is native to South Australia and Polynesia, regions with humid climates. But then, I also know they can be found in secondary forests—woodland that has regrown after a timber harvest. I know the area he's talking about, and I remember my father telling me it used to be a log farm, long before the Viscontis moved into the Cove and turned it into the Pacific Northwest's answer to Vegas. That, plus the mangroves in the caves closer to Devil's Hollow—

"Nah."

I look up. "Huh?"

Dante throws me a bored expression. "No, I won't be contacting Fish and Wildlife. They are a bunch of tree-hugging hippies just like you—"

"You can't be serious?"

"You've interfered with our building plans enough, don't you think? If it was up to you, the whole of the Devil's Coast would be a goddamn swamp."

Before I can bite back, there's a loud crash from the patio. Dante leaps to his feet, hand brushing over the gun tucked in his waistband. Amelia shrieks and grabs her husband's arm. At the far end of the table, Vittoria lets out a loud sigh, then turns back to her cell.

The French doors fly open and Tor saunters through them, his date's arm slung over his shoulders. She's giggling, wobbling on her heels, her eyes half-lidded.

Alberto mutters something under his breath in Italian.

"Apologies all round," Tor says through a chuckle. "Skyler fell over. She says her heel got caught in the patio slats," he says as he brushes his lips over her hair, "but I say she's had one too many dirty martinis."

With a giggle, Skyler wobbles off in the direction of a bathroom, and Tor sinks back down in his seat.

"Skyler," Dante mutters darkly into the bottom of his glass. " *Gesù Cristo.* That's a stripper name if I've ever heard one." He glances to the swing doors. "She's been to the bathroom three times and we haven't even had our appetizers yet."

"She's probably nervous about being on a date with such a hearthrob," Tor shoots back, throwing me a wink. The one thing that makes Tor slightly less insufferable than Dante is that at least he includes me in his jokes, even when I'm not the brunt of them.

"More like she's trying to see how much powder she can get up her nose before the crab cakes are served. I hope she knows you cut your coke with horse tranquilizer, because I'm not removing her body from the guest bathroom."

Tor's fist thumps the table, anger flashing across his face. "Fuck you. My blow is cleaner than a nun's browser history."

"*Basta,*" Alberto hisses. His voice is low and quiet but it slices through the dining room like a hot knife in butter. His hand finds its way back to my thigh, and the heat of his palm makes my fresh wound burn. "I have had *enough*. This family can't get through one goddamn dinner without arguing. If your mother was still here—"

"If our mother was still here, there wouldn't be a capo chaser sitting opposite me."

Silence.

Tor lets out a low whistle. Amelia's fingers gently brush my forearm, and Alberto groans.

I should sip my wine and smooth down my hair and let the comment go over my head. But being *that girl* doesn't come easy to me.

"A capo chaser?" My eyes dart to the steak knife, then up to Dante's scowl. "What does that mean?"

Donatello drops his files onto the table with a heavy thud. "Dante, don't—"

"It means you're marrying my father because it's the only hope you have of getting out of your peasant town. There's loads of girls like you in Devil's Dip," he spits, jerking his thumb in the direction of the lobby. "I bet Tor's whore is from the same slum as you." Leaning his elbows on the table, he closes the gap between us. The way his eyes dance with pure hatred both terrifies me and excites me at the same time. "You're all the goddamn same. Tits bigger than your IQ and a smile just as fake. You know what I find funny? You've never broken a law in your life, but you're happy to look the other way and spread your legs, as long as your Amex doesn't have a limit, right?"

"Dante," Alberto snarls. "If you say another word, I'll—"

"You'll what?" Dante says sourly, eyes never leaving mine. "Find somebody else to do your job for you?"

Alberto leaps to his feet and Dante follows suit, squaring up to him.

Jesus. I'm still coming to grips with this whole mafia hierarchy thing, but even I know it breaks every Cosa Nostra code to go up against the clan's capo. Even if you're the underboss who pretty much runs the entire business, and even if the capo is your drunk, womanizing father.

The air swirls hot and heavy with unspoken gripes and inflated egos. This is bigger than me. Balling my fists, I dig my nails into my palms and mentally scream a bird-word. I'm too sober for this, and what's worse, *dinner hasn't even started yet.*

It's going to be a long night.

Eventually, Donatello breaks the tension. "All right, all right," he sighs, scraping back his chair and rounding the table to wedge himself between them. "Let's all calm down and talk about this tomorrow." He pries his father's whiskey glass from his hand and sets it on the table. "We've all had too much to drink and said things we didn't mean."

The three of them lower their voices and start muttering in harsh Italian among themselves. Tor catches my eye and smirks, then slinks outside for another smoke.

There's a nudge against my leg. "Aurora? Are you okay?"

I turn to meet Amelia's kind gaze and realize I'm not.

This is not me.

I'm not the dumb, gold-digging blond everyone in this family thinks I am, and I'm sick of playing that part. I'm sick of these stupid high heels and short dresses that Alberto forces me to wear. I'm sick of the sneers and eye rolls and the insults from people who wouldn't pee on me if I was on fire. The escorts and itineraries and the sleepless nights staring at the gilded ceiling of Alberto's bedroom, wondering if his fat belly will suffocate me when he finally clambers on top of me on our wedding night.

I hate the Viscontis.

And I hate that I have no choice but to suck it up and smile.

"Aurora?"

And I'm sick of being called Aurora. My name is Rory.

"Let's put this down, shall we?" Amelia slips her hand over mine and gently pries the steak knife from my grip. She flashes me a pitying smile and says, "Don't listen to Dante. He and his father have their own issues going on and he's just dragging you into the mud."

Before I can gather enough semblance to reply with a forced smile and a polite dismissal, the swinging doors crash open and a security guard with an earpiece crashes through them. He makes a beeline for Alberto and whispers something in his ear. Immediately, Alberto, Donatello, and Dante rip their guns from their waistbands and storm through the doors without another word.

"Oh, fuck," comes a hiss from the patio. I turn to see Tor flick his half-smoked cigarette into the darkness and cross the dining room, also disappearing into the lobby with a gun in his hand.

The hairs on the back of my neck stand to attention. "What's going on?"

"Your guess is as good as mine," Amelia whispers.

A few heavy beats pass, before a gruff voice and a burst of laughter slice through the tension. Beside me, I feel Amelia relax, slumping in her chair and taking a slug of her wine. The collective noise is light and cheery, and it travels back into the dining room, bringing the Visconti men with it.

"Look who's come for dinner!" Alberto roars, face pink with delight.

Before I can turn to see who it is, a gentle hand rests on my shoulder and I look up to meet the gaze of a server. "*Signorina, Signor* Visconti has requested to move you to the other end of the table to make room for his guest."

I glance down to the far end of the table, where Vittoria and Leonardo, Alberto's teenage twins, are glaring moodily at their phones. There's an empty setting to the right of Vittoria, and next to it sits Max. He catches my eye and grins.

Great. I scowl back at him, but then I shrug. Whatever. I'm more than happy to get away from Dante's laser-like glare and out of the reach of Alberto's ruby ring.

More servers swarm me, plucking at my silverware and replacing it with a fresh setting with the speed of a Formula One pit stop team. When I settle in next to Max, he nudges my shoulder and grins. "Well, isn't this a nice surprise. Now, I don't have to just admire you from afar." His eyes glitter, running over my red dress and coming to a stop at my chest. His throat bobs. "You look lovely tonight, by the way."

I'm grateful that the server tending to this end of the table didn't get the memo about my alcohol ban. He fills up my glass with red wine and I take a desperate gulp before turning back to Max. "You know I'm engaged to your boss, right?"

"You know me," he purrs, pressing his knee against mine under the table. "I like living life on the edge." But the way his eyes dart feverishly to the head of the table suggests otherwise.

Max isn't a Visconti, but he sure wishes he were. He's what they call an associate—he doesn't have a drop of Italian blood in his veins but works for the mafia nonetheless. He's just a lackey of sorts, doing whatever odd jobs the "made men" don't want to dirty their hands with, including escorting the capo's fiance to Devil's Dip twice a week.

Max makes my blood boil. He has leering eyes and groping hands and he reminds me of the boys that *made me like this*. He went to the same school as them, too—the prestigious Devil's Coast Academy—so I know he's heard the rumors.

He's only a year older than me, with big brown eyes and floppy hair that he huffs out of his face when he gets nervous. The only reason I haven't done a *bad thing* to him yet is because we have a deal. I tolerate his lewd comments and lingering stares in exchange for two hours of alone time once we get to Devil's Dip. We both know he'd get into serious trouble if Alberto found out he wasn't trailing me at all times, so it's our little secret.

Clink, clink, clink.

The sound of silverware bouncing off the side of a crystal glass. Of course the noise comes from Alberto—the only thing he loves more than young women and anecdotes is a long, boring speech. I look up at him as he clears his throat, and then immediately, my eyes are drawn to the man who took my place at the table.

A weird sensation creeps over my body, one my brain is racing to make sense of. It starts at the base of my spine and works its way up to my neck, before settling around my throat like a chokehold. I force myself to swallow and focus on the man's profile. That sharp cheekbone, the stubble lining his jaw...

And then, as if he can feel my stare boring into the side of his face, he turns and locks eyes with me.

Oh, flamingo.

It's him. The man from the cliff's edge. The one with the cigarette and the wingtips and the indifferent tone.

Suicide is a sin.

He pins me with a disinterested stare, and then his gaze darkens.

I look away, fussing over the napkin on my lap with shaky hands. My heart is thumping like it's trying to escape its cage, and I can feel the sweat pooling under my thighs, causing me to sink further into the chair. By the time I find the courage to look back up, he's turned his attention to Dante. Still and silent, he listens to him talk with a neutral expression on his perfect features.

Alberto clears his throat, clinking on the glass with more force. The room finally settles.

"Attention, everybody," he booms. With a shark-like grin, he turns to the dinner guest and raises his glass. "We have an unexpected but very welcome visitor. So, cheers to my favorite nephew, Vicious Visconti!"

Nephew. Vicious.

I'm drowning in the cheering that floods the room.

I bring the wineglass to my lips and sink every last drop of blood-red liquid, then hold it out for a top-up.

I have an uneasy feeling I'm going to need it.

CHAPTER
Three

Rory

THE EXCITEMENT IN THE dining room eventually mellows, and the fight between Alberto and Dante seems long forgotten. With a snap of my fiance's ring-clad fingers, dinner begins.

A lazy version of *Ava Maria* drifts out of the piano, serving as a backdrop to the easy chatter. Wine and whiskey flow, as much into my glass as anyone elses, but it does nothing to dull the unease brewing under my skin.

I can't take my eyes off him.

At first, I watch his every move because I'm waiting for the moment he tells Alberto he recognizes me. The girl in the sweatpants balancing with one foot dangerously over the edge of a cliff. *Alone.* I'm waiting for Alberto to pin me with that blistering glare, jaw grinding, just like he did last Friday when I embarrassed him by pulling down his curtains. This time, the consequences will be a lot more severe than a slap across the face or a sharp tug on my ponytail.

But as the fourth glass of merlot warms the pit of my stomach, the fear gives way to curiosity.

He's barely said a word. Barely moved. When the appetizer arrived, he slipped off his suit jacket and folded it neatly over the back of his chair, revealing a cream-colored sweater that hugs his body like a second skin. Ever since, he's sat there with a steel-like spine, fists clenched on either side of his untouched plate, while Alberto and Dante do all the talking.

He hasn't looked at me once.

Maybe it's the initial shock wearing off, or maybe it's the wine working its way around my nervous system, but I start to allow myself to believe that I imagined his dark glare when Alberto introduced him. It was fleeting, I was probably just in his line of sight. What are the chances he recognizes me, anyway? He only looked at me once on the cliff, just as he was turning to leave, and I had my hood up the whole time.

Yes. This is okay. It's all going to be okay.

"Do I make you nervous?"

It's no more than a whisper and I almost don't hear it. I tear my gaze away from the head of the table and look at Max.

"Huh?"

He licks his lips. "You're jiggling your leg and you haven't touched your food. Does sitting so close to me make you nervous?"

If I didn't need him to visit my father twice a week, I'd cut his car brakes.

Instead of biting back, I turn my attention to my left, where Vittoria sits. She's pushing a crab's leg from one side of her plate to the other, her silky black hair covering her face.

"Vittoria?"

"I'm becoming a vegetarian," she announces, giving the limb a disgusted shove. "Crabs scream when they get boiled. Did you know that?"

"Good thing they are pan-fried, then," Leonardo says dryly from the other side of her, not looking up from his iPhone.

"Jerk," she mutters under her breath, setting her fork down.

She and Leonardo are twins, and at just sixteen, they hate these dinner parties almost as much as I do.

I lightly touch her arm and lower my voice. "Uh, is that your cousin?"

She tosses a napkin over her butchered crab and glances up moodily. "Angelo? Yeah, haven't seen him in ages."

Angelo. At least his name's not really Vicious. "And he's part of the Hollow clan? I haven't seen him before."

Stepping across the threshold of this mansion was like falling into a scene from *The Godfather*. I learned the family tree pretty quickly, but I still only have a loose grasp on who owns what. Alberto and his sons are often referred to as the Cove clan, while his brother, Alfredo, runs the Hollow clan, in Devil's Hollow, just twenty minutes down the road. They have their whiskey company there, as well as other businesses I know little about. But I've met Alfredo's sons a few times, and this new guy certainly isn't one of them.

"Nah, he's from Dip."

I blink. "Dip?"

She looks at me like I'm stupid. "Angelo's from the Devil's Dip clan. You know, the town you're from?"

My blood turns to ice. "There's no clan in Devil's Dip," I almost whisper.

No. There can't be. There's no Visconti presence in Devil's Dip; that's literally the whole point of this agreement.

"Not anymore, there isn't. He was meant to take over when Uncle Alonso died, but he never did."

"Uncle Alonso? Alberto has another brother?"

"*Had.* Like I told you, he died."

"So why didn't Angelo take over?"

She sighs in that loud, bratty way spoiled teenagers do. "Why don't you just ask him? He's like, right there."

"Shh," I hiss.

I chase down this new information with a slug of wine, but it doesn't make it any easier to swallow. I glare at the head of the table over the top of the glass. *Angelo Visconti.* So, the mysterious jerk has a name. My eyes follow him obsessively as he finally moves for the first time since appetizers were served, only to lean back in his chair and rub his hands together in a way that makes his huge biceps flex.

He looks bored.

The servers clear the plates and top off my wine. The conversation flows, but it sounds distorted, like I'm listening to it underwater. The breeze creeps in from the crack in the French doors and gently tickles my neck, taunting me, teasing me with the idea of running away from this murderous dining room and never having to see a Visconti again.

Slowly, my disgust for this family turns toward one member in particular. My eyes scorch the side of Angelo's cheek.

Suicide is a sin. But Devil's Dip has a way of making you want to throw yourself off the edge, doesn't it?

My next gulp of wine sours on my tongue. Now that I've managed to convince myself he doesn't recognize me, my fear about him telling Alberto I was alone in Devil's Dip melts away into something darker: hatred.

He thought I was going to jump, and yet...he did nothing except tell me it's a long way to fall. He left me there, toeing the edge. He didn't even glance back.

If the last two months have taught me anything, it's that the Viscontis are cruel. But this one? Holy Crow, there's not a single ounce of humility in that sculpted body.

Maybe that's why Alberto referred to him as Vicious.

"Aurora? Uh, maybe you should slow down. You're looking a little tipsy."

"Shut up, Max."

My pulse thrums in my ears to an unsettling rhythm. I've given up pretending not to stare, and now my eyes are boring into the side of his head. *What an A-Hole.*

Suddenly, I hear my name.

"What?"

I know that slipped from my lips loud and brash, because everyone has paused their conversations to stare at me.

There's a scrape of a fork. Someone coughs.

"I was just telling Angelo you're from Devil's Dip," Alberto says carefully, pinning me with a wary glare. A *don't-you-dare-embarrass-me* glare. "Angelo grew up there too. I'm sure you two will have much to talk about."

Angelo checks his watch, then returns his gaze to the wallpaper above Dante's head.

"Not much to discuss," he drawls. "That place is a shit hole."

Tor lets out a loud laugh, and next to him, Dante smirks into his lowball glass.

"Why'd you go back then?"

Silence. It's hot and heavy and my comeback hangs in the dining room like an ugly painting.

Oh, sparrow. What have I just done?

Not only did I back-talk in front of Alberto, but I just let it slip that I'd seen his nephew in Devil's Dip. Which implies I'm not being escorted just to see my father and back like I'm supposed to be. My heart quickens, my throat goes dry, and I wish I could gobble up those words as quickly as I let them out. Especially when Alberto pops his knuckles and hisses something in Italian.

It suddenly dawns on me that something is off. I'm the only one looking at Alberto for his reaction. Everyone else? Their collective focus is on Angelo. It's almost as if they are waiting with bated breath to see what he's going to do next.

I force myself to look at Angelo too, and realize that now he's staring right at me. His gaze is heavy and cold. Indifferent. Like he's looking at a McDonald's dollar menu rather than the girl who just challenged him.

The next few seconds stretch on for what feels like forever. Then he lifts his whiskey to his lips, takes a lazy sip, and turns to Dante.

"Rafe said you're renovating the Grand. Sounds expensive."

And just like that, the tension dissolves into conversation about the Viscontis' latest business venture. Everyone's forgotten my tiny act of rebellion, but I can't seem to shake the feeling that the consequences of my smart, drunken mouth will rear their ugly head later on.

After the servers clear away dessert, Alberto pats his fat stomach, claps his hands, and announces, "Time to party!"

Great.

Chairs scrape back and everyone filters through the swinging doors and down to the basement. Instead of following suit, I break away and stagger toward the guest bathroom next to Alberto's study, the one in which Tor's date has presumably been snorting coke off the gilded sink.

I just need a moment to gather my thoughts. To sober up a little. The wine has gone straight to my head and I can barely keep upright on these stupid stilettos Alberto insists I wear. I just need a moment away from this family. To sit in a quiet room, then I'll splash my face and—

"Ouch!"

There's a sudden vise-like grip on my wrist. It spins me around and shoves me against the wall of the corridor. Despite the darkness and the drunken haze clouding my vision, I can smell the cocktail of cigars and liquor on Alberto's hot breath. I twist my head away, gasping at the weight of his enormous body pinned against mine.

Is this what it's going to feel like on our wedding night?

"Alberto!"

I'm cut off by his fat hand clamping my jaw. "Don't ever embarrass me like that again," he hisses, stooping down so his wet lips graze my nose. "If you want to act like a brat, I'll punish you like a brat." His grip tightens, threatening to break my jawbone. "I'll take away your father's care team and I'll stop your visits. Understood?" Despite the pain, I can't help but feel a flicker of relief. He doesn't realize I saw Angelo in Devil's Dip; he's only angry about the back-talk. I jerk my head in his hands, because I barely have any room to nod. "Good," he purrs, seemingly happy with my sudden obedience. I think he's going to release me but he doesn't. Instead, he pushes farther into me.

Is that... *Holy crow.* The bulge now pressing against my thigh suggests he's *more* than happy. Bile rises in my throat, and I fight the urge to connect my knee with his erection.

"Or perhaps, I won't wait until our wedding night to take what's mine."

My heart stills. Alberto's threat is loaded like a gun, and he lets it marinate in the tiny gap between us. His breath scorches my cheek, growing more and more labored in the silence.

"Understood," I croak.

Never one to miss a party, he pulls himself off me and stomps down the corridor. "Seen and not heard, Aurora," he grunts over his shoulder. "Learn to keep that pretty little mouth shut."

I stay there, frozen to the wall, until the sound of heavy footsteps slapping against the marble dissolves into nothingness. I scurry away to the bathroom and lock the door behind me. Panting, I lean my weight against the sink and gaze up at my reflection.

Three years of doing bad things. Maybe weekly confession to an anonymous voicemail service isn't enough? Maybe I have to repent for my sins, too. Maybe having to look in the mirror every day and not recognize the girl staring back at me is my punishment.

Who is this girl? I silently ask the mirror. Because I don't recognize her with the inch-thick makeup and the poker-straight hair. Despite the fact that I signed my name in blood on the dotted line of Alberto's contract, I'll never be Aurora Visconti. I'll always be Rory Carter from Devil's Dip. The Rory who wears her hair curly and lives in *Lululemon* and sneakers. Who can start a fire with a soda can and can identify over three hundred birds by their tweets alone.

I allow myself a sigh. A long, desperate one. It takes everything out of my lungs and swirls around me like a hug. I flop down on the edge of the toilet seat and put my head in my hands. *Holy sparrow, my jaw hurts.*

When I struck a deal with Alberto Visconti, he promised me everything I begged for in exchange for my hand in marriage and the untouched space between my legs. Being sliced open with his ring and assaulted in dark corners weren't anywhere in the contract.

I'm in too deep.

Sucking in a lungful of air, I scrub away the wine stains on my lips with a tissue, smooth down my dress, and brace myself for the basement.
Remember why you're here, Rory.
Remember why you're here.

CHAPTER
Four

Rory

THE BASEMENT BAR IS flooded with low lighting, lighthearted chatter, and new guests deemed not important enough to attend the actual dinner. The music has switched from classical to jazz, seeping through the speakers behind the oak-clad bar.

Behind the green velvet booths and sofas, floor-to-ceiling doors lead out to the patio area, where Tor and Donatello are in deep conversation under a heat lamp.

I hate that I immediately look around for Angelo. When I scan the sea of faces and don't spot him, or my disgusting fiance, for that matter, the panic zig-zags up my spine. What if Angelo's pulled him into the cigar room, or the games room, and is telling him what he saw? Because surely, after my outburst, he's made the connection now.

I glance in the direction of the cigar room and see Dante standing outside the closed door, one hand in his pocket, the other wrapped around his whiskey glass. He's pacing.

Dante Visconti isn't the type of man who paces.

Swallowing hard, I push my way toward the bar and slip in next to Amelia. The bartender turns around, locks eyes on me, and laughs. "Rory Carter," he purrs, twisting a cloth around the inside of a beer glass. "I heard you were hanging out with the Viscontis these days. Didn't believe it."

I squint under the amber glow and realize it's Dan. He works with my friend Wren at The Rusty Anchor, the port bar in Devil's Dip.

Instinctively, I slip the hand with my engagement ring off the bar. "Dan, hey. What are you doing here?"

"Picking up a few extra hours doing private bar work." He slings the cloth over his shoulder and narrows his eyes. "I didn't have you down as one of these girls."

My temples thump. *One of these girls.* I don't even need to look around the bar to know what girls he's talking about. There's a running joke in Devil's Dip that every girl's life goal is to either get out or marry a Visconti. And if you can't snag a Visconti, then at least one of the very rich men that can afford to frequent the Visconti-owned establishments in Devil's Cove.

I was always in the first group of girls; my goal was to get out the second I turned eighteen. I guess life doesn't always pan out the way you want it to.

"What can I get you?"

Anything that'll make me numb. "Gin and tonic, please."

"Make that two," Amelia chimes in, coming up beside me. "These Friday nights are so boring, aren't they? I can just about put up with the dinner, but these after-parties..." She stifles a yawn. "They just go on forever."

"I know," I groan, bending down to rub the fresh blister on my heel. "What I'd give to be in my fluffy pajamas watching *Grey's Anatomy* right now."

Her gaze rolls over me in disbelief. "You don't strike me as the type of girl who owns fluffy pajamas. I bet you sleep in Chanel No.5 and go for your morning run in a Versace gown."

My snort is ugly, and if Alberto had witnessed it, he'd have dragged his ring over more of my flesh. I want to tell her that everything she sees in front of her is made in Alberto's image. That this darn thong is slicing my butt in half, and I've lost track of how many times I've caught my skin in too-tight zippers. But even though Amelia is my only tie to the normal world within the gates of this mansion, she's still part of the family. So I smile and shake my head, my snort melting into the pretty little laugh I've managed to perfect over the last two months.

We take our drinks and find a sofa by the patio doors. As soon as we flop down, Donatello and Tor saunter through the doors, both with big grins on their faces.

"Ladies, we're taking bets. Want in?" Tor asks.

Amelia looks up at her husband with a scowl. "I swear to God, Donnie. How many times have I told you to stop getting involved with these stupid bets? Your family are a bunch of scammers—you'll never win."

Donatello stoops to chuck her under the chin. "Relax, *mio amore*. We are betting on how long Dante will stand outside the cigar room before he breaks the door down."

I glance over. Dante is still pacing, and now he's muttering something under his breath.

Tor laughs. "He's pissed he hasn't been invited to the meeting."

"What meeting?" Amelia asks.

"Father is in there with Angelo. Apparently he wanted a private chat." Tor sticks two fingers in his mouth and whistles. Dante looks up and glares at him, but when he beckons him over, he comes.

"What?" he snaps.

Tor clamps a hand on his shoulder. "You know how pathetic you look standing there, bro? Like you're in high school and your girl is in *seven minutes in heaven* with another dude."

There's a ripple of laughter, and warmth fills my stomach knowing that, for once, it's not at my expense.

"Father's always been obsessed with him," Dante growls, stealing another glance at the door. "What the fuck do they have to talk about? He's barely a made man these days." Gulping the remaining brown liquid in his glass, he slams it on the nearest table and growls, "Fuck it. I'm going in."

We watch him storm toward the cigar room door. Tor checks his watch, smirks, then sticks his hand out. Donatello grunts and pulls a money clip from his breast pocket. He mouths *sorry* to Amelia, who looks like she wants to punch the both of them.

"He's thirty-fucking-two," Tor chuckles, counting the bills in his hand. "And he's still bitter about it."

"About what?" I find myself asking.

Tor glances down at me and smirks. "Angelo fucked his prom date."

"Why?"

He looks at Donatello, and in unison they say, "Because he's Vicious Visconti."

The hairs on the back of my neck stand up. "Vicious?"

"Yeah, he's a nasty fucker," Tor chuckles. "Well, he was before he went straight." Nudging Donatello's ribs, he adds, "Remember when he blew out his driver's kneecap 'cause he took the wrong turn?"

Donatello nods. "Mmm. And when he locked all those port workers in a shipping container and blew it up, all because there was one boat log they couldn't account for." He shakes his head in disbelief. "Of all the made men to go straight, I never thought it'd be Vicious."

Tor slaps Donatello on the back. "Speaking of dates, I should probably find Sarah."

"Skyler," Amelia corrects him with an eye roll. "Her name is Skyler."

"Whatever. I haven't seen her in a while. She's probably got her hands on the family china." And with that, Tor slices through the party-goers and disappears. Throwing an apologetic grin to Amelia, Donatello follows suit.

"Every time," Amelia mutters, stabbing an ice cube with her straw.

But I'm not listening. Instead, I'm watching as Dante thumps his fist against the cigar room door. It flies open and reveals Alberto's looming silhouette. They have a short, heated discussion before Dante turns around and pins me with a blistering stare.

I freeze, my drink halfway to my lips, and when he makes a beeline for me, my palms start sweating. *This is not good.*

"It's you," he growls, coming to a stop just inches away from where I'm sitting. "He wants to speak with you."

My heart skips a beat. "Me?" I croak.

But Dante is already halfway to the bar, and Amelia is now tapping furiously on her cell. My stomach drops, and for the briefest of moments, I consider slipping out the patio doors and disappearing down the beach, but the impatient scowl smeared across Alberto's face tells me my presence is non-negotiable.

I abandon my drink and make my way to the cigar room, my heels threatening to give way on the plush carpet. Alberto steps to the side, snakes his arm around my waist, and plants a cold, slithery kiss on the curve of my neck, as if he didn't have his hand clamped around my jaw while he sprayed my face with saliva and venom less than ten minutes ago.

He pushes me into the room. When Greta, the head housekeeper, showed me around the Visconti manor for the first time, she told me women weren't allowed in here. *It's for the men.* But I haven't been missing much—it's just a smaller version of Alberto's office. Mahogany cabinets and plush armchairs, all sitting under a heavy cloud of tobacco smoke.

It looks even smaller with Angelo Visconti spilling out of the armchair by the fire.

"Aurora, I didn't have the pleasure of formally introducing you to Angelo over dinner."

Behind me, the door clicks shut, plunging us into a deafening silence.

In the short time I've been engaged to the head of the Cosa Nostra, I've done this dance countless times. Different men, same suits. Kisses on the back of my hand, a frozen smile on my lips. But this time, it feels different.

It feels like I can't breathe. Why? Because for some inexplicable reason, I'd rather throw myself off the cliff in Devil's Dip than do this dance with Angelo Visconti. *Vicious* Visconti.

Taking a deep breath for courage, I force myself to look up from the carpet.

A weight pushes down on my chest as I meet his heavy gaze. *Oh, holy crow, he's handsome.* Maybe it's because he's no longer standing dangerously close to the edge of a cliff, or perhaps it's the way he reclines in that armchair, an irritated sneer on his face, but I can't believe I never realized he was a Visconti. Green eyes glitter against his tanned skin, and black hair that looks like silk gleams under the spotlights built into the low ceiling. That jaw and those cheekbones; they are as sharp as I remember them, and they still have the effect of snatching the air from my lungs.

He's beautiful in the most untouchable of ways. Not that I'd want to touch him. And even if I *did*, judging by the disdain on his face and the reputation that precedes him, he'd snap my fingers off if I even tried.

"Angelo, meet my fiancee Aurora, and Aurora, meet Angelo. He's my favorite nephew. Of course," he adds with a chuckle, "don't tell Raphael or Gabriel I told you that."

I don't know who they are and I don't care to ask. Instead, I tear my gaze from Angelo's, because the unease creeping up my arms is telling me something bad is going to happen if I don't. But then my liquor-fueled stubbornness forces me to do the opposite. I swallow the knot in my throat and tilt my chin higher, reinforcing eye contact.

"Fiancee," he drawls, settling back in his armchair. His eyes bore into mine and I can't help but notice he's the only man that Alberto has formally introduced me to that hasn't immediately turned his attention to my chest or legs. I also can't help but notice that for some unknown reason, this makes me despise him even more. "I'm losing count of how many wives you've had, Uncle Al."

I blink. I've never heard anybody aside from Dante talk to Alberto like that. Heat prickles at my skin, but before I can regain some composure, Alberto wraps his arm around my waist and plops down in an armchair, bringing me crashing into his lap.

I gasp. Angelo looks mildly disgusted.

"This wife is special," Alberto huffs, his arm clamping me to his lap like a safety belt. "She's a virgin."

Oh my goose. Did he really just say that?

My head swims with disbelief and heat scorches my cheeks. It's hard to fight the urge to elbow him in the gut, but I know I'm too drunk and my heels are too high to run away from him if I do. Instead, I break the eye contact I was determined to keep and choose the safety of the photograph hanging on the wall behind Angelo.

After a few seconds, I realize I'm staring at an aerial photograph of the Devil's Coast. It was named that because of the jagged cliff faces and steep drops; it looks like the Devil himself took a bite out of the land. At the top, Devil's Cove sparkles like the Crown Jewels. The bright lights from the hotels and the casinos twinkle up and down the perimeter of the sandy semi-circle. Below it is Devil's Hollow, the landscape so black that it's almost navy. All of the excitement of Hollow is buried deep below ground, in majestic caves where the Viscontis age their whiskey in barrels and host illicit parties for the rich and depraved. A little way back from the coast, you can see the grand structure that is the Devil's Coast Academy, which is practically Hogwarts for the super-elite.

And then there's Devil's Dip. *Home.* It sits on the small curve of land right at the bottom of the coast. My heart aches looking at the bird's eye view of the small port and the cobbled, narrow streets, both set against the backdrop of the sprawling, forested Devil's Preserve. It's crazy that I'm less than forty minutes from home, yet I might as well be a million miles away.

A pinch on my hip brings me back to the room. I clamp my aching jaw together and say, "My apologies, I missed that. What did you say, darling?"

Darling. Perhaps my playing into Alberto's sick fantasy will get me out of another punishment. I turn to him and flash my sweetest smile. It seems to work, because the fire in his eyes simmers and he grips my hand.

"Show him the ring."

Swallowing hard, I meet Angelo's gaze again, slowly inching my hand into the space between us. It's trembling. *Must be all the wine.*

He regards my hand like the whole idea of having to look at my engagement ring is more boring than a long bus ride on a rainy day. Then he drinks a lazy sip of whiskey, taking his time to set it down on the side table. The shells of my ears feel hot, and the drawn-out silence is suffocating.

The clock on the mantelpiece chimes. Alberto's chest wheezes against my back.

With a small, sudden huff, he leans forward and slips his hand around my wrist.

My breathing shallows. I didn't expect him to *touch me*. I look down at his fingers wrapped around my wrist. They are so long that the tip of his thumb meets the knuckle of his index finger. My hand sits tiny in his palm, looking ridiculously childlike.

I don't like it. It feels wrong. *Dangerous.*

"It looks heavy."

The indifference in his voice sends static down my spine, and a strange feeling of exhilaration coasts down after it. The diamond is *huge*. It weighs down my ring finger like an anchor and Amelia once joked that the clarity is so high, it doesn't just catch the light, but the darkness, too. Every man Alberto has forced me to show it off to has gushed over it, and yet…

Angelo couldn't give two swans about the million-dollar rock on my finger. As much as I dislike him, the little act of rebellion against the almighty Alberto excites me.

Alberto clears his throat. "I'm not sure how long you'll be in town for, but the engagement party is next week and we'd love to have you there. Up." To my horror, Alberto slaps my ass twice, catapulting me to my feet like I'm a darn mule refusing to work. "Come, Angelo. There's something I want to show you."

He bristles past me and disappears through the door. The sound of the party briefly fills the room before the door swings shut and plunges us back into silence.

We're alone and the heat is suffocating.

His gaze burns up at me. I force myself to stare back down at him.

His eyes flicker with something I can't give a name to as he rubs his fingers over his lips.

"Aurora Visconti," he murmurs from behind them.

My chest hitches. I've heard that name aloud before, even just hours ago at the dinner table, from Amelia. But the way it rolls off his tongue and into the silence between us sounds...*inappropriate*.

And yet, my ears crave to hear it again.

He stands, uncurling himself from the chair and stretching to his full height. Despite wearing these stupid heels, my eyes are level with the thick trunk of his throat. I'm transfixed by the sight of his Adam's apple bobbing under the shadow of his jaw.

"Heavy enough to weigh you down."

My eyes lift to his. "Excuse me?"

He drops his gaze to my hand, then drags his teeth over his bottom lip. Heat floods between my thighs, unwanted yet unstoppable.

"Your ring. It looks heavy enough to weigh you down if you choose to fall."

My heart collides with my rib cage, and my breathing stops. The only noise I can hear in the room is my blood pounding against my temples. I'm hyper-aware of his presence, feeling every heavy footstep as he moves around me to head toward the door.

But then he stops right by my side, just like he did on the cliff. The stubble of his jaw grazes against my cheek, and his now-familiar scent makes my head spin.

"It was a pleasure to meet you, Aurora."

The delirium that comes with the unknown transports me back to the cliff edge.

And for the first time, I genuinely wish I'd jumped off it.

CHAPTER
Five

Rory

"D<small>OUBLE</small> S<small>MUGGLERS</small> C<small>LUB</small>," I rasp to Dan, unable to look him in the eye. "Hold the ice."

He lets out a low whistle and slides a crystal lowball glass across the bar. The warm whiskey hits the back of my throat, trickles past my thumping heart, then joins the bitterness in the pit of my stomach. It does nothing to cool the fever scorching my body.

While the ghost of Alberto's grip on my jaw aches, the memory of Angelo's hand around my wrist *burns*.

"Another," I demand. Dan raises a brow, but tops me up regardless.

I slam it, wipe my mouth, and stagger through the crowd, making a beeline for Max.

He's sitting in a booth, alone, nursing a beer. If I didn't strongly dislike him, I'd feel sorry for him, because he's dedicated his life to a family that couldn't give two flying flamingos about him.

"Tell me everything you know about Angelo Visconti."

"What do you need to know?" Max purrs, his beer breath tickling my neck.

Let's start with: why does he make me so nervous?

"What I said. Everything."

He sidles up closer, and the heat from his thigh pushing against mine makes my skin crawl. "What's it worth?"

"Your life, Max. He saw me alone in Devil's Dip. You know, when you were meant to be escorting me at all times?"

It takes a few moments for the penny to drop. "Vicious did? Fuck," he groans, running his hands through his hair. "Alberto's going to kill me."

I've learned that when somebody says that around here, they mean literally, not figuratively.

"Dante said he's not even a made man anymore. I thought Visconti men were made men by default?"

Max glugs his beer, making a gross gasp as he sets it back on the table. "Alright, here's the rundown on Angelo. His father, Alonso, was the capo of the Devil's Dip outfit. He ran imports and exports out of the port. Super lucrative business—what he was raking in over in Dip makes Cove look like a shanty town."

I frown, thinking of all the five-star hotels and glitzy casinos that line Devil's Cove. Then an image of the Devil's Dip port comes to mind. Nothing more than a creaky old dock, a few sorry-looking boats, and an abandoned shipping container turned into a bar. "Really? What did he trade?"

"Anything and to anyone. He had cocaine coming in from the Colombians, guns going out to the Russians. Nothing was off-limits."

I shake my head. Not a chance. The thing about living in a small town is that you grow up knowing everyone and their mamas. I know lots of the port workers—Bill, my dad's best friend, Old Riley who married Wren's mom—and they'd *never* get involved with something illegal like that. No, the only thing coming in and out of Devil's Dip port are crayfish and canned food.

When I tell Max this, he laughs and playfully bumps his shoulder against mine. "Now, hold on. I haven't finished the rundown, have I?" He reaches up and brushes a stray strand of my hair off my shoulder. A move that makes my bones cringe. "Alonso was very, very clever. You know the church up on the cliff?" For a moment, I can taste the salty air, feel the wind blowing through my curls. Smell the cigarette smoke. I nod. "When the Visconti brothers came to the Devil's Coast, Alonso immediately bought that church, got ordained, and established himself as the parish deacon." He sits back and crosses his arms. His eyebrows are raised, like he's waiting for me to connect the dots.

"And?"

He sighs. "And, why do you go to church?"

"Uh, to pray?"

"To *confess*. Alonso knew Devil's Dip's deepest and darkest secrets. With that ammo hanging over their heads, they'd do anything he wanted them to, illegal or otherwise."

There's a strange ringing in my ears as I process what he's saying. "Jesus," I mutter. "That's..."

"Genius."

"Cruel, was the word I was going for."

"That too," he says with a sip and a shrug.

Suddenly, goosebumps spread across my arms like a nasty rash, and heat prickles my left cheek. It's instinctive to turn, and that's when I find myself staring into the eyes of Angelo Visconti. He's leaning against the bar, holding a whiskey glass so loosely that it looks like he's about to drop it. Dante is in his ear, talking animatedly while he remains still and silent. The contrast between them is like fire and ice.

Our eyes lock and his stare is cold enough to give me frostbite. *What is with this guy?* When somebody is caught staring, they usually avert their gaze—if not out of embarrassment, then at least to be polite. But he's regarding me like he has every right to, like I'm a painting hanging on the wall, or a statue in the lobby.

Just not one he likes the look of.

Then his eyes slide to my right. To Max. The storm that clouds his expression makes me look away.

I clear my throat and mutter, "Let me guess: the reason he didn't take over as capo was because he didn't agree with his father's seedy blackmail tactics."

He doesn't pick up on my sarcasm.

"No. It's because he watched both his mother and father die in the same week."

The hairs on the back of my neck stand up. "They were murdered?"

"Nope. Maria had a heart attack, and a few days later, Alonso had a sudden bleed on the brain. We're big on family around here, you know? He took it hard. After the funeral, instead of being sworn in as capo, he got on a flight back to London and has lived clean ever since."

"Clean?"

"Guess that's what Dante meant about him not being a made man anymore. Before his parents' deaths, he was running a very successful loan shark business in England, waiting it out until his father retired and he'd take over. But after? He didn't come back. Instead, he chose to stay in England and turned the whole business legit. Rumor has it he doesn't even carry a gun anymore."

When I turn to look at Angelo again, it's with a slightly brighter light. I watch as he cocks his head and slowly swirls the liquid around his glass with a lazy roll of his wrist. A flicker of sympathy ignites in my stomach, and guilt settles on my skin like dust.

I really am a horrible person. Losing my mom was hard enough, but the cancer crawled through her body as slow as syrup, at least giving us the time to say goodbye. I can't imagine losing both my mom and father in the same week.

There's a sharp stab in my chest. *That's not entirely true.* When mom died, a big part of my father died with her.

"And his brothers?" I say suddenly, remembering Alberto's quip to Angelo in the cigar room. *You're my favorite nephew, but don't tell Raphael and Gabriel I said that.* "Why didn't they take over Devil's Dip instead?"

"Rafe and Gabe?" he asks in a breezy manner that suggests they are the best of friends, which, I highly doubt. "Nah. It goes against tradition to pass on the position of capo through the bloodline. The only exception is death or incarceration. Besides, the Dip brothers..." he sticks his finger in his beer, scoops out some froth, and sucks on it. *Gross.* "They are fiercely loyal. Only a few years between them but you'd think they were triplets by the way they behave."

"Do they live in London, too?"

"No, no. Rafe owns most of Vegas's skyline. You'd have seen him about—he often comes to Cove to play poker with Tor and the Hollow brothers. But Gabe?" He laughs. "You won't have seen him."

The scoff that punctuates his sentence piques my interest. "Why? What does he do?"

"Dunno. I'm not brave enough to ask."

Before I can continue my interrogation, Vittoria slides onto the bench opposite us and drops her head on the table. "God, I'd rather gauge my eyes out with a rusty spoon than be here."

Max raises his lukewarm beer in a toast. "Wait 'til your twenty-one. Being drunk makes these parties a little more bearable."

"I *am* drunk," Vittoria says, cutting me off. "Tor's girlfriend isn't as useless as she looks. She keeps slipping me vodka shots from her hip flask. At least, I *think* it's vodka."

"Oh no," Max mutters, rising to his feet. "If your brothers find out I knew you were drunk..." He scurries away into the crowd, not before shooting me a pleading look. "You haven't seen me, okay?"

I roll my eyes and turn my attention back to Vittoria. After a few moments, she emerges from under her curtain of black hair and looks up at me with bloodshot eyes.

"My dress is too tight. My feet hurt." She sits up straight and grabs the pearl necklace around her neck. "And this fucking thing is itchy." With one swift motion, she rips it off her neck and slings it onto the table. "And..." She suddenly pales, pursing her lips. Without another word, she slides out the booth and darts up the basement stairs.

My gaze lands on the necklace, and I mutter a bird-word under my breath. She yanked it off her neck like it's made from macaroni and string. It disgusts me that even the youngest member of this family has no concept of their wealth or privilege. She'll grow up to be a spoiled brat, just like the rest of them.

I sweep my gaze over the room.

Then, when I'm sure nobody is looking, I slip the necklace into my bra.

The party continues, a storm of music and laughter. Sometimes being around the Viscontis feels like it's Christmas Day, and I'm peering through the window of their living room while shivering in a snowstorm. An outsider who'll never be invited in to sit by the fire. It always makes me sad, but just for a moment.

Because I know I'd rather be bitterly cold and lose all my toes to frostbite than join them.

As I scan the room, Amelia catches my eye. She smiles and makes her way over. When she's just a few feet away, Donatello shoots out his arm and grabs her wrist.

"Baby. The villa we just bought in Tuscany, you didn't even like it, right?"

Amelia's jaw juts. Her nostrils flair. Then she takes a deep breath and sweeps her gaze over me with a frozen smile. "Aurora, sweetheart, would you excuse us for a moment? I just have to remind my husband that if he continues making bets with his brothers, we'll soon be living in a cardboard box under the pier."

"I'll go check on Vittoria," I mutter, clambering to my feet.

As I leave them bickering in the booth, the familiar pang of longing knocks the wind out of me. They have the same thing my parents had—true love. I always promised my mom I'd marry for nothing less, and even as I hovered over the dotted line of Alberto's contract, the ghost of her soft voice whispered a reminder in my ear. Breaking that promise to her is a sin that has weighed me down ever since, and no matter how many times I've confessed, it's too heavy to shake.

Jesus, I'm drunk. The floor breathes as the amber lights glow low and hazy. Each step through the sea of suits and stilettos is unsteady and reckless; it'll take only one misstep to buckle on these stupid heels, and I don't need to give Alberto another excuse to punish me.

The stillness of the lobby feels like taking off my bra after a long day. I let out a lungful of air and slink back into the shadows of a connecting hallway, pressing my back into the cold mahogany paneling. The party hums beneath my feet, like the residents of hell are banging on the ceiling, trying to escape.

I bask in the tranquility for a while, before deciding that I should probably get around to checking on Vittoria. A large part of me doesn't care that a Visconti—even the youngest, most innocent one—might be currently choking on their own vomit, but I guess there's still a small fraction of me that isn't a monster.

I smooth down my dress and take a deep breath. As I turn the corner, I collide with something large and stone-like. At first, I think I've turned too early, crashing into one of the gaudy statues that lurk in the alcoves. But then a hand shoots out and grabs my forearm, stopping me from tumbling backward.

Angelo Visconti.

We lock eyes. Then the shock snatches the air from my lungs, and I rip my arm from his grip like it burns.

He slips the hand he grabbed me with into his pocket; the other holding a cell to his ear. Obviously he stepped out of the party to take a private phone call. There's a faint hum of chatter on the other side of the line, but he doesn't seem to be listening. Not anymore.

Oh, boy.

Here's when I mutter an apology. When I sidestep him and scurry back to the party, where the laughter and the music and a fresh glass of liquor will warm the chill on my skin.

But I don't, *can't*, do anything but stand and stare at him.

Jesus, was he this tall and broad on the cliff? Maybe this hallway is narrower than I remember, or maybe it's the darkness. Monsters are always bigger and scarier in the dark.

I swallow the lump in my throat and shake my head. *Get a grip, Rory.* Angelo Visconti isn't a monster. Dante said he's barely a made man, and Max said he doesn't even carry a gun.

But when he hangs up without a word, slides his phone in his pocket and takes a step forward, I take a step back. Growing up in the Preserve has sharpened my instincts, and standing in a dark corridor with this man gives me the same sense of unease as hearing a leaf crunch on the forest floor, or a howl in the distance.

He might not be much of a made man, but it feels like I'm face to face with a predator.

The silence that served as a respite just a few minutes ago is now suffocating, crushing my chest like a brick. Eventually, his eyes release mine, moving down my neck and settling on my chest. His gaze burns even more than his touch. It's so *brazen*, so shameless. Like my body belongs to him, instead of me.

"It's rude to stare." The retort flies from my mouth, haughty and slurred, before I can stop it. *Oh, swan.*

I know better than to speak to a Visconti like that, especially twice in one night. What's worse, he's the one Visconti I should be trying to butter up, or at the very least, avoid. There's nothing stopping him from telling Alberto he saw me in Devil's Dip, *alone*, teetering on the edge of the cliff. How many times has Alberto hissed in my ear, *don't you dare embarrass me*. I'm sure everybody finding out your fiancee would supposedly rather throw herself into the sea than marry you is the ultimate humiliation. I have no doubts he'd follow through on his threats. Take away my father's care team. Stop my visits.

So, I should apologize. I should bow my head, turn on my small-town charm and act like I don't have two brain cells to rub together. That's what he and the rest of his family think of me anyway, right?

But I'm hot, feverish. Stupefied under the intensity of his attention. As he drags his gaze back to mine, my skin grows hotter, like I'm standing in front of an open fire. It's dangerous but *oh-so-enticing*.

He takes another step forward, and I, another step back. Now in the vast foyer, the stained glass in the entryway windows cast a kaleidoscope of colors over his face. Greens, blues, pinks, warming his cold features and softening his sharpness.

He runs a thumb over his bottom lip. Gives a slight shake of his head. Then he reaches out toward my chest, his knuckles grazing the silk fabric cutting across the curve of my breasts.

What the—

I glance down and my blood freezes. Before I can protest, his thumb and forefinger grip onto the lone pearl poking out of the neckline, and he pulls.

Pearl by pearl, Vittoria's necklace unfurls from my bra and into his hand. Despite the panic starting to seep through my veins, I can't ignore how each cold bead grazes past my nipple as he slowly pulls. I can't ignore the flame flickering between my legs, or the way my breathing shallows under his touch.

When the clasp finally falls from my chest, he holds up the necklace by the end pearl, in the same way people hold a bag of dog poop from a dog that isn't theirs. He's also regarding me like I'm said dog—with a sneer that deepens the cleft of his chin, and frosty, narrow eyes.

The lump in my throat is too big to swallow, and I know it's way too late for fake smiles and halfhearted apologies. I should sink to my knees and beg him not to tell Alberto, and if it was Tor, or even Dante, that's exactly what I'd do.

But for some inexplicable reason, this man makes me want to be stubborn. I have the urge to go toe to toe with him, to prove I won't be the one that backs away from the edge of the cliff before he does, no matter how many rocks crumble under my sneakers, or how strong the wind blows.

Annoyance flickers in his irises, like I'm a fly he can't swat away.

"If you looked more enthusiastic when sitting on your fiance's lap, then perhaps he'd buy you a pearl necklace of your own."

The colors on his face shift as he closes the gap between us.

I stop breathing.

His silhouette looms over me like a storm cloud, and I have this strange, conflicting feeling swirling around my body. I don't know whether I want to turn on my heel and run for shelter, or tilt my head back, close my eyes and embrace the rain.

It's all the liquor in my system. It has to be. I'm going to wake up with a pounding head and a chest full of regret. And probably some more serious injuries when he tells Alberto what I—

His hand finds my wrist, stopping all of my racing thoughts in their tracks. Now, all I can focus on is the burning band of fire on my skin; like a venomous bracelet. He pulls my hand up to my side, and we both look down at it.

He turns my fist over. Instinctively, I uncurl my fingers to reveal my palm.

To my surprise, he lets out a small hiss, like something about my action bothers him. Then he pools the necklace into my palm, creating a small, careful coil of pearls, and closes my hands back into a fist. I can feel his gaze, a heavy burden, against my cheek. But I don't lift my eyes up from his hand wrapped around mine. It's so *big*. Thick fingers and a heavy, hot touch.

He clears his throat, and when he finally speaks, his voice has a rasp to it.

"Stealing is a sin, *Aurora*."

I wince at how he wraps his lips around the vowels in my name.

And then with a heavy brush of his shoulder against mine, he's gone. He strides across the lobby, the stained glass creating rainbows against his suit jacket, and disappears into the shadows.

Just like on the cliff, he didn't even glance back.

I stand there in the darkness, with a stolen pearl necklace and a pounding heart.

CHAPTER
Six

Angelo

THE RUSTY ANCHOR BAR and Grill.
 The sign slapped above the door is missing most of its vowels, and I'd bet my Bugatti the inside is just as neglected. Ever since I was a kid, it's always been the type of joint that makes you want to wipe your feet on the way out.
 That's the thing about Devil's Dip. The places, the people. *The fucking weather.* Nothing about this shit-hole town ever changes. Stepping out of the storm and into the shipping container, I'm immediately proven right. The same splinter-laden bar made from washed-up wood; same old-timers propping it up. Even the bullet hole in the roof is still there from where my father shot his pistol into the air to restore law and order among disgruntled port workers.
 And the bloodstain on the rug from when one of the stupid bastards didn't take his threat seriously.
 I stare at the rainwater sloshing into the bucket in disgust. Dante must have slipped something into my whiskey last night, because I can't see any other logical reason why I agreed to meet him here.
 Or why I would have agreed to meet him at all.

The armchair by the fireplace grunts as I sink into it. Twisting my head toward the bar, I signal to the girl behind it to come over. She startles, points to her chest and mouths, *me?*

Yeah, I guess table service isn't the done thing in bars made from abandoned shipping containers.

By the time I've dusted the rain from my coat and raked a hand through my wet hair, she's hovering over me, wringing her hands.

"Y-yes?"

"*Smugglers Club* on the rocks."

There's a hiss from the other side of the room. Looking up, I lock eyes with an old man hunched over a table made from a crate. I know his type. Too old to still be slinging cargo on the docks, but he comes here every day to drown his sorrows with cheap beer, watching the port run fine without him through the rain-streaked window. Around here, men like him don't have anything else to do.

The girl flashes me an apologetic smile. She's blond, all sunny smiles and nervous energy. "Sorry about that. Uh, the *Smugglers Club* factory is in the town over, and the people around here aren't too fond of the family who owns it."

I ignore her in favor of holding the man's gaze. I rake my teeth over my bottom lip. Crack my knuckles. It'd be so easy to take the two strides over to him, wrap my hand around his throat and make sure he's unable to ever fucking hiss again.

I break my blistering glare and turn back to sunny smile girl. "He'll have one too. And make it a double."

Guess I'm not that loyal to the Visconti name.

She shifts her weight from foot to foot, then scurries away. She disappears into a back room, the sound of rummaging and clinking even louder than the rain hammering on the tin roof. I wonder what her story is. Girls with the biggest smiles harvest the darkest secrets. And besides, you must be repenting for *something* if you're working in this joint.

"You."

My eyes flick lazily to my left. Another old man, regarding me with fascination rather than a scowl.

"Is it really you? One of the Angels of Devil's Dip? I haven't seen you in years, kid."

Yeah, and I haven't heard that nickname in years. I huff out a laugh, one that tastes like bitter nostalgia, and turn my attention back to the pathetic excuse for a fire.

The Angels of Devil's Dip. That's what the locals used to call me and my brothers growing up, because we were the deacon's sons. That and the fact we were pale, blond, and angelic-looking. Back then, we didn't look like we had an ounce of Sicilian blood running through our veins, but as we grew upward and outward, our hair turned black and our skin more tanned, despite living in a town that saw about thirty minutes of sunshine a year.

"It's an honor to see you back in town, kid," the man says, tugging the beanie hat off his head and clutching it to his chest. "Your father was a great man."

Kid. I could tell him in not a fucking kid anymore. I'm a thirty-six-year old man, founder and CEO of a multi-billion-dollar investment firm.

I could also tell him my father was *not* a great man.

But I don't. I can't be fucked. Getting into scraps with the locals was always beneath me and it isn't the reason for my visit.

The bar girl brings over a dusty bottle dug out from the depths of the storage room, sloshes the brown liquid into a glass and sets it down on the three-legged table in front of me.

She glances at my Rolex. "If you're looking for Devil's Cove, you got off the interstate two junctions too early."

"Wren," the beanie-wearing man hisses, "that's Alonso Visconti's son."

I don't tear my gaze away from the fire. I don't need to, because I can hear the cogs whirring in her brain. She mutters a curse word, followed by a mumbled apology, then scurries back to the safety of the bar.

I turn back to the man who hissed. There's now a large glass of Visconti-produced whiskey next to his half-drunk beer. With a nasty grin spread across my face, I lift my glass to him, then take a large gulp.

He isn't scowling anymore.

Both he and the doe-eyed bastard who's up my father's ass. They represent the entire population of Devil's Dip. You either loved or hated my father, and in the rare event you were impartial, you still sure as hell knew who he was.

He and his two brothers were the first generation of the Sicilian Cosa Nostra to cross the Atlantic. New York was overcrowded and Boston was dominated by the Irish, so they traveled up and west until they found the isolated Devil's Coast. It had nothing but three shitty towns running along the length of it. They drew straws to decide who got what turf, and my father got Devil's Dip, seemingly the worst of a bad bunch. The waters were choppier, the cliffs were rockier, and the people were more...*simple* than they were further up the coast. But the port? It was perfect for black market cargo.

Nobody docks in Devil's Dip unless they have to. The waves are relentless, and the cliff curves around to hug the dock, making it invisible to incoming ships that have no business being there. It's small, nondescript, and draws no attention from local authorities. Plus, it's got easy trade routes along the West Coast, as well as Canada and even Russia.

The smallest towns have the biggest secrets, Angelo. That's what my father would always say when I was growing up. When I'd look at the bright lights of Devil's Cove or see my cousins in Devil's Hollow sealing seven-figure deals in business meetings with investors from New York, and ask him why he's still here.

And the bigger the secrets, the more power we have.

Over the rim of my glass, I study the two men. One shiny-eyed with nostalgia, the other growling into the bottom of his beer. No doubt one benefited from my father's reign, while the other lived in fear of it.

In other words, one had a bigger secret than the other.

Behind me, the door flies open and Dante's voice carries in with the blistering chill. Both snake down the back of my lapel in the most uncomfortable of ways.

"You're early, Vicious."

I roll my eyes at the nickname, slam my drink, and wave in the direction of the bar for another. I'm going to need it. But then, another voice takes the edge off my mood.

"I've found it."

"Found what?" Dante grunts.

"The most depressing place on earth. I bet even the cockroaches have fucked off."

My lips curve at the sound of Tor's cocky voice. I turn to see him approach the bar and slam his fist against it. "*Bastardo,*" he mutters, bringing his hand up to examine it. "I got a fucking splinter."

The bar girl appears from the back room, clutching the *Smugglers Club* bottle, the frozen smile on her face not doing a good job of hiding the panic in her eyes. She might not have known me, but she sure as hell will know Tor and Dante.

"Oh look, it's the Good Samaritan."

"I have a name, you know."

"Yeah, yeah, just give us that." Tor grunts, lunging over and grabbing the bottle from her.

"Uh, okay. Um, anything else?"

"Yeah, a tetanus shot."

I shake my head, mildly amused.

"Can't bring him anywhere."

I hadn't noticed Dante sink into the armchair opposite. He leans back, regarding me. As always, his tight smile doesn't reach his eyes.

Just like his father, he represents everything I hate about being tied to the Visconti name. The Cosa Nostra runs through his veins like a nasty virus, and he dresses like he's just wandered off the set of a Marlon Brando film.

Tor saunters over and slams the bottle on the table between us. "Good to see you, *cugino*. You usually only grace the Coast for Christmas and funerals, so I was surprised to see you turn up to dinner last night. You here for your parents' memorial service? 'Cause that's over two weeks away."

"No," Dante says quietly. "He wants to come home."

Behind the rim of my glass, I bite back a smirk. So *that's* why he was so insistent last night on meeting me today. When everyone was asking me why I was in town, my answer of "just visiting" wasn't convincing enough for him.

He's wrong. I'd rather shit in my hands and clap than move back to Devil's Dip and take my rightful place as capo, but the way his beady gaze shifts around my features, the way he white-knuckles his glass, it makes me realize he's nervous. So, I'll let him sweat it out a little longer.

Tor whistles. "Is it finally the return of Vicious Visconti?"

My jaw works. Just like Angels of Devil's Dip, Vicious Visconti is a nickname from a different lifetime. For the last nine years, there's been nothing vicious about me. But I can't deny it—hearing Tor call me that sends a zap of adrenaline down my spine.

It felt *good* to be vicious.

"I'm not moving back. Like I said last night, I'm just visiting."

Lie. You'd have to be lobotomized to visit Devil's Dip without an agenda. Tor's right—I fly back for Christmas and funerals and very little in between. I stay just long enough to shake hands with my uncles and fist-bump my cousins. To kiss aunts on the cheek and to let them pinch mine as they tell me how big I've grown. Being in this town for too long makes me feel like I'm losing brain cells. Plus, there's only so many times I can hear the question: *When are you coming back?*

Everyone always wants to know when I'm fucking coming back.

I don't like Dante even nearly enough to tell him that I'm here because of a goddamn fortune cookie.

Relief flickers in his eyes, and I have the immediate urge to distinguish it.

"But when I do decide to take over Devil's Dip again, you'll be the first to know," I add. "Thanks for keeping it warm for me."

He damn near chokes on his whiskey. Smoothing down his shirt—Italian, no doubt—he sets down his glass and glowers up at me. "Warm? I've completely transformed it. I've overhauled the infrastructure, bought a whole fleet of private-use vessels. Hired round-the-clock security to patrol the town. Hell, I have the port officials wrapped around my little finger and I've secured new trade routes to Mexico and the Middle East." His nostrils flare. "I've done more than keep it warm," he growls.

His outburst lingers in the air like a bad smell. Basking in the heat of his glower, I slowly roll my wrist, swirling the brown liquid around my glass. I let him sweat. Then, when the tension is deliciously thick, I meet his glare with one of my own.

"So, when I decide to return, you'll show me how it's done."

"Return? It must be nice, having the luxury to come and go as you please while I hold down your territory for you."

And there it is—one of the many reasons why Dante despises me. The sneers and the loaded comments, they've been a wedge between us for as long as I can remember, and being a whole continent apart for almost a decade hasn't changed a thing. It started when we were just kids; he always thought my brothers and I were childish because of the special game we'd play. And then that disdain turned into jealousy when our game meant we killed a man long before he was even allowed to pick up a gun.

Oh, and then I fucked his prom date. Can't remember why, though.

Now, the moment I step foot on the Coast, I feel his hostility. He hates that I went against his beloved tradition, and he hates that it's the same tradition stopping him from taking over Devil's Dip entirely and having full, unprecedented access to the port.

I raise my glass and wink. "That's what family is for, right?"

The silence blisters hotter than the fire. His jaw ticks and his throat bobs as he swallows the bitter retort he was about to spit out.

We glare at each other, and I can feel that familiar darkness swirling in the pit of my stomach. The adrenaline buzzing around the edges of my brain. I lick my lips, ignoring the rattling sound of Vicious Visconti trying to escape his cage. Since going straight,

I've tried to chase the high with fast cars and whores that don't have the word "no" in their vocabulary, but nothing comes close to the feeling of being a cruel fucker.

I swapped this life for a penthouse office and boardrooms and *fucking spreadsheets*. But it hasn't been easy. At least I get to indulge in my dark side once a month. That's probably the only reason I'm not stuffing my fist through his face.

Tor clears his throat and rises to his feet. "I'm going for a smoke. Come on, perhaps standing in the pissing rain with me will cool you two dogs down."

Without a word, Dante and I follow Tor through the bar and to the patio at the back. The porch is nothing but four slats of timber wood tied together with fisherman's rope, and the only things shielding us from the storm are a couple of crates that form a makeshift roof. Tor casts his eyes upwards, mutters something about OSHA under his breath, and lights his cigarette.

Wedged a few yards up the side of the cliff, the patio of the Rusty Anchor offers an uninterrupted view of the port. Despite my disdain for it, I can't deny that it's glossier than when I was a kid. The harbor is twice the size, the gangways and the ramps have been fully restored. Hell, even the harbormaster's office has been renovated—it used to be nothing but a creaky old hut that'd groan in the wind, and now, it's made from bricks and even has windows.

Tor offers his cigarette pack to me but I shake my head.

"What are you guys running through here now?"

"Still what you agreed to. Ammo goes out. Coke and party pills come in. Along with the usual restaurant and hotel supplies for Cove, of course." He blows out smoke into the rain and grins at me sideways. "Don't worry, if we decide to start trafficking Russian whores, we'll make sure to run it by you first."

"Sounds lucrative."

"Sounds like you want a cut," Dante growls. I glance over to see him leaning against the corrugated iron walls of the shipping container, hands stuffed into his pockets. "What were you talking to our father about last night?"

I don't bite. Instead, I turn my back to the stormy sea and look left, taking in the glittery lights of Devil's Cove in the distance. In front of it, Devil's Hollow looms like a dark shadow, and our old school, the Devil's Coast Academy sits on top of it like a poisonous cherry on top of a cake. I crane my neck directly upward, eyes landing on my father's church. Then focus on the headland in front of it, where, Wednesday morning, I came across my uncle's latest whore standing too close to the edge. I'd barely gotten a glimpse of her, just a shock of blond hair peeking out from under her hoodie and a brief glance at her face as I'd turned to leave. Usually, it wouldn't be enough to recognize her from across the dining table like I did last night. But then when she glared at me from the other side of the room, I knew those eyes instantly. They are the color of warm whiskey.

I stuff my hands into my coat pockets, bracing my back against the howling wind. Fair play to the old bastard—she's a smoke show for sure. That fucking red dress she'd poured herself into; *Jesus*, any man with a pulse would get a hard-on at that visual.

"Speaking of your father, I see he has another gold-digging whore already," I drawl, lazily dragging my gaze back down the rocks to Tor. "They get younger every year."

He huffs out a laugh. "Yeah, younger and hotter. Fuck knows where he picked her up."

"Meaning?"

"Usually Big Al's girls are club rats. You know, lingering around the VIP area in my clubs trying to find a meal ticket. But Aurora? I'd never seen her before." He flicks the butt of his cigarette into the rain and tucks his chin into his jacket. "Trust me, I'd have spotted that hot piece of ass a mile away," he mutters.

I chew on this nugget of information for a moment. *Interesting*. Sure, she has all the same components as the others that came before her—blond hair, big tits, and legs as long as a Monday—but she's definitely different. A smarter mouth. A smirk prickles my lips as I remember pulling Vivi's pearl necklace out of her ample cleavage. *And a dirty little thief.*

I glance back up at the cliff edge and an uninvited thought seeps into my brain. *Why did she want to jump?* But I shake it off as quickly as it arrives. I truly don't give a flying fuck about my uncle's latest leech. And besides, I'd kill myself too if my only way out of Devil's Dip was to hand my virginity over to a seventy-year-old sleazeball.

Tor's cell buzzes in his pocket. He pulls it out, looks at the screen and groans. "Work," he grumbles, before dipping back inside. Now, it's just me and Dante, and I realize he's been awfully quiet over the last few minutes.

We lock eyes and his glare darkens. "Why are you really here, Angelo?"

Turning my attention back to the sea, I drag a knuckle through my beard and steel my jaw.

"Dante?"

"Yeah?"

"Mind your own fucking business."

Without looking back, I shove past him, head into the bar and stroll toward the door. As I pass, Tor grabs my arm, pulls his cell away from his ear and mouths, *where are you going?*

I pull out a stack of cards from my breast pocket and toss them in the tip bowl. "Meeting the Hollow clan for lunch."

"Tell Benny he owes me forty-grand from last week's poker game, yeah?"

I nod, then keep walking.

"You coming round for Sunday lunch tomorrow?" he calls after me.

A groan rumbles in my chest. The Cove clan loves a fucking get-together. I'd rather stick my dick in a car door, but instead of telling him that, I lift my hand up in a half-wave and crash out into the parking lot.

Slipping into the car, I let out a hiss of breath. The rain falls in sheets against the windshield, and the wind threatens to rip off the side mirrors. *Man, this weather.* I start the car and slice through the storm, snaking along the road cut into the cliff face, which I'll take until I'm at the highest point of Devil's Dip. To get to Devil's Hollow, you have to come up to the top of the cliffs and cut across them, before taking the narrow, winding lane that leads down to the town below. Locals call it Grim Reaper road, because the slightest oversteer will have the man himself looming over your shoulder.

This should be a fun drive.

The engine groans up the incline, and the radio crackles as it struggles to find a signal. I strum my fingers against the steering wheel and try to remember the last time I saw the Hollow Viscontis—I don't see them nearly as much as my brother Rafe does. Seems like he's partying with them every other week.

Ah, yes, it was a few months ago. Castiel's engagement party. He's marrying a sour-faced Russian who hates him as much as he hates her. She's the heir to the Nostrova Vodka company, so, another business arrangement. No surprises there—the only people in this family dumb enough to marry for love are Donatello and Amelia.

And my mother.

On the top of the cliff, a familiar building looms in the distance, getting closer with every swish of the wipers. A groan escapes my lips. *Of course.* I'd forgotten I have to pass my father's church on the way to Hollow, and I can't be fucked to deal with all the memories it drags up right now. When I arrived on the coast on Wednesday, I decided to do what I always do: head straight to the church even before dumping off my bags at the Visconti Grand hotel. Get all the anger and the bitter nostalgia out of my system before I dive into the family gatherings and the air kisses and the small talk. But then a certain somebody was already in my usual spot, and she proved to be quite the distraction.

As I round the graveyard, I notice a car parked at the entrance. Strange. The only people buried here within the last century are Viscontis, and the only reason a local would visit a Visconti grave is to piss on it. Maybe it's the territorial instinct in me, left over from when I actually gave a shit about this place, but I slow down, then come to a complete stop under the willow tree. Upping the speed of the wipers, I squint through the windshield and the low-hanging branches, trying to figure out who's in the car. The headlights are on high-beam, casting a yellow glow over lop-sided headstones that are sinking into the mud, and a small trail of smoke escapes the gap in the driver's side window. A man's hand pokes out, flicking cigarette ash onto the gravel.

Gripping the steering wheel, I frown and lean closer, trying to get a better look at who's in the car, and realize their head is turned, as if they are looking to the right. I follow their gaze across the road. The bus stop is empty, but the phone booth next to it is not.

My frown deepens. *Jesus, who the fuck uses a phone booth these days?* The flickering bulb built into the roof of it illuminates a silhouette. A female with long blond hair and a willowy figure.

Letting out a huff of air, I slump back into the seat and mutter under my breath. *You've gotta be shitting me.* It's Alberto's girl, Aurora. Sure, her hair is different—wild curls instead of poker-straight strands—and she's in sweats and sneakers instead of that sexy red dress, but it's definitely her. I turn down the crackling radio, as if it'll magically help me hear what she's saying, and watch her for a moment. She twirls the phone cord around her fingers and talks animatedly into the mouthpiece. Whoever is on the other side of the line clearly doesn't have much to say, as she's doing all the talking.

What the fuck are you doing here, girl? And who are you talking to?

Shaking my head, my fingers graze the key in the ignition. I don't give a flying fuck who she's talking to. It's clearly someone she doesn't want my uncle to know about, otherwise she'd use her cell. Whatever. Alberto's sugar baby is none of my business, and I couldn't care less what she gets up to behind his back.

I'm just about to start the engine when she abruptly hangs up, turns to the car, and knocks on the glass door of the phone booth. The car lights switch off, and the figure gets out the driver's side, holding an umbrella. He hustles across the road, opens the door, and holds the umbrella above her head with one hand, then snakes the other around her waist. As he guides her across the road, I get a good look at him.

It's that kid, the lackey. Max, or whatever his name is; he must be her escort. My knuckles whiten over the steering wheel and annoyance prickles my skin. He's holding her close, really fucking close, and by the way he's gazing at her under the streetlights, I can tell it's not just because he's trying to keep her dry.

None of my business. This is not why I'm here.

But I can't shake the irritation that itches under my collar like a rash. It must be another instinctual thing, just like being territorial over my father's church. I might not be the biggest fan of Alberto or his sleazy love life, but he's still family.

I'll wait. Just for a minute.

They reach the car, and to my surprise, Aurora doesn't get in. Instead, they have a short conversation, Max hands her the umbrella—fingers brushing against hers—then he gets in the car and drives off.

A low whistle slips through my lips. Leaving the Don's fiancee on the side of the road alone? In a shit hole like Devil's Dip? That kid's asking for a bullet in his head.

If I were a better man, I'd kick this car into gear and take her home.

Too bad I'm not.

Instead, I watch as she stands there, eyes following the car until the lights disappear into the fog, before she turns her attention to the graveyard.

I freeze, and an icy thought trickles into my brain, slower than syrup.

The cliff edge. Is she going to finish what I interrupted?

There's a lump in my throat and I'm not sure how it got there. Or how my hand moved from the steering wheel to the door handle. I've seen people kill themselves dozens of times. Hell, I forced some of them to write their suicide notes.

My fingers drop off the handle and into my lap. *Not my problem*—I have enough of those. I'm not getting out the car.

She takes a step forward, toward the path that cuts through the graveyard and to the cliff headland.
Fuck it, I'm getting out the car.
Just as I yank on the handle, she comes to an abrupt stop, then turns. Walks down the road.
"Fucking hell, girl. Make up your mind," I grumble to myself. Before I can talk myself out of it, I start the vehicle, flick my lights off, and crawl down the street behind her.

I'm not a patient man, never have been. And as the owner of the largest supercar collection in Europe, I'm not used to driving at this speed. Nor am I used to following young women down empty roads without their knowledge. Not really my bag.

After what feels like forever, she turns off, and I realize she's heading into the Preserve. First the phone booth, then the forest. What the fuck is this girl up to?

I don't mean to wait. I tell myself just a couple more minutes, but an hour ticks by, and I still haven't moved.

And then I see her. She steps out from behind the trees, then Max's car crawls back down the street to greet her. He gets out, plants a kiss on her neck, and guides her back to the car.

As they drive off, I realize I'm grinding my jaw. There's something bitter on my tongue, a taste I don't recognize. Steeling my spine, I start my car and spin my wheel into full lock to head in the direction I just came, all stealthiness out the window.

So, she's a gold-digger and a thief.

She represents everything I hate about this life. To my uncle, she's nothing but a piece of pretty pussy and something to brag about over a poker game. To her, my uncle is a walking, talking Amex, with a spend limit worth spreading her legs for.

Whatever. I have more important things to do than spy on my uncle's whore.

CHAPTER Seven

Rory

THE DRESS GRETA IS trying to squeeze me into is two sizes too small, but she's not the type of woman to back down from a challenge. Women who wear tweed pencil skirts and half-moon spectacles, and scrape their hair back into the tightest bun possible, never are. She folds my flesh with one hand and yanks up the zipper with the other.

"Oh, flamingo," I hiss, glowering at her in the full-length mirror. She looks up and pins me with a glare of her own.

"You need to stop with all the candy," she snaps, bending down to tug on my hemline. It's pointless; the dress still barely covers the curve of my ass. "You think I don't see all those wrappers in the garbage? Stuffed inside your purses? Cut them out and your waistline will thank you."

"Or you could stop buying me dresses meant for a twelve-year-old," I snap back.

Of course, with its plunging neckline, it'd be *very* inappropriate for a twelve-year-old. It's also incredibly inappropriate for lunch, but I'm not feeling very argumentative today; I never am on Sundays. It bridges the gap between Saturday and Wednesday, which are the days I get to see my father. Also, these Sunday lunches are much more civilized than Friday dinners. Everyone is quieter, meeker, especially if they've partied hard the night before.

Greta's hand clamps my shoulder as she nods to the vanity. "Sit."

My heart sinks. "Aw come on. Can't I just have one lunch where I don't have to—"

"Aurora, sit in the chair and keep your mouth shut."

Nostrils flaring, I slowly sink in front of the mirror.

"I don't know why you always insist on arguing," she mutters, ripping open the dresser drawer and pulling out her torture tools: the straightener and the hairbrush. "*Signore* Alberto likes your hair straight. He doesn't ask much of you but gives you so much in return. The very least you could do is wear your hair how he likes." She punctuates her sentence by dragging the brush through my curls. A million strands of my hair scream for help. I suck in a lungful of air and clench my fingers over the hem of my dress. "You don't realize how lucky you are."

"You marry him, then."

My retort is met by a swift *thwack* on my head with the back of the brush. I squeeze my eyes shut and mutter a bird-word under my breath. The bitterness swirls in the pit of my stomach, and my fingers ache with the need to curl into a fist and connect it with her stupid face. But Greta is Alberto's head housekeeper and most brainwashed follower, so I know she reports everything back to him without fail. I'd rather a crack around my head from her than something more sinister from Alberto.

She's worked for him so long that she speaks fondly of changing Dante's diapers. It's obvious that she's been in love with him for just as long, too. My guess is she's bitter that somewhere between all the wives, she never got a look in. Maybe she had the chance when she was younger, but now she's way past her sell-by date in Alberto's eyes, and she missed the window.

"Don't move, I need to grab the anti-frizz serum." She twirls around and stalks into the en-suite attached to the dressing room. Naturally, my eyes fall to her Cartier watch on the vanity, which she always takes off when tackling my mane. With a cursory glance to the bathroom door, I pluck a pin from a sewing cushion and scratch the pointed end deep into the watch face. I've considered stealing it several times because I'm sure it's worth a hefty amount, but it was a gift from Alberto, so I'm sure she'd notice.

I lock eyes with myself in the mirror and afford myself a sigh. Bad things, *petty* bad things, are what keep me from going insane in my new, messed-up version of reality. Little acts of revenge keep me calm. Those, and candy.

Picking up my purse from the vanity, I rummage around for a sweet treat. There's always *something* in here, whether it's a stick of blueberry bubblegum or a pack of Nerds. My fingers brush over a half-melted Reece's peanut butter cup. That'll do. As I pull it out, a small, glossy card falls into my lap. Absentmindedly, I pick it up and flip it over.

Sinners Anonymous. The letters are embossed in gold, and underneath, the number is printed in silky black numerals. The card has taken a battering; there's a crease in the middle where I once sat down with it in the back pocket of my jeans, and the edges curl in, like they are protecting my special little secret. I don't know why I still carry the card with me after all this time, because I'd be able to recite the number in my sleep.

Whether or not I believe in fate, I don't know, but I do know it was more than just a coincidence that I found this card on the darkest day of my life.

I remember it like it was yesterday.

A mouth full of blood, not all of it my own. Fresh finger-shaped bruises forming on my throat, and an ache between my thighs I didn't ask for. I'd stumbled out of the Devil's Coast Academy and into the parking lot. Got in my car and drove, until I could no longer see the school's Gothic spires in my rear-view mirror. I made it as far as the church in Devil's Dip before the reality of what they'd done to me—*what I'd done to them*—hit me like a tsunami. I couldn't breathe. Wasn't sure if I wanted to. If I deserved to. I staggered out of the car and into the rain, just to feel something other than the crushing sensation on my chest. As I leaned against the bus shelter, sobbing, I looked up, and that's when I saw it. The small card pinned to the board in the phone booth opposite.

Sinners Anonymous.

I'd heard of it—everyone on Devil's Coast had. A few years earlier, these cards had started turning up in tip jars in coffee shops and bars. Pinned to the walls of bathroom stalls in clubs, tucked in with the check at restaurants. When you called the number, it took you straight to an automated voicemail service, which prompted you to confess whatever sin or secret was weighing on your mind. It was so mysterious, and the excitement of it all rippled down the coast for a while, until the hype settled down like dust, and eventually, Sinners Anonymous just became entwined into the fabric of the area.

That first call, I made it on my knees, the phone tucked between my chin and shoulder as I clasped my hands together like a prayer. Now it's become part of my life. Just like how religious people go to church to confess every Sunday, I call the Sinners Anonymous hotline twice a week from the same phone booth by the church. I confess everything I've done, from the slightly gray to the dark.

Greta bustles back into the dressing room and brings me back to present day. The next hour crawls by in a painful storm of tugging and muttering and the occasional burn mark on my neck. By the time Greta steps back and claps her hands, I'm the girl Alberto wants me to be again. Smokey eye makeup, blood-red lipstick, and a dress that clings to my curves like second skin.

Time for Sunday lunch.

Refusing to utter another word to Greta, I storm past her and click-clack into the hall. But just before I descend the marble staircase, a hushed voice makes the hairs on the back of my neck stand up. Two voices, and something in the tone of the conversation makes me freeze, my foot hovering over the first step.

"It's a standard contract. Just add the fucking clause and be done with it."

Holding my breath, I peer over the railing and see a familiar silhouette in a corner of the lobby. *Alberto.* I can't see the man he's talking to, but as soon as he speaks, my blood runs cold.

"She's already signed it. You know I can't tamper with signed contracts, Alberto."

That's Mortiz, his lawyer. The one that breathed over me in Alberto's office as I signed my life away.

"Oh, please. We both know she's too stupid to have read it. Just draw up a new contract, add her signature to the bottom and we'll be done with it."

There's a stagnant silence, followed by a nasal sigh. "Give me a few days to find another way. In the meantime, read through the new clause and let me know if there's anything else you'd like to add." There's a shuffling sound and I brave leaning over the railing just enough to get a glimpse of Mortiz handing Alberto a brown folder. Then, he clears his throat. "You understand, don't you, Alberto? If she realizes the contract is not the one she signed, she could sue. And you know the Superior Court isn't your biggest fan right now— "

Alberto cuts him off with a laugh so loud it echoes off the domed ceiling. "That girl doesn't have two dimes to rub together. She's a nobody, Mortiz. Besides, who'd believe her? Everyone knows her father is an old quack, so it'd be easy to convince everyone else she hasn't fallen far from the tree."

My ears start to ring so loudly I can't hear the rest of the conversation. I duck into an alcove, trying to stop myself from panting like a darn dog. *What the hell is Alberto up to? Changing the terms of our contract?*

Heat prickles under my skin and the lone Reese's peanut butter cup in my stomach threatens to make an appearance. I *knew* I shouldn't have trusted him. But he's right. I'm a nobody, especially in this world. I don't come from money or power. If he wants to screw me over, the three hundred dollars in my bank account will do nothing to stop him. He and his family own everything and everyone on this coast; nobody will help.

Over the thumping of my pulse, I hear Alberto's booming footsteps head in the direction of his study, and I glance down just in time to see him leaving it again, empty-handed.

The decision is a split-second one, fueled by anger and determination. I do a quick sweep of the lobby, then make a clumsy sprint down the stairs and into his office. Inside, the air is thick with the smell of stale cigars and musty books. Heavy drapes on the bay windows keep out sunlight and keep in all the secrets, and although it's so dark in here that I can barely see the desk, I don't dare turn on the lamp. Instead, I shuffle blindly through files, bringing them up to my nose to read the first few lines. I rip open drawers. Even give the darn safe under the desk a frustrated kick. Nothing.

"Snooping is a sin, Aurora."

The voice melts out of the shadows like butter on a warm day, gluing me to the spot. *Oh, holy crow.* Forcing myself to look up, my eyes land on a silhouette in the arm chair, one darker than the corner it's occupying. *Angelo.* Christ, why is he still here?

Sucking in an unsteady breath, I steel my spine and try to keep the wobble out of my voice. "I'm not snooping, My fiance asked me to fetch him something," I say, attempting a breezy tone. I continue to rustle through papers I care nothing about.

The floorboard groans as he rises to his feet. I hate how hyper-aware I am of his presence, how I can feel every heavy footstep he takes toward me in my chest, like the beating of a drum.

He leans his palms against the desk and looks up at me with hooded, lazy eyes. "Really?"

One simple word, loaded like a gun. I swallow the lump in my throat. "Yes."

I drop a hip in an attempt to look natural. It's instinctive to twist a curl around my finger when I get nervous, but as I reach up to my hair, I'm met with nothing but poker-straight strands. Awkwardly, I let my hand go limp by my side. "Lurking in dark corners isn't a sin, but it's still weird as hell."

His eyes flash with dark amusement. While he irritates me, I mildly amuse him, and it's a feeling that makes the flame of annoyance flicker brighter in my stomach. Mildly entertaining. Like a rerun of a sitcom playing in the background as you make dinner, or a waving toddler in the car next to you on the freeway.

For some reason, I want to be anything but his mild entertainment. *Anything but mild to him at all.*

"You're right. It's not a sin. But you know what is?" He leans closer, closing in on the gap between us. My breathing shallows, but I don't dare pull away. Don't dare give him the satisfaction. "Cheating on your fiance. But cheating on Alberto Visconti with one of his lackeys? That's a death wish." His gaze drops to my lips, and I fight the urge to lick them. "You really *do* like living life on the edge, huh?"

His words contain too much information to process. Cheating with a lackey? He must mean Max, and that means...he saw us yesterday in Devil's Dip. And by living life on the edge, he's referring to the first time we met, on the cliff. My cheeks grow hotter by the second, and I feel like I'm burning and blistering under a dark sun, but I refuse to scurry back to the shade.

"For someone who hates Devil's Dip so much, you're sure there often," I rasp.

He's still and silent, gaze moving over my features like he's waiting for more.

I hate that I give it to him.

"Alberto knows I spend Saturdays and Wednesdays in Devil's Dip, and Max is my escort." My voice is almost pleading, "I'm *not* cheating."

"And you are not snooping."

"Exactly, I'm not snooping."

I hear footsteps in the lobby. They grow heavier and closer, until they are so close they rattle the golden ornaments on the desk between us. Angelo's face is a network of hard lines, but even in the dim light, I can see his gaze dancing wildly.

"Well, let's ask him."

The doorknob turns and the light from the lobby floods the room. I drop the stack of papers in my hand, take a step back from the desk and turn to face the silhouette darkening the doorway.

I swear I hear Angelo chuckle.

Alberto pauses when he sees me. His eyes narrow, then flick to Angelo and back again. "What are you doing in here?"

Oh, flamingo. My brain and tongue can't connect quick enough to come up with an answer. He raises a bushy eyebrow, his jaw ticking as he waits for my reply. But all I can think about is the bruising on my wrist, the cuts on my thigh. They burn with the ghost of his violence, which is getting worse by the day. There are only so many nightcaps I can spit in, only so many important legal documents I can steal and run under the bathroom tap.

Alberto takes a step forward. "Aurora—"

"I caught her on the way to lunch," Angelo drawls, dragging his hands off the desk and unfurling his spine to his full height. He towers over his uncle and makes his office feel smaller than a matchbox. "Had a few questions about Dip."

I steal a glance at him, but he's looking down at his cell, expressionless. Like he's already bored with the conversation. Bored with me.

My ears ring with his lie, and my mind races with all the reasons why he'd bother to lie for me at all. And then a small hit of adrenaline zaps down my spine. It rolled so easily off his tongue, like lying is second nature to him, and something about it...

I ignore the heat spreading between my thighs. *Don't be so ridiculous, Rory.*

"Well, I hope you got what you needed," Alberto says breezily. "Now if you don't mind, I'd like to have a quick chat with you before lunch." He looks at me pointedly. "*Alone.*"

I can't get out of there quick enough. Before the door slams shut behind me, I feel the heat of Angelo's gaze follow me out.

The brightness of the lobby feels like a hit of fresh air. I take a moment to steady my breathing and smooth down my dress, before heading toward the dining room on wobbly legs. Laughter and lighthearted chatter spill out from underneath the swinging doors, but another voice steers my attention to the right.

In the kitchen, Vittoria stands with her arms crossed, a lanky-looking boy of around the same age, opposite her. His suit is too big, his hair too floppy. He huffs it out of his eyes and says, "That necklace cost me my entire weekly allowance, Vivi. What do you mean you lost it?"

She rolls her eyes in a way that suggests this is the millionth time he's asked. "I don't know, Charlie, I was drunk. Besides, I'm like, sixteen. What sixteen-year-old do you know who wears pearls?"

Jesus. I need to start keeping a diary of all my sins, because I'll end up forgetting what I need to confess to.

I slip into the dining room and the laughter gets louder. Today, the decor is less *The Adam's Family* and more *Architectural Digest*. A white lace tablecloth runs the length of the dining table, adorned with checkered silk napkins and bell jars filled with carefully stacked pumpkins and squash. Outside the French doors, the sky is clear and the fall sun bright, making the Pacific ocean glitter.

There's only one person at the table, and when I take my seat next to him, he gives my thigh a squeeze.

"Hey, gorgeous," Max mutters.

"Jesus," I mutter, swatting his hand away. "What have I told you? No touching."

He leans his elbows on the table. "About that no touching rule…"

"Don't start—"

"Hear me out." He glances up toward the head of the table, and when he realizes it's just us, he turns his attention back to me. "Angelo hasn't said anything to Alberto about me leaving you to your own devices in Devil's Dip, has he?"

I shake my head. I don't bother telling him that he saw us yesterday, too.

"Good," he purrs. "But that whole ordeal, it got me thinking. Leaving you to see your father on your own is a big risk, you know? If Alberto finds out, he'll kill me."

Twisting a napkin in my fists, I shoot him a scowl. "What's your point?"

"My point is that big risks deserve big rewards." He drags his eyes down to my chest, then a shit-eating smirk splits his face in two. "I need more from you, Aurora."

It takes a few moments for his insinuation to click. But when it does, the rage spills out of my gut and through my arms and down to my hand, which curls into a fist and makes a beeline for his jaw. I catch the shock on his face before he grabs my hand.

"What the fuck?" he spits.

I try to snatch my hand back, but he refuses to let it go. "You're all the same," I hiss back, feeling my hand tremble against his palm. I yank it back again, but he curls his fingers tighter around my bones. "All you boys from that stupid school, you're all the same."

"Aurora, what the hell—"

"Let *go* of me," I demand, not caring that my voice is growing louder, echoing through the empty dining room.

Suddenly, the doors swing open and Angelo strolls in. He pauses. He glances from me, to Max, then to our hands entwined between us. Max squeaks something inaudible and drops my hand like it's burning him, but it's too late. Panting with the weight of my outburst, I hold Angelo's gaze as it grows as dark as an incoming storm.

It's not what it looks like, I want to scream. I can't have him tell Alberto what he just saw, or have him voice his suspicion that I'm sleeping with Max. Because hell, this man has enough over my head already.

Under the heavy silence, I study the table cloth and wish I could take my outburst back. It's not just Max being a creep, it's also Alberto being a damn snake about this contract, and it's Angelo being...well, *Angelo*.

I'll drown in the actions of this family.

Before he can say anything, the doors swing open again, and Alberto stomps in, two men strolling in after him.

"Drinks," Alberto booms to no one in particular. But of course, only seconds after he sinks into his seat, a server appears holding a tray with a bottle of *Smugglers Club* and four glasses. Angelo sits in my usual seat and the two men sit next to him.

"Aurora, these are my two other nephews, Raphael and Gabriel," Alberto says without looking up at me.

Through weary eyes, I turn to regard them. I'm in no mood for pleasantries. Max was right, and I recognize Raphael because he hangs around with Tor and the Hollow brothers. He has the same glittering, green eyes and silky, black hair as his brother, but he looks like he's been put under immense pressure and came out the other side a shiny, diamond version of Angelo. Smooth, tanned skin, and when he flashes me a dazzling smile, dimples crease his cheeks, giving him a mischievous charm. He looks younger than Angelo—dresses younger too. His suit is sharp: a crisp slim-fit and a collar pin with two diamond dice on either side of it instead of a tie. When he lifts his drink to his lips, his matching cuff links glint at me.

"A pleasure, Aurora," he drawls over the rim of his glass. He punctuates it with a wink that I bet makes most women drop their panties.

I force a polite smile and shift my attention to the other brother, Gabriel. Instantly, a chill runs down my spine. He has the same cold, unrelenting stare as Angelo, but there's something darker behind it. More sinister. I don't know…maybe it's the thick beard, the angry scar carved into his face, or the tattoos crawling out from underneath his turtleneck sweater, but if I definitely wouldn't want to bump into him in a dark alley.

He doesn't say a word.

Slowly, the rest of the Viscontis pour in, plus a few extras, like the teenager in the too-big suit, who follows Vittoria into the dining room with the air of a recently kicked puppy, and to my surprise, the same girl Tor brought to dinner on Friday night.

And so Sunday lunch begins.

The pianist plays light jazz, the servers bring out honey-roasted hams and herb-crusted lamb, accompanied by glazed vegetables and potato Dauphinoise. Whiskey and apple cider cocktails flow, and I refuse them every time they pass, deciding it's probably best to remain sober today, especially considering my mood. One swipe from the wrong Visconti, and I'm afraid I'll lunge for the carving knife.

I'm drawn to the hum at the top of the table and through the curtain of my hair, I watch Raphael hold court. He's telling a story, one so gripping that even Alberto isn't interrupting with an anecdote. My eyes shift to Angelo, just in time to see him throw his head back and laugh.

My heart stills. *Whoa*. It's deep, throaty, and genuine. The type of laugh that carves a mark in your memory. There's a sudden dull ache under my rib cage, and briefly, I allow myself to wonder what it'd feel like to be the recipient of it.

Darn it, Rory. Cut it out.

Goose. Not only will this family drown me, they'll turn me insane, too.

A sharp elbow in my ribs brings me back to reality. "Well?"

I shift my gaze to Max. "Well what?"

"You thought about what I said?"

My jaw hardens, that rage brewing in my gut again. I lower my head and shuffle my seat closer to whisper in his ear. The last thing I need is to draw Alberto's attention.

"The only way I'll touch you is when I put my hands around your throat and choke you in your sleep."

He recoils, shocked. Stares at me for a few stunned seconds. "Are you drunk?"

"No, I'm just sick of you. All of you."

"All of us?"

"Men. Everything is a damn exchange to you. News flash—when a woman wants something from you, she shouldn't always have to pay with her body. Whatever happened to a good old-fashioned favor? You know, like when I begged Alberto not to log the Devil's Preserve, he could have just agreed, instead of anchoring me to him with this damn ring on my finger. And when I asked you to give me some peace and quiet for a few hours in Devil's Dip twice a week, you could have just agreed, instead of deciding that it's an ask worthy of getting to grope my boobs in the back of your Lexus."

I rip away from him and stare up at the gilded ceiling, taking deep, deliberate breaths. *Is this it? Have I reached my limit?*

As my attention falls back down to the table, I lock eyes with Angelo. He's no longer laughing at his brother's story, nor is he eating. Instead, he's staring right at me, his hands clenched into fists on either side of his untouched plate. Once I acclimate to the chill of his gaze, I realize what he sees. Me and Max, shoulder to shoulder, heads huddled and having a private, heated conversation at the end of the table.

Panic claws at my throat, and I immediately put some distance between us.

"Aurora—"

"Not now, Max," I mutter, picking at bits of ham.

"But—"

Ting, ting ting.

His plea is interrupted by the sound of a knife hitting crystal. A sound I've come to know all too well since having the misfortune to be engaged to Anecdote Alberto.

With a stifled sigh, I look up and prepare myself for a long speech. But Alberto is still sitting and looking to his left.

It's Angelo who's standing up, holding his whiskey glass in one hand and a knife in the other.

"May I have everyone's attention, please."

His voice is low yet commanding, and triggers immediate silence.

He basks in it for a few seconds, then shifts his attention to me. "Aurora, isn't it?"

My eyes narrow. I know this jerk knows my name, because the way it rolls off his tongue is etched into my memory. But with a wary glance at Alberto, I nod.

"Aurora. Stand up."

A soft laughter ripples around the room, the type tinged with uncertainty. *What's he playing at?* With all eyes on me, I know I can't cause a scene, so begrudgingly, I scrape back my chair and slowly rise to my feet.

"Perfect. Now, take three steps to the left."

My cheeks grow hot, and everyone's laughter gets louder, like he's telling a joke and I'm the only idiot who doesn't realize I'm the punchline. With a huff, I take one step back so I'm behind Vittoria's seat, then take three deliberate steps to the left.

"Happy?"

But if Angelo replies, I don't hear it.

There's a glint in his right hand. Then the *bang* is too loud. The smell of gunpowder too strong, and the taste of blood splatter on my lips too tangy.

The bullet enters Max right between the eyes and exits out the back of his skull, taking half his brain with it. His head hits the table with a heavy thud, his blood turning the lace tablecloth crimson.

There are a few gasps. One scream from Tor's date, Skyler. Vittoria mutters, 'Oh, for fucks sake," in the same tone you might use if you'd missed the bus. But it's less than five seconds before silence settles around the table.

With my ears ringing, I look up at Angelo. As calm as a spring day, he sits down, sets the gun next to his napkin, and stuffs a forkful of ham in his mouth. He chews. Takes a sip of whiskey. Then he catches Alberto's eye and waves his fork in his direction.

"The kid's been selling your business plans to the Russians." Then, lazily glancing around the rest of the table, he adds, "Eat up, your food will get cold."

Raphael sniggers.

Tor lets out a low whistle.

The word *vicious* flashes behind my eyelids.

And I black out.

When I come around, I'm lying on the sofa in the family room. Harsh sunlight streams through the window, and on the other side, the branches of a willow tree scrape against the glass, like it's trying to wake me up gently. A bird chirps. Without looking, I know it's a Black-capped Chickadee. They are hardy little things that never migrate for winter. They never flee from their hometowns, even when things get cold and tough and uncertain. No, they stay with their families and do what it takes to survive.

I've always liked Black-capped Chickadees.

"If you want to be a part of this family you really can't be so squeamish."

I roll my head to the side and see Leonardo, Vittoria's twin, spread across the armchair opposite. He's tapping lazily on his phone, his floppy hair concealing one of his eyes.

"Huh?"

But then the memory floods back and I bolt upright, ignoring the pounding on the back of my head. *Angelo shot Max.* Looking down, there's a red splatter against my dress. I lift a trembling hand to my lips, and sure enough, when I pull my fingertips back, they are covered in blood that isn't mine.

"Oh my god," I gasp, digging my fingers into the velvet fabric, trying to clamber to my feet. "*Oh my god.*"

The door opens and Amelia hurries in. "No, no. You stay right there, sweetie. You've had quite the nasty fall and I need to check your head." She touches my arm. Sinks into the seat next to me. "Does it hurt?"

"He killed Max."

It's not a question, and Amelia doesn't answer it. Instead, she gently tilts my head forward and brushes my hair away from the tender spot at the back of my head.

One second he was alive, eating herb-crusted lamb and drinking whiskey cider cocktails, and then the next…

Jesus. The last thing I remember before my world went dark is the image of his body slumped over the family's fine china. Through the headache, a small, niggling voice in the back of my brain speaks to me. *Did I do this?*

But I bat it away. It's a stupid, self-centered thought. Angelo Visconti wouldn't pee on me if I was on fire, just like he wouldn't have grabbed me if I jumped off the cliff. And even if he truly believes I was cheating on his Uncle with Max, he doesn't strike me as the type to shed blood over something that doesn't concern him.

"Hold still," Amelia murmurs. I wince under the touch of her cold fingers. Eventually, she pulls away and pats my lap. "No blood, just a big bump. Take it easy for the next few days, okay? Oh—and if you start feeling sleepy, let someone know."

I take in her sorry smile and calm demeanor. "Are you serious?"

"Yes, concussion is no joke."

I blink. "Amelia, Max just got *shot*. Dead. As in, he's literally not alive anymore. And you're..."

"You heard what Angelo said," she says quietly, glancing to Leonardo, who's now smirking under his hair. "He was a traitor."

Slowly, I shake my head. "No," I murmur, "Max wouldn't—"

"Well, he did," she interrupts in a firmer tone. Then her eyes soften, like she regrets being so harsh. "I'm sorry, Aurora. I remember my first time like it was yesterday..." She huffs out air, slumps her shoulders. "But it gets easier, I promise. You have to remember the Visconti world is different from the one we're used to." With one last pat on my leg, she rises to her feet. "I'm here if you need to talk. In the meantime, try to rest."

She crosses the carpet, ruffling Leo's hair as she passes. "But how did he know that Max was a traitor? He doesn't even live on the continent, let alone on the coast."

The question slips from my lips before I realize I'm even thinking it.

She pauses, holding on to the door frame. "The same way he knows everything." Then she slips out of the room, her heels click-clacking on marble in the distance.

I turn to Leo. "What does that mean?"

With a sigh, he tears his attention away from his phone and looks at me. "The Dip brothers have this hotline. Anyone can dial it and confess their secrets. Max probably called it. Snakes like him usually have a guilty conscience."

No.

No, no, no.

"A hotline?" I croak.

"Yeah, you've probably seen the cards around." *Please god, no.* "It's called Sinners Anonymous."

Not for the first time today, my world goes black.

CHAPTER
Eight

Angelo

Saint Pius Church, Devil's Dip.

It's a small, modest building, bar the towering spire that can be seen all the way from Devil's Cove on a clear day. It sits stupidly close to the edge of the cliff, and the stones are eroded by the salty sea air and years of neglect. In front of it, ivy-covered tombstones clutter the graveyard, including those of my parents.

Standing in front of the rotting oak door, I tighten my grip on the crowbar and take a deep breath. Nine years ago, I threw the key off the side of the cliff and I can't be fucked to find out if either of my Uncles have a spare. Instead, I jimmy the bar in between the wood and the iron lock, and unsurprisingly, the rot makes it easy to pop open with a good shove.

The musty smell hits me first, followed by a wave of bitter nostalgia.

Fucking hell. I haven't stepped in this church since my parents' funeral. Slowly, I stroll down the aisle, my footsteps echoing off the broken beams in the ceiling. My fingers graze over the benches, gathering a carpet of cobwebs as I pass.

It's a shit hole in here, and I'm solely responsible for that. The Cove clan offered to maintain it, just like they do the port, but I insisted they burn the entire fucking thing to the ground.

We compromised by sealing it off.

I take my old seat—on the edge of the left front bench—and I wait.

It's not long before the wind carries in a purr of a car engine. I hear footsteps. The groan of the door. Then my brother's booming laugh fills the church, a sound that brings me right back to my childhood.

"Out of all the churches in the world, you chose this one."

"I was in the neighborhood."

It's fascinating to watch Rafe unlock a million memories. None of his are poisoned like mine. Hands in his pockets, he strolls down the aisle, a lopsided grin on his face as he gazes at the vaulted ceilings, drinks in the altar and finally seeks out the confession booth in the far right corner.

He gives a small shake of his head and comes to a stop next to me. "We've been doing this for nine years, and yet, we've never met here," he mutters in disbelief. "Unbelievable."

He's right, it *is* unbelievable. Westminster Abbey in London, St Peter's Basilica in the Vatican. *La Sagrada Familia* in Barcelona. For the last nine years, we've met in a church somewhere around the world on the last Sunday of every month, but never the one we grew up in. Ironic, because it's this very church where our game started.

I was twelve, Rafe ten, and Gabe eight when my father sat us down in Sacristy and told us it was time we became men. We'd been listening in on confessions for months, crawling into the gap between the stone wall and the confession booth and straining to hear all of the townspeople's darkest sins and secrets. Most were pathetic—married men paying whores, Devil's Coast Academy students cheating on the school's entrance exams—but some made me sick to my stomach.

Among all the candles, robes, and dusty stacks of Bibles, our father told us that from then on, on the last Sunday of every month, we'd have to decide which was the worst confession we'd heard.

And then we had to do something about it.

Our special game bonded my brothers and I together like glue. While the locals called us the Angel's of Devil's Dip, they didn't know that we were the judge, jury, and executioners of this town too, and throughout our teens we buzzed with our secret power.

We continued this ritual, all the way up until I was eighteen, which was when I left the Coast to study business at Oxford University in England. Rafe and Gabe didn't want to continue the tradition without me, so it fizzled away into nothing more than a fond memory we'd drag up whenever we came home for the holidays.

And then our parents died. A few months after the funeral, Rafe turned up at my London office, unannounced. He was drunk and bleary-eyed, fresh off a jet from Vegas.

"I miss us," he'd slurred, leaning against my desk to stop himself from swaying. "I miss the game."

Sinners Anonymous was all his idea. A bigger, shinier version of the game that forced us to become men. He'd hatched a whole plan as he flew thousands of feet above the Atlantic, fueled by liquor and nostalgia. An "anonymous" voicemail service instead of a church confession booth. A reach that touched all four corners of the globe—not just the cobbled streets of Devil's Dip. We wouldn't meet at Saint Pius's at the end of every month, but a different church anywhere in the world each time.

My first instinct was to shut him down because I'd meant what I said when I left Devil's Dip—I was going straight. But the ache to be bad throbbed under my skin, and I was experiencing withdrawals akin to a crack addict. And when you're sweating and shaking and glaring at your bedroom ceiling at 3:00 a.m., then you always find a way to justify your bad habits.

Mine came in the form of our mother's favorite expression. Ironically, it's the reason I went straight in the first place. *Life is all about balance, Angelo. The good always cancels out the bad.*

Sure, I'd play my brother's game, and not just because I needed to scratch the itch, but because I owed it to our mama to cancel out the bad.

I told Rafe I was in.

Now, he sinks down on the bench next to me, and I can hear the *click-clack* of his dice as he rolls them between his thumb and forefinger in his pocket. Our childhood game shaped him a lot more than it did me. In fact, his whole life is a game—he owns half the hotels and casinos in Vegas and collects protection from the ones he doesn't. He wins when others lose, and when others win, well, they'd better hope it wasn't because they cheated. There's nothing Rafe hates more than a cheat.

My brother is a fucking shark. All pearly white teeth and charm, but nobody survives his bite.

A few moments pass, then the growl of a Harley Davidson seeps through the open door and down the aisle.

"Here he is," Rafe mutters, a sly grin splitting his face.

Gabe's heavy footsteps make the old stained-glass windows rattle.

"Fuck me, brother," Rafe barks down the aisle. "Do you own any footwear that aren't steel-capped boots? You stomp around like the Big Bad Wolf from *Little Red Riding Hood*."

Gabe looms over us like a storm cloud and scowls down at Rafe. "All the better to kick your head in with, my dear," he growls.

"Holy shit, that's the most I've heard you talk all year," Rafe shoots back with an easy smile. "Good to see you, bro."

Gabe grunts something unintelligible, then shifts his gaze to me. "Nice stunt at lunch today."

"Thanks."

"Not gonna tell us why you pulled it?"

"Nope."

He nods, then pulls out an iPad from under his jacket.

"Let's get on with it then."

Rafe's gaze heats the side of my cheek. "Hold the fuck on. You're shitting me, right? You take down a lackey at Big Al's Sunday lunch, follow it up with some bullshit excuse about the Russians, and you're not going to tell us why?"

I huff out a lungful of stale air and drag a knuckle through my beard. Truth is, I don't know why the fuck I did it. And the reason I *think* I did it is utterly fucking insane.

Her.

I wish I could say I walked into the dining room and saw that kid's hand gripped tightly around her wrist and the fear in her eyes. That I was protecting my uncle's honor, or at the very least, stopping his fiancee from being manhandled by his lackey. But that'd be bullshit, because I'd already picked up the gun from Alberto's office and tucked it into the back of my waistband before that, when the only information I knew, or thought I knew, was that she was fucking him behind Alberto's back.

But as I sat there eating lunch, listening to Rafe describe his latest poker game with the Hollow clan, I was watching them—the way he was all over her like a fucking rash, how she squirmed uncomfortably under every touch—and I realized I was wrong.

But I was going to kill him anyway.

Like I said, utterly fucking insane.

"My trigger finger was itchy," I drawl, lazily checking the time. "Can we get on with this? I've got shit to do."

"Shit to do in Devil's Dip?" Rafe quips back. "That's how I know you're bullshitting."

I ignore him and turn back to Gabe. He unlocks the iPad and holds it up so we can both see the screen. "You know the drill. We've each chosen four callers." He stabs the big "Generate Random Numbers" button on the screen. A spreadsheet populated with twelve names appears, each with a number between one and twelve beside it. "Over to you, Rafe."

Rafe chuckles and brings the dice out of his pocket. "My favorite time of the month," he murmurs, bringing his fist up to his mouth and blowing. With a flick of his wrist, he releases the die, letting them scatter and bounce over the wooden floorboards and iron grate.

Silence. Then Gabe takes the three steps over to inspect them. "Six."

"Yes!" Rafe hisses. "Lady Luck never lets me down, baby."

"So, who we got?" I ask.

Rafe reaches for the iPad and peers down at the screen. "Phillip Moyers. Some old bastard in Connecticut. Called to confess to a hit and run."

"Big fucking deal," I mutter, rolling my eyes. "Out of all the calls you got around to listening to this month, that was the best you could find?"

"He was off his tits on coke. Didn't realize she was wrapped around his bumper until he'd dragged her for three blocks. When he finally heard the screaming, he peeled her off and left her for dead." He scoops up his dice, gives them a small kiss, and slips them back in his pocket. "The coroner's report said it wasn't the accident that killed her, but the exposure of being left in the dirt overnight for seven hours. Oh," he adds, rising to his feet and pinning me with a sour glare. "She was eight months pregnant."

Gabe pops his knuckles. "Mine."

I shift my gaze to him. "Yours?"

He nods. Tucks the iPad back in his pocket and strolls out the church without another word. A few moments later, his motorcycle engine roars to life, then melts into the howl of the wind as he rides off.

Rafe and I stand shoulder to shoulder, staring at the open door.

"What happened to him, man?" Rafe says, more to himself than me.

I don't reply, because, like him, I don't have an answer.

Gabe's a goddamn mystery. Has been since he came back to the Coast one Christmas, shortly before our parents died, with a whole new personality and a fresh scar running from his eyebrow to his chin. He won't share his shit. Everything we've pieced together comes from Chinese whispers and half-baked rumors. Some say he's building and testing new weapons out of a Siberian military base. Others say he's working as a hitman for the Palermo outfit. All we know for sure is that on the last Sunday of every month, he'll turn up wherever in the world you ask him to.

Rolling back his shoulders and cracking his neck, Rafe turns to me. "What you really doing here, bro?" As I open my mouth, he lands a sucker punch on my shoulder. "And don't fucking lie to me. I'm not Dante."

I snarl at his hit and he's lucky I don't disconnect his jaw from the rest of his skull for that cheap shot. Instead, I take a few steps down the aisle, and then turn around to look back up at the predella. I can practically see our father standing behind it, banging his fist against the altar, his voice booming around the nave.

If he was really there and I had a gun, I'd put a bullet between his eyes, just like I did to Max hours earlier.

"Bro?"

My eyes fall back to Rafe. "I won't lie to you." *I just won't tell you the truth.*

"I know."

"So I won't say anything at all."

I feel his gaze burning between my shoulder blades as I stride toward the door. Just before I step out into the blistering wind, I stop and turn back around. He's still standing in front of the altar, arms crossed over his chest.

"Dad wasn't the hero you thought he was," I say quietly.

He stays silent, his jaw as hard as steel.

"And Mama?"

I pull my collar up, dig my hands into my pockets and get ready for the fall chill.

"Mama was a fucking saint, and don't you ever forget it."

CHAPTER
Nine

Rory

It's Tuesday night and I'm practically crawling the walls of the Visconti mansion. Every secret and sin committed within them, including my own, weakens their foundations, bringing them one step closer to tumbling down on top of me.

I'm worried sick. Haven't eaten since Sunday lunch. I can still taste Max's blood on the corner of my lips, still see his lifeless figure slumped over the dinnerware. But it turns out I'm even more selfish than I thought, because Max's death is the thing I'm worried least about.

Angelo owns Sinners Anonymous. I've spent the last two days trying to remember every word I've ever spoken down that line, every bad thought and feeling and action that I've confessed to it. Not only do I despise the fact that he now has that hold over me, I'm scared out of my mind that he'll tell Alberto what I've confessed.

Because there's one confession in particular that will be enough to get me killed in a heartbeat.

And then what'll happen to my father?

Calm moments are fleeting, but when they roll over me, I somehow manage to convince myself that maybe it'll all be okay. It's Sinners *Anonymous*. An anonymous voicemail service that should, in theory, have no way of tracking who called. And it's not like I ever used my own cell phone, and even after Alberto took it away from me, I've never called from the small burner phone he insists I carry.

But I've learned quickly that it's not out of character for a Visconti to go back on his word. Alberto is already trying to change the terms of our contract—yet another stress weighing me down.

I've spent the last two days moping on the bottom steps in the entryway, one eye on the front door in case Angelo darkens the doorway with my confessions in his pockets, and the other eye on Alberto's office door, trying to listen to his conversations. In this time I've heard several hushed exchanges between Dante and him, something about if Angelo comes back, it's going to ruin all of Dante's plans.

Seems like I'm not the only one rattled by his sudden appearance.

It's late Tuesday afternoon, and the sun is just beginning to set on the other side of the stained-glass windows in the lobby. I'm curled up on the bottom step, leaning against the wrought iron railings, holding a book that serves as nothing more than a prop. Alberto's on the phone in his study, barking rapid Italian to someone he deems less important than him. Tor strolls out of the family room, briefcase in one hand and a wool coat slung over his arm.

He comes to a stop in front of me.

"Fucking hell, girl. I've had enough of you moping about like a kicked puppy. It was only *Max*, for Christ's sake." He runs a hand through his hair and shakes his head. "Get up."

"W-what?"

Ignoring me, he turns on his heel and strolls into his father's study without knocking. They have a quick exchange in Italian, then he turns back to me and jerks his head. "*Up.* You're coming with me."

I blink. "To where?"

"Work."

"In Devil's Cove?"

"No, on Mars." He breezes toward the front door, calling over his shoulder. "Last chance."

My heart thumps double-time in my chest, a plan slotting into place. "Just grabbing my purse," I yell, before taking the stairs two at a time up to my dressing room.

When I burst out into the circular front drive, I'm relieved to see Tor hasn't left without me. The engine of his Bentley is running, and he's leaning against the driver's door, smoking a cigarette. His gaze drops to my purse. "You really need all that?"

I freeze. Curl my arms protectively around my large tote. "Uh, yeah. I've got my makeup and my wallet…"

I trail off, my lie lingering in a puff of condensation in the chilly air, but Tor just takes a final drag on his cigarette, rolls his eyes, then flicks the butt onto the grass. "Women," he mutters under his breath. "Come on, get in."

I clutch my bag tightly as we snake out of the Visconti grounds and onto the coastal road that runs parallel to the beach. I've lived on the Devil's Coast my entire life, and yet every time I drive through Devil's Cove, I'm always surprised by how glamorous it is. A complete contrast to Devil's Dip and Hollow. Out of the window on my side, it's the picture of tranquility; the navy sky melts into the black sea, and a strip of white sand in the foreground remains untouched. Tourists don't exactly come to Devil's Cove to sunbathe on a freezing cold beach and take a dip in the choppy ocean. No, the lure of Cove can be seen from Tor's window—the row of shimmering hotels and casinos and Michelin-starred restaurants. A promenade connects them, paved with marble that gets dangerously slippery in the rain, and hardy-variety palm trees that struggle to survive the harsh winters.

Tor slows the car and cranes his neck to look up at the sky. "Cheeky bastard," he laughs. I follow his focus, up to a lone plane cutting through the sky. "Vicious is up to something."

My heart stills at the sound of Angelo's nickname. "Huh?"

He jerks his chin up. "That's his jet." He cocks his brow at me, amusement dancing on his lips. "Would you have your jet flown in all the way from London if you were *just visiting?*"

My head swims with the idea that Angelo's presence on the Coast could be permanent. I can't imagine it, having to see his scowling face at every Friday night dinner and every Sunday lunch. Feeling his heavy gaze follow me around the basement bar. Holding my secrets over my head like a rain cloud. I rest my burning face against the cold window and close my eyes. A worse realization suddenly suffocates me. What happens to Devil's Dip if Alberto hands the reins back to Angelo? Would this stupid agreement have been all for nothing?

"If you're gonna be sick, let me know so I can pull over. These seats are nappa leather," Tor drawls, not taking his eyes off the road. Then, he lets out a low chuckle and adds, "A fucking Bombardier Global Express. Why he needs a jet that big, I'll never k now."

"It's a Gulfstream," I find myself whispering.

Tor drags his gaze to me and scowls. "What?"

"That jet. It's a Gulfstream, not a Bombardier. The nose and the wings are a different shape."

Silence swirls the car for a few moments, then he lets out a low whistle. "And there I was thinking you were just bird-crazy. Are you obsessed with anything that flies, kid?"

I swallow the lump in my throat and drag myself upright. "I had a place at the Northwestern Aviation Academy."

"What? Pilot school?"

"Uh-huh."

He finds this so hilarious that he thumps the steering wheel with his fist. "You're shitting me. And you chose to marry my old man instead of going?"

"No, I applied three years ago, when I was eighteen."

"But then what? You decided to hold out for a sugar daddy?"

I steel my jaw, feeling my nostrils flare at his jab. When I signed that stupid contract, Alberto warned me that only Dante knew the reason why I agreed to marry him, and not to bring it up to anyone else. He said it's because it's purely business, but after knowing him for a few months, I now realize it's a power thing. He wants people to believe he could genuinely win over a young woman like me, despite being old and gross.

He's fooling nobody. Instead, everyone just thinks I'm a gold digger.

"Not quite," I growl back.

"What happened, then?"

What happened? The smell of old books and chalk assaults my nose. The ghost of strong hands pinning me to the blackboard. The sound of screams oozing out of the classroom echo in my ears.

I shake my head and mutter, "I wanted to stay in Devil's Dip."

"Ha. Devil's Dip is the dead-end of dreams, kid." When I don't respond, he glances over at me. "Aw come on, your life could be worse. My dad kept his last wife locked up in the beach house. She was technically my stepmom and I met her twice, once at Christmas, and once when she kicked through the glass window and made a run for it. Well, three times, if you count her open casket." He slows the car, then swings into an alley. "Here we are."

I glance up at the window and notice we're next to a half-built building, propped up by scaffolding and covered with tarps. I thin my eyes in Tor's direction. "Did Alberto ask you to kill me?" I'm only half-joking.

He leans over and opens my door. "Not yet."

Inside, the building is dark and damp; the smell of sawdust and cement swirls the air. Tor leads the way, guiding me over broken floorboards and under low-hanging beams. With every step he takes, he gets more and more agitated. "Lazy *bastardi*," he snarls. "This joint was meant to be knocked up a week ago."

We burst into a room that looks like it belongs in a different building entirely. A games room, filled with five velvet poker tables and a fully stocked bar in the corner. The cluster of men gathered around one of the tables jump to their feet, dropping their cards and knocking over low-ball glasses.

A few beats of silence. Then one of them dares to speak. "Boss—"

But Tor doesn't let him finish. In a flash, he crosses the room, whips his gun from his waistband, and strikes the man's face with the butt of it. "What do I pay you for, huh?" He snarls, gripping him by the base of his neck. I look away, squirming at the sight of the man's blood dripping down his temple. "'Cause I know it ain't to sit around like a bunch of jack-asses and—"

"*Calmati, cugino.*" A back door opens, and a suited figure strolls through it, immediately chilling the air in the room. "He's lost enough money in the last hour; he doesn't need to lose his life too."

Tor pauses. Drops the man like a sack of bricks. "Rafe! You're still here?"

He nods to the door behind me. "Benny and I are planning a poker tournament in the Hollow caves next week."

"*Bastardi*—without me?"

"When do we do anything without you?"

Tor's amused; mutters something lighthearted under his breath. Rafe turns his gaze to me, and I shift uncomfortably under his megawatt smile. "You brought company."

"Yeah." Tor waves in my direction. "Thought she might want to see something other than the inside of Big Al's bedroom."

Rafe doesn't laugh at his crappy joke. Instead, he stares at me with sea-green eyes too similar to Angelo's. But it's not just his likeness to his brother that makes me uncomfortable. Behind the charm and the smile, there's something scarily stoic about him. He oozes power out of every perfect pore, filling the room with his presence. Tonight, he wears a navy suit, pinstripe shirt, and a rose-gold collar pin, complete with a small chain. He has that same untouchable air as his brother. I can't ever imagine him doing anything normal, like standing in line at Starbucks, or driving his car through a car wash.

He shifts his attention back to Tor and they start talking business. I stand there for a few moments, awkwardly clutching my bag, waiting for a break in the conversation.

Eventually, it comes. "Um, Tor? Did you need my help with anything?"

He flashes me an irritated look. "Yeah, if you know how to plaster walls, that'd be great." When greeted with my blank stare, he rolls his eyes and adds, "I'm kidding. Disappear for a bit—but be ready when I want to leave."

Before he can change his mind, I scurry back through the rubble hallways and crash out into the main Devil's Cove strip. I breathe in the salty sea air in an attempt to steady my heartbeat, and turn right, breaking into a half-walk, half-run down the promenade. Tourists spill out of fine-dining restaurants and bars, and I catch the tail end of carefree laughs and anecdotes in foreign languages as I pass, my bag clutched to my chest and my chin tucked into the collar of my jacket. After a few minutes, I reach my destination.

When I step inside Devil's Ink, the doorbell dings, announcing my arrival.

Apart from the name above the door, there's no clue that this place is a tattoo shop.

It's small and clinical-looking, like the waiting room of a high-end dentist. Recessed white lights bounce off shiny floors, and everything gleams like it's sterile. In the middle, Tayce straddles a chair, hunched over a man's bulging bicep with a tattoo gun in her hand.

"It's appointment only," she snaps, not looking up.

Her client turns to scowl at me. "Don't distract her. I've waited three years for this."

"Keep still, Blade."

I let out a huff of air. "Okay, but I really can't come back later."

The whirring of the tattoo gun stops. Tayce jerks her head up and her eyes grow wide the moment they land on me. "Oh my god, Rory!" she breathes, leaping out of her chair and running over to give me a hug.

I squeeze my eyes shut in the crook of her shoulder, breathing in the familiar scent of my friend. God, if I ever cried, this would be the time my tears would fall. She grabs my arms and takes a step back, studying my face. "Are you okay? You're okay, right?"

My eyes dart over her shoulder to her client. Every inch of his body is inked, from the dragon slithering up the side of his jaw, right down to the rosary beads tattooed around his ankle. Tayce is the best tattoo artist on the continent. Some would argue the world. Her waiting list is as long as the Bible and people clamber over each other to get on it.

Including the members of the world's most powerful mafia families.

Ones that have names like "Blade."

Sensing my unease, Tayce twists her neck to face her client.

"Blade, you'll need to come back tomorrow."

"You're shitting me, right? I've been on the waiting list forever—"

"So forever and one day won't kill you. Out."

He growls. Clenches his fits. But Tayce doesn't falter. "Something to say?"

He swallows his retort and shakes his head. Then he rises to his feet and, with a lingering scowl in my direction, reluctantly trails out of the shop, half a Grim Reaper etched into his bicep.

Tayce follows him to the door and locks it behind her. "Oh my god, Rory. I'm so happy to see you. You never called." She takes a step forward, fury replacing the relief in her eyes. "Why *the fuck* didn't you call?"

With a heavy sigh, I sink down on the tattoo bed, curling my body around the bag. It's been two and a half months since I crashed through the doors of Devil's Ink and told my best friend I'm getting married to Alberto Visconti.

Her first instinct was to slap my face. The next was to wrap her arms around me and beg me to reconsider. She knows the family well—there's not a tattoo on any inch of Visconti skin that wasn't inked by her gun—and that's exactly why I couldn't tell her why I was signing my life away. I knew I'd only drag her and her business into the darkness with me.

But Tayce didn't pry, because she knows the value of a secret. We met three years ago, when I'd just turned down my place at aviation school and taken a job at the diner in Dip. She'd turned up on a rainy Thursday afternoon, everything she owned in a small duffel bag at her Doc Martens. With her jet-black hair stuck to her forehead and her heavy eye makeup dribbling down her cheeks, she looked like a girl that'd just left a life behind.

I poured her a cup on the house and asked her name. She'd paused for too long before she said it was Tayce, and when I asked if she was visiting, her gaze had shifted uncomfortably toward the door.

I'll never forget what she said to me then.

"Please don't ask me any questions, because I'm sick of telling lies."

And so I didn't. Fast forward three years and she has her own tattoo shop, despite not having a single drop of ink on her own porcelain skin. The tattooless tattoo artist, the press call her.

"I couldn't call because Alberto took my phone and I don't trust the burner he gave me," I say simply. I work my jaw, trying to ignore the aching in my chest. Oh, goose, how I'd love to tell Tayce everything. But what good would it do?

"Jesus, Rory, you're shaking."

With a glance at the clock above the cash register, I shove my bag into her chest. "Listen, I don't have much time. I need you to do something for me."

"Anything. You know that." She peers inside the bag and narrows her eyes. "What the hell is this?"

It's the collection of things I've stolen from the Viscontis over the last few months. Vittoria's necklace, an Audemars Piguet watch I managed to slip off Alberto's wrist while he was sleeping. Lots of silverware. Anything of value I could get my hands on without raising suspicion.

"Tayce, if anything happens to me, I need you to sell all of this. Use the money to move my father somewhere, *anywhere*, that isn't on the Coast." I meet her gaze and swallow the sob creeping up my throat. "To a care home."

She lets out a hiss of breath. Studies me with sadness in her eyes. "Can I ask why?"

The smile on my lips feels bittersweet. "No," I say softly. "Because I'm sick of telling lies."

Her mouth opens and then closes just as quickly. Me repeating her own plea from three years ago is enough to buy her cooperation.

"You have my word."

"Thank you," I breathe, feeling like at least some of the weight has been lifted off my chest. When I rise to my feet, Tayce takes a desperate step toward me.

"You can't stay? Just for a little while? I've got a bottle of vodka out back. We could put on Whitney's greatest hits and dance around the shop like we used to." She all but whispers. "Remember when we'd do that? I fucking hate Whitney," she adds with a bitter laugh.

Emotion prickles at the corners of my eyes. *I will not cry. I will not cry.*

"I can't, but I'll try my best to come and see you soon."

I turn to go, but Tayce grabs my arm. "Wait. What about the club opening on Halloween?"

"What?"

"Tor was here a few weeks ago for a touch-up. He invited me to his new club opening next weekend. He's going to be your step-son soon." We both recoil at the thought. "So you'll be there, right? I'll see you then?"

My mind bounces a few blocks down the street, to the half-built club, still propped up by metal bracing. It'll be a miracle if it's open by next weekend, but I don't tell Tayce that. Instead, I nod and flash her a tight smile. "I'll do my best to come, but I don't know..."

I let the rest of my sentence dangle between us, unspoken. *I don't know if Alberto will let me.* She nods, understanding, and pulls me in for a hug. "Nothing's going to happen to you, Rory. And if it does, I'll look after your father, okay?"

"Thank you," I whisper into her neck. I bought her the perfume she's wearing for Christmas, and it smells like happier times. As I pull away, she only grips me tighter.

"And if anything *does* happen to you," she says, dropping her voice to a menacing whisper in my ear. "I'll burn down every one of their hotels, restaurants, and bars to the ground. Everything."

A chill ripples down my spine. There's so much I know about Tayce, yet so much I don't. One thing I do know, though, is that she's deadly serious.

Before I break down on her shiny, sterile floor, I dart back out into the bright lights of Devil's Cove and hurry back to the half-built club. As I round the corner into the alley, Tor steps out from behind a tarp and almost crashes into me.

"There you are." He dusts down his sharp suit. "I thought perhaps you'd had the good sense to run away."

"I don't think your father would be too happy about that."

"Nonsense. He'd just replace you with a hotter model." He glances down at my empty hands. "Where's your bag?"

Oh, swan. My mind races with a million lies, none of them convincing enough to try out on the smartest brother in the Cove clan. "I—"

A yellow light creeps over the walls of the construction site and lands on Tor's face. He scowls, lifting his hand up to shield his eyes. "Somebody has a death wish," he growls.

I turn to follow the light and see a car crawling toward us. Their high-beams are on, lighting up the alleyway.

The engine cuts off, plunging us back into darkness and silence. Then a lone, imposing figure gets out and Tor's scowl melts into his signature grin. "Two out of three Dip brothers in one night? I must be dreaming."

My heart leaps into my throat. *Angelo.* It's instinctive to want to run away, and I gaze out of the alley, across the promenade, and to the dark ocean, wondering how far I'd get down the beach before I got caught.

But I don't move. Instead, I settle for staring down at my feet.

"Rafe's here?"

"Well, it ain't gonna be Gabe. I'm guessing after Sunday lunch he crawled back to his cave."

"I like you Tor, but you know I have no problem dislocating your jaw."

The calmness in Angelo's voice forms an icicle along the length of my spine. I steal a glance up at him. He's standing under a streetlight. The yellow glow shines off his dark hair and casts a dark shadow under his high cheekbones. Makes his green eyes glitter like emeralds. Tonight, he's wearing a black wool jacket, with a gray turtleneck sweater poking out from underneath the collar. He looks warm, strong.

Scary.

We lock eyes and I immediately turn my attention back to the gravel road.

"See," Tor drawls, pulling a pack of cigarettes out of his pocket. "That's not the attitude of a man who pays his taxes." He flicks a lighter and lights the cigarette tucked into the corner of his mouth. "Nice shot on Sunday by the way. You've still got it."

"Like riding a bike," Angelo shoots back, looking bored. "You never forget."

A mix of annoyance and disgust swirls in my stomach like a bad bout of food poisoning. But I keep my face neutral. This man has my life in his hands and now is not the time to draw attention to myself, or piss him off any more than I already have.

Tor blows out a billow of smoke, then holds out the carton to Angelo.

"I don't smoke."

My eyes shoot upward, locking on his. *What?* He was smoking up on the cliff; that's how I knew he was there in the first place.

We stare at each other. His expression is disinterested as always, but behind his eyes something dark glitters. A challenge.

Like he's silently goading me to dispute his lie. I tilt my chin up and he cocks an eyebrow, as if to say, *go on. I dare you.*

The hairs on the back of my neck stand up, but strangely, not in fear. It feels...*exhilarating*. The same adrenaline rush I got in Alberto's office, when Angelo covered for me. A secret between enemies.

Well, I doubt he thinks of me as his enemy.

I doubt he thinks of me at all.

"Rafe would give his left nut for you to return to Dip," Tor says, cutting through my racing thoughts.

Angelo smirks. "He told you that?"

"He's my best friend, he tells me everything. Seems like you're thinking about it."

"Yeah?"

"Yeah. I've noticed you've been having meetings with my old man."

"Hmm."

"And I saw your Gulfstream fly in earlier."

"Uh-huh."

"Not gonna get anything out of you, am I?"

"Nope."

Tor drops his cigarette butt and grinds it into the gravel. "I hope you think about it." *I don't.* "I know you live this fancy life in London, but just think about it, all right?" He bumps his fist against Angelo's, then slaps his shoulder with his other hand. "Even if it's just to piss off Dante."

"Tempting."

Tor strides towards his Bentley, waving over his shoulder. I scurry after him, not wanting to be left alone with the Devil himself. Being alone in a dark alley with a monster is never a good idea.

"Goodnight, Aurora."

The baritone in his voice sends a hot flush through my body. The shells of my ears burn, and I find that I close my eyes, just for the briefest of moments.

The passenger seat of Tor's car feels like a refuge, even when he kicks the car into gear and peels off out of the alley.

I shouldn't glance in the side mirror, but I do.

Angelo stands under the streetlamp. Before we turn the corner, I see the flick of his lighter. A billow of smoke oozes out from his parted lips.

Oh, swan. I'm in over my head.

CHAPTER
Ten

Rory

"ALBERTO, PLEASE."

I dig my fingernails into my palms, which are getting sweatier by the second. As I shift uncomfortably from one foot to the other on the Persian rug, Alberto doesn't even look up from his files. Instead, he swats me away like a fly.

"You no longer have an escort."

"That's not my fault."

"It's not mine, either."

"We had a deal, Alberto!"

The anger in my voice makes him slam down his *Mont Blanc* pen and regard me with a warning scowl. "Aurora," he says low and steady. "I won't tell you again. You're not going to Devil's Dip on your own today, and everyone on the grounds is too busy to take you. I'll try to find someone for Saturday." He takes a sip of whiskey, not caring that it's not even 9:00 a.m., mid-week. "No guarantee, though," he adds over the rim of his glass.

I whip around to glare at the bookshelf. First editions that have never even had their spines cracked stare back at me, and I will myself not to cry. I seem to have that down to a fine art these days.

I'm being punished for his nephew's hotheadedness and it's *not fair*. Max was the only associate Alberto had who'd humor me. Nobody else in the family would give up their precious time to drive me all the way to Devil's Dip and wait around for an hour while I visit my father. And even if they did, they certainly wouldn't let me go and see him on my own. Christ, I can't imagine how scared he would be if I turned up flanked by a sour-faced Italian with a weapon tucked into his slacks.

I suck in a lungful of air, trying to think of a solution that doesn't involve me clubbing Alberto around the head with one of those paperweights on his desk.

Then I remember last night. In bed. The way his bulge pressed against my lower back as he pressed himself up against me. The way his hot, whiskey breath tickled my ear as he told me he can't wait for our wedding night.

My eyes flick up to the chandelier, and I mutter a bird-word under my breath.

What other choice do I have?

Rolling my shoulders back, I harden my jaw and turn back to face him. In three steps I'm at his desk, leaning over it. His attention falls to the 'V' neckline of my top, and he lets out a soft grunt.

"Alberto. What do I have to do to go and see my father today?" The words feel sticky in my mouth. I hate how desperately they spill out into the space between us. "Because, perhaps we can come to an...*agreement.*"

He shifts back in his leather armchair and rakes a hungry gaze over the length of me.

But then, his face darkens. "You'd be a lot more tempting if you weren't dressed like such a fucking hobo." I recoil from the venom of his words. "Why must you let your hair get so frizzy like that? It looks like a bird's nest. And would it kill you to put on a slick of lipstick?"

Rage thumps in my temples and instinctively, my eyes dart to the paperweight.

Oh my goose, how tempting it is to pick it up, and slam it against his skull.

Alberto's attention shifts over my left shoulder.

"Angelo." He clears his throat and bolts upright, mildly embarrassed.

You have got to be kidding me.

I stay there for a few moments, my eyes closed, leaning all my weight against the desk. *Is this guy ever not lurking around?*

Inhaling deeply, I turn and brace for the weight of Angelo Visconti's disgusted sneer. In the handful of days I've had the misfortune of knowing him, I've come to expect it. In fact, I'd say I've almost acclimated to the heat of it; how it turns my skin feverish and twists my stomach into uneasy knots.

But the moment he lifts his gaze from Alberto to me, I know I'm only lying to myself. I'm anything *but* used to it. Today, his stare is indifferent, scornful. Like he'd come into *his* office and found servants in the middle of a lover's tiff. But I can't keep my eyes off him, and because I'm watching him so intensely, I peel back his layers and notice something harder underneath his disdain. The thumping pulse in his jaw. The flair of his nostrils.

He's angry.

He pushes off the door frame and takes three steps into the room. Drops a file on the desk. It's nothing more than a slither of paper, but it sounds like it weighs a ton.

"The names you wanted."

Alberto's leather chair groans as he shifts his weight. "*Grazie.*"

Angelo doesn't move. Instead, he shifts his attention down to Alberto's face and pins him with a glare so dark I'm immediately relieved I'm not the subject of it. He's still and silent, unwavering in his intimidation as he looms over his uncle like a bad dream. My gaze moves between them, my heartbeat increasing with every tense second that ticks painfully by.

I don't dare breathe.

This is the first time I've ever seen Alberto look...*small*. Angelo's shadow engulfs him, and suddenly he's not the larger-than-life mafia boss who sits at the head of the table, commanding obedience with his booming voice and enormous silhouette. For the briefest of moments, he doesn't look like the Almighty Alberto that has me bent at the knees, chained to him with a contract I know he'll break.

For the briefest of moments, I'm not scared of him.

It's him who slices through the tension. He glances toward the door and confusion flashes over his face. "Everything okay, kid?"

A heavy beat passes. Then Angelo drags his knuckles off the desk and returns to his full height.

The study crackles with static. There's a hot itch under my collar now, too. It's crazy; I've been in a hundred rooms with a hundred made men, and yet, they've never made me feel as *nervous* as Angelo does. It feels like I'm standing on the edge of the cliff and I can taste the danger again.

"Aurora." I jump at the sound of my name. "I'll take you to Devil's Dip."

My ears ring. "Y-you will?"

I steal a glance at Alberto and notice a steady flush creeping up his neck.

"I'm heading that way."

Angelo strolls out the door without looking back. I stand awkwardly, suspended in limbo between the two men who each hold broken pieces of my life in their hands.

Alberto has the power to ruin my father's life.

Angelo knows all of my sins.

I turn back to Alberto and study his face. It's instinctive to want to ask permission, but I swallow the question in a small act of defiance. He stares after Angelo for a few moments, before looking up at me.

Then he nods. It's so small that if I'd blinked, I'd have missed it.

"Thank you," I breathe, but it's quiet and I'm halfway out the door so I doubt he even heard it. Heart racing, I run across the lobby, crash through the front door, and come to a stop on the steps.

Angelo stands leaned against the bonnet of his car, hands tucked into his coat pockets. He's staring intensely at something in the distance, and disappointment starts to chip away at the edges of my excitement.

Did he mean it? Or am I just a pawn in this weird power play between him and Alberto?

Before I can pluck up the courage to ask, he pushes off the hood and strolls to the passenger side. He holds the door open. "Get in."

I don't have to be asked twice. I scurry down the steps and inch past him, feeling the burn of his narrowed eyes as they trail me, and slide into the passenger seat before he can change his mind.

He slams the door a little too hard, plunging me into silence. I try to ignore the warm, masculine scent engulfing me—a cocktail of new leather and his oaky aftershave. The way it heightens my instincts, raising the hairs on the back of my neck and sharpening my senses.

Danger is imminent.

The car dips as he slides into the driver's side and I regret my haste even more. The interior is sleek and sporty and feels infinitely smaller the moment he slams his door. In retrospect, perhaps I could have waited until Saturday to see my father. Until Alberto found someone else to escort me, someone more...*appropriate.*

I swallow the lump in my throat.

The engine comes to life under my seat, purring like a tiger. Clenching my hands in my lap, I keep my eyes trained ahead, on the lone water droplet snaking its way down the middle of the windshield. I don't dare steal a glance at Angelo; his anger radiates off him so hot and heavy that steam is starting to gather on the windows.

"You know, being a whore is—"

"A sin," I blurt out, my voice too loud for the tiny gap between us. I cringe and clear my throat, lowering my volume as I add, "Yeah. I know."

Silence. I can feel my face turning crimson. So, he saw my desperate attempt at flirting with Alberto in the office, which means he also saw how venomously he shut me down. *Goose, how embarrassing.* Did he agree to escort me to put me out of my misery? He doesn't seem like the type to feel second-hand embarrassment.

He hooks his thumbs onto the steering wheel and speeds up, taking the road out of the Visconti grounds with the speed and control of a Formula One driver. I bite my lip and try to keep my stance neutral, like I'm totally used to traveling at a million miles an hour all the time.

"I was going to say, unattractive."

Frustration claws at my throat, threatening to cut off my air supply if I don't let it out. "I'm not a whore."

"You're not unattractive, either."

I freeze.

What?

Only when my heart decides to beat again, I steal a glance at him. He's staring at the road ahead, jaw clenched too hard for any misspoken words to have slipped out of it. I imagined it. I *must* have. It was nothing but the sound of a low-hanging branch scraping against the windshield, or a passing car with a radio turned up too loud.

It was anything but a twisted compliment from Angelo Visconti's lips.

But his next comment, although nothing more than a mutter, I hear loud and clear.

"What the hell does he have over you?"

I stare ahead, eyes fixed on the wrought iron gates creaking open, revealing the coastal highway behind them.

What does he have over you? It suddenly dawns on me like a new day; Angelo has more over me than my fiancé does.

And I need to find out exactly what he knows.

Steeling my spine and wiping my sweaty palms on my *Lululemon* leggings, I edge toward the subject.

"You have things over people, too."

He cocks a brow, waiting for me to elaborate. I fight against my nerves and add, "I heard about your voicemail service. It's why you killed Max, right?"

A smirk curves on his lips, deepening the angle of his cheekbones. "Apologies if I got blood on your pretty little dress," he drawls. Then he shifts his gaze from the road to me. Runs a cold eye over the curl I'm twirling between my thumb and forefinger, then dips his eye line lower, to the curve of my breasts. His glance is over as quickly as it began, but leaves me breathless.

He turns back to the road, taking a sharp right toward Devil's Hollow. "Seems like you only get that dressed up when you want something, Magpie."

I pause. "Magpie?"

Another smirk. *Oh, right.* He thinks I'm attracted to shiny things, like my fiance's will and Vittoria's pearl necklace. But I don't bite, because I can't let the annoyance thrumming in my veins push me off track.

"Sinners Anonymous, right?" I rasp. "How does that work, then?"

He frowns. "Why?"

"I'm just wondering. I've seen the cards about and—"

He cuts me off with a low chuckle. It's soft and dark. Deliciousness underpinned with ill intentions. "You've been calling the number."

My head swims. *Oh, swan.*

When he laughs again, I realize I said that aloud. "Don't worry. No sin of yours is going to be interesting enough to ping my radar."

"Perhaps I'm not as innocent as I look," I snap back. Immediately, I regret my outburst. *Darn it.* Why can't I just be relieved that he's unaware of my obsession with the hotline? But the way he looks at me so condescendingly, like I'm a child, makes my skin itch with the desire to prove I'm not.

"Let me see. You're a twenty-one year old virgin who swears using bird puns. The worst thing you've done is steal Vittoria's necklace, and I already knew about that. And yet, your conscience is so heavy you want to throw yourself off a cliff."

My fists clench. "Not true."

His stare scorches my cheek, hot and unrelenting. When I turn to meet it, my heart stills.

"Are you a bad girl, Aurora?"

I swallow. His eyes dance with dark amusement, but his tone is more sinister. Dripping with an insinuation that ignites a flame between my thighs.

"Sometimes."

The car rolls to a lazy stop outside the church. The engine cuts out, plunging us into silence. All I hear are my shallow breaths; all I feel is the path his eyes carve down to my lips. Any hint of humor in them is long gone.

"Do you like being bad?"

Our gazes clash. I give a slow, small nod.

He releases a puff of air through his parted lips and rakes his fingers through his hair. The action reveals an inch of tanned, toned flesh above his pants. It's a visual that suddenly makes me wonder what else is underneath that expensive-looking suit.

My stomach flips.

"Be back in an hour," he rasps.

Face burning with a cocktail of frustration and embarrassment, I unclick my seat belt and grab the door handle. "Are you going to insist on coming with me?"

"You're a bad girl; you can handle it."

I pause, grinding my teeth to stop myself biting back. As I open the door, his hand locks around my wrist.

Oh, holy crow.

The ability to breathe escapes me, and I force myself to look at him. His gaze is turbulent, flashing like a lightning storm against a starless sky.

"I could listen to every secret you have with a tap of a button."

My blood runs cold. "But you won't."

"But I *could*." He tilts his head in the direction of the phone booth. My phone booth. "I know exactly where you're calling from. It'd be piss-easy to trace."

My breathing quickens. I'm torn between begging him not to listen to my sins and ripping myself away from his touch.

His grip tightens around my wrist. *So I guess that eliminates my second option.*

I dig my nails into the palm of my free hand and swallow. "What do you want from me?"

"A sin."

I blink. "W-what?"

"Tell me a sin, Aurora," he drawls. His tone drips in syrup, thick enough to drown in. I briefly close my eyes from the twisted pleasure of it.

"You're serious?"

"Deadly."

Racking my scrambled brain, I bite down on my bottom lip. For some reason, I have the urge to tell him something of substance. Nothing *too* bad, but just enough to show I'm not the blithering little girl that replaces swear words with bird puns.

"Last week, I went into Alberto's closet and cut a hole in the pocket of every suit." My eyes dart to his expressionless face. "Small ones, the size of a dime. But big enough for him to lose his car keys four times in the last seven days."

The silence is suffocating, stretching out like there's an endless void between us. Within it, all I can hear is my heartbeat thumping against my rib cage, and all the blood from my fried brain rushing around my ears.

And then, his laugh. A delicious, throaty laugh that lights up my skin like a live wire. I can't stop *staring* at him. At the way the hard lines of his face soften, all except the cleft in his chin, which deepens under the weight of his broad smile. It's the same laugh from the dinner table, moments before he shot Max—the one I'd craved to hear again.

He's so handsome it makes my teeth ache.

I have to get out of this car before I lose my mind. When I tug out of his grip, he lets me go and I dive out onto the road, feeling his gaze follow me through the windshield as I head into the forest.

CHAPTER
Eleven

Angelo

I HAVE A RULE book as thick as my dick when it comes to women, but all rules can be boiled down to one word:

Don't.

Don't stick your dick in crazy.

Don't let them stay the night.

And *definitely* don't let them leave something they'll want you to return the next day.

A fat raindrop falls on my windshield, followed by another. Eventually, they merge together and obscure my view of Aurora's perfect ass in those gym leggings as she hot-foots it away from my Bugatti.

Oh, and don't ogle your uncle's fiancee.

A bitter laugh slips through my lips. It tastes like disbelief.

Big Al is one lucky fucker and he doesn't even realize it. Turns out, his latest squeeze is more than a smoke show—she's a guilty conscience locked in a tight, stubborn body. If she wasn't so fucking hot, the fact she thinks petty theft and being a little scissor-happy warrants a confession to Sinners Anonymous would be kind of adorable.

I glance to the phone booth opposite the church, then down to my cell in the center console. I could find her calls to the hotline within seconds. It'd certainly pass the time while I wait for her to emerge from whatever the fuck she's doing in the Preserve.

Spinning my iPhone between my thumb and forefinger, I entertain the idea for a few minutes. My cock stirs at the thought of having something, no matter how trivial, to hang over her head. Perhaps I could convince her that atoning for your sins is better than confessing them.

Maybe she'd let me punish her by bending her over my knee, pulling down those obscenely tight gym leggings, and giving that ass a good spanking.

Or maybe I can elicit other trivial confessions out of her by winding my fist in those golden curls my uncle seems to hate so much, and—

Jesus fucking Christ. I thump my steering wheel in an attempt to beat those thoughts out of my brain. My cock is aching now, straining against my slacks like I'm a goddamn school boy who can't control his urges.

Get a grip, Angelo. I'm a thirty-six year old man, perving on a girl nearly half my age. I'm not my damn uncle, and I like to think I skipped the sadistic gene that the Cove Viscontis all have. To them, women are a currency, something to buy and sell, barter for, and trade. How proud Alberto was to tell me that the latest in his long line of fiancees was a virgin, like that makes her worth sky-rocket. The sad thing is, all the other old fucks in his Rich Boys Club would have been impressed by that. Jealous, even.

The image of my uncle humping on top of her tiny body on their wedding night is enough to short-circuit my boner. *Fuck.* Now I'm all worked up in a different way. Hot, itchy annoyance prickles under my collar like a heat rash. Up until nine years ago, I would have probably started a Visconti civil war on this feeling alone, but I'm different now.

I'm not a part of this world anymore; I'm merely visiting it. Here to tie up a loose end.

I don't chase the thrill of violence or dish out revenge that's way greater than the crime. I don't explode over barely anything and cause irreparable damage.

I am not Vicious anymore.

Burning up, I whip off my jacket and toss it on the passenger seat. Loosen my tie. Despite the rain falling in sheets, I inch down all the windows to let some cold air in, and also to drive the sweet scent of her vanilla perfume out. *Christ, she's fucking irritating.*

If Viscontis are sadistic for treating women like currency, then what does that make me?

I treat them like they are nothing at all.

A wet hole to plunge my dick into. A mouth to face fuck. But at least I don't pretend they're anything more than that.

The minutes tick by on the digital clock on my dashboard. I check emails from shareholders, texts from my assistants—panicked messages asking me when I'll be back. Skim through notes taken in meetings I should have been chairing. Through my cell, Visconti Capital goes on without me, and my corner office overlooking Hyde Park in my London Head Quarters seems a lot farther away than just the other side of the Atlantic.

When I see Aurora's blond curls emerge from between the trees, I toss my cell in the console and twist the key in the ignition. She has a spring in her step, practically bouncing in her muddy sneakers as she cuts across the road. It's still raining, and if I was a better man, I'd step out with my jacket to shield her from it.

But I'm not. Instead, I watch as droplets turn the white top under her unzipped hoodie transparent, revealing the outline of her bra.

Pink. *Lace*. Of course it is. I bet her panties always match, too. In fact, I bet her whole underwear collection is as sweet and silly as her stupid sins. The girl wouldn't know a real sin if it slapped her in the face.

God, I can't stand girls like her.

As she approaches the car, we lock eyes and she slows to a stop. She stands there in the glow of my headlights, shuffling from one foot to the other, like she's just remembered I'm her ride and she's contemplating if it's safer to run back to Cove instead.

I last three seconds before impatience gets the best of me and I lay on my horn. She yelps, then mutters one of her stupid bird puns, and I hide my smirk behind the back of my hand when she flings open the passenger door and scurries inside.

Yeah, you're real bad, girl.

The car tires screech as I turn the wheel into full-lock and peel out back in the direction of Devil's Cove.

"Is your father *Stig of the Dump*?"

Next to me, I feel her still. "What?"

I glance in my rear-view mirror, just as the forest disappears behind a bend. "He lives in the woods. Nobody lives in the fucking woods."

"How would you know if anyone lives in the woods? You're not exactly the Mayor of Devil's Dip." She shuffles in her seat. "Bet you don't even know who the mayor of Devil's Dip is."

Another smirk prickles on my lips, and I chew the inside of my cheek to stop it from forming. The only thing bad about this girl is her bite.

"You kiss my uncle with that mouth?"

"Unfortunately."

Something flickers in the pit of my gut. Something I don't want to name.

I clear my throat. "Smart-assed women don't go over too well in the Cosa Nostra, Magpie."

"So I've noticed," she mutters.

The tone of her voice urges me to steal a glance at her, and I immediately wish I hadn't. She's staring straight ahead, my jacket draped over her lap and her hands absentmindedly stroking the wool fabric. I forgot I'd tossed it onto the passenger seat, and she didn't mention anything when she got in the car. And now she's sitting there, using my fucking jacket as a blanket like it's the most natural thing in the world.

My hand hovers over the heater dial, but then I pause. Move my hand back to the wheel without turning it up. My jaw's grinding so hard my teeth ache.

"He's a ranger."

"What?"

Aurora rummages around in her purse and pulls out a chocolate bar. She peels back the foil wrapper and, watching me with big, doe eyes, she takes a bite. If she's doing that on purpose, it's fucking working. I shift in my seat to stop my dick swelling.

"My father. He's the Devil's Preserve ranger. Well—he was. He's retired now, but still lives in the cabin by the lake."

I frown. "A ranger of what? A few shitty trees and a swamp?"

"Are you serious?" she splutters. "Devil's Preserve is a world-renowned nature reserve. It has more than three hundred different species of trees and is home to thirteen pairs of American Bald Eagles. You know the only place in the world that has more nesting Bald Eagles reported than Devil's Dip? *Yellowstone*. Oh, and you know what else?" She leans forward, clenching her fist around the fabric of my jacket. My jacket. "It's home to other rare birds, too. The Trumpeter swan. Ospreys. Marbled Murrelets. Not to mention all the other animals—otters, the cougars, the British Colombian wolves." Flopping back in her seat and taking an angry chomp of chocolate, she adds, "It's a lot more than a few trees and a swamp."

Rain hammers on the windshield. Radio static crackles between us.

And suddenly, it all makes sense.

"Alberto wants to build a hotel in the Preserve."

Aurora stiffens, then turns to look out the passenger side window. Her shallow breathing mists up the glass, and she uses the heel of her palm to wipe it away.

Letting the silence blister between us, I turn my attention back to the road, head pounding. A few months back, Big Al called my office, requesting an urgent meeting. I sure as shit wasn't flying all the way back to the coast for no damn reason, so he came to me in London, blueprints tucked under his arm, Dante nipping at his heels like a loyal dog. He unrolled the plans over my desk and stabbed a fat, ring-clad finger in the middle of the expansive forest of the Devil's Preserve.

A woodland retreat, he'd said, practically spitting with excitement. *Russian and Saudi tourists love shit like that.*

I'd taken one glance at the blueprints, another glance at my watch, then told both he and Dante I wasn't interested. Sure, I don't give a flying fuck about Devil's Dip, but I know what Alberto and his slimy son are like. Give them an inch, they'll take a mile. One hotel in Dip will turn into two, and before I know it, Devil's Dip will be Cove Clan territory, just like Dante always wanted.

And so what if it was? I'll never come back here. The right thing to do would be hand over the land to Alberto and his sons, let them do whatever the fuck they want with it.

I have no reason to say "no" except I'm a malicious, stubborn bastard.

A few days ago, Alberto dropped the idea into conversation again in the cigar room. He said they were still going ahead with it—not in Devil's Dip of course—but up on the north headland in Devil's Cove.

I'd nodded and grunted in all the right places, but I couldn't give a flying fuck what Alberto does within the borders of Cove. Come to think of it, it *was* strange that he didn't push it further. That he didn't try to lay on the pressure, offer me the world until I agreed to give him what he wanted, which I've noticed is his usual tactic in business.

No, he just let it go. And now I realize why. He's tricked Aurora into believing the preserve is *his* territory, and he's dangling it over her head as an excuse to get between her legs.

My knuckles whiten over the steering wheel. I could bring this whole engagement crashing down with one sentence of truth. My mind goes to a darker place: if she's marrying Alberto because she thinks it'll save her precious nature reserve. What would she do for *me* if I told her I was the one with the real power?

Static travels the length of my cock. *Fuck.* I wouldn't waste time with petty shit like the pretense of marriage. Instead, I'd put that smart mouth to work.

Suddenly, her eyes dart back at me. "What's funny?" she snaps.

I realize I'd huffed out a laugh. One swimming in disbelief.

I pause, running my tongue over my teeth. What my uncle does is none of my business. Besides, let's be real—if she doesn't give him what he wants, contract or not, he'll just pop her off anyway. This chick doesn't need to hear my opinion, but that doesn't stop it rolling off my tongue.

"You're marrying Alberto Visconti to stop him cutting down a few trees in the Preserve. Jesus Christ," I rake my fingers through my hair, shaking my head. "You're even stupider than you look."

I wait for her to bite back, but her retort doesn't come. Out the corner of my eyes, I watch her pink mouth open and close just as quickly. Then she twists her hands together, and turns her attention back to the Devil's Cove promenade passing in a blur outside the window.

Whatever. I don't give two shits what this chick does. Whether that's marrying my seventy-something-year-old uncle or chucking herself off the side of the cliff.

Heat prickles under my collar, and I pop the top button. I never pop my damn top button.

We ride in heavy silence until we arrive at the gates of Alberto's beach-side mansion. Then Aurora sits up a little straighter. Starts coiling that curl around her finger again.

She clears her throat. "So, uh. We have a deal?"

My gaze slides lazily to hers. "Deal?"

"Um, my calls...you won't listen to them, right? That's what you said?"

Pulling onto the front drive, I kill the engine and look at her. *Really* look at her for the first time, not just with stolen glances from the head of the dining table, or over my whiskey glass in the basement bar.

Looking like that, she could never be a sinner. Her eyes are too big. Each of her pitiful secrets swirls in her irises, which are the color of warm whiskey. Her skin is too pale and perfect. The slightest sin will make her flush a beautiful shade of pink. My gaze drops to her plump, parted lips. *And that fucking mouth.* The only sound inside the car is the small, shallow breaths escaping it.

A familiar feeling swirls through my veins like a nasty virus. It threatens to poison the moral compass I've tried so hard to build over the last nine years.

But I'm fooling nobody. My moral compass: it's as weak as a house of cards, and if Aurora lets out *one more fucking breath like that*, she'll blow it down.

Fuck. My dash says it's forty-eight degrees outside, but it's a fucking furnace in here. I wish my Bugatti wasn't so small. Maybe then I wouldn't feel the heat rising from her, or smell the sweetness of her perfume.

Curling my hands into fists, I tear my gaze away and glare at the car logo embossed on the center of my steering wheel.

"A deal goes both ways, Aurora." Her hot, shallow breaths stop. *Thank God.* "What do I get in return?"

"What?"

Her whisper goes straight to my dick.

"Nothing is free in this world. How are you going to buy my silence?"

The air is so thick I could stick out my tongue and taste it. *What the fuck are you doing, Angelo?* I shouldn't be playing these games with my uncle's fiancée. I should lunge over her, kick open her door and tell her to get out. Rid the car of her fucking vanilla and chocolate scent and heavy breaths and those shiny blond hairs I know I'm going to be finding strands of everywhere for the next few days.

But then her voice comes out in a low, sultry rasp. "Well, what do you want?"

Fuck.

I drag my eyes from the steering wheel back to her face. Her stupid, girlish face and those big amber eyes, which are now wider than usual.

Heat crawls under my skin like an itch I can't scratch. I pop another button. Rub my hand over my jaw. Then I laugh a small, bitter noise that doesn't belong to me.

This is ridiculous. I eat girls like Aurora for breakfast. Only I don't, 'cause I'm not going to lay it on my uncle's girl. Even if that uncle is Alberto, and even if his girl looks like...

That.

I'm not going to grab her by the base of her nape, pull her closer, and see how those soft lips taste. I'm not going to wind my fist into that hair and scrape my teeth along the length of her neck until she moans all of those silly little secrets of hers in my ear.

"Get out."

Aurora doesn't move. But if I sit in this car with her any longer, I'll either cave or put my fist through my dashboard. Or both. So I pop my door and get out and stride toward the house. Rain pelts down on me, sizzling against my skin yet doing nothing to cool me down. Behind me, I hear a car door slam.

"Wait!" Aurora's soft voice carries through the wind, and I hear the crunching of gravel under her sneakers as she tries to keep up with me. "Angelo, please, don't—" Looking up, I realize what has cut her off. The front door opening and her fiancee, my uncle, darkening the doorway. His eyes look to me, then to Aurora and back again. He folds his arms over his enormous gut and frowns.

"Jesus Christ, kid," he mutters. "You could have got the girl an umbrella."

The girl. I stare into the amber glow of the foyer behind him and lean against the pillar propping up the roof of the porch. "I'm not your associate, Alberto."

His gaze skims over me warily. "Of course, of course. Well, I appreciate you helping me out in a bind. She would have been bleating on all week if I hadn't let her see her father."

Aurora climbs the steps, panting. She glances over at Alberto, then to me, sheer panic clouding her eyes. I slip my hands in my pockets and hold her gaze.

"Sweetheart, you're back." Alberto steps out from under the doorway and pulls her slender frame against his. "Give your fiance a kiss, then."

My heart thumps against my rib cage, but I keep my expression neutral. Unbothered. Aurora takes a step back, but Alberto's grip only tightens.

"What?" she says, with a tinkling little laugh.

"A kiss, Aurora."

Her eyes shoot up at me, and I refuse to back down from her gaze. Refuse to help her, either. *You got yourself in this damn mess, get yourself out of it.*

Alberto leans in and presses his wrinkly lips against hers. My fists clench in my pockets, but I force myself to watch. It feels like watching is punishment for my own sins. She recoils under the weight of him, holding her hands out in the air at an awkward angle as he lays it on her. It feels like fucking forever until he pulls away.

I have the sudden urge to punch something, and if I don't get off this porch right now, it'll be my uncle's face. And that'll cause a war I can't be fucked to get into.

I push off the pillar and trot back down the steps. "I'll leave you two love birds alone," I say icily.

"Thanks again, kiddo." Every time he calls me that I want to remove his teeth.

The rain trickles down my unbuttoned collar as I stride toward the car.

And then before I can stop myself, I stop. Turn on my heels and pin my uncle with a blistering stare through the sheet of rain.

"I'll take her to Devil's Dip every Wednesday and Saturday."

He looks up from Aurora's tits. "What?"

"Your fiancee. I'll take her to see her father."

His eyes thin. "Why?"

I stare up at the gray sky, looming over the Visconti mansion like a nightmare. "There's some shit I need to take care of in Devil's Dip. She's a local, so she can show me around. In exchange, I'll drop her off at her father's house twice a week."

He frowns at me for a few seconds, then a sly grin stretches across his face. "You coming back, kid?"

A groan rumbles deep in my chest. *Hell no.* But I don't say that. Instead, I suck in a lungful of damp air and steel my jaw. "Thinking about it."

His laugh rips through the storm, dirty and distorted. With a small wave, he turns and heads back into the house. I turn too, my fingers brushing over my car key in my pocket.

As I pass, I slip the key between my thumb and forefinger and drag it along the driver's side of Alberto's Roll's Royce Phantom.

When I get in my car and flick my wipers on full speed, I look up and see Aurora still standing on the porch. It's growing dark, and the glow from the foyer turns her into nothing more than a dark silhouette. But when I swing the car around, my headlights wash over her.

And for the first time since we met, I see her smile.

I think I like it when she smiles.

CHAPTER
Twelve

Angelo

THE MOMENT I STEP out of the elevator and into the cave, nostalgia hits me. The kind that puts a hole in your stomach and a small grin on your face. It's the smell; damp and metallic, it reminds me of playing hide-and-seek down here when we were kids, long before Castiel and the other Hollow brothers turned it into one of the most prestigious clubs in the world.

Whiskey Under the Rocks. It's a secret buried deep within the caves of Devil's Hollow, a far cry from the glitzy strip of clubs over in Devil's Cove. Over there, money will buy you entry to any club or casino, but this joint is invite-only. Once a month, Rafe, Tor, and Benny come together to hold a poker night. It's a partnership that's worked seamlessly over the years. Tor brings in the biggest spenders from his casinos in Devil's Cove. Rafe has a reputation that has any gambler begging for a seat at one of his games. And Benny, the second oldest Hollow brother, is a fixer. From the finest Russian whores to the purest Peruvian cocaine, there's nothing he can't, or won't, source to give his guests a good time.

Tonight isn't the usual poker night, but Rafe decided to pull one together last minute, because our meeting at our father's church meant that he was going to be in town for the week, anyway. I'm not much of a gambler, and I'm not just here to support my brother and the cousins that I actually *do* like. No, I'm here because the Cove and the Hollow clans want to talk shop. No doubt they want to renegotiate the terms of the port usage.

I stroll down the narrow tunnel, running my fingers over the craggy walls and remembering all the hours we spent down here as kids. When I reach the entrance to the main room, I huff out a laugh. It's so fucking different. The exposed cave walls still drip with moisture, but now, the chandeliers built into the jagged ceilings light up all of my old hiding places. Booths line the walls, and a bar is built into the farthest alcove, selling every top-label liquor available, including, of course, the whiskey that's made just a few caves over.

Hearing a familiar bark echo through the empty club, I twist my head to the left, a lazy smirk forming on my lips. Tor's here already, acting like the big nightclub boss, a role he assumes so well. Behind me, the elevator dings, and a loud Russian voice spills out of it.

"Well, what the fuck am I supposed to do for the next three hours, Castiel?"

I glance over my shoulder and spot a long-legged blond in an impossibly tight dress. In front of her, my cousin Cas storms ahead, a face like thunder. He catches my eye, mutters something in Italian, and spins on his heel. "Here," he spits, taking a wedge of bills out of his pocket and tossing it at the woman's stilettos. "Go play."

She yells at him in Russian and storms off. Judging by the weary gaze settling on his face, Cas is used to it by now.

I jerk my chin up. "Lover's tiff?"

He pinches the bridge of his nose. "Lovers war, more like. My father's on his death bed and won't let me take over Smugglers Club until I find a wife. He seems to think that stupid Russian bitch is the most suitable."

"So I've heard," I drawl, raking my teeth over my bottom lip in amusement.

"So you've also heard that if I don't marry her before he dies, the factory goes to the board of investors." He shakes his head. Tightens his cuff links. "At this rate, I'll be dying before he does."

I clap him on the shoulder. "Speaking of Uncle Alfredo, I should go see him at some point before I leave. He's always been good to me."

"Yeah," he grunts. "If you could shove a pillow over his face while you're there, that'd be great."

As much as I hate to admit it, warmth spreads through the pit of my stomach. Cas is the oldest Hollow brother; I've always liked him and admired his business acumen. He's calm, money-minded, and single-handedly turned Smugglers Club whiskey from "mafia juice" into a global brand. He's got a few nicknames along the coast, one being The Silver Fox—thanks to his George Clooney-esque good looks and salt-and-pepper hair, and the other being Mister Moonshine. He's always experimenting with new liquor concoctions, and made men around the world go nuts for it. Owning a special-edition Smugglers Club liquor bottle, brewed by Castiel Visconti himself, is the ultimate status symbol.

We stroll toward the bar and he pours us two whiskeys. We chink glasses, and over the rim of his, his eyes glitter with mischief. "When you finally get your ass back to the coast and take over Devil's Dip, you'll need a wife yourself."

"Yeah, not going to happen."

"Moving back, or getting a wife?"

"Both."

He laughs, but I'm deadly serious. I can barely tolerate a woman staying longer than it takes for her to make me come, let alone having one around permanently. Aside from the concept of love being absolute bullshit, I find women...*boring*. Weak-willed and weak-minded, they always seem to agree with what I say and do what I want. That's what assistants and employees are for. I need a woman with a damn backbone, both in and out of the bedroom. But especially in the bedroom. I like to fuck rough, but rough's boring when she lies back and takes it.

An unsolicited image of Aurora bent over my knee, bare-assed and red-faced, pops into my head. I wonder if she'd lie back and take it, or if she'd writhe under the palm of my hand. If she'd scream in the way I'd want her to.

Fucking hell.

A booming voice saves me from my dirty thoughts.

"I can't find you a wife for life, but I can give you a wife for the night."

Cas groans. I turn around to see Benny, the middle Hollow brother, stroll into the club, a gaggle of half-naked women on his arms. He shoots a wink at me. "What's your type, *cugino*?"

Curly-haired and unavailable. But I don't reply. Instead, I down the rest of my drink and lean against the bar. I loosen my tie. Since when were the caves so hot? But I'm only fooling myself. I know what's got my skin burning up like I have a fever—the thought of spanking my uncle's fiancee. Maybe I *should* get laid tonight. Find a blond, curly-haired babe and have her mutter dirty bird puns in my ear.

Cas cocks a brow. "What's so funny?"

I hadn't realized I was laughing. Shaking my head, I turn my eyes to the jagged ceiling. "Nothing, man."

This isn't about Aurora; it's just the Coast. It's always made me lose the plot.

Cas glances over my shoulder toward the elevator. "Guests are starting to arrive. Come—I have a private room set up, and we can wait for the others in there."

I oblige. The room is an alcove off the main club, with little but a cluster of deep-seated armchairs around a low table and a private bar in the corner. I take a seat, and a few moments later, Rafe walks in, his men forming a wall around him.

"Fucking hell, Rafe," Tor drawls, storming in behind him and slapping him on the back. "It's just family; you didn't need to bring the cavalry."

"I'm an important man, *cugino*," Rafe shoots back, throwing me a wink as he sits down next to me. He nods to his men, who then take guard by the door. "I don't expect you to understand."

Before Tor can reply, there's a strange gurgling noise and a click of a safety catch. When I look up, one of Rafe's men has a thick arm around his neck and a gun to his temple. It's gold, with a dragon etched along the barrel. While everyone in the room jumps up and draws their own weapons, I smirk into the bottom of my whiskey glass.

I'd know that ugly fucking Glock anywhere.

Gabe's gruff voice comes from the shadows. "Your cavalry are pathetic." He drops the man like a sack of shit and shoves the others out the way.

Rafe sinks back into his chair, glaring at Gabe as he takes his place next to me. Rafe leans over the table and hisses, "*Grazie*, dickhead. You really had to embarrass me like that in front of the whole family?"

I can't remember the last time I saw Gabe smile, but I swear, the corners of his mouth turn up before he picks up my whiskey glass and downs it in one. A server hurries over and immediately fills it back up.

"Always a barrel of laughs when the Devil's Dip brothers come to town, isn't it?" I look up to see Dante striding in, looking like a miserable fuck as usual. Donatello's by his side, a huge grin on his face and a thick stack of files tucked under his arm.

My eyes dart behind them. "Where's Uncle Al?"

Dante's gaze darkens. "At home. Probably groping up his jail bait." He smooths down his shirt and sinks into the chair opposite. "You know, I take care of most things these days. Going forward, you should expect to be dealing with me."

"Did Daddy finally give you keys to the kingdom?" Rafe asks mockingly. "Or did he just lend you a booster seat so you can sit at the table tonight? Don't worry, I'll keep an eye on the clock to make sure you don't miss your curfew."

Everyone around the table laughs except Dante. The tension between him and my brother crackles like static. No one on this earth hates Dante more than Rafe does, because he swears he caught him cheating at one of his poker games years ago. The only reason he didn't put a bullet in his head is because he's Tor's brother. The feeling is mutual, but not because of that fateful night. No, Dante hates Rafe because he's everything he wishes he could be. As successful as Devil's Cove is, it'll never be Vegas, and as cut-throat as Dante is, he'll never be as powerful as Rafe.

"All right, all right," Donatello interrupts, fighting a smile. "Let's get down to business so we can go and play. I have a *lot* of money to claw back off you assholes. I'll go first." He flips open his files and studies them. "Angelo, all I need is approval to open a trade route to and from Japan. One vessel a week, the only cargo is fish."

Tor snorts, muttering something about him being a loser. Donatello probably is the only one around this table that doesn't know what it feels like to snuff the life from a man.

Donatello turns pink and steels his jaw. "It's pufferfish. Fugu. I can't fly it in because it's one of the most poisonous and rarest sushi dishes in the world and highly illegal to prepare if you're not fully trained—"

I cut him off with a lazy wave of my hand. "I'll allow your little fish shipment, Don." I turn to Castiel and Benny. "And what does the Hollow Clan want from Santa this year?"

Cas clears his throat. "Well, it has nothing to do with the port, actually." He cocks his head to the back wall of the alcove. "There's a network of caves we want access to a few miles over, but it falls under Dip territory—"

"Done. Anyone else?"

"Hold on," Dante growls. "You're giving them access to Dip land? Yet when my father and I wanted access to the Preserve, you flat-out refused?"

"What the fuck am I going to do with a cave?"

"What the fuck are you going to do with a forest?"

Nothing. And if it'd been the Hollow brothers who'd asked for the land, I'd have probably given it to them. But now I know Alberto wants it to hold over his hot, young fiancé, there's not a chance in hell I'd even consider it. I darken my glare and recline in the armchair.

"Did you know, there's thirteen pairs of American Bald Eagles in that park? It's more than just a few shitty trees and a swamp."

"What do you care?" His eyes thin. "You sound like that bitch Aurora."

Bitch. An unnecessary amount of fury threads through my veins. I wash it down with a gulp of whiskey. "I care about the environment."

Tor bites out a laugh. "Tell that to your private jet."

Dante's blistering stare doesn't waver. "All right, what do you want?" His eyes move to Rafe. "Tell you what. I'll let you build a hotel and casino in the Cove. There's a great plot of land on the south headland. Has uninterrupted views of the beach."

Rafe's chuckle is deep and sinister. "Build a Raphael Visconti hotel and casino on your land? You wouldn't know how to deal with the sudden spike in tourism."

Dante slams his fist against the table. Rafe's men step out of the shadows. I rise to my feet and put a hand on my brother's shoulder. "Enough. Dante, I'll think about your request." *Lie.* "Now, is there anything else you leeches want from me before you drown yourself in whiskey, debt, and whores?"

A cocktail of music and laughter seeps under the door, signaling that the games are in full swing. Rafe's shoulder twitches under my palm, and as I look around, I notice everyone's eyes are glancing toward the party.

"Then I say this meeting is officially over."

Everyone pours out of the room. Everyone except Dante, who sinks back into his chair and fiddles with a pen Donatello left behind. Only when the door slams shut behind Gabe, muting the music again, does he speak.

"There's something else I want from you, Angelo."

Sucking in a lungful of air, I sit back down and signal to the server behind the bar for another refill.

It's going to be a long night.

The poker games are in full swing. Croupiers deal out cards with the flair of up-close magicians, and glitzy watches flash under the chandeliers as gamblers scoop up their chips. Girls in lingerie and lace work the room, weaving in between tables looking for their next John.

I watch as Rafe's eyes follow a petite red-head, then he leans against the bar and whistles. "She'd do well on the strip, that one."

"You buying?"

He eyes me sideways. "When have you ever seen me pay for a whore?" He looks over my shoulder and his gaze darkens. "What did Dante want?"

"You don't want to know."

"Oh, but I do."

I roll the glass in my hand, watching the brown liquid slosh up the sides. "He wants the records for any calls made to Sinners Anonymous on the coast. Me taking out that dumb lackey over Sunday lunch gave him the idea. He seems to think it'll help weed out traitors and gain intel on business partners."

He huffs out a laugh. Runs a finger over his bottom lip. "Doesn't he realize I've been doing that for years? I hope you told him to fuck off."

"Word for word, brother."

Although silent, I can feel the rage blistering off his body as he watches Dante from across the room. He's in deep conversation with Nico, the youngest Hollow brother, who just graduated from Stanford and is still learning what it means to be a made man.

"God, I hate that cunt," Rafe hisses, before sinking his whiskey and slamming the empty glass on the bar. "I swear, if you ever wanted to take over Dip, I'd be back here within the hour, drawing up hotel and casino plans that'll make Cove look like Coney Island."

"Let's go for a walk."

"Hold on." Rafe turns toward the bar, pulls out a wedge of Sinners Anonymous cards from the breast pocket of his suit, and tosses them in the tip jar. "All right," he says with a wink. "Let's go."

We amble around the club, silently observing the different games. We watch Donatello lose his Omega Seamaster to Benny in blackjack, then come to a stop behind one of the poker tables, just as the dealer sets up a fresh round.

"My money's on Gabe," Rafe mutters, nodding to our brother on the opposite side of the table. His leather jacket is slung over the back of his chair, and he's wearing his signature aviators. Not that he needs them—nobody has a poker face like our brother.

My gaze shifts around the table. Dante and Nico sit to Gabe's right, and two young guys I've never seen before have their backs to us.

The one with the blond hair and the too-big suit leans into his friend. "Dude. Playing against Dante Visconti is totally going to psych you out."

Rafe and I exchange smirks. How the fuck these kids ever got into this party, I'll never know, but at least they'll provide a level of entertainment.

"I know," the other one hisses back. "All the Viscontis must have grown up on a diet of full-fat milk and steroids. They are fucking *huge*."

"And all look like MMA fighters."

"Hey, I like these kids," Rafe murmurs to me with a lop-sided grin. "Maybe I can hire them to follow me around and kiss my ass."

I nod toward the suited guards skirting the perimeter of the room. "You have enough of those."

He huffs out a laugh, and we go back to eavesdropping.

"They must be loaded," the blond kid sighs, flicking a poker chip between his thumb and forefinger. "And they always get the hottest girls."

"Even the old dude. And he must be like, seventy by now."

"Uh-huh. Have you seen who he's marrying?"

My ears prick up, but I force my face to remain expressionless.

"Oh yeh, that Rory chick? From Devil's Dip High?" He lets out a low whistle, shuffling closer to his buddy. "You know he thinks she's a virgin?"

Blond-boy glances over at Dante, then puts his hand in front of his face. But from behind him, I can still see and hear what he whispers. "I know. Hilarious. Remember when she let Spencer and his crew run a train on her?"

"Who could forget? She didn't even go to Devil's Coast Academy and yet everyone knows her name. Spencer and his friends were the richest kids in school, so obviously she's one of those girls that'll do anything to secure a paycheck."

"Literally, *anything*."

Their whispers continue but I can't hear them any longer over the blood thumping in my temples. The ghost of whiskey now tastes bitter on my tongue, and my fingers twitch. So much so, that I slip my hand in the pocket of my slacks and curl it into a fist.

So, Aurora's a whore. A far cry from the virgin she's pretending to be for my uncle. I run my tongue over my teeth and take a slow, deep breath. Rafe's silent now, and I can feel his gaze heating my cheek.

And what do I care? Why does this revelation have me feeling all hot and itchy, have me feeling like I want to connect my fist to a jaw just to hear it crack?

And then I realize why these dumb kids have got under my skin.

In the car ride back to Alberto's house yesterday, she let me believe she was different, even just for a moment. She let me believe she wasn't like all the other girls in Dip, just looking for a Visconti paycheck. That her motive for marrying a man three times her age was completely altruistic.

I huff a laugh into the bottom of my glass. To stop Alberto plowing down the forest. *Yeah, right.* That impassioned spiel she gave about all the fucking birds and the otters—she knew exactly what she was doing. Had me eating out the palm of her hand, and now I'm no fucking better than my dirty old uncle, believing her lies.

Sure, she might not have said anything, but she tricked me. Those big, doe-like eyes and flustered skin and pathetic sins tricked me.

"Everyone place their bets," the dealer drawls, spreading his hands out above the cards then turning them upward, showing the camera above the table he has nothing up his sleeves.

Stacks of golden and silver chips slide across the green velvet. My gaze falls to the back of the blond boy's head.

"Angelo, don't—"

But Rafe's voice sounds like it's in the cave over. Before he or my own common sense can stop me, I take a step forward, loom over the kid's shoulder, and slam my hand down on top of his poker chips.

He yelps in surprise, recoiling from the table. Then he studies my hand, my watch. The citrine ring on my pinky. He gulps, before reluctantly dragging his eyes up to meet mine.

Unlike the rest of my family, I'm not much of a betting man, but I'd bet every chip in the joint that he's just pissed himself.

"I saw that."

The table falls silent. The kid's gaze widens, then moves around the table and back to me again. "W-what?"

"You slipped these chips out of your pocket." I shoot a loaded look in the direction of his shit-talking buddy. "Both of you did."

He pales and his bottom lip gives into a quiver. "No! I didn't, I swear—"

I scoop up one of his chips, cutting off his protests. They are made from pure 24-carat gold, my family's crest embossed into the middle. Ignoring the heat of everyone's attention, I hold it up to the low lighting and let out a hiss. "Yeah, counterfeit."

"It's not! It can't be, I got it from over there!" He stabs a shaking finger in the direction of the cashier booth. The chick behind it holds up her hands in protest. She doesn't want to get involved in this shit-show and I don't blame her.

"Let's ask the guy who created them." I toss the chip behind me to Rafe. He catches it with one hand. "What do you think, brother? That look real to you?"

Rafe pins me with a blistering glare. His jaw locks and he gives a shake of his head so slight that I know it's only meant for me. But I hold my ground and wait. Flaring his nostrils, he eventually looks down, flicking the chip between his thumb and forefinger.

The silence stretches over canyons. Eventually, he looks up at me through half-lidded eyes and rakes his teeth over his bottom lip. "Faker than a three-dollar bill."

The club comes back to life. Chairs scrape against the cave floor, and the *click-clicks* of safety catches releasing echo off the low ceiling. Rafe's men emerge from the shadows and clamp their hands on both the boys' shoulders and drag them away. I can hear their screams all the way until they are bundled into the elevator at the end of the long tunnel.

"*Bastardi,*" Tor growls, dusting down his suit jacket and sinking back into his seat at the Blackjack table. "They work at Delirium and constantly beg me for an invite to a private poker game." His diamond nose stud glints as he shakes his head. "They've barely got hair on their dicks, let alone balls big enough to try a stunt like that."

The music starts again, and slowly, the incident settles like dust and everyone falls back into having a good time. Feeling heat on my back, I turn around and see Rafe standing in the shadows, glaring at me. As I walk past, he pulls a hand out of his pocket and grabs my arm.

"Vicious Visconti is back," he murmurs in my ear. I stare straight ahead, spine steeled, until he lets me go and moves off into the crowds.

Maybe Vicious never really left.

CHAPTER
Thirteen

Rory

"**H**OLD STILL."

"I *am* holding still."

"No, you're fidgeting like an innocent man on trial." Greta emphasizes her point by slamming a bony hand on my shoulder and squeezing. "If I stab you with this needle, don't go running to Alberto crying, because it'll be your fault."

Once again, she's chosen a dress too small—so small, in fact, the back zipper won't go past the curve of my hip. Instead of letting me wear something else, Greta's solution is to physically sew me into it. I'll probably have to sleep in it too, because I have no idea how I'll get it off tonight.

"You're nervous."

Greta's observation shoots down my spine like a laser beam. I lock eyes with her in the mirror and swallow. Silently begging my skin not to flush. "Why would I be nervous? It's only a Friday night dinner."

She frowns at me like I've lost my mind. "Nervous about next Saturday, you stupid little girl," The point of her needle grazes over my flesh. "Your engagement party."

"Oh."

I watch as she glances at my left hand clutching my stomach. More specifically, at the rock on my ring finger. "You don't know how lucky you are," she murmurs softly.

My eyes flutter shut. "So you've said, Greta. Thousands of times."

The moment I step into the Visconti Grand Hotel on Alberto's arm next Saturday, the countdown to the wedding will begin. It'll start with the engagement party, then it'll be the wedding dress fitting and the cake tasting, meetings with the pastor and dinners with extended family, and then it'll end in exactly two weeks with me walking down the aisle.

Or, more likely, being dragged down the aisle. Potentially kicking and screaming.

One week and one day. That's all the time I have left to pretend that this isn't really going to happen.

"Before you leave, remind me to put some more powder on your nose." Greta stands to her full height and thins her eyes. "Why are you so shiny?" She takes a step back. "Are you sick?"

I hiss out a breath through the gap in my teeth and smooth down the front of my dress. "I'm fine."

I'm not fine, and haven't been fine since the car ride with Angelo on Wednesday. Ever since I stood on the porch and watched his tail lights melt into the gray horizon, there's been a thick unease trickling under my skin. Like being in a small car with him on a rainy day has turned my blood to syrup. It's an uncomfortable feeling, akin to when I step outside first thing in the morning, and although the sky is clear and the weather forecast predicts sun, I know it's about to rain. It's inexplicable. Ominous. It raises the hairs on the back of my neck and tension clots between my shoulder blades, and yet, I can't put a finger on why.

It's only rain.

And Angelo is only a man. One I don't even *like*.

I sit in blistering silence as Greta teases my curls. The cocktail of burnt hair and hairspray burns my nostrils, and my temples sting under the brunt of her comb. When she's finished, she takes a step back and treats me to a tight smile.

"You look like Marilyn Monroe."

It'd be a compliment if her tone weren't so bitter.

My eyes fall lazily to my reflection. I'm usually unbothered by the unrecognizable face staring back at me, but I have to admit, tonight I do look particularly impressive. The silver dress shimmers under the white vanity lights, and my hair, for once, isn't poker straight and boring. Greta has styled it into big, loose waves, which cascade down my bare back and bounce when I walk.

I bite back my smile because I'd *never* give the miserable old hag the satisfaction of being happy. I bristle out of the room without a glance back.

Tonight, the pianist has started early; lively jazz drifts from under the swinging doors of the dining room and fills the domed ceiling. I descend the stairs slowly, because, as always, my dress is too tight and my heels too high to do anything in a hurry. Peering over the banister, I notice there are more guests than usual. Several of the Hollow brothers have turned up, crowding in the foyer and swiping *amuse-bouche* off passing trays without breaking pace in their conversations.

I study each and every suit. And I hate how my stomach drops a few inches when I realize none of them belong to Angelo.

Stop it, Rory. I swallow the disappointment and steel my spine. The only reason I feel like this is because, even though I despise him, I can't deny that he makes these long-winded gatherings more interesting. He gives me someone other than Dante to glare at.

Yes. That's all it is.

As I hop off the last step, something moves in the corner of my eye and holds my attention. It's coming from the gap in Alberto's office door. Two figures, back-lit by the moonlight shining through the window behind them. I slow down to a stop and squint under the curtain of my hair, trying to get a better look.

It's Alberto and Mortiz, deep in conversation. My heart skips a beat as I remember their conversation last week about changing the terms in our contract. I've been so distracted by...*other things*, that I totally forgot about it.

Well, doomsday is coming. In less than three weeks I'll be chained to this sleazeball in sickness and in health, and I *really* need to find out what the hell he's planning before I decide what I'm going to do.

Before I decide if I'm going to go ahead with my own plan.

With a glance toward the lobby, I take a sharp right down the hallway behind the stairs. There's access to the pool from the game room, so I'll slip out, skirt around the side of the house, and see if I can hear Alberto and his lawyer's conversation from outside the office window.

Holy crow, it's cold. As I step out onto the deck, the mid-fall chill blasts me, raising goosebumps on my arms and legs. It's not even Halloween yet, but frost is already settling on the pool cover, and wisps of fog dance in the glow of the landscape lighting.

I creep left, hugging the wall of the house as I round the corner. Suddenly, there's something soft underfoot, which causes my heel to sink into the ground and my ankle to buckle underneath me.

"Gah," I yelp. I shoot out fingers and grasp for something, anything to stop me from tumbling over. They brush over a drainpipe and scrape down some bricks, but before I can find something, something finds me. A hand. It's big and strong and I shouldn't be able to recognize who it belongs to so easily.

Warmth brushes my bare back, a wave of adrenaline chasing after it. I twist around to find Angelo Visconti so close I can probably guess the thread count of his crisp, white shirt. I shift my gaze higher, meeting his eyes. He slips a cigarette between his lips and inhales.

Then he blows.

Hot and heavy smoke swirls between us; I find myself briefly closing my eyes, basking in the heat grazing my nose and cheeks. I open them again just as the cloud evaporates into the darkness, revealing the network of hard lines that make up Angelo's expressionless face. I can't be sure—the starless sky provides little light—but there's something licking at the edges of his stare. Irritation, perhaps. I'm sure the last person he wants to bump into is me.

"Those silly little shoes of yours are very...*inappropriate.*"

Suffocating under the intensity of his stare, I glance down at my feet and swallow. I'd forgotten that the corner of the house is where the deck meets the beach.

"Sand." I mutter, trying to control my breathing. "I'd forgotten there was sand."

A grunt, low and sinister, rumbles in his chest. I'm so close I can feel the frequency of it. The cherry of his cigarette glows, and then I'm surrounded by his smoke once more. This time, I part my lips and slowly suck. It's not lost on me that this smoke was in his mouth just seconds before it enters mine, and the thought feels so incredibly naughty that my face starts to burn.

"That's not what I meant."

My heart stills for a second, before reality brushes the comment away. He's only saying what everybody in the house behind me is thinking: at Friday night dinners, I dress like a whore. My skirt is too short, my heels too high, and my makeup too thick. Too *inappropriate.*

Angelo's gaze is too heavy, and it's instinctive to try to crawl out from underneath it, but when my eyes dart around, I notice there's nowhere to go. In front of me is the brick wall of the house, and behind, Angelo's imposing figure. Sucking in a lungful of air, I slide my arm out of his grasp and twist around, so my back is flat against the wall.

Big mistake. He takes a step forward, closing the gap between us as quickly as it appeared. I force my expression to remain neutral, unbothered, even though I'm sure I'm not fooling him. I was never very good at acting, and if I can hear my heart beating like that, then he probably can too.

I clear my throat. "What are you doing out here?"

"Smoking."

"Thought you didn't smoke?"

His gaze rises up to mine, confusion crossing his face for a split second, before he realizes I'm referring to the night in the alley beside Tor's half-built club.

His lips twitch. "You keep my secret—I'll keep yours."

"All of them?"

The moment the question tumbles from my lips in a puff of condensation, blood rises to my neck and chest. The memory of being in his car on Wednesday makes my bones cringe. A *deal goes both ways, Aurora.* I'd misread what he'd meant by that so badly that I almost did something...*highly inappropriate.* The worst part was that when I was sitting in the passenger seat contemplating it, my heart rate had quickened, and heat had pooled between my thighs in the most delicious of ways.

It felt like it would have been the best bad thing I'd ever done.

Flamingo, what must he think of me?

He doesn't answer my question. Instead, his gaze drops to my lips as he rakes his teeth over his own. I really wish he'd stop doing that; it makes my head feel all funny. In a bid to look at anything but the delicious curve of his cupid's bow, I glance down at the cigarette glowing faintly in his right hand.

He must have noticed, because he brings it up into the small space between us, and twists it around so the filter is facing me.

He wants to share? My pulse flutters. It's one thing sharing the same cloud of smoke, but putting my lips where his were...

It feels dangerous.

Goose, I'm pathetic. Truth is, I have almost no experience with boys, let alone *men.* Before that awful day three years ago,

I'd never even been intimate with a boy. And I'd never had a childhood sweetheart growing up because all the boys in my class and in my town were so...*familiar*. I'd known them since kindergarten, just like my parents had known their parents and so on. There was nothing new or exciting to discover about them. Their memories were also mine, as were their experiences. That's why I was so excited for college—not only would I be one step closer to my dream of becoming a pilot, but also I'd get to meet boys outside of the Devil's Coast.

"I don't smoke."

Dark amusement dances in his eyes. "I thought you were a bad girl."

Bad girl. The way he spits out those words, harsh and heated, makes me want to be just that. It's easy to ignore the blatant mockery, and without another word, I take the cigarette from him, watching him watching me, and I bring it to my lips and inhale.

Immediately, the back of my throat starts to burn, and I drop the cigarette in the sand in the middle of my coughing fit.

I can barely hear his chuckle over the sound of my own labored breaths.

"Jesus Christ," I wheeze, tilting my head back against the brick wall.

With a smirk that deepens the cleft of his chin, he pulls the pack from his slacks and tugs out a fresh cigarette. The flame of his Zippo lighter dances majestically against the dark night as he lights it.

"Watch me." *As if I ever do anything else these days*. He slips it between his lips and takes a slow, sensual drag. This time, he has the courtesy to blow the smoke out above my head. I feel mildly disappointed. "Here." He hands it to me. "Not so much this time, magpie."

I like the way he watches my mouth as I slowly inhale. A few seconds later, smoke smoothly escapes my lips, coasting over the planes of his face.

"Better," he purrs.

I smile, passing it back to him. He glances down at the red ring of lipstick around the filter and pauses. His Adam's apple bobs in his throat, and I swear, I see his pulse in his jaw.

"Oh—"

But before I can finish my sentence, he slides the cigarette between his lips and inhales. For some silly reason, my heartbeat skids to a stop at the mere sight of his mouth in the same spot where mine just was. It feels wrong. Too intimate.

In fact, standing out here with him, *alone*, feels too intimate. Wrapping my arms around myself, I glance toward the garden.

"I should probably get going."

"Stay."

It's not a suggestion. Despite turning his back on the Cosa Nostra, Angelo Visconti doesn't strike me as the type of man that merely suggests. I lean back, my heels sinking farther into the sand, anchoring me between the house my fiance built and the man who could blow it down with a huff of his sarcastic breath.

Faint jazz drifts out from inside the house. Down by the sea, the waves crash angrily against the shore. Both serve as a backdrop to the sound of my heavy breathing.

"Alberto will wonder where I am."

"So, tell him."

I huff out a bitter laugh. "Yeah, that'll go down well." He cocks a brow, waiting for more. "How would you feel if you found your fiancee in a dark corner, sharing a cigarette with a handsome man?"

He stares at me. At first blankly, then his eyes thin. "You think I'm handsome."

Oh, flamingo. Despite the chill coasting around us, my skin instantly burns up with embarrassment. *I'm meant to hate him as much as he hates me.*

I steel my jaw. "Don't get too excited. I usually wear glasses."

His laugh feels good against my skin. "Am I more handsome than your husband?"

"It's not hard."

"So, who would you rather kiss?"

I blink.

What?

My breathing shallows, eventually coming to a stop altogether. I'm burning up, blistering under the intensity of his attention, yet he's as cool as a cucumber. We're like fire and ice. He takes another drag on the cigarette and regards me with the indifference of a man who just asked me the time.

Don't look. Don't look. Don't look.

My gaze drops to his lips.

Oh, swan.

A look can tell a thousand words, and judging by the smug grin that splits Angelo's face, my glance at his lips have written him a whole frickin' essay.

I feel the urge to clutch back some footing, and the only way I know how to do that these days is to be nasty.

"I don't know. You're almost as old as him anyway."

Annoyance coasts across the planes of his face, but he rearranges his features immediately.

"I'm thirty-six."

"Almost twice my age."

"I suppose when you're still a silly little girl, everyone above the age of thirty seems old."

I'm glad it's dark, because hopefully, he can't see me fluster under the navy sky.

"Besides," he continues, his voice hardening, "only silly little girls would think grown men would want to kiss them."

"And only dirty old men would ask their uncle's fiancee about her kissing preferences."

Silence swirls us, thicker than the smoke escaping Angelo's parted lips. "I was joking, *Aurora*." So, he's back to saying my name like *that*. "Alberto is family, and while we may not always see eye to eye, I'll always respect him."

I tilt my chin up. Now that my stilettos are halfway in the sand, he feels even taller than usual. "You can't respect him that much. I saw you key his car."

"When?" he asks, without missing a beat.

"On Wednesday, when you dropped me off."

"Wednesday..." he murmurs, scratching his jaw as he pretends to think. "You mean the day you kissed him in front of me? "

My stomach churns at the memory, but I'm irritated about playing his game. "Yes."

"Hmm. I don't know what you're talking about."

His face is deadpan; as emotionless as his tone. But still, a little firework sparks inside my chest. I was disorientated by Alberto's sudden PDA, and the rain was so heavy it distorted Angelo's body as he moved toward his car. I thought perhaps I'd imagined the childish act of vandalism, but now, I know I didn't.

He keyed his uncle's car because of that kiss.

Confusion prickles on my skin but I ignore it in favor of the adrenaline skating down my spine.

This is bad. Three-thousand feet in the air, *toeing a tightrope no wider than dental floss* type of bad. I have the weight of my world on my shoulders, and if I fall, there's more than just my own life on the line.

It's excitingly dangerous, but still, dangerous.

I should be more afraid of heights.

"I have to go," I whisper.

This time, he doesn't tell me to stay. He takes a final drag of his cigarette, then closes the gap between us. Instinctively, I push myself further into the wall, flattening my palms against the cold brickwork. He looms over me like an incoming storm, placing one hand next to my shoulder, using the other to grind the butt into the wall, just inches from my ear.

He stays there for a moment. And then another. Trapping me in with the weight of his body and the intensity of his gaze. Time seems to crawl; even the music drifting out of the house sounds slower.

I don't think I want it to speed up.

"Tell me a sin, Aurora."

The gravel in his voice grates me in places that it shouldn't. I swallow the thick lump in my throat and close my eyes. *Jesus, is all that heat radiating from his body?* It's October, and yet he's out here in little more than a suit and feeling like a furnace.

And yet, I realize I'm not cold anymore, either.

"Is this what it's going to be like now?" I rasp. "Me drip-feeding you sins so you don't listen to the ones I dialed in?"

He licks his teeth. Slowly nods.

I suck in a lungful of air and drag my gaze up to the starless sky. I'm trying to concentrate on anything that'll give me respite from the dull ache forming low in my stomach, but the feeling of his hot breath grazing my nose makes it impossible.

"Every time he makes me kiss him like that, I spit in his whiskey."

My sin lingers in the air, filling the tiny gap between us. As his body stills against mine, I tear my gaze from the sky and land on his. It's darker than the night and just as cold. *Oh no.* My heartbeat thrums; perhaps I've overstepped the mark. Perhaps I should have gone with something lighter; perhaps—

But then a laugh trickles from the parting of his lips, a cocktail of velvet and nails. Husky and raw. It lights up my nervous system, like I've just heard a song that was once my favorite, yet I hadn't heard it in years.

I laugh too. And I laugh more, harder, leaning into his hard body.

Until something dawns on me like a new day.

I'm utterly, madly, unacceptably obsessed with Angelo Visconti. My fiance's nephew, near-stranger, and keeper of my darkest secrets.

And suddenly, my sin isn't so funny anymore.

CHAPTER
Fourteen

Angelo

NO MATTER HOW CLOSE to the shoreline I get, I can't escape the Whitney Houston ballad that spills out of the basement bar. I can't escape *her*, either.

Jesus Christ, she's everywhere. I crossed the line earlier, and now I'm forcing myself to keep my distance. Which is near-impossible, because tonight she's a walking, *dancing*, disco ball with legs. It's like she put on that damn dress to irritate me. The sequins shimmer and flash every time she moves, commanding my gaze like a magnet. And then I find myself watching her. Watching her sway her hips and flip her hair to cheesy ballads. Watching the hem of her dress ride up her ass as she leans over the bar to talk to the server. Even when she sits in the shadows, twirling the straw in her gin and tonic, with a lop-sided smile, observing Don and Amelia dancing to the slow songs, she forces me to watch her.

It's all too easy to forget she's a gold-digging whore.

I catch her watching me, too. I feel it, her heavy gaze brushing against my back while I'm talking to Cas or Benny. I clench my fists and try to concentrate on whatever business shit they are rattling on about, but it's near impossible when her laugh trickles over my shoulder, or she teeters past and I catch a whiff of her vanilla and bubblegum scent.

When it's too much, I come out here to smoke to get away from her. Yet, I'm so pathetic, I can't help but hope she'll follow me out. The moonlight cuts a path across the sea, which spills out onto the shoreline and onto my shoes. The late night breeze is a welcome chill, snaking down the collar of my shirt and cooling the heat on my skin. With a snap of my wrist, the Zippo lighter in my fist comes alive, and I wave the flame under a fresh cigarette.

I'm almost out.

A shadow crosses the moonlit sand, and the suited figure it belongs to comes to a stop by my side.

"I haven't seen you smoke this much since the funeral."

Taking a long, much-needed drag, I exhale a cloud of smoke up into the sky and pass the pack to Rafe.

"Stress."

"Huh." He takes a cigarette. Lights it. "You've spent nine years resisting the urge to pop a cap in everyone's ass. Nine years as the boss of a billion-dollar company, where you can't make your problems go away by burying them six feet under." He pauses to take a drag. "And yet, in nine years, I haven't seen you smoke once."

"Yeah, well it's been nine years since I spent more than a weekend on the Coast. I'm surprised I haven't turned to the crack pipe."

Rafe doesn't laugh. Instead, he stands shoulder to shoulder with me, smoking his cigarette and watching the waves roll in.

"Tell me why you're back, bro."

A long sigh escapes through my nostrils. I drop my gaze to the sand and roll my shoulders back.

Fuck it. It'll all come out eventually.

"Last week, I had a meeting in San Jose. A tech company we'd invested in a couple years ago has been defaulting on the dividends. I was getting sick of the disrespect, and we weren't making any headway with conference calls, so I decided to just fly over there. Shit the bastards up a little." I drop the cigarette and grind it into the sand with my foot. "Anyway, I turn up to this office in Silicon Valley, and I'm met by some asshole claiming to be the CEO. You know the type—lives in a hoodie and wears flip flops Monday thru Friday." Out the corner of my eye, Rafe grazes a finger over his collar pin and shakes his head in disgust. "He leads me into this glass boardroom, and I tell him he's got seven days to pay up. And you know what he said?" I grind my teeth together, hot, angry flames licking the walls of my stomach. "*Make me.*"

Rafe's face stretches into a sly, sideways grin. "And then what? You slammed his head against the desk and forced him to eat his own flip flops?"

I huff out a bitter laugh. "No, I left. Told him he'll be hearing from our lawyers, and then I got into the fucking elevator and I left. No broken bones, no chokeholds." I rake a hand through my hair and shake my head in disbelief. "I *left*, Rafe."

Rafe's laugh is louder than mine. "Jesus Christ. That's what happens when you go straight—you spend your life paying taxes and getting shit on." He fills the silence with a cloud of smoke. "So, let me guess: you decided you'd had enough of playing Mr. Normal and diverted your London-bound jet to the Coast to remind yourself of how the other half live?"

"No. I walked out the building and started pounding the sidewalk. I had no idea where I was going and I didn't care. I just had to *think*. I was angry, not even at that tech asshole, but at myself. At this family. Viscontis—all of us—are hard-wired to do bad things, be bad people. It's entwined in our DNA, and no matter how many fucking spreadsheets I fill out or how many hours I spend in boardrooms, I'll never be normal." I crack my knuckles and glance up at my brother. "An intern put sugar in my Americano and my first thought was to dislocate his jaw."

Rafe smiles. "But you've always been like that; that's how you got your nickname. It's instinctive for you to deal out revenge that is always greater than the crime." He hitches a shoulder, smirking. "Like the time Dante told dad you missed a drop-off, so you fucked Dante's prom date. You're *vicious*."

I bite back a smirk. "So *that's* why. I couldn't remember."

"*He* sure does." Rafe drops his cigarette and smooths down the front of his shirt. "We're bad people, Angelo. You can run from that fact, but you can't hide from it, even all the way in England."

"You know what Mama always used to say," I say quietly, tugging another cigarette out the carton and lighting it. "Good cancels out the bad."

My brother is silent for a beat, but I can hear the cogs in his brain clicking into place. "That's why you left. You thought Mama would have wanted you to turn good, because it'll cancel out all the bad from the rest of the family. You left because of Mama."

It's not a question, it's a fact. I nod anyway. "I'm back because of Mama, too."

He whips around to face me. "What?"

I keep my gaze trained on the horizon. "That day in San Francisco, I walked and walked and eventually, I found myself in

China Town. I was crossing the road when a woman jumped out in front of me rattling this big sack." I glance over at him, lips pursed. "She was selling fortune cookies. Broken ones from the factory she worked at. You know I don't believe in any of that shit, but I was just thinking about Mama, and you know how much she loved those fucking fortune cookies..."

"You bought one."

"Uh-huh."

"Angelo," he says seriously. "For the love of God, don't tell me you came back to the Coast because of a fortune cookie. Christ," he huffs, tilting his head to the sky. "I wish I'd never asked."

"And hopefully, you won't ask again."

"What did it say?"

"Don't worry about it."

"Seriously?"

I offer him nothing more than a curt nod.

If I told him what was inside the fortune cookie, then I'd have to tell him why it made me come back to the Coast. And that would mean peeling back the layers of the lie I'd built to protect him and Gabe from the truth.

At least talking about it reminds me why I'm here. I landed on the Coast exactly a week ago, a man on a mission, and have done fuck-all since. I've been too...*distracted.*

"All right, another question."

I groan, dragging a knuckle across my jaw. "Come on—"

"The kids at the poker game. What were you playing at, man?"

I steel my jaw and slide my hands into my pocket. "They were shit-talking family."

"They were shit-talking Uncle Alberto's plaything."

"She'll be family soon enough."

I ignore the punch in my gut.

"Yeah. That's why you've been staring at her all night? You're just checking out the latest addition to the Cove clan?" His eyes drop pointedly to the cigarette pack poking out my top pocket.

In my slacks, my hands clench into fists. His gaze burns my cheek as he waits for an answer, but when it's clear he's not going to get one, he lets out a hard sigh.

"Papa always used to ask me and Gabe, *if Angelo jumped off a cliff, would you jump, too?*" He smirks at the memory. "Know what I'd always say?"

Behind us, the Whitney Houston ballad picks up into something more up-tempo.

I shake my head.

"Without a parachute." He laughs into his hand as he wipes his mouth. Then, he turns his back to the sea, brushing his shoulder against mine. "Look," he says, lowering his voice so I can barely hear it over the Marvin Gaye song blaring out the house. "I'll always be your ride-or-die, and I know Gabe feels the same way. You want to burn this fucking coast down, I'll lend you my lighter. But please, for the love of God, don't make me go to war with our cousins over a piece of pussy."

And with that, he strolls back up the beach toward the bar, leaving me alone on the shoreline with all my sins.

CHAPTER
Fifteen

Rory

I WAKE BEFORE THE sun with Alberto's fat slug of an arm pinning me to the bed like an anchor. His stale whiskey breath tickles the curve of my neck in sickly, rhythmic waves. Every bone in my body cringes. He always insists on going to bed holding me, whispering dirty thoughts and desires in my ear as his belly and bulge press uncomfortably against my lower back. I always lie there, still and silent, until he falls asleep, and then I slip out from underneath him and curl up on the corner of the bed, making myself as small as possible. Somehow in the night, he's managed to find me again and drag my body flush with his.

Nausea hits me, and I know it's not just because I went too heavy on the gin and tonics last night. As I shuffle out from under Alberto's heavy limbs, I glance at the watch on his wrist. It's barely five-am, and yet I'm wide awake, unease and uncertainty buzzing through my veins.

Stopping in the doorway to throw a cautious glance at Alberto, I slip out of the room and pad down to the kitchen. Then, I pour myself a cold glass of water from the fridge and lean against the sink, watching the first rays of light make an appearance over the ocean through the kitchen window.

I'm anxious I won't get to see my father today. Hell, I'm anxious about everything. About Alberto meeting with his lawyer, *again*, and the fact that I still don't know what he's planning. I was on a mission to find out last night, but I happened to get...*distracted*.

Drawing in a slow, deep breath, I roll my neck around my shoulders but it does nothing to loosen the knots in my back. I need *release*. Yet, the only outlet I have comes in the form of Sinners Anonymous.

And obviously, that's out of bounds now.

Taking another gulp of water, I look over the rim of the glass to the ocean. Lazy waves lap against the shore and recoil just as slowly. It looks calm and cool, while I'm disturbed and hot.

With an obscene thought racing through my brain, I pour the rest of the water down the sink and dart back up the stairs. Instead of turning right into Alberto's wing, I head left, into my dressing room, and make a beeline for the closet. Less than three minutes later, I'm bounding down the stairs in sweatpants, my bikini on underneath and a towel tucked under my arm.

Snaking through the house, I marvel in the silence of it. Usually, there's always *someone* lurking around. Always noise floating through the halls—the low murmur of ever-present guards, the maids vacuuming non-existent dust. Alberto himself, barking demands at skittish servers. But this morning, the tranquility is like a breath of fresh air.

I almost regret my impulsive decision the moment I step out of the patio doors and my bare feet sink into the sand. It's *freezing*. An icy chill whips my cheeks, working its way up my sleeves and down my collar. But I force myself to ignore my teeth chattering and the little voice in my head telling me to crawl back to the warmth of the house.

There's no comfort for me there.

Instead, I rip off my sweats like a band aid and trudge toward the waves. As I get closer to the shoreline I break into a run, because I know if I slow down, I'll stop, and if I stop, I'll never extinguish the heat blistering through my veins.

I gasp when the water breaks at my ankles. Damn-near choke when it sloshes against my chest, forming an icy claw around my lungs and stopping me from taking anything but short, labored breaths. It burns my skin like frostbite, but I keep going, until I'm fully submerged and fighting against the current with long, strong strokes.

It was my mom who taught me to swim. Years later, she said it was because she was so bitter that my father got to teach me everything else—riding a bike, how to start a fire, how to build shelter from discarded wood—and she wanted to pass a skill onto me, too. She took me to the lake by our cabin, bundled me into our boat and rowed us out into the middle of the water. *Jump,* she'd said, before folding her arms and staring at me, expectantly. I'd laughed. Mom was known for her sense of humor. But when she didn't crack a smile I realized she wasn't joking, and the panic started to seep in around my edges, I reached for the oars to row back to shore, but she pushed me back down on the boat bench with a firm hand.

Jump, she repeated. *Because when you jump, you'll find your wings as you fall.*

I glanced up at my father, who was hovering nervously on the bank, clutching a life buoy. I swallowed the fear rising up my throat, balled my fists, and I jumped. Not because I thought I'd miraculously be able to fly, but because I knew that if I fell and couldn't get back up my parents would always be there to save me.

I owe them the same. And while I couldn't save my mom from the cancer, I sure as hell will save my father from Alberto Visconti.

When my lungs start to ache, I stop swimming and flip onto my back, letting the waves carry my body. The sky is starting to pale, morphing from a dark gray to a light blue, and I wonder how long it'll last before the day's storm rolls in.

Breathing low and slow, I close my eyes for a moment and listen to the squawking of the cranes circling the cliffs for early morning prey. I realize I'm smiling. This feels good. I feel *free.* Although I can't escape the Coast like I've always wanted to, at least my mind can, even just for a few minutes.

The serenity lasts for a while, my mind as clear as the sky above me, my conscious as weightless as my body in the ocean.

But as the dark clouds roll in over the Cove, dark thoughts come with them. One dark thought in particular—Angelo Visconti.

No, no, no.

But it's too late. The image of him appears, fully formed, behind my eyelids. I can feel the heat of his body against mine; feel the weight of his loaded question between my thighs.

So, who would you rather kiss?

I groan, submerging myself under the surface again, but this time, the shock of cold water does nothing to extinguish the heat. It comes from deep within, a burn that starts low in my stomach and spreads south to a place it shouldn't. And then I remember the way he raked his teeth over his bottom lip, how his heavy gaze dropped to my mouth. The burn spreads up, back over my stomach and tightening my breasts. Absentmindedly, my fingers slide along my collarbone and under the fabric of my bikini top, then graze over my nipple. It's hard and sensitive, and I shudder with excitement as I roll it between my thumb and forefinger.

I bet it'd feel even better if he did it. Especially with those large hands and thick fingers that make a cigarette look as small as a needle. I bet his palms are rough and his touch heavy.

And then, I wonder what would have happened if, in the darkness of the walkway, I'd answered his question truthfully.

You.

I'd rather kiss you.

My hand trails down my stomach and slides between my legs. It's a different wetness that coats me down there; it's warm and slick and when I dip a finger deeper into it, my whole body reacts.

What would he have done if that one word had fallen from my lips? I imagine his square jaw sharpening, his gaze darkening. One hand trapping me against the wall, the other gripping the hemline of my dress and impatiently dragging it up my bare thighs. He wouldn't be gentle, and deep down, I know I wouldn't want him to be.

Letting out a hiss of air toward the sky, I slide my finger up to my hardening clit and start rubbing in slow circles around it. It's not how Angelo Visconti would touch me. No, I irritate him too much for him to go slow and soft. He'd rip my thong to the side and cup my sex. He wouldn't tease out an orgasm, because men like him don't tease. He'd *demand* one with long, thick fingers.

I bite my lip as I slip a finger into my hole, imagining it was his stretching me open instead. I move on it, bucking my hips against my palm to build up friction, chasing that release I need so badly. The back of my head and my ears bob in and out of the water as I kick my legs to stay afloat. *God, it feels good.* My eyes flutter open, just as a seagull glides overhead, and when my gaze falls back to shore, I freeze.

There's a figure standing on the beach. A man. Sharply dressed in a navy suit and a crisp white shirt.

My blood runs colder than the water around me.

No. It can't be...

But Angelo's silhouette is impossible to overlook, standing tall and wide against the backdrop of the house. He's staring straight ahead, feet shoulder-width apart, and his hands are tucked into the pocket of his slacks. I've stared at him enough to know it's definitely him.

Swan, swan, swan.

When the salty water brushes over my lips, I suddenly realize I'm not treading water anymore, and I quickly flap my arms and kick my legs to stay afloat. *What the hell is he doing here? Can he see me?*

Of course he can. It's the first rule my father taught me when camping: If you can see a predator, assume they can see you, too.

A wave picks me up and carries me a few feet closer to the shore, but I lie on my back and kick against it, trying to get further out to sea.

Sinking a little lower under the surface of the water, I peer up at him through wet lashes. My memory of him from last night is shrouded by a cloak of darkness, gin, and nicotine, making him bigger, sexier, *scarier*. Perhaps the way he made by head spin and clit pulsate could have been brushed under the carpet, if he didn't make me feel the exact same way in the cold light of day. There's about a hundred feet and an ocean between us, and yet, just the blurry outline of him makes hot, itchy, lust crawl through my veins, and the network of nerves between my legs beg for pressure.

Just the darn image of him drains my brain of all rationale. My hand slides back into my bikini bottoms. This time, I don't need to close my eyes to imagine him, I simply stare across the waves. Him, in all of his untouchable glory. I imagine him spotting me, his gaze darkening and his fists ripping off his Armani suit as he impatiently strips to join me in the water. I imagine what he looks like under those tailor-made clothes. What muscles will flex and contract in his back as he swims to reach me in a few quick, strong strokes. How hot and hard his body feels when he presses it against mine.

The wind is picking up now, and I groan into it, my eyes never leaving his imposing silhouette on the shore. Then my hand becomes his hand again, and he slides one of those thick fingers into me. The walls of my passage burn deliciously as they stretch to accommodate him, molding to his thickness and adjusting to his speed. His touch is rough but the space between his neck and shoulders is warm—*God, he smells good*—and I nuzzle into his damp skin to get more of it, all of it.

With two fingers inside my now, I grind the heel of my palm against my clit, riding the crest of my sick fantasy. And then my free hand reaches back into my bikini top, pinching and twisting my nipples until every nerve ending in my body is pulsing with an electric current. My orgasm is *so close*, and I look up at Angelo through blurry, half-lidded eyes, rubbing harder, faster.

I'm frantic. God, I want him. I want him on me. I want to know what he feels like.

My orgasm builds and builds, tingling deep within my pussy and threatening to spill out and flood my entire body.

One more stolen glance at Angelo's indifferent expression and I come, *hard*, the lust washing over me like a wave. I ride it in delirium, throwing my head back and crying out in the wind. The adrenaline zaps through my spine like a lightning bolt, and I realize—this is what I live for. I chase *this* high. It's why I continue to do bad things; why I want to fly planes thousands of feet in the air. Why I find myself balancing on the edge of a cliff, one sneaker hovering over nothingness.

Why I'm fingering myself at the thought of Alberto's nephew, while he's a mere few feet away, oblivious.

I live for living dangerously in a place that barely lets me live at all.

The throbbing between my thighs dies down to a subtle ache, and my breath slows to its natural rhythm. But I'm still high on the sin, so as I swim back to shore I'm biting back a smile.

When it's shallow enough for the pebbles to graze against my stomach, I tilt my chin and allow my gaze to flicker up to Angelo's. He's lifting a cigarette to his lips, but he stops in his tracks when I stand up.

We stare at each other. Almost a gawp, as you do when you see an exotic animal in the wild for the first time. It's like I've never seen a man in a bespoke suit, and he's never seen a girl nearly naked. I come to a sudden stop, my heart pounding a mile a minute in my chest. My legs are still shaky from my orgasm, but that's not what's making it impossible to walk.

His stare hardens into a glare, and slowly, he slips the cigarette back into the pack and tucks it into his pocket. He palms his jaw. Swallows. Then his gaze drops to below my collarbone, where it trails the drips of water running down my chest and disappearing into my cleavage.

My pulse flutters, and I feel my nipples hardening underneath my bikini top; knowing that the fabric is thin enough for him to notice.

Simply for something to do, I drag my heavy hair over one shoulder and twist it, squeezing out the seawater. Something about this action elicits a low growl from his half-parted lips.

Feeling bold after sinning in the sea, it's me who slices through the heavy silence first.

"What are you doing here?"

He purses his lips, then tears his eyes from me and turns his attention to the horizon over my shoulder. "I told you. I'll be taking you to see your father on Wednesdays, and Saturdays."

For some reason, his tone doesn't sound as indifferent as usual.

"Oh, yes." I aim for nonchalance, but my acting skills don't stretch that far. "I'll go get changed, then."

He doesn't say a word. Instead, he stares ahead with a smolder hot enough to set the Pacific on fire. I side-step him, brushing my wet shoulder against his dry suit as I pass. But then I feel a strong tug on the side tie of my bikini bottoms and come to an abrupt stop next to him.

What the hell?

Confused, I look down to see his forefinger is hooked under the thin bow tying my bikini bottoms together. My heart stops beating so suddenly that I feel as if I may pass out. *He's touching me.* The back of his knuckle scorches my bare skin, and it doesn't escape me that all it'd take is a slight tug and my panties would be in the sand.

Blood drums in my ears. I glance up, but he's still glaring out to sea. The only thing moving on him is the pulse thumping in his jaw.

"If you belonged to me and dressed like that around other men, I'd pull down those skimpy bottoms and spank your ass until it was raw."

His voice is thick and raspy. Each word is short and bitter, and yet, his expression remains emotionless.

We stand like this, side by side, for what feels like minutes.

Eventually, with his threat lingering between us, he unhooks me and lets his hand fall to his side.

Trying to catch my breath, I stumble up the beach, gathering my sweats as I go, and try not to collapse under the weight of his words.

CHAPTER
Sixteen

Rory

BY THE TIME I slide into the sports car on the front drive, I've managed to convince myself I imagined the entire exchange. It doesn't matter that my hip burns like I've been branded with a hot iron, or that I can't think about anything except for the pulse ticking in his jaw. No, Angelo Visconti would never get himself worked up over a girl like me. At the very most, I annoy him. At the very least, he doesn't think of me at all.

I'm staring out the windshield when the door swings open and makes me jump.

Propping his arm against the roof, Angelo leans in and pins me with an annoyed stare. *See, annoyed, Rory. You're an irritating little girl to him.*

"I don't think you can handle something so big."

I blink. "Huh?"

He jerks his head toward the dash, and that's when I realize I'm sitting behind the steering wheel.

"Oh, uh..." I glance around, confused. "I—"

"It's a British car." He pushes himself off the door frame and steps aside. "Out."

I scoot past him, round the car, and reluctantly get into the passenger seat. As I fumble with the safety belt, he stares at me impatiently, drumming a steady rhythm on the wheel. At the sound of the click, I meet his gaze and he cocks a brow.

"Good?"

No. "Yes."

He peels out of the driveway toward the gravel lane, heat blistering off him. There might as well be a warning sign above his head that flashes "Do not talk to me" in neon lights. But the tension is tangible, and if I sit in silence, rubbing my sweaty palms against my leggings for any longer, I'll go insane.

"This is the third car I've seen you in. Why do you have so many cars?"

"Same reason you can't keep your sticky fingers off the family jewels, Magpie." He slows to meet the iron gates, resuming the impatient tapping as he waits for them to open. "I like the thrill."

"I don't steal for the thrill," I snap.

"Ha."

My cheeks grow hot. "It's *true*."

"What do you do it for, then?" he asks in a way that suggests he's not interested in the answer. "You're marrying a very rich man, Aurora. You don't need the money."

I stop rubbing my hands up and down my thighs and curl them into fists in my lap instead. "I'm not marrying your uncle for the money," I hiss. Slamming back on the headrest, I close my eyes and grit my teeth. *Christ.*

But if Angelo notices my annoyance is starting to level with his own, he doesn't say it. "Then why the fuck are you marrying him then?" he growls back.

I pop a lid open. Raise a brow. Jesus, there was so much venom in that retort that he's practically spitting fire. From the corner of my eye, I watch as his Adam's apple bobs. "Is it 'cause you like getting your pussy pounded by dirty old men?"

What the hell is his problem? I'm about to ask him, but something else slips through my lips instead.

"Is that wishful thinking? Do you think you'd have a chance if I did?"

A beat passes. The silence echoes loudly off the ceiling and makes my bones cringe.

Then he laughs. The type of laugh that reveals too many of his pearly white teeth. It sounds so easy, so care-free, that I immediately feel stupid for daring to read between the lines every time I'm forced to share the same air as him.

I'm an idiot if I thought he was jealous. If I thought he actually wanted to kiss *me*.

There's a sudden itch under my skin: a familiar one. It makes me want to do something spiteful and revengeful to him, like scrape the alloys of his fancy car, or, you know, lace his stupid cigarettes with cyanide.

Okay, maybe not *that*, but the urge to be bad tingles inside me, and I feel the same frustration I woke up with. I can't do anything awful, because now I have no way to confess anymore.

Instead, I lean against the window, the early-morning condensation cooling my forehead, and I close my eyes.

Angelo manages to halve the journey to Devil's Dip by driving like a psycho, and in less than thirty minutes, we're pulling up beside the church. I gaze at the phone box wistfully, wishing I could dive in and dial the number, even if it's just to hear the familiar tone of the robotic answering machine message. Anger licks at the walls of my stomach, but at the same time, the phone box serves as a reminder that I can't be too nasty to Angelo. Just because he hasn't listened to my sins, it doesn't mean that he *can't*. I'm sure just tapping a few buttons on his cell phone sitting in the center console is all it'd take.

He kills the engine and reclines the chair. "You've got an hour."

Without another word, I hop out of the car and stride down the road, refusing to look back.

What is with that guy? He blows hot and cold like a broken heater. One minute he's teaching me to smoke in a dark walkway, the next he's back to calling me a gold-digger and a thief.

Whatever. As the pavement morphs into a carpet of gold and red maple leaves under my hiking boots, I brush Angelo's comments off my shoulders. Stepping into the forest is like entering a different world. *My* world, and every time I'm in it, I force myself to forget everything that exists outside of it.

As I head further into the woods, the noise from the road disappears behind me. Instead, fallen leaves crunch underfoot, melting into mush when the branches of maple and ash trees grow thicker above my head. They let enough light seep through to guide my way, but it wouldn't matter if they didn't, because I know the forest better than I know my own body.

At the start of the hemlock trees, I take a sharp left, veering off the trail and into the thick of the forest. I jump over the small stream my father and I would play "Pooh Sticks" on when I was little, and brush my fingers over the trunk of the lone old oak that sits in the middle of an empty clearing. Mom used to read Enid Blighton's *The Faraway Tree* as a bedtime story, and she'd tell me it was based on this oak tree. I'd stand under it for hours, squinting up at the topmost branches through my binoculars to see if I could spot the magical lands up there.

When the brush starts to thin, I slow down. I pull my cell out of my hoodie and fire off a text to one of the three pre-programmed numbers in the phone book:
I'm here.
The reply comes back almost immediately.
We're in the bird blind.
Nerves flutter in my stomach, just like they always do before I see my father, because there's always a chance that today's the day he's...*different.*

I step out onto the bank and round the lake to get to the wooden pier, then walk down it toward the small hut right at the tip. When I'm a few feet away, I twist the ring off my finger and slip it into my pocket.

The breeze carries Melanie's soft voice out of the hut and down the pier. "Your daughter's here, Chester. Are you ready to see her?"

No response. No response is never good.

My heart drops a few inches in my chest. I pick up the pace, coming to a stop outside the entryway and *rap, tap, tap* on the wooden wall.

"Hi, Dad!" I chime with a smile so big it makes my cheeks ache. And then I wait.

He's hunched over, peering out the window, with a pair of binoculars pressed against his eyes. He doesn't move at the sound of my voice. I wait a little longer, my pulse quickening. Melanie flashes me a small smile, then her eyes dart toward my father, to o.

"Chester? Rory's here."

He sighs, then drops his binoculars so they hang by the cord against his chest.

"For flamingo's sake, Mel. You scared off the belted kingfisher. I heard you the first time."

Relief escapes my lungs, slumping my body over. Then I break into a smile—a real one—and step into the hut to throw my arms around my father.

"Sorry, Dad," I say into his neck, breathing in his familiar scent of soap and Old Spice. "I know how much you love a kingfisher."

He pats my back, his chest vibrating against me as he chuckles. "We interrupted his breakfast, I suppose. He flies down to the lake this early every morning to munch on the tadpoles." When he pulls away, he adds, "Good to see you, Rory-bear."

My heart swells, and I have to turn away in case the prickling sensation behind my eyes turns into anything more.

Chester Carter. If you say that name to anyone from Devil's Dip, their face will stretch into a fond smile. Everyone knows him as the forest ranger, but younger locals also know him as "Bird Man" because he used to go into schools up and down the coast and teach kids all about the birds that inhabit the area. Despite having retired both jobs a few years ago, he still wears his uniform every day. Under his quilted jacket, his gray shirt hangs a little looser than it used to, and I've had to punch a new hole in his belt to hold up his black slacks, but he still very much looks the part.

"You missed it. I saw a blue heron yesterday," he says proudly, gazing out the window across the lake. "Remember the last time we saw one of them? It was with your mom."

"Uh-huh," I reply, swallowing the lump in my throat. Then I slide my arm into his and guide him back out onto the pier. "Perfect day to take the boat out, don't you think?"

He pats my hand and chuckles. "Sure, sure. I could do with the exercise. Mel?" He cranes his neck to find her. "Would you like to come out on the boat with us?"

"Mel's fine right here," I say, before she can answer. I don't look over at her. Although she and her team of nurses take care of my father well, they've been hired by Alberto. I don't know if I can trust her, or if she's another Greta and reports everything I say or do back to him. That's why I always insist that we go out on the boat—away from prying eyes and ears.

She hovers awkwardly on the dock as I help my father into the boat and settled him on the bench opposite me. He waves and smiles at her as I push off, using the oars to steer us into the middle of the lake.

"Lovely day for it," he muses, squinting up to the gray sky. "Not like last week, when it was pissing down with rain and you made me come out here anyway." He shoots me a mischievous look and we both laugh.

"You love the rain."

"No, I just love spending time with you," he says softly, reaching over and squeezing my hand. When he lets go, I realize he's slipped a peppermint humbug into my palm. "So tell me, Rory-bear, how's school going?"

I breathe in slowly, trying not to let my smile falter. Telling him I finally accepted my place at the Northwestern Aviation Academy a few months ago was the easiest excuse as to why I couldn't live here anymore. Of course, I hate lying to my father; it makes me sick to my stomach. But it's a hell of a lot easier than admitting the truth.

"It's going good," I say breezily, popping the hard candy into my mouth. "Everything's good. So—tell me more about the blue heron you saw yesterday."

"It's very good of them, letting you leave twice a week to come see me," he says, ignoring my attempt at changing the subject. "Very flexible for such a prestigious school. Have you flown on your own yet?" The lines around his eyes deepen. "Oh, Rory. Your mom would be so proud of you."

His words weigh on my chest like a ton of bricks, making it hard to breathe. Mom wouldn't be proud of me for so many reasons. Although she was always bitter that my father got to teach me so many skills, there's so much she taught me too. Like, not to lie—especially to family—and the only man worth marrying is the one you love.

I've let her down on all accounts.

Time flies in a whirlwind of bitter nostalgia and memories that make my heart ache. When my father's teeth start chattering, I glance down at the time on my cell and sigh. "We better get you back, Dad."

I row back to the dock, throwing the rope to Mel so she can help tie us up.

My father stops at the end of the pier and rubs his hands together. "Come on then, my love, let's get back to the cabin for a hot tea. You must be freezing without a proper jacket."

I grind to a halt. *Goose.* What I'd give to go back to the cabin with my father right now. To sit in front of the living room fire with a tea and a tray of cookies, listening to his stories.

Our eyes lock. His warm and expectant, mine threatening to leak. "I can't," I whisper.

His bushy brows knit together. "No? You have to go already?" He glances at his watch. "But it's not even lunchtime."

My stomach twists in knots, and this time, the lump in my throat is too big.

"Rory?" He takes a step toward me and puts his hand on my shoulder. "What's wrong, my love?"

"I—"

"She has a very big exam on Monday," Mel interrupts, stepping between us and gently touching my father's back. "She needs to go and study. Isn't that right, Rory?"

Eyes fluttering, I nod. "Sorry, dad." My apology is loaded with so much more than just this little white lie. "Maybe next time."

Another lie. I won't go to the cabin next time, either. Because what we have out here doesn't exist in there.

I say the cheeriest goodbye I can muster and with the ghost of his kiss against my cheek, hurry back into the thick of the woods before he can see me cry. Tears sting the back of my eyes, but I refuse to let them fall. I haven't cried since my mom died, and I don't plan on starting again now.

The forest floor leads into gravel again, signaling that I've made it back to the main road. Squinting in the sudden sunlight, I look up and see Angelo leaning against the hood of his car, taking a phone call. His eyes follow me as I make my way toward him, and when I'm close enough to hear his conversation, he abruptly hangs up.

He slips his cell in his breast pocket and drops his gaze to my feet. "You're not getting in my car with those on."

I look down at my boots, caked in mud. "I'll walk then."

As I turn on my heel in the direction of Devil's Cove, his hand grips my wrist. "Not a chance," he growls. Steeling his lips into a thin line, he presses a button on his car keys and the trunk door lifts up. "Sit."

I'm too emotionally drained to argue, so I perch on the edge of the trunk. Angelo stands in front of me. Muttering darkly under his breath, he hitches his slacks and sinks to one knee. Then, without warning, he grips my thigh.

Holy crow. Every muscle in my body tenses. I don't know what I was expecting when he demanded I get in his trunk, but it wasn't that. I steal a glance down at his hand. It's hot and heavy, burning through the thin fabric of my leggings. And if he moved just half an inch higher...

My head swims. Instead of letting my thoughts go there, I focus on his shoulder as he rips off my boot with his other hand. He pauses and sits back on his haunches. Amusement makes his lips twitch.

"What?" I snap.

But then I follow his eye line to my socks. They are gray, with little orange pumpkins on them. Immediately my cheeks start to burn. "It's nearly Halloween," I mutter. "They're festive."

"Festive," he huffs, running the back of his hand over his mouth to hide his smile. "Cute."

Cute. For some reason, that word stings. I'd rather be annoying than be cute. Being cute puts me in a different box altogether, one a man like Angelo Visconti wouldn't bother to open.

I squeeze my eyes shut. *Stop it, Rory.* I'd already overstepped the mark today with my little stunt in the sea.

I bet the women he dates back in England look like supermodels. I bet they are super successful—lawyers, doctors, accountants—and they wear heels all the time and not just because they're forced to. I bet they never wear fluffy stocks. Only garters and sexy stockings.

Envy prickles under my skin as I glare at the top of Angelo's head. He places his hand on my other thigh, higher this time, and removes my other boot. When he stands to his full height again, he peers down at dirt on his knees in disgust.

"This is why you don't live in shitholes like this," he grunts, bending over to dust himself off. "It's *messy*."

"You grew up here too," I shoot back. "What the hell did you do when you were a kid?"

His expression sours, a sneer forming on his cupid's bow. "Counted the days until I could get the fuck out."

"Figures."

"You never wanted to leave?"

I let out a huff of air, turning my attention to the sky. Just then, a plane flies over the cliffs in the distance. Before Alberto took away my cell, I had an app that let me track the fight path of any plane that flew near me, and I always loved checking it. This one is probably going down to Central America; it's heading that direction.

"Of course. But not because it's *messy*. I love all the nature in Devil's Dip." I tuck a stray curl behind my ear and add, "It's the people who make me want to leave."

He lets out a humorless laugh. "People like me and my family."

"Did you go to the Devil's Coast Academy?"

"Of course."

"Yes, then. People like you and your family."

His gaze narrows. He opens his mouth, then closes it again. Like he wants to ask a question but decides I'm not worth it.

To be fair, I don't know why I brought up the academy at all. My past is none of his business.

"Let's go," I mutter. I go to hop off the edge of the trunk, but realize I'll be stepping on dirt, which I'll then tread into Angelo's precious car. And then his whole display of yanking off my muddy boots would have been all for nothing. He comes to the same conclusion, because he turns his attention to my sock-clad feet then dips his head in the trunk.

Without warning, he slips one arm around my waist, the other around the back of my knees, and lifts me up in the air. *Oh, flamingo.* Suddenly, I feel drunk, being this close to him. My cheek grazes against the stubble on his neck, and I fight the urge to nuzzle into it, to breathe in his warm scent of aftershave and danger.

He's holding me like I weigh less than a feather, and when he drops me into the passenger seat all too soon, he does so surprisingly gently.

I try to catch my breath as he rounds the car and gets into the driver's seat. He peels off without another word, and because my temples are still thumping wildly, it takes me a few minutes to realize he hasn't turned off to take the coastal highway back to Devil's Cove. Instead, we're heading down to the main town of Devil's Dip.

"Um, where are we going?" No answer. "Hello?"

"How old are you, Aurora?"

I swallow. "Twenty-one."

His jaw locks. "Twenty-one. Christ."

"Your point being?" I snap back, my face growing hot.

He chews on the inside of his lip as he pulls out onto Main street. The car rattles and rocks over the cobbled road.

"I want you to think about the kids in your class at school. The years above you and the years below you too. Know any man around here that has a scar on his cheek?"

"What? Why?"

"Shut up and answer my question."

The venom in tone pins me to the seat. I blink, then shake my head. "A lot of people around here have scars on their face. It's a port town—everyone has manual jobs. That, plus the forest...everyone's a little scuffed up."

"And anyone who's a complete cunt?" I recoil at the sound of *that* word. He glances sideways and smirks. "I mean, anyone who's a complete..." He waves a hand around. "Canada goose?"

"I would have gone with "cuckoo" myself."

"Don't make me ask you again."

I huff a wayward curl out my face, my head pounding. "Jeez. Okay, let's see...well, there's always Ryder Sloane. He has a scar. Or is it a burn mark? Anyway, there's something on his face. He was a total jerk in school. Just got out of prison, too."

He cocks his head. "I'm listening."

"Um. It was an acid attack on his girlfriend. Ex-girlfriend, I mean. She left him; he got angry and followed her home from the bar one night." I rub the base of my throat, thinking about poor Nicole. Nobody's seen her in more than a year. Some people say she only goes out at night because her face is so messed up. "He got four years in prison."

Angelo nods, absorbing my rambling. "Okay. Ryder Sloane. Any idea where he lives?"

"No. But I know he works at his dad's bike shop."

"Where?"

I crane my neck and glance out the rear window. "We've just passed it, actually."

The speed with which he spins the car around throws me against the window. And then when I realize what he's doing, my blood runs cold. "Angelo—"

"Stay in the car."

My heart is beating a mile a minute, but all I can do is gawp as he swings the car onto the sidewalk outside the bike shop, almost crashing into a mailbox.

As he unclicks his seat belt and lunges for the door, my hand shoots out and grabs a fistful of his suit jacket. He stops in his tracks. His eyes skid down to my fist and then they harden, like he can't believe I have the nerve to touch him.

But he doesn't bark, nor does he bite. Instead, he does something so small and stupid that it has no right to snatch the oxygen from my lungs.

He puts his hand over mine and lifts it to his face. Grazes his lips over it. "Stay in the car, Aurora," he murmurs into my knuckles, making every nerve ending in my body buzz.

Winded, I fall back and watch helplessly as he slams the door and strides into the bike shop. Through the window, I see Ryder step out from behind the cash desk to greet him.

What the hell are you doing, Angelo?

Even as he takes the three steps toward Ryder, I still don't know. They exchange a few words, then Ryder's eyes shoot up. Before he can open his mouth again, Angelo grips his jaw, using it to slam him into the shop window.

Oh my goose. Blood rings in my ears, making the low chatter of the radio sound like it's in a different vehicle altogether. Even though Ryder's back is now facing me, I can see how scared he is. His arms flail next to him, and when he drags his palm against the glass, it leaves a smear of sweat.

But I'm barely looking at Ryder, because I can't take my eyes off of Angelo. I thought I knew what it felt like to bear the brunt of his glare, but boy, was I wrong. The hard lines of his face are sharper than a blade, and his lips curl over his teeth with every venomous word he spits out. I should alert someone. Hell, if I had any sense, maybe I'd even call the police. But it's like passing an accident on the freeway—morbid curiosity makes it impossible to look away. And then, as Angelo rolls up his sleeves to reveal his thick, tanned forearms, that feeling morphs into something hotter.

The pulse between my legs flutters. My nipples tighten.

I've never craved Angelo Visconti more than I do right now.

Christ, Rory. I'm burning up like I have a fever, suddenly wearing too many items of clothing even for a late Fall day. Before I start salivating like a rabid dog, I close my eyes and let out a hiss of air in an attempt to claw back some sort of composure.

And that's when I hear the crash.

My lids pop open in time to see Ryder's body flying through the window, glass exploding out onto the sidewalk. I lurch forward, then freeze with my hand hovering over the door handle. But then Angelo's body blocks my view out of the window as he ducks into the car.

As cool as a cucumber, he clicks on his seat belt, starts the car, and peels out, hand resting on the gearshift.

My jaw swings open. "What the hell was that about?"

"Wrong person." His eyes flick to the rear-view mirror. "Any other suggestions?"

Even if my brain functioned well enough to think, there's no chance in hell I'd give Angelo Visconti another name. He knows so, too, because without a word, he takes the turning off to the coastal highway and heads toward Devil's Cove.

My heart thumps wildly against my rib cage, like it wants out of this car as much as I do. But I'm still so damn hot. So...*turned on.* I find myself squirming against the leather seat, my clit begging for any type of friction.

Jesus.

I slump against the window, but this time, the cold glass does nothing to dial back my temperature. Instead, I watch the ocean pass by in a blur of blue and gray and try to not to moan every time the side of Angelo's hand brushes my thigh when he switches gear.

It makes sense to me now, why they call him Vicious Visconti. It's not a singular act of ruthlessness from his previous life, like sleeping with Dante's prom date, or shooting his driver in the knee because he took the wrong turn. No. It's a personality trait. It's how he can flick it on and off like a light switch. How he thought nothing of shooting Max dead over a presumption, or shoving Ryder through a shop window over little more than a loose description, then going back to normal like nothing happened.

He's a cold-blooded killer.

By the time the iron gates to the Visconti mansion open, I already have my seat belt off, and I'll jump and roll out of this darn car if I have to. Angelo slows to a stop on the circular drive and kills the engine.

"I'd say thank you for the ride home but—"

His hand clamping my thigh ends my sentence like a full stop. I hold my breath and peer down at his hand through my lashes. It's higher than it was when I was sitting in the trunk. So high, the back of his pinky is grazing the seam where my mound meets my leg.

I swallow. Let out a staggered sigh.

He stares ahead, regarding the house with indifference through the windshield. "You know the drill."

"I—"

"A sin," he rasps. "Tell me a sin."

"Uh, okay." I lick my lips. "Greta is horrible to me. So, when she does my hair, I use a dress pin to scratch the face of her watch."

He remains still. "Tell me a real one."

I blink. "That *was* a real one."

A gasp escapes me as he squeezes my thigh, hard. *Holy crow.* I hate how my mind is so far in the gutter that I wonder what it'd feel like if he squeezed even higher up. I curl my fingers over the curve of the seat to stop myself from pushing against him, and concentrate on the house ahead.

"Give me a better one, Aurora," he growls.

"I..." *I can't concentrate with your hand there.* "I, um. I didn't just steal Vittoria's necklace. I stole Tor's cufflinks, Leonardo's Nintendo Switch, Dante's—"

Another squeeze. It sparks up to my pussy, making it pulsate. This time, the anticipation is too much, and I can't help but throw my head back onto the seat and moan. "Stop, *please.*"

"Not until you give me a real sin."

I glance up at him, and even from his side profile, I can tell he's wearing an expression darker than thunder. "Like what?"

"You know what."

My chest hitches. He knows what he wants me to say. What he wants to hear me *confess*. Has he listened to my calls? I dismiss the idea immediately; I'd be dead if he had. My head thumps with a million sins he might be interested in, but as my breathing gets more and more ragged, I can't pin one down.

Behind my fluttering lashes, I see the front door open and Alberto darkens the doorway. He squints toward the car, then starts descending the steps.

"Angelo—"

He tightens his grip. Moves his pinky up a millimeter. "A sin. *Now.*"

Holy crow. Alberto is crossing the drive toward us and Angelo's hand is practically on my pussy. "I don't know. I don't know—"

"Yes, you do."

"Please," I whisper, my gaze frantically watching Alberto's own. He's just feet from the car now. "Let me go."

"Then tell me."

"I can't."

"I'm not giving the option, Aurora."

"No—"

"*Now.*"

Alberto is passing the front tires.

"This morning, in the sea. I was fingering myself thinking about you."

It tumbles from my lips thick and fast, sucking out all the oxygen in the tiny space between us. Angelo turns his head and stares at me. The tiniest flicker of something passes through his gaze. Shock, maybe. Anger? I don't know and I don't have time to decipher it, because Alberto's stooping to peer through the window.

Gasping, I slap Angelo's hand away, and thankfully, he doesn't take any more convincing. He moves it a mere few inches, so it's resting easily on the center console.

Rap, tap, tap. Alberto's ring-clad fist thumps on the window.

Angelo's jaw ticks in annoyance, then he begrudgingly rolls down the window.

"There you two are." Alberto pauses. Shifts his gaze between the two of us. "Everything okay?"

"All good, Uncle Al," Angelo drawls, emotionless.

"Good, good. Was my fiancee useful to you today?"

"Very useful." His gaze flickers to mine. "In fact, she gave me some good information that I can use."

"Great. Are you coming in for a drink?"

"Can't. I have shit to do."

"Oh, all right. Well—" he raps his knuckle against the roof again "—I'll see you next week, kiddo."

He walks back to the house, and panic rises in my chest again. I *have* to get out of this darn car. Away from Angelo, away from my god-awful confession lingering between us. My fingers trip up over the door handle, but eventually I tug it open and slam the door shut behind me. I don't care that I'm only in my fluffy Halloween socks.

His gaze scorches my back.

"Aurora." I come to a reluctant stop and tilt my head to the sky.

"I don't care what Alberto says. Wear your hair curly."

CHAPTER
Seventeen

Angelo

M**Y UNCLE'S TWENTY-ONE-YEAR-OLD FIANCEE** emerging from the sea in a tiny black bikini is temptation personified. But her telling me she fingered herself while watching me on the shore?

A death sentence.

Holy fuck. The way she just stood there. Dripping wet and next-to-naked. She was a contrast of extremes—a body like a damn porn star, soft brown eyes conveying innocence. *Feigning* innocence, actually. Little did I know that while all I could see was her blond hair and big eyes bobbing above the waves, underneath, she was *finger fucking* herself. I'm glad I hadn't found it out then and there, because the sight of her alone had wound me up tighter than a drum. If she'd told me her pussy was still fresh from an orgasm, there's not a chance I would have been able to resist picking her up and dragging her back into the fucking sea and giving her the real deal.

Family etiquette be damned.

Rafe kills the radio. Leans over the steering wheel to squint out the windshield of his Model X. "Are we in the right place?"

I push all thoughts of Alberto's fiancee to the back of my brain and look up. "Beaufort Cherry and Apple Orchard, Connecticut," I read off the big sign hanging off the gate. Beyond it, rolling hills, flecked with red, greens, and oranges, create a dramatic landscape. "Gabe picked this place?"

Rafe chuckles darkly. "I'm as surprised as you are. Every time he picks the location, we usually end up in a cement basement."

I rub the scruff of my beard. "Yeah, this is very unlike Gabe. This is…"

"Beautiful," he finishes, a sly grin stretching across his face. "I'm glad he's finally embracing the theatrics of the game." He flashes me a sideways glare. "You could take a leaf out of his book."

Sinners Anonymous is more than just a game to Rafe, it's a fucking show. Every time he's tasked with picking the location to bring our sinners, I know we're going to end up in the craziest places. The Colosseum in Rome. The Fjords in Iceland. He always wants to carry out the kill in the most dramatic of ways, against the most memorable backdrops. Me, on the other hand, I'm good with any old place, as long as I can use our sinner as a human punching bag. Each bone that cracks under my fist, each tortured scream that escapes their lips, relieves more and more tension built up throughout the month.

Being good is stressful.

Gabe's different. He's sadistic. If it were up to him, he wouldn't kill the sinner, he'd find new and exciting ways to torture them for as long as possible. He'd use them like a guinea pig, testing out new additions to his toolbox on them, and wouldn't put them out of their misery until they'd literally gone insane from his psychotic wrath.

So when I hear the chug of an engine coming up behind Rafe's Tesla, a cocktail of excitement and unease swirls my blood.

"What the fuck are you planning, Gabe?" I murmur from behind my hand, watching him get out of the van in the wing mirror.

The excitement radiating off of Rafe is palpable. "Let's fucking go!" he booms, hopping out of the car.

Gabe emerges from the van and strolls toward us, like he has all the time in the world. "Good morning," he drawls. He casts a stony eye over our suits. "You're not dressed for a hunt."

Rafe glances at me. "A what?"

Without a word, Gabe strides back to the van and comes back with three rifles, the straps slung over his shoulder. He slams one into my chest, another into Rafe's. "Hunting. It's what real men do."

"Ha, ha," Rafe snaps back. But he lifts the rifle up to the early morning light and studies it with fascination. "Fuck. What have you done to it?"

"Modified it, obviously. It's just a Barrett M107A1, but I've removed the scope and bought high-power .50 cartridges."

"And in English?"

I turn to Rafe. "Removing the scope means there's now no viewfinder to help with accuracy. And a .50 BMG is big enough to splatter someone all over the trees." Shifting my gaze to Gabe, I add, "So, you want us to shoot blind and with a bullet the size of a fucking grenade." My lips twitch. "You're a psycho."

He holds his hands up in mock-surrender, expressionless. "Just doing my job."

"Which is *what*, exactly?"

Gabe pins Rafe with a hard stare. Neither of us has a concrete idea of what Gabe does these days. Not since he came back to the Coast for Christmas that year with a huge, mysterious scar running down his face. All we know is that now, he can speak better Italian than the both of us combined, and every time we see him, he has new battle wounds. Today, it's a purple-green mark creeping across his eye socket, and deep cuts on his swollen knuckles.

"Worth a try," Rafe mumbles to himself.

I jerk my chin toward the van. "He's awfully quiet."

"Yeah. That's 'cause I've already had my fun with him."

"For fuck's sake—"

"Relax," he drawls, cutting off Rafe's protests. "He's still fighting fit."

He turns and strolls back toward the van. "Meet me at the beginning of the path."

We stand there and watch the van drive out of sight.

I shake my head. "He's nuts."

"But *why*?" Rafe shoots back. "Since *when*?"

"Why'd you care?" I gesture to the orchard behind us. "This is your wet dream."

But I know how he's feeling. Gabe's our brother, after all. One of us. Our own flesh and blood. And yet, we don't even know where he lives, or what he does on the three Sundays a month he's not with us. He never answers his cell. We just text him and he turns up.

Rafe chews on the inside of his cheek, keeping silent as we pass through the gate and walk to the mouth of the path. It's a long, gravel road, lined with perfectly trimmed apple trees. In the distance, it rolls upward over a hill, where a white Colonial house sits proudly on top.

The early morning air is mild; a far cry from the ever-present chill in Devil's Dip. I slide my hands into the pockets of my slacks and tilt my chin up to the clear sky. Birds circle overhead: little blue ones with an annoying chirp.

I bet Aurora would know exactly what fucking bird it was. She probably uses its name as a curse word.

"What are you smiling about?" Rafe snaps next to me.

I rearrange my features back to my default expression: indifference. "Just excited to play."

"That's what I like to hear."

Through the trees, the black van emerges. It drives down the path toward us and parks in a small turnoff a hundred feet or so away. A few seconds pass, then Gabe hops out, our sinner in tow. Tape covers his mouth and rope binds his wrists. Gabe looms behind him like the Grim Reaper, marching him forward. They come to a stop a few feet away.

Gabe slams his hand on the man's shoulder and squints at us through the harsh sunlight. "All right, lads, welcome to the hunt." The sinner squeals and tries to rip himself away from Gabe, but he only tightens his grip. "The rules are so simple that even you two idiots can follow them. Phillip here gets a thirty-second head start, and then it's fair game."

My eyes are trained on Gabe, who's muttering something in the man's ear. He's crying now, his sobs muffled by the tape over his mouth. With a final clap on his back, Gabe comes to stand next to us.

I glance at him. "You're expecting him to just run straight down the path?"

"Uh-huh."

"Bullshit. He's going to dive into the trees the first chance he gets."

A huff comes through his nose. "I promise you, he's running straight."

Rafe leans forward to get a better look at him. "He looks kinda old. Hope those legs still work, because I want him to gain a good distance before we begin."

"Makes no difference to you, you've always been a shit aim," I taunt.

Anger flashes in his eyes as he glares at me, but it's soon replaced with a hint of mischief. "A hundred grand says I hit him first."

"Make it two that you don't."

"I bet half a mil neither of you hits him at all," Gabe cuts in, not looking up from his rifle.

"Deal," Rafe and I say in unison.

The air is thick, the gentle breeze carrying over the man's muffled pleas.

"Thirty," Gabe's voice suddenly booms without warning. "Twenty-nine. Twenty-eight. Twenty-seven…"

The man freezes as Gabe counts down. Eyes darting between the three of us, he finally turns on his heels and runs.

"Jesus, bet he never ran track in high school," Rafe mutters next to me.

He's staggering, tripping up over his sneakers in his attempt to get away from him. I guess I wouldn't be practicing perfect form, either, if I had three men pointing shooting rifles in my direction.

"Nineteen. Eighteen. Seventeen…"

"Hope business is going well, bro, 'cause I'm about to hit your wallet where it hurts," Rafe chuckles, cocking the gun and squinting over the guard.

"Seven. Six. Five…"

Showtime. A familiar bolt of adrenaline zaps through my spine, and I'm salivating with the knowledge that I'm about to experience a high I'll be feasting off for days. Grinding my jaw in concentration, I ready my gun, my finger brushing over the trigger.

"Three. Two—"

At the last second, the man takes a sharp right, running toward the trees. In unison, Rafe and I swing around our rifles round to follow him, but Gabe drops his to the floor.

"What a fucking idiot," he growls, punching the air.

I whip around to face him. Confused. "Huh?"

And then I'm deafened by a roaring explosion. Feel the heat of it scorching the side of my cheek. It's instinctive to shield my eyes from the burning yellow light and the gravel raining down around us. Eventually, it settles down to a crackling fire, thick black smoke lazily drifting up to the cloudless sky.

I pull my hand away from my face, and all three of us stand there, staring at the scene in silence.

"Stupid bastard," Gabe eventually spits. "I told him to run straight." He shifts his gaze to us and a wry smirk on his lips. "Well, looks like both owe me half a mil."

Rafe blinks. "What?"

"I bet neither of you would hit him at all."

I let out a hiss of air through my teeth. "You rigged the path with explosives and told him so. You thought it'd force him to run straight."

"He must have thought I was bullshitting."

The silence makes the ringing in my ears sound louder. Then, Rafe starts to laugh. A loud laugh that starts from the bottom of his gut and spills out onto the charred gravel.

"Jesus Christ, that was incredible." He presses the unfired gun into my hands and breaks into a slow jog down the path. "Just want to see the damage up close!" he calls over his shoulder.

I turn to Gabe and pin him with an annoyed stare. "Your brain is fucked up."

"Played too many video games as a kid," he says dryly, his eyes trained ahead.

I follow his gaze, landing on Rafe kicking a limb that landed halfway down the path. "I want to ask you something."

"Don't bother."

"Not about *you*," I mutter back. "I've given up trying to figure you out these days."

"Hit me with it then."

I smooth down the front of my suit, but I know there's no saving it from the amount of gravel and human debris splattered across the lapel. "I've been thinking about renovating our old house."

He stiffens. "In Devil's Dip?"

"Yeah. I passed it the other day and it's a mess up there. I'm sick of staying at the Visconti Grand every time I visit. Hate being in Cove territory," I add, tasting bitterness in my words.

"You're moving back."

I grind my jaw. I'm sick of hearing everyone in this fucking family say this. I expect my brothers to know me better than that, at least. "I'm not moving back to Dip, Gabe. I'd rather stick my dick in a car door."

"You're moving back. You just don't know it yet."

"No. I just thought it'd be nice to have a base that isn't under Dante's roof—"

"No. You won't leave her here, not with him."

I spin on my heel to face him. "What? Who?"

He doesn't move a muscle. "Uncle Al's fiancee. You can't take your eyes off her. Staring at her like a lion spotting his prey in the bush. I know you better than you know yourself. You flew in to the Coast because you're haunted by some unfinished business there. You're a smart man, so whatever you came back for you'd have figured it in a weekend and flown back to London the first chance you got, if that's what you wanted to do." His eyes focus on me. "But it's not. You saw her, and you decided to stay." He rakes a hand through his hair, still staring ahead. "You just don't know it yet."

Shaking my head in disbelief, I take a few steps back toward the car. "You're insane, my brother. I don't give a flying fuck about what Uncle Al does, or who he marries." Heat prickles under my collar. I clear my throat and add, "As if I'd give up my life in London for a piece of pussy."

"Uh-huh."

"I mean it."

Gravel crunches under his feet as he turns around to join me. He claps his hand on my back and leans into my ear, even though we're the only two people around. "Wanna know how I know? Because you can't stand someone else having something you want. Even if it's family. You know as well as I do, you'll go back to London, to your fancy penthouse apartment overlooking Hyde Park, and you'll lie in your posh-ass bed staring at the ceiling, and you'll be thinking about Aurora. Thinking about Uncle Al fucking her." His lips graze my ear. "Thinking about what would have happened if you'd stayed nine years ago and taken over as Capo like you were meant to." Raking my tongue over my teeth, I close my eyes and brace myself. Because I know what he's going to say. "She'd be begging *you* not to chop down the forest, not your uncle."

With a hard shove, I push him away from me. "Is that what you've been doing these days?" I snarl. "Training to become a fucking counselor?" A satisfied smirk crosses his face. "Anyway, I left Dip for a reason. I'm not coming back, especially not to steal Uncle Al's chick."

He pauses, glances at Rafe, then lowers his voice an octave. "I know what you did."

My hands curl into fists. "I don't know what you're talking about."

"You do. I know what you did, and I know why you left Devil's Dip all those years ago." He takes a step toward me, pinning me with a glare all too similar to my own. "You committed a sin bigger than any of those fuckers that call the hotline."

Blood thumps in my temples. Rage blisters the lining of my gut. *How the fuck does he know what I did?*

Fuck. If I stand here for another second, I'm going to crack my brother in the jaw, so I turn to storm back toward the car.

But Gabe's hand shoots out against my chest, stopping me. "Thank you," he rasps.

Confused, I look up to meet his eyes. There's something soft in them. It looks out of place under his perma-scowl and above his bruised socket. "If you hadn't done it, I would have done it myself."

He swallows. Looks away. "But for different reasons," he mutters darkly.

I feel like I've been stung. Putting both my hands on his head, I lower my forehead to his. "What the fuck happened to you, bro?" I hiss. "What did he do to you?"

He pushes me away, his gaze hardening, morphing back to his signature stare. "When you realize you're moving back, let me know." His jaw ticks. "Because when you steal Uncle Alberto's girl, I promise you, you're going to need a fucking army."

CHAPTER
Eighteen

Rory

Friday night. Dinner is winding down, and with a final glance over my shoulder into the foyer, I scurry down the steps and make a beeline for Tor's car. "Wait," I hiss, my heels bucking against the pebbles as I half-run, half-trot toward him. "Wait for me!"

Tor's leaning against the passenger door, tapping away on his cell. He looks up from the screen and squints into the darkness. He stills. Runs an eye over my body, then pushes himself off the car. "Oh, hell no, girl."

I hurry after him, slamming my back against the driver's door before he can reach it. "I'm coming with you."

"Like fuck you are. Not tonight, and not dressed like *that*. Move." But when I don't, his eyes thin. "You have a death wish?"

"Aw, come on, Tor. Alberto won't even notice I'm gone. He's got all those old men from the country club over and they are playing bridge."

"And when he does notice, I'm fucked. Now, *move*."

"All right," I huff. "What do you want?"

He pauses, cocks a brow, then his eyes shift to my chest. He lets out a little laugh, like he's just stopped himself from saying something he shouldn't. "Don't tempt me, little girl. Get out of my way."

As he reaches to grab my arm, I catch his wrist. I stare at the colorful tattoos poking out from his sleeve, stopping just before his watch strap, and my heart thumps a little harder.

"Tayce did these."

Irritation flickers through his irises. "Obviously. I don't let anyone else ink me. What's your point?"

I can feel a grin spreading across my face. "Even you can't skip the waiting list."

"God himself couldn't skip her fucking waiting list."

"But I can."

He hitches a shoulder. Purses his lips. "You have half a second to get to the point."

"Tayce is my best friend. I can get you an appointment like *that*," I snap my fingers for emphasis, and he looks down at them like he wants to bite them off.

He's still glaring at me, but he's suddenly still. He's weakening. "No waiting list?"

"Uh-huh."

"Never again?"

I pause. *Swan*, Tayce might kill me for this. "Never again."

His eyes narrow. Then he takes a step back. "Get in the fucking car." Jabbing a finger in my direction, he adds, "No talking to men that don't have the "Visconti" last name. In fact, don't even look at them. No more than three drinks. And I'll have Amelia take you home at midnight." He slides into the driver's seat, muttering under his breath. "Otherwise you'll turn back into Cinderella."

"Thank you, thank you, thank you."

"Yeah, yeah," he grunts, tapping out an email as he peels out of the circular drive. "You don't think I've done you enough favors this week?"

My stomach drops a few inches. I came downstairs on Wednesday morning to find Tor waiting for me instead of Angelo. He was pacing, irritated. Said Angelo was out of town, and that he'd asked him to take me to Dip instead. Of course, I was happy that I still got to see my father, but ever since, I haven't been able to shake the unsettling feeling crawling underneath my skin.

One day, Angelo will leave for good without warning and he won't come back. And that thought shouldn't make me feel so sick.

As we speed down the Coastal highway, I unzip my purse and fish out a box of Nerds. Tor side-eyes me in disgust, but then holds out his hand for the carton. "Fucking hell, haven't had these in years," he mutters, tossing them into his mouth. "You get these trick-or-treating? You're still young enough for that, right?"

I laugh. "Shut up."

A few seconds pass. As we slow to meet a red light, I feel the heat of his gaze on my dress. "I'm sure I'll have a few spare shirts lying around in my office," he mutters. "You'll have to put one on."

"Not a chance."

"Aurora, don't push your luck. You're not walking into my club dressed like that. It's opening night, and it's Halloween. I'll be too busy mingling with sexy nurses and slutty Lara Crofts to be fighting men off you. What are you meant to be, anyways?"

I look down at my black leather dress. It's strapless and plain, bar the large, silver zip that runs down the middle, all the way from the hem to the neckline. I've accessorized with a pair of chunky velvet boots and a small pointed hat pinned onto my curls. "Isn't it obvious?" He pins me with a blank stare. I sigh, pull out the wrinkly rubber nose from my purse and slip it onto my own. "What about now?"

A beat passes. Then he bursts out laughing. "All right, fine. Keep that nose on all night, and I'll let you forgo the shirt."

Smiling triumphantly, I settle back into the seat, watching the ocean pass in a navy blur. As we pull onto the boulevard, butterflies start to flap their wings against the lining of my stomach and nervous energy buzzes through my veins.

I'm not the type of girl who dresses all sexy for Halloween, and I know the only reason I'm doing so tonight is just in case Angelo turns up. I'll avoid him of course—I'm too mortified about my confession last week to actually speak to him yet—but still. I have visions of him seeing me from across the club. Seeing me dancing and drinking with Tacye, having a good time. For just one last time, I want to feel his eyes follow my every move. I know it's wrong and I'm playing a dangerous game, but I want him to see I'm not the silly little girl he thinks I am. The one who wears fluffy, festive socks, gets worked up about stupid bad things I've done, and hasn't said a real curse word in her life.

Just once. Just for tonight. Because tomorrow is my engagement party, which signals the beginning of the rest of my miserable life.

Tor pulls up in a parking space out front, one that has a sign with his name embossed in gold. I glance out the window at the entrance to the club, and my nerves intensify.

Jesus, it's *packed*. Cats, Devils, Skeletons. Every Halloween cliché clambers to get in, while the heavy music thumping from the entrance sounds like it's trying to get out.

"Here we fucking go," Tor chimes excitedly, killing the engine and rubbing his hands together. He leers out the window at the girls in fishnet stockings and thigh-high boots. "Halloween is better than Christmas."

"Hey, where's your costume?"

"I'm wearing it."

I take in his three-piece suit. The silk handkerchief folded elaborately in his top pocket. His little diamond nose ring. "Well, what are you supposed to be?"

"A made man," he shoots back with a wink.

He rounds the car and helps me out, then pushes me toward the entrance of the club by the small of my back. Skipping the line, we stop at a wall of burly, suited men with earpieces. Tor slaps one on the chest and points at me.

"See this girl? It's Big Al's fiancee." The man's eyes grow wide. "You keep an eye on her at all times, got it? Anyone touches her, you take their hand."

I swallow the lump in my throat. Jesus, by take their hand, I doubt he means "hold it." He turns back around to me and cocks his head inside. "Let's go."

We walk down a small corridor, which opens up onto a large room.

Whoa. I halt in my tracks and recoil, my eyes trying to adjust to the sudden bright lights. It's an enormous, round space with cavernous ceilings. The mirrored floor sparkles under the sweeping strobe lights, casting a silver shine on the black walls and velvet drapes that separate the main room from the private booths. Everything is centered around a raised dance floor in the middle—and when I squint, I realize it's *rotating*. I blink, and then something above it catches my eye. *Holy Crow.* Dancers in black leather leotards twirl and fall from orange and green ribbons, coming so close to the top of the crowd's heads that I physically flinch, before they sexily climb back up again.

Just under two weeks ago, I was standing here in the rubble and the dust and was convinced there wasn't a chance in hell it'd be ready to open in time for Halloween.

Tor chucks me under the chin. "Sure you don't wanna go home, little girl?" I manage a slight shake of my head. Feeling something behind me, I glance up, and notice one of the burly guards from outside lurking over my shoulder. "My man here will take you to

VIP. Should be a few friendly faces there already." He sweeps his hand up and around, pointing to a balcony that snakes the entire perimeter. Then his finger lands on me, along with a serious glare. "Remember what I said. No men. Three drinks."

As he turns to leave, I grab his arm. "Wait—when Tayce turns up, can you get your men to send her up to me?"

He murmurs in the guard's ear and nods. "Sorted." Then he shouts over the music, "Now if you'll excuse me, I have...*business* to attend to."

Flanked by two more guards who seem to have appeared out of nowhere, he disappears through a door off the main room.

I glance up at my own guard, as if to say, *what now?* He responds by wrapping his arm around me and bowling through the crowd, until we reach a glass elevator on the far side of the room. We ascend, high above the sea of party-goers, and emerge onto the balcony.

It's only slightly quieter up here, but a hell of a lot less busy.

"This way, *signora*."

I wince at the name, suddenly reminded of what Amelia said to me a few weeks ago. *They'll be calling you Signora Aurora Visconti soon.*"

Very soon. As in, just two weeks from now. The thought swells in my chest and threatens to stop my lungs from working. But as Amelia herself and a handful of other Viscontis come into view behind a red rope and yet another guard, I push down the panic and force a smile.

"I wasn't expecting to see you here," Amelia laughs, flipping her long black wig over one shoulder and side-stepping the bouncer. She plants a flowery kiss on my cheek. "Cute costume," she squeals, flicking my prosthetic nose. I grin, and nod down to her black vampy dress.

"Morticia Adams, right? Which means..." I turn and lock eyes with Donatello. He raises a champagne flute in my direction, a grim smile underneath a thin faux mustache. "Donatello is Gomez. Nice. How'd you manage to convince him to play along?"

"He lost our yacht in a poker game the other evening," she says tightly. "He didn't really have a choice. Anyway, does Alberto know you're here?"

I flash her a coy smile. "No, and he won't unless you tell him."

"Or I tell him." The ice threading through a voice behind me makes me spin around. Dante. *Swan, I forgot about him.* He's sitting on a cream couch, glaring at me. "You shouldn't be here, Aurora."

"Don't be such a snitch, *cugino*." Benny, one of the Hollow brothers, flops down next to him and picks up the bottle of Dom Perignon from the ice bucket. "In two weeks, she'll be one of us. And we don't snitch on our own." He winks and hands me the glass of champagne. "Welcome to the family, *bella*."

I smile, feeling my cheeks heat at the kindness of his words. I don't hear them very often from any Visconti, and especially not from the scarier members, like Benedicto. Like Tor, he and his younger brother Nicolas are well-known to women up and down the coast. I don't think they have the same mom as Castiel, because they are fairer in complexion, with chocolate brown hair and stormy gray eyes. Even so, they are known as the Hollow enforcers, carrying out hits on anyone who dares get in the way of the Smugglers Club's expansion.

One glass of champagne turns to two. Then three. The bubbles go down easy and take the edge off the music; soften the harsh silver lights. Amelia and I laugh and dance to cheesy pop songs. Then we drift over to the balcony, pointing out our favorite costumes from the crowd below. When Donatello taps me on the back, holding out the bottle for a refill, I'm surprised to see how busy the area has become. It's Viscontis only on this side of the red rope, but all the other booths snaking around the balcony are filling up with sharp suits and slutty outfits.

"Who are all these people?" I shout at Amelia over the music.

"Stupidly rich hotel and casino guests," she calls back. "They are paying thirty-grand a booth."

I balk at the amount, that familiar disgust swirling in my stomach. Devil's Cove is swimming in wealth, yet forty minutes down the road, there are people in Devil's Dip that work twelve-hour shifts doing hard labor, but can barely make ends meet.

Life will never be fair.

The thought leaves me the second I recognize a familiar figure strolling toward me, a guard looming behind her. *Tayce*. Grinning, I duck under the red rope to meet her.

"You made it!" She laughs in my ear, bringing me in for a big hug. "*And* you've hooked us up with VIP. Win-win!" Pushing me out to arm's length, she runs an eye over my outfit. "What the hell, Rory? Last year, you dressed as a dinosaur. The year before, a giant tube of toothpaste. Why so sexy this year?"

I laugh off her question, but my cheeks grow hotter. "And you've gone for the less is more approach, as usual."

She does a little twirl, flaunting her black corset, fishnet tights, and tiny tutu skirt. If she hadn't scraped her long black hair into two pigtails and painted stitches on either side of her mouth, I'd have no idea she was meant to be a dead doll. As she comes to a stop, her eyes land on something over my shoulder, and then her gaze widens. "Holy shit, is that Vicious?"

Ice trickles down the length of my back. Between dancing with Amelia and seeing Tayce, I'd forgotten to keep an eye out for him. But at the sound of his nickname, the hairs on my arms stand to attention and I'm suddenly hyper aware of my surroundings.

I swallow and force my features to remain neutral. And I *definitely* don't turn around. "How do you know Angelo?" I ask, as calmly as I can muster. She moved to the Coast three years ago, which was long after he left.

"Everyone knows Angelo," she says with a little laugh, not taking her eyes off him, even when Benny brings her over a glass of champagne and hovers awkwardly next to her. "Christ, he's definitely the hottest Visconti. And have you *seen* those muscles?"

"How have *you* seen those muscles?" I snap back, sounding angrier than I meant to.

Now, her gaze shifts back to me, accompanied by a frown. "I haven't. He's the only Visconti that has never stepped foot in my shop."

"Really?" I almost spin around in surprise, but instead, clutch onto my flute glass a little tighter. "He doesn't have any tattoos?" When suspicion narrows her eyes, I clear my throat and add, "Just weird, that's all. Every Visconti is so inked."

"Yeah," she sighs, shooting Benny a sideways glare. "Not like this idiot, who doesn't have an inch of flesh left on his body to tattoo. What do you want, Benny?"

He flashes her a dazzling grin. "Is that how you speak to all your customers?"

"Just the ones that hover uncomfortably close to me on my days off." Before he can reply, she tiptoes and clamps her hand over his mouth. "I don't talk shop outside of business hours. Those start on Monday, nine a.m." *Guess this isn't the time to tell her what I promised Tor.* Grabbing my arm, she leads me over to the balcony and rests against it. "Honestly, why are men so annoying?"

"You must be the only person who can speak to a Visconti like that and not get a bullet in your head."

She laughs breezily. "They are all pussy cats masquerading as lions." Her eyes darken as she takes a sip of her drink. "I've known worse."

Her remark prickles on my skin. I'm desperate to ask her what she means by that, but I know Tayce. She'll completely shut down if I pry.

Before I can bring up the subject of Tor's new exception from her waiting list, something behind me catches her attention, making her brows shoot up. "Looks like we've got front row seats to some drama."

I spin around to see Dante on his feet, glaring to the left. I follow his gaze and spot Angelo. He's closer than I thought he was, cutting a sharp figure just a few feet past the red rope. He leans casually against the railing while next to him, a long-legged cat talks animatedly in his ear. As usual, his expression is indifferent, bored. He takes a lazy sip of whiskey and stares out into the crowd.

The sight of him winds me.

"Who is she?" I mutter more to myself than Tayce. But of course, she knows the answer.

"Lucy. One of the go-go girls at the Burlesque club. Everyone and their mama knows she's been fucking Dante for over a year, because she'll tell anyone who'll listen." She chuckles into her flute glass. "I suppose she's finally set her sights on bigger and better things."

My head swims, and not because of the champagne. *This* is not how the night was meant to go. I had this stupid, schoolgirl fantasy that he'd be watching *me* all night, while I pretended like I couldn't feel the heat of his gaze on every inch of my body. Instead, I hadn't even known he was here, and he hasn't looked up at me *once*.

I feel hot. My dress is too tight and my stomach has tangled itself into knots. "I'm just going to the bathroom."

Before Tayce can insist on coming with me, I storm off toward the back of the VIP area. Donatello grabs my arm as I pass. "Where are you going all by yourself?"

"Just the bathroom! Jeez."

He points to a velvet curtain. "There's an en-suite in Tor's office. Use that."

Gritting my teeth, I force a nod and slip behind it. There's a small corridor then a door with Tor's name embossed on it in gold. He likes gold signs with his name on them, I've noticed.

Inside, I take a moment to bask in the silence, realizing my head is spinning and my ears are ringing.

Damn him.

I quickly use the bathroom and run my wrists under cold water in an attempt to cool myself down. It does nothing. Sighing in frustration, I fling open the bathroom door.

And come to a crashing stop.

There's a dark figure standing on the other side of Tor's desk. He's leaning on his knuckles against it, and when I open the door, he looks up at me through half-lidded eyes. They take their time scraping over every inch of my body, coming to rest on my face.

Angelo Visconti.

A barely audible puff of air escapes his lips.

"You wore your hair curly."

My heart forgets to beat. After the initial shock, I suck in a lungful of air, steel my spine, and turn my attention to the door. Now, all I have to do is will my legs to walk toward it. One step. Two steps. I can feel Angelo's heavy gaze following me. *That's what I wanted, right?* But now, I don't feel like basking in it, not after seeing him talk to that supermodel-esque blond.

When I pass him, I breathe a little easier. That's the hard part, and now I'm so close to the door, I can hear the hum of music—

"No!"

But Angelo doesn't listen to my weak-willed protest as he grabs my wrist and spins me around so fast the lights spin in a golden haze. When I blink and steady myself, my back is flush with the door, and Angelo's heavy body is pushing me against it.

Gasping, I dare myself to look up at him. He's not looking at me like a piece of meat anymore. No, something darker licks the walls of his irises. Something dangerous.

Hatred.

He lunges forward. I squeeze my eyes shut, bracing myself for the unknown, but all I hear is the *click* of the lock turning.

"I need to know what the fuck you meant when you said you touched yourself in the sea thinking about me," he growls. His hot whiskey breath grazes my nose, and my knees threaten to buckle underneath me. I can barely breathe, let alone reply. In response to my silence, he winds his hand through the roots of my hair and yanks my head back.

A moan escapes me before I can stop it.

He hisses something dark in Italian. "Fuck, you're annoying."

"You don't sound convinced."

I pop a lid, catching his eyes trail hungrily down the length of my throat. Wet heat pools between my thighs, and the pulse in my clit is thumping harder than my heartbeat.

His hand tightens on the nape of my neck. I feel his grip as if it's on the nerve endings *down there.*

Angelo grits out, "*Tell me what you meant.*"

I bite my lip, knowing I shouldn't be entertaining this. But champagne and adrenaline flow through my body like a dangerous cocktail, making me feel reckless and wild.

Duck it. This is the last chance I'll get to do something crazy. Because after tonight, wedding celebrations begin, and I'll live the rest of my life tethered to an old man.

I swallow the thickness in my throat. Steel my jaw. "What I said. I fingered myself in the sea, thinking about you."

His eyes squeeze shut. "Thinking *what* about me?"

"Thinking about your fingers inside of me. Wondering what they'd feel like."

His Adam's apple bobs. "And?" he rasps. "What was your conclusion?"

A sly grin spreads across my face and I squirm as his gaze automatically drops to my lips. "That it would feel incredible."

I gasp again as his fist slams the door just inches from my head. He pushes himself off me and turns around, running his hand through his hair. Then he stands there, glaring at the back wall.

Dizzy on the excitement, I take a few steps closer, clenching my hands into fists. "At first, I used just one finger, but then…" I trail off, flustering.

His shoulders hitch. "But then?"

"I realized one of your fingers is equal to two of mine."

"Fuck, Aurora." When he turns around, his eyes are as wild. Hungry. "You're my uncle's fiancee. I can't touch you."

"Who are you trying to convince—me or yourself?"

The vein in his temple ticks. His gaze mists over. In one, large step, he closes the gap between us.

"Do. Not. Tempt. Me."

We stare at each other, the seconds feeling like minutes. I'm basking in every delicious moment of it, because it feels like we are standing on the edge of the cliff again. I can practically smell the smoke; taste the danger. Every nerve in body is buzzing with the desire to *jump.*

I know he feels it too. I can see it in the way he clamps his jaw shut. Hear it in the heavy breaths escaping his nostrils.

They say be careful what you wish for, and tonight, I got my wish. Angelo Visconti wants me as much as I want him.

His gaze carves a trail down to my collar bone. To the silver zip keeping my dress closed. And then, slowly, he reaches out and hooks his finger in the zip ring.

His eyes meet mine. "Show me."

My breathing shallows. "What?"

"Show me what you did to yourself."

My heart pounds against my rib cage, and my first thought is to run. My second, is that I'm about to explode with excitement.

I've never done *that* in front of anyone. In fact, only one guy has done it to me. It was rushed and felt more like a clinical experiment rather than sex.

My attention drops to his thick finger, knuckle white as it grips around the zip ring. A pink flush decorates my chest, and suddenly, I feel mortified. He's probably been with a million women who've done this for him...what if I do it wrong? Or worse, what if he's toying with me? What if I take off my dress, and then he regards me with that condescending smirk I hate so much?

You're a silly little girl, Aurora.

"You said you couldn't touch me."

"I won't," he says thickly. "I'm going to watch."

And then he tugs. The zip opens inch by inch, revealing my breasts, stomach, panties. Then it falls to the floor at my feet.

Oh, goose. Swallowing hard, I let my eyes flutter closed. I can hear his sharp intake of breath, feel his gaze scorch every inch of my flesh.

He shakes his head in disbelief. "Do you always wear pink panties?"

I pop a lid, my eye landing on his lips. No smirk. That's good. When I look up, his gaze snatches my breath away. It's clouded with desperation. Desire. *For me.*

A new-found confidence swirls through my veins, and without breaking eye contact, I sink to the leather couch behind me. Without blinking, I lift my heels up onto the seat and slowly slide my hands up the inside of my thighs.

Angelo hisses. Runs a hand over his jaw. "Take them off."

With trembling fingers, I lift my hips and slide my panties off. He turns to look at the thin pink lace crumpled up on Tor's rug. "Christ," he mutters. Then his attention moves back to my face. My eyes and body follow him as he moves to the edge of the sofa and leans his palms on the armrest.

"Lie down," he demands. "And. Show. Me."

Biting my bottom lip, I slide my back down the sofa and part my knees, baring everything to him. When a groan rumbles deep in his chest, a wave of pleasure washes over me.

"Fucking hell, Aurora. You're perfect. Of course you'd be perfect."

My pussy throbs under his compliment, and I start circling my clit with two fingers.

"Is that what you did? In the ocean?" Angelo chokes out.

Biting back a whimper, I nod. "To begin with."

His gaze flashes dark. "To begin with?"

Taking a deep breath, I nod again. "Yeah," I rasp. "And then…" My fingers carve a path through my wet lips, from my clit down to my entrance. "And then I slipped a finger inside of myself."

"Show me."

I slide my finger in, heat flooding my insides. Holding his lustful stare, I say, "And then I put in two fingers."

He drops his eyes back to my pussy expectantly. I slip a second finger in, moaning in pleasure as my walls stretch to accommodate the extra digit.

"Does it feel good, baby?"

Baby. Heat rises from my pounding clit. "Yeah," I whimper, fingering myself faster. Then I catch his eye and smile coyly, "I bet it'd feel better if you did it." Dark amusement flashes in his eyes, but his hands clawing over the curve of his arm rest tell me he's restraining himself. Seeing him so worked up is driving me wild. "Tell me what you'd do to me."

His nostrils flare, and for a moment, I think he's about to come to his senses and shut this down. But he doesn't. Instead, he pushes himself off the armrest and lowers himself to his haunches by my hip.

Oh, goose. He's so close now, I can smell his aftershave, feel the heat radiating off him. His sleeve brushes over the side of my bare thigh and my heart hitches. *Please touch me. Please, for the love of God, touch me.* But he clamps his hands together and rests his elbows on his thighs, turning to watch me intensely.

"First of all, I'd take that silly little bra off," he growls.

Arching my back, I reach around and unhook it. With a mischievous grin, I toss it onto his lap. He groans, fisting the fabric and bringing it to his face. I pump my fingers into my pussy harder, faster, getting off on the sight of his big hands clawed around my lingerie.

"And then what?" I whisper.

His gaze falls to my chest, and he rakes his teeth over his bottom lip. "And then I'd take those perfect tits in my mouth, see if they taste as sweet as they look."

"Mmm," I moan, tugging at a nipple, hard.

His eyes glitter. "You like it rough, baby?"

I hitch a shoulder, drawing out my fingers and running my juices over my clit. "I don't know," I whisper shyly.

"Then I'd want to find out," he growls, inching closer. I raise my hips up so he can get a better look at what's going on between my legs. "I'd slap that tight little cunt just to hear you scream."

Muffling a sob, I slap my pussy, bucking under the shockwave of pleasure that rolls from my clit and up to my lower stomach. *Holy crow.*

"Harder," he demands.

I slap it again, an orgasm cresting inside me. "Oh, swan," I mutter, turning my head and biting down on a cushion.

"Don't you dare look away from me, Aurora. I want to see the look on your face when you come." I turn back to him and he cocks his head, satisfied. "Good girl. Now, rub your clit as hard as you can."

I nod frantically, rubbing my nub harder and harder, squirming under both the pleasure and Angelo's heavy stare. My orgasm builds and builds, making me lightheaded and breathless.

"Don't you dare fucking stop," he snarls, leaning over my knee and not taking his eyes off my pussy. "I want to see your cum trickle out of that cunt and down your thigh."

My clit beats like a drum, until every muscle in my body tightens, and pure, adulterated pleasure explodes inside of me.

"Oh, God!" I cry, my body taking over as I grind against my palm to release every last bit of my orgasm.

My eyes close and I try to catch my breath, as the fireworks inside my stomach and between my thighs come to a slow stop.

After a few seconds, the sofa dips. Through my lashes, I see Angelo stand to his full height. A huge bulge strains against the crotch of his slacks. *Christ.* He runs a final, hungry gaze over the length of my body and lands on my face, a dark smirk playing on his mouth.

"I was wrong about you, Magpie," he says huskily, licking his lips. "You *are* a bad girl."

With one last lingering stare, he turns toward the door and unlocks it. Just before he slips through it, I see something pink and lacy in his hand.

My bra.

He subtly slides it in his pocket and leaves me reclined on the sofa.

Fully naked and spent.

CHAPTER
Nineteen

Angelo

THE IMAGE OF MY uncle's fiancee naked and fingering herself last night is burned so deep into my retinas that I fucking see it every time I close my eyes.

The ghost of her shallow breathing still rings in my ears. The damp *thwack* as her hand slapped her swollen pussy haunts me. And when her face flushed and her whole body shook as she came, I knew I had to get the fuck out of there before I did something I couldn't take back.

Christ himself doesn't have as much restraint as me.

The moment I walked out of Tor's office I left the club. Not just because I had a hard-on that wasn't going away anytime soon, but because I knew the night had peaked. I couldn't go back to seeing Aurora wriggle around in that obscenely tight dress now that I knew what shade of pink her pussy was. And besides, I was in no mood to deal with Dante, who, for some reason, was glaring at me from the other side of the VIP booth like I fucked his prom date all over again.

Today, as the wrought iron gates open, my cock twitches in anticipation. I know I'm playing a dangerous game, but I'm past the point of caring. I just want to see her, even if just fully clothed. Even if it's just to take pleasure in how she'll squirm with embarrassment after baring her all to me last night.

Rolling up to the entrance, I can immediately feel the buzz of activity surrounding the mansion. Servers come and go out of the front door, loading boxes into trunks and talking animatedly into cell phones.

There's more going on inside the foyer, too. There are women with earpieces and Greta's holding a clipboard, barking at a gaggle of young maids. *What the fuck is going on?*

Something catches my eye at the top of the stairs, and when I look up, I see Aurora. She spots me too and freezes, her foot hovering in the air, ready to descend to the next step. A woman is in her ear, but I can tell by the flush creeping out from underneath her silk robe that she's not listening.

I bite back my smirk and cock my head. "You're not dressed."

"And you're not meant to be here," she whispers back. Eyes darting toward Alberto's closed office door, she scurries down the steps and comes to a stop in front of me. She glances up and recoils, like she forgot how tall I was compared to her. Or maybe she remembers last night as vividly as I do.

"You don't want to see your father today?"

"I can't." She shifts her attention to her bare feet. Of course her toes are painted pink too. "It's...my engagement party tonight."

My stomach flips. I'm surprised at how quickly her comment digs under my skin, carving a bitter, angry path around my body. I lock my jaw in an attempt to keep my expression neutral. "Cool, but that's tonight."

She glances around at the sea of people falling over themselves to get shit done. "There's a lot to be done."

"That's why you have servants."

"But—"

My hand around her jaw cuts her off. Her eyes widen, cutting back to Alberto's office. "What happened to no touching?" she breathes.

I let out a dry chuckle and reluctantly drop my hand to my side, dragging my thumb down her soft cheek as I go.

"Right," I say dryly. "I can look but I can't touch." Christ, I was so hard for her last that I'd have made up any excuse just to see what she had going on under that slutty dress. "Do you want to go and see your father or not?"

"I can't—"

"That's not what I asked."

Again, she glances over at Alberto's office and the pulse in my temple ticks. Fuck, I hate how much power he has over her.

"I'm not allowed today."

Without another word, I turn on my heel and burst into Alberto's office without knocking.

His expression clouds with rage, until he looks up from his files and realizes it's me. Then he shifts in his leather armchair and cocks his head. "Ah, hi, kid. You're early. Party isn't until tonight, and we're having it over in the Visconti Grand." His wrinkly lips form a tight smile. "You didn't need to come all the way over here, you just had to take the elevator down to the ballroom."

I don't engage in his light-hearted small talk. Instead, I kick the door shut with my heel and stroll over to his desk. It's not lost on me that he recoils. "I need Aurora today."

"It's our engagement party—"

"I've been thinking about your offer on the Devil's Preserve. Perhaps you're right. It's so much wasted space, maybe we should do something about it."

His eyes light up, then a shit-eating smirk crosses his face. "Finally. Fuck, how many times have we spoken about it this week alone?"

A *fuck ton*. Every time Alberto gets me behind a locked door, he asks about the damn Preserve.

"A lot," I say sourly. "I'd like to scope it out before we discuss it further. Aurora knows the forest like the back of her hand, so I'd like to take her out there with me."

"Excellent idea. But uh..." His eyes dart toward the door and he lowers his voice a few decibels. "You should know that she thinks the Devil's Preserve is my territory." Holding his hands up in mock surrender, he adds, "I know, I know. I'm a naughty boy. Gotta do what you gotta do, am I right? So, uh. If you could just not mention that it's yours, I'd appreciate it."

White heat licks the lining of my stomach. I run my tongue over my teeth and give a curt nod, before turning on my heel.

"Angelo?" I still. "You and me, we'd do amazing things together on this coast, kid."

Shut up, shit-face. I fling open the door and find Aurora directly on the other side of it. She yelps one of her stupid bird puns and jumps back.

"Well?" she whispers, eyes adorably big.

"Get dressed. I'll meet you in the car."

Less than ten minutes later, she slides into the passenger seat of my Aston Martin in a pair of gray leggings and an oversized hoodie. Fuck. I don't think I've met a girl who looks as good in sweats as they do in leather. Her hair falls in loose curls around her shoulders, and she must have just washed it, because the smell of her cherry shampoo fills the whole car and makes my damn dick ache.

I peel out of the driveway, trying to concentrate on keeping the car on the road, which is near impossible. All I can think about is the shape of her tits under that hoodie, and the small strip of golden hair on her pussy mound.

I tug at my collar. Drum my fingers against the steering wheel.

"Hungover?"

Aurora tenses. "No." Her gaze brushes my cheek, then her voice lowers. "I wasn't even that drunk."

"Right."

She coughs. Fidgets. Then she pulls out a pack of Mike & Ikes from her purse and shoves a whole handful into her mouth, before offering me the carton. I sneer down my nose at her and shake my head.

"Suit yourself," she mutters. "So, uh. Where were you on Wednesday?"

"Why? Did you miss me?"

"Yes." Her answer comes quick and thick. It's followed by the most adorable little laugh.

Coming to a halt to meet the gate, I drop my head against the backrest and close my eyes.

"Don't test me today, Aurora. I've spent nine years resisting temptation. You're making it very hard for me to get to a decade." The moment I dare to look up at her, I immediately wish I hadn't. She's gazing up at me under those thick lashes, breathing heavily through her plump, parted lips. I harden my glare. "I mean it."

She shakes out another handful of candy and stares down at them. "Last night was bad…real bad." She catches her bottom lip with her front teeth. "We shouldn't have done…*that*."

"We? I didn't do anything."

She scowls, her pale skin turning a darker shade of red. "*You* watched. Anyway, it can't happen again." She swallows and twists in her seat to glare at me with surprising venom. "And if you tell Alberto, I swear, I'll set fire to your car."

I bite back a laugh. "You'll what now?"

"You heard."

"Jeez. Who are you and what have you done with Aurora? It was less than two weeks ago that you were on the verge of tears, begging me not to listen to your secrets."

"Well, I know you'll keep this secret, because you'll be just as screwed as me if you don't."

"Nothing happened, Aurora. I didn't touch you; you didn't touch me. Chill out." I'm forcing my face to remain unbothered, but inside, my blood is pounding hot and fast against my skin.

She nods, visibly relaxing, like this was the confirmation she needed. "You're right. We didn't touch. It's fine. Everything is going to be fine. It's Rory, by the way."

"Huh?"

"My name is Rory. I just thought you should know. I mean, now you've seen me naked and all."

What?

Biting my tongue, I shake my head and focus on the coastal highway. Fuck, this was a bad idea. I knew I shouldn't have picked her up today, but a sick, twisted part of me wanted to see her, just so I could bask in her embarrassment. I thought she'd be flushed and squirming, unable to meet my eye knowing what she did for me last night. I thought she'd be climbing the walls, horrified that she finally has a real sin under her belt.

But this girl? She's "Rory" all of a sudden. She has a bite, and it's irritatingly hot.

We drive the rest of the way in silence, and I pull up in the usual spot outside the church.

"An hour," I remind her. She nods and dives out of the car, bounding toward the forest without looking back.

When she emerges from the trees sometime later, her expression is sullen. Her steps are quick while her hands clench the sleeves of her hoodie.

I still, gripping the steering wheel as I watch her approach the car.

"What's wrong?" I snap, the moment she opens the door.

She drops to her seat and stares out the windshield blankly. "Nothing. Let's just go."

My eyes narrow. "Aurora, look at me." She shakes her head. "I dare you to make me ask twice," I growl.

She tenses, but still stares head. Irritation flickering in my gut, I follow her gaze and realize she's staring at the phone box.

"I was wrong. It's not fine." Her soft voice is barely audible, but it shoots me in the stomach. "I have too much on the line to be doing stupid things with you."

"Forget about it—"

"I can't," she interrupts, her tone firmer. "That's not how it works. I can't help but do bad things, but it always ends up being okay because I confess and rid myself of the guilt." She swallows and scrapes a curl away from her face. "And now I can't, because *you* own the thing I was confessing to."

I lean back in my seat, rubbing my hand over my jaw. "I told you, I won't listen, Aurora. I got bigger things to worry about then your stupid confessions. Go call the line. I don't care."

"But you're not the only person with access to Sinners Anonymous, right? Your brothers have it, too."

She has me there. No doubt she'll talk about what happened last night, and if Rafe or Gabe hears it, they'll put two and two together, and that'll start a whole shit show. Rafe's words bounce around my brain: *Don't make me go to war for a piece of pussy.* And Gabe? Well, he seems to think he's psychic these days, and I can't be assed for his slew of *I told you so.*

Pinching the bridge of my nose, I groan. "And you can't just keep a fucking diary like everyone else?"

She laughs bitterly. "I'm not even allowed a passcode on my phone. What makes you think I'll be able to hide a diary?"

Fury burns low and slow in the pit of my stomach.

Not my problem. Not my problem. Not my problem.

I can't get attached to this girl. Even just allowing the thought to live in my brain rent-free is ridiculous. "And if you can't confess? What happens then?"

For a moment, I swear her focus moves left. Over the graveyard. Past the church.

To the cliff.

My blood runs cold. *Fuck.* She's all sass and mouth, but can she really not deal with her guilty conscience? Hell, I've heard a sample of her sins and they are the dictionary definition of petty. If she can't deal with it when she has an outlet to confess to, how is she going to deal with last night's sin with no means of confessing?

"Get out."

Killing the ignition, I round the car and storm up the path toward the church. When I don't hear her door shut, I turn around, annoyed.

"Do you need a leash?"

By the time I break into the church, she's at my heels, scurrying into the darkness after me.

"Whoa," she breathes, slowing to a stop in the middle of the aisle. "You know, this place has been closed since I was twelve." The thought makes me shudder. Fuck, nine years ago, she wasn't even a teenager. "I've always wondered what it looks like inside."

"You weren't missing much," I grunt back. "Come."

She follows me down the aisle, round the altar, and to the confession booth on the far right. I thump the mahogany door with my fist, then lean my back against it. "Here. A real-life confession booth, knock yourself out."

But she's not listening; she's too busy walking up the steps to the altar, running her fingers over patterns carved into the pulpit. "You grew up here?"

I pause. "Yeah. My father was the deacon."

"So I've heard," she says with a sour scowl. "He had quite the hold on the town, apparently." She stops, then whips her head around so fast that her curls form a wave across her back. "Wait." Her eyes dart back to the confession booth. "So, your father used to listen to confessions. You do too. You've modernized your father's confession booth."

"Wow. Gold star for Detective Aurora."

Her gaze thins, but then it softens. "So, is Sinners Anonymous an homage to your late father?"

"No," I spit with more venom than needed. I push myself off the booth and join her on the chancel. "Growing up, my brothers and I would spend our Sundays listening to everyone's sins." I turn, pointing to the wall behind the booth. "There's a pretty big gap behind it. All three of us would squeeze in and eavesdrop. What we deemed to be the worst sin, we'd...*take care of it.*"

I study her face, waiting for her reaction. At first, she's confused, and then when the penny drops, her brows shoot up. "You mean..."

"Yes."

She lets out a hiss of air and glances up to the domed ceiling. "I don't think God would approve of that."

I huff out a laugh and shake my head. "God wouldn't approve of a lot of things I've done. Anyway, after our parents died, Rafe had the idea to modernize our childhood game. And that's how Sinners Anonymous was born."

Her body tenses, and instinctively, she takes a step back from me. *Good.* Aurora would do well to stay away from me.

"So you still eavesdrop, and what you deem to be the worst sin, you..."

"Take care of it. Once a month."

She staggers backward, like the weight of this revelation is too heavy. I can barely hide the smirk on my lips. See, this chick wouldn't know bad if it slapped her around the face. But then she steels herself, and something animated flashes across her face.

She takes a step forward.

So do I.

"You find it hard to be good."

My gaze drops to her mouth. The need to run a finger over my bottom lip makes my hands itch.

"Impossible."

We stare at each other. She swallows and palms her cheek, like she's checking her own temperature. "And on Wednesday?" she rasps. "Were you...*taking care of it?*"

For a moment, I leave her question to hang in the air between us. Then slowly, I nod.

She sucks in a sharp breath. "How?"

"Don't ask questions you don't want to know the answer to, Aurora."

"I want to know."

Her voice is coated with something thick and delicious, and it's enough to make my dick swell. I study her more intently and realize her breathing is ragged and her pupils are expanding in those cinnamon eyes.

She's enjoying this.

Fuck.

Taking a deep breath, I rake my hands through my hair and glance up at the ceiling, like I'm hoping God will save me from this temptation. *Yeah, right.* Like I've ever given him a reason to help me out. When I turn my attention back to Aurora, my gaze darkens.

"We blew him up."

Her eyes flutter shut for a brief moment. "Did you enjoy it?"

I take another step toward her, dropping my head so my lips almost brush against the tops of her golden curls.

"Yes."

Her breath skitters across my shirt. "I thought you went straight."

"I did."

She dares herself to look up at me, but there's an edge to her gaze. "But—"

"I need release, Aurora. Avenging sins gives me the same release you feel when you confess them."

She nods slowly, eyes falling to my Adam's apple. When she talks, it's barely a whisper. "Some of my sins are so bad that I don't feel release when I confess them anymore."

I bite back a smile. *Fuck, she's adorable.* "Like what? Telling your teacher your dog ate your homework, when, really, you just didn't do it?"

With a flash of anger in her eyes, she widens the space between us. Before I can stop myself, my hand shoots out and I drag her back against my chest. I'm not done having her so close. She glares at my grip on her arm pointedly.

"Oh, yeah," I drawl, dragging my hand back to my side. "No touching. I forgot."

Flustered, she turns her attention to my shoes. "I'm not as innocent as you think I am, you know."

Ice prickles in my chest, and just one question bubbles up my throat: *Because you fucked half of Devil's Coast Academy?* But I swallow my retort. As much as it pisses me off, her sex life is none of my business. "Then, tell me what you did."

"I can't," she mumbles. "Because I haven't done it yet."

I laugh. "What? Then what have you got to confess to?"

"Just thinking about it. Knowing I'll eventually do it. It's bad enough."

I open my mouth to make another sarcastic comment, but the way her hands are clenched into tight fists stops me. Whatever it is, it's really haunting her. Slipping my hand under her chin, I tilt her head up to look at me. "You're a silly little girl, Aurora," I grind out.

Her gaze hardens. I feel her jaw flex against my thumb pad. "That's not what you said last night."

A hiss escapes through my teeth. "Seems like you can't get last night out of your head." Pinning me with a steely glare, she doesn't reply. I cock my head over to the confession booth. Rub my thumb pad over her soft cheek. "Is that what you're so desperate to confess? That it felt so good to have me watch you finger-fuck yourself last night?" I tighten my grip, stifling a moan when her breath skitters over my hand, hot and hard. "Or that you're wet at the thought of it happening again?"

Silence. It fills the space between us, suffocating me with sickly sweet tension. "Both," she finally whispers.

Darkness licks at the walls of my stomach. I breathe in, breathe out. Shift my gaze to above Aurora's head, because if I look at the torment in those big fucking eyes I'll know I'll lose my shit. I'm not this guy anymore. I'm not Vicious Visconti. He's locked in a box somewhere at the back of my brain, but now, I can hear him thumping against the lid, desperate to get out.

The suggestion tumbles from my lips, coated with a husky lust, before I can stop it. "There's an alternative to confession, you know." Our eyes clash. Hers sweet and innocent, mine dark and corrupted.

"What's that?" she rasps. But by how fast her chest is rising and falling, I know she already knows.
"Atonement."

CHAPTER
Twenty

Rory

A TONEMENT.

One word, yet it sounds so darn loud, echoing off the ceilings and making my ears grow hot.

Through half-lidded eyes, I look up at Angelo and swallow. Not even for a *second* can I convince myself that I've got the wrong idea. Not when I see the storm raging behind his eyes, nor when the line of his jaw sharpens as he clenches it.

He takes a step forward. I take one back. This amuses him, thinning his lips and making his gaze shine as black and slick as an oil spill.

Finally, I find my voice, although it's not as strong as I'd hoped. "Do you mean…?"

He pauses. Cocks a brow. My cheeks grow hot. *He's waiting for me to say it.* But I can't. The idea is so obscene that I can't physically put the word out in the open.

"Do you mean what I think you mean?"

"I'm not psychic, Aurora. What do you think I mean?"

I grind my jaw, irritated at how much he's enjoying this. Well, I won't give him the satisfaction. Sucking in a lungful of air, I roll back my shoulders and match his gaze. "Spanking me."

His Adam's apple bobs, but his expression remains neutral. "Another gold star for Rory."

My eyes flutter shut at the sound of my real name. It's the first time he's used it, and I hate how it warms the pit of my stomach.

"Well?"

My gaze snaps back to him.

"Well what?" I snap back. "You can't *spank* me. Christ, you're not even allowed to touch me."

But even as my protests slip through my lips, my heart starts to thump wildly, and a new pulse I've never felt before pounds behind my clit. In a sick, twisted way, the idea excites me.

He looks bored, like I'm too stupid for him to engage with. "So I won't."

Confusion crinkles my features for a split second, but then when I realize what he means, my blood turns to ice. It's instinctive for my gaze to drop to his belt. Then, to the bulge straining against the fabric underneath it.

Holy crow. Angelo Visconti wants to spank me with his belt and he's hard at the thought of it. My head spins, perhaps because I keep forgetting to breathe. I turn around, placing my hands against the altar to steady myself. Staring at the glossy wood surface, I beg myself to claw back some sort of composure.

But I can't *think*. I'm now delirious, drunk on the thought of Angelo's cold belt grazing over my bottom. *Why the hell does it turn me on so much?* I can already feel the wetness pooling in the fabric of my panties.

"Okay."

I agree before my brain can sign off on it. Like there's a visceral urge deep within my being, so desperate that it spoke on my behalf.

Crackling heat brushes against my back, making my nipples tighten. Large hands come to rest on the altar on either side of mine.

Angelo's breath coasts over the shell of my ear. "Okay?"

I swallow. Nod.

A slow, dark chuckle comes from behind me, coasting up my spine and forcing all my hairs to stand to attention. "Rory." Angelo's voice drips in syrup. "Okay is not good enough."

"I don't understand."

"Silly girl," he murmurs, "Did your mother never teach you to say *please*?"

My breath catches in my throat. My eyes fall shut and I grip the edge of the table. "You're really going to make me ask you to spank me?" I ask with a little laugh. "Are you serious?"

"Deadly," he growls.

I should shove him away from me. This is so wrong on so many different levels. But I'm in too deep; I've walked too far into the danger zone. And it's made me feel so *alive*.

Pulse pounding in my temples, I stare up at the image of the Virgin Mary above the altar. Shake my head in disbelief. *Forgive me.*

"I want you to spank me. *Please.*"

Behind me, Angelo breaths deep, and a small jolt of satisfaction stabs me in my gut. Of course he didn't think this "silly little girl" would really go through with it. He didn't think I'd call his bluff.

But my smugness is fleeting, evaporating the moment I hear the clink of his belt buckle. The *thwap* as he slides the leather out of the loops of his slacks.

Something rough catches in his tone. "Bend over."

The pulse in my neck quickens. Slowly, I bend over the altar, pressing my cheek against the cold wood.

Angelo clears his throat. Then, his voice drops an octave. "Now, I need you to reach down and pull your leggings and your panties down."

All of my muscles recoil, and I squeeze my eyes shut. *Oh, swan. This is really happening.* But there's no turning back now, even if I wanted to. Which, I know in my heart of hearts, I don't.

Nobody will find out.

Trembling, I hitch my thumbs into my waistband and roll the fabric over the curve of my ass.

Bent over and exposed to Angelo, I've never felt so vulnerable. *So alive.* The anticipation makes my skin prickle, and when he finally lets out a low, lustful groan, I bask in it, letting it warm my skin like sun rays.

"Fuck," he breathes, gripping the back of my hoodie. "Your pussy is the most perfect thing I've ever seen." The fronts of his thighs graze against the back of mine, and the feeling of cold, soft fabric sends a shock of pleasure up to my clit.

He steels his tone. "This is going to hurt. If you tell me to stop, I'll stop. If you don't, then…" I shiver as he drags the folded belt down my spine. "I'll stop when I see fit. Understood?"

I nod.

"No," he growls, pushing his weight against me, bending over so his breath scorches my ear again. "Use your words."

"Yes," I croak. "I understand."

My mouth is watering. My heart is slamming against the altar. The wait is agonizing and—

The belt whistles in the air and comes down fast and unexpected on my ass. The pain explodes on my skin, the welt throbbing and stinging at the same time. A scream bubbles up my throat and spills out over the altar.

Behind me, Angelo stills. "Use your words, Rory."

Clenching my molars together, I take a few moments to steady my breathing. The throbbing on my cheek melts into a dull ache, and to my surprise, a wave of pleasure washes over me.

"Again."

A groan rumbles deep in Angelo's chest, and my pussy clenches around it. Without another word, he kicks his foot against mine, forcing me to spread my legs wider, and then his belt hits again. This time, I jerk forward, moaning at the feeling of my nipples rubbing against the lining of my hoodie. My pussy aches for the same type of friction, and I find myself on my tip-toes, arching my back toward the belt.

"I think you like being punished," he drawls. He kicks my foot again, and this time, I open my legs so wide that a cool breeze coasts over my wet lips. Behind me, the floorboards creak. Then I feel a whisper of a breath against my clit; a graze of stubble against my inner thigh.

Oh, holy crow. Angelo's on his knees behind me, his mouth just millimeters from my pussy. It's instinctive to arch my back and lower myself onto him. But a strong hand grips the top of my thigh long before I get to feel the heat of his lips on my clit.

"Now, now, Rory," he rasps, voice strangled with lust, "that would count as touching. And it'd be wrong to touch you, wouldn't it? You're a taken woman." His voice darkens. "Reach over and spread yourself for me."

Panting, I do as I'm told, reaching around and pulling my cheeks apart. My knees buckle under the vibrations of his moan against my pussy. "You like atoning for your sins, don't you, baby?" I rake my teeth over my lip. *Christ, I like it when he calls me baby.* "You know how I can tell?"

"How?" I croak, although I know what he's going to say. Because I can *feel* it. Carving a wet, hot trail down the seam of my leg.

There's a rustle, and then suddenly, something soft and silky cups my sex, dragging over my clit and through the folds of my pussy. With a strong finger behind it, it swirls the entrance of my hole, lighting every nerve ending in my body on fire.

Angelo extends to his full height, then tosses something in front of me on the altar. It's his silk pocket square, and to my embarrassment, the pale blue fabric is now stained dark navy with my juices.

"Getting so wet for a man that isn't your fiance?" He leans over, holding the fabric and bringing it up to my face. "That deserves another spanking."

He whips me again without warning, and white, hot pain shoots through me in the most delicious of ways. *What the hell is going on?* But now that I've felt the cocktail of pain and pleasure swirl through my veins like an I.V., I crave more.

When a breeze flutters over my flesh as he brings the belt back into position, I brace myself again. But then, it falls lax against the curve of my ass.

"I think you've had enough punishment for one day, Rory," Angelo whispers, malice lacing his voice.

Already? "No," I beg. Squeezing my eyes shut, I can feel the start of an orgasm cresting, and I'd give anything, *do anything*, to see it through. "Don't stop."

"One more whip of my belt, and you'll be coming in a church. No amount of confessing can save your soul from that."

In the aching silence, I hear the rustle of his slacks. The clink of his belt fastening. Then his heavy footsteps taking the stairs, growing quieter as he heads toward the door.

Is he seriously leaving me like this?

His deep, commanding voice echoes down the aisle. It has a harsh edge to it. "Do what you have to do, whether that's finish yourself off or use the confession booth. I'll meet you in the car."

And then with the heavy thump of a door closing, he's gone.

CHAPTER
Twenty-One

Angelo

THE BALLROOM OF THE Visconti Grand Hotel is as tacky as Alberto himself. Gilded portraits of dead ancestors I've never heard of glare down at me. The center dome features a knock-off version of Michelangelo's painting on the Sistine Chapel, and gold glitters on every visible surface.

It's giving me a headache. Just another fucking reason I shouldn't be here.

With my back to the navy sea, I lean against the open patio doors, crumpling a pack of cigarettes in the pocket of my tux. It's not too late to leave. I'm sure Alberto wouldn't notice; he'll be too busy showing off his hot young fiancee to any old fucker that'll listen.

Bitterness burns my throat, and despite the salty chill coasting over the planes of my shoulders, I'm starting to burn up.

A soft punch on my arm makes me grit my teeth. I slide my gaze lazily to my left, landing on Benny's shit-eating grin. He's got a cigarette tucked into the corner of his mouth, as if he's just about to head outside for a smoke.

"You're becoming quite the regular round here, *cugino*. Where's the other two musketeers?"

"Rafe has business in Vegas, and Gabe's..." I trail off, running my tongue over my teeth. Gabe turned up at my penthouse suite two days ago, demanding the keys to our parents' house. He's been there ever since, ripping out walls and fixtures, while listening to the type of rock music that makes my ears bleed. "Busy," I finish.

He huffs out a laugh, taking a step out onto the patio to light his cigarette. He offers me the carton but I shake my head. "Gabe's always fucking busy. Ah, well. I'm sure they'll make the next one."

Frowning, I tear my eyes from the ballroom and glare at him. "What did you say?"

He takes a long drag, then points his cigarette in the direction of the guests littered around the dance floor. "This isn't Big Al's first engagement party and sure as shit won't be his last. I'm sure Rafe and Gabe will catch the next one."

Irritation digs under my skin. He's right, of course. Rory isn't the first young, hot thing Alberto's sunk his claws into, and when he's got what he wants out of her, she'll be cast aside and the next will take her place.

He's crazy. *I'm* crazy.

"Hey, where are you going?"

But Benny's voice is already a whisper in the wind. With my back to the ballroom, I take the steps to the beach below. Fast and two at a time, heading farther into the shadows where the gold lights of the ballroom can't reach me. When concrete turns into sand underfoot, I stop and lean against a tree.

A cloud of condensation leaves my lips as I let out a heavy breath.

Fuck, I hate this place. I hate the Cove Clan, and I hate *her*.

I especially hate her. I hate that she's exactly what I like: a girl who doesn't back down when I have my wicked way with her. I hate the sound she makes when my belt meets her ass. I hate the shade of red her skin turns, and how that *fucking ring* glints on her finger when pleasure makes her hands clench into fists.

I hate that "look but don't touch" is a hard and fast rule. It has to be, because I know the moment I taste those lips—either set of them—there's no way I can go back to London.

I know I'll have to stay and fight for her.

"Jesus fucking Christ," I hiss into the darkness, popping my knuckles. I've been on the Coast for over three weeks and I can't tell if being here is solidifying the wall I've put up between myself and the rest of the Viscontis, or if Aurora is softening the cold, black mass behind it.

As I stare out to the dark sea, something to the right of the shoreline catches my eye. Instinctively, my hand reaches for the back of my waistband, only to find there's nothing there. I close my eyes, mutter a curse word under my breath. *See?* The Coast is fucking with me, making me revert back to being the typical made man; reaching for a weapon I no longer carry at the mere sight of something mildly suspicious.

I need to get back to boardrooms and spreadsheets, sooner rather than later.

Steeling my gaze, I hone in on the silhouette. It's a girl sitting on a large rock, her legs tucked up underneath her. My heart beats on the double, and I rake my fingers over my jaw.

Rory.

Mild irritation flickers over me. At her own fucking engagement party, she's managed to slip away unnoticed. All those assholes up there care more about the champagne and caviar floating around on golden platters than they do about her safety. In fact, I bet Alberto will only notice she's gone when he's full of liquor and fancies something tight to grope.

Slipping my hands in my pockets, I stroll across the sand and come to a stop next to her. She slides a stick of Big Red into her mouth. As I follow her attention out to sea, I hear her breathing still.

"Is your ass still sore from this morning?" Nonchalance flecks my voice, like spanking Rory's ass is something I have the pleasure of doing on the daily. Like I didn't last just three strokes of my belt before having to get the fuck out of there.

Like I didn't go home and fuck my fist in the shower.

"Not sore enough."

I smirk at her attempt to match my indifference. It's fucking adorable when she tries to act unfazed, because her body language always betrays her.

So, I call her bluff. "Then perhaps I'll have to spank you harder next time."

"Holy crow," she hisses. "Angelo, there can't be a next time."

My jaw works, because I know she's right. Of course she's right—she's my uncle's fiancee and I live an ocean away.

Finally, I dare myself to look at her and immediately wish I hadn't. She's irritatingly beautiful, just like I knew she would be on the night of her engagement party. The fabric of her red dress spills over the rock she's sitting on, and her long, blond hair falls over her shoulders in tight spirals. Her gaze clashes with mine, just as she pops a bubble.

My chest tightens.

"Why are you looking at me like that?"

Huffing quietly, I shake my head. "You wore your hair curly again."

Even in the moonlight, I can see her skin flush. "Yeah, Alberto wasn't too happy about that."

"Good."

Under the heat of her bewildered stare, I shrug off my jacket and slip it around her shoulders. She pauses, wide-eyed, then pulls it tighter around herself, hiding a small smile in the fabric of the lapel. *Fuck.*

Without a word, I sink down next to her and pull the cigarette carton from my pocket. I slide one out and slip it between Rory's parted lips. As my knuckle grazes over her chin, I fight against the instinct to grip her there. The flame of my Zippo casts a soft shadow over her face, and when I light the tip, she draws a slow sensual inhale that goes straight to my cock.

"Tell me a sin, Aurora."

As soon as it leaves my lips, I wish I didn't ask. Every time I've coaxed a sin from her, I've hoped it'll be about her sluttiness. But if she tells me about it tonight, I might put my fist through a tree. No, tonight, I have a strange urge to get something deeper from her. I want to know what goes on inside her head.

She looks at me through the cloud of smoke, sadness swirling her irises. A long silence stretches out between us, before she passes me the cigarette and leans back on her palms, staring up at the starless sky.

"My mom died two years ago. Cancer. It started as a small spot on her lung but spread down to her liver and up to her brain. She fought like hell, but eventually, there was nothing more the doctors could do, apart from keep her comfortable. So, they sent her home." She swallows. "Set up a full hospital bed in the living room, and nurses came twice a day to care for her. When the nurses weren't there, she had this buzzer she could press, so my father and I would always know if she needed something. Well, one night, it went off. I leaped out of bed and ran into the family room to check on her. She was fine—in fact, she looked the most alive I'd seen her in weeks," she adds with a soft laugh. "She'd only pressed the buzzer because she wanted to talk to me. She wanted me to promise her something."

My back tenses as she shifts closer to me. Rests her head on my shoulder. I briefly close my eyes and swallow the thickness in my throat. I should tell her that this counts as touching, but I don't. Instead, I bite out, "Promise her what?"

The top of her head grazes my jawline, and when she speaks, I feel her soft, hot breath on my throat. "That I'd never marry for anything but love." She slumps against me. The urge to snake my arms around her and drag her into my chest is all-consuming, so I distract myself with a long drag of the cigarette. "The same night, she night passed in her sleep."

I drop my head on top of hers, twisting to breathe in her cherry shampoo. "I'm sorry," I murmur, my lips brushing over her golden strands.

"I always thought I'd keep that promise. No one ever thinks they'll marry for anything but love, right? Well, the guilt started after I signed Alberto's darn contract. And no matter how many times I called your hotline, I've never been able to shake the horrible feeling that I've let her down." She sucks in air, then releases it in a shaky breath. "This is why we can't go on like this, Angelo. He'll find out eventually, and when he does, he'll kill me and do whatever he wants with the Preserve anyway. Breaking my promise to my mom can't be in vain."

He'll kill you anyway.

We sit in silence for a while, passing the cigarette back and forth. The tide's coming in, the waves now breaking gently against the rock we're sitting on. Above us, a brass brand breaks into an acoustic version of Stevie Wonder's "Isn't She Lovely." Cheers and laughter float down the steps and through the trees, and by the time they reach the quiet of the shore, they sound sinister.

As the water covers the sand around us, I tuck the cigarette into the crook of my mouth and bend down, drawing a line in the wet sand. "There."

Rory glances down at it. "What's that?"

"A line in the sand."

Her mouth twitches. "Right, and we can't cross it."

The waves roll back in, lazily lapping over the line and melting it away.

"I know what it feels like to let down your mama."

The statement slips from my lips comfortably before I can stop it. Rory drags herself upright, pins me with a curious stare. "You do?" she whispers.

With a heaviness brewing under my rib cage, I lean back on my elbows. It doesn't go unnoticed how Rory's eyes trail down my torso.

"Nine years ago, my mom died of a heart attack." My gaze cuts over to hers, and when I realize she's not shocked, I smile bitterly. "I'm sure you already knew that, because if there's one thing the Cove Clan are good at, it's gossiping. But what they don't know is that the heart attack wasn't natural." Now, she looks shocked. "I was twenty-seven, had just landed in Devil's Dip for the Holidays.

I really didn't want to come home that year, because I knew my father and uncles were planning to sit me down and have a serious talk about me taking over as Capo. I always knew I'd have to eventually, but business was booming in London, and I wasn't ready to give it all up. The day I landed, I decided to take my mama to the fair. Remember the one that used to sit on the north headland over there?" I jerk my chin to the right side of the shoreline. "The one that burned down?" *The one I burned down.* She nods. "Every time I came home, I'd take her there. It was tradition." I let out a sour laugh; run a hand over my face. "She fucking loved that fair. Not 'cause of the rides and games, but because of all the fortune tellers in their wagons, promising to lay out her future for five dollars. She lapped all that shit up—anything to do with fate or fortune. In fact, she lived her life by it."

A cold gust of wind off the Pacific whips past us, and I hear Rory's teeth chatter. Instinctively, I turn to face her and wrap my jacket tighter around her.

"Eventually, Mama had visited all the psychics she wanted to see, so we turned to leave. But it was getting dark, and the fair was starting to get busy. We were heading out, going against the flow of the crowd as everyone poured in, so it wasn't the craziest thing when a kid spilled a coffee all over her blouse." I grind my molars together at the memory. It still burns, all these years later. "Of course, my first instinct was to crack this kid square in the jaw. It was a no-brainer. But Mama begged me not to." My knuckles graze over the rock as I clench my hands into fists. "She always hated violence, which was why she always such a fucking saint to everyone. She believed her being good would cancel out the rest of the family being bad. She went to the bathroom, and I shit this kid up a little, but let him go." I turn to face Rory, my nostrils flaring. "I fucking let him go," I growl.

Her small hand curls over my fist. Warm and soft. "And what happened to your mom?" she whispers.

"I waited outside the women's restroom for my mom to clean herself up. Five minutes ticked by. Then ten. Eventually, I started feeling uneasy. Something wasn't right, I just knew it. So I went in, broke down the cubicle door and..." I glance up at the sky. Shake my head. "She was just lying there, slumped against the toilet. Dead."

Rory's gasp rings around my ears. "The coffee—"

"It was a poison solution that caused her to have a heart attack within minutes."

"Oh my goose. Angelo. I'm so sorry," she sighs. "And then your father…"

"Had a bleed on the brain three days later." I sit upright, steeling my spine. I don't want to talk about my fucking father right now. "Anyway, I couldn't find the cunt from the fair for love nor money. It must have been a local, because I remember they had a Red Devil's football team tattoo on their neck. But nobody on the Coast would talk. Especially not to a Visconti."

"Is that why you left?"

"I left because Mama was gone. Somebody else in the family had to be the good to cancel out the bad. That's what she would have wanted. Don't get me wrong. I'm far from a saint. But I live by the law and keep on the straight and narrow, even though it's near-impossible most days."

"But Sinners Anonymous…"

"Yeah, I know." I shoot her a look and lick my lips. "We all have our vices, Rory. Pulling a trigger or beating some asshole to a pulp once a month is mine. Hell, it's the only thing that keeps me sane. And I justify it because everyone we kill deserves what's coming to them. I've managed to convince myself Mama would approve—her sons are doing something good to cancel out the bad."

Silence swirls between us. I can practically hear the questions bouncing around Rory's head, all begging to be asked. But when we lock eyes, only one slips through her lips.

"So why are you back, Angelo?"

I can't help but laugh. How many fucking times this question has been put to me since I touched down on the Coast. And yet, Rory is the only person who will get the truth.

"For the last nine years, my guilt has been an itch I can't scratch. I need to find the man who killed my mom, and then I need to kill him." Shock crosses her perfect features, but it's gone as quickly as it arrived.

She nods. Buries her chin into the collar of my jacket. "When you told Alberto you'd take me into Devil's Dip twice a week in exchange for my help, you meant it."

My lips twitch. "You sound disappointed."

Her chuckle comes out muffled. "I am."

There's that fucking feeling in my chest again. The heavy one that pushes against my rib cage, threatening to break what's underneath. It solidifies what, deep down, I already know: I've been on the Coast too long and now I'm in too deep.

When I stand, Rory looks up at me, expectantly.

"Help me find him, and I'll be on the next flight off the Coast. You'll never have to worry about me ruining whatever deal you have with Alberto again. I won't cross the line in the sand," I rasp. Each word comes out strained, but I force myself to keep my expression neutral. But I can't resist sliding my hand over her jaw, tilting her chin up to look at me. "Promise me something, Rory."

I feel her pulse flicker against my thumb. "What?" she whispers.

"We'll find him before your wedding."

She pauses. "Why?"

"Because seeing you in your engagement dress is hard enough. But seeing you in your wedding dress?" A growl vibrates deep within me. I tighten my grip. "That'll be fucking torture."

A few minutes later, I'm standing at the bottom of the stone steps, hands in my pockets, watching Rory walk back up to her engagement party, taking a bitter part of me with her.

Something shifts behind a tree, catching my eye.

"Who's there?" I growl, reaching for that *fucking* imaginary gun again.

Tor steps out from behind the brush, zipping up slacks. He sees me and stops, gaze thinning. His eyes dart up the stairs just in time to catch the trail of Rory's red tress disappearing into the hotel.

Behind him, a blond emerges from the shadows, tugging down her dress, giggling. She steadies herself on Tor's arm, but he brushes her off, not taking his eyes off me.

"Go upstairs."

She looks at him, then to me and back again, and staggers up the stairs without another word.

Silence swirls us. I harden my jaw.

"Aurora's a good kid," he says icily, "and my father is a cunt. But don't make me choose."

My teeth graze over my bottom lip. "What's that supposed to mean?"

"It means I respect you, Angelo. You've been more of a brother to me than my own brothers ever have. And fuck, Rafe is my best friend. But the fact of the matter is, Big Al is my father." His fists clench at his side, his eyes flashing dark. "Don't go after his girl. Don't make me choose."

We glare at each other for what feels like minutes, before he stalks up the stairs and back to the party.

I should have told him that it won't come to that. He won't have to choose because we drew a line in the sand.

But that's the thing about lines in the sand. Eventually, they wash away, and you can't remember where you drew them.

But when there are no boundaries, no lines to box you in, bad things happen. Wars happen, murders happen. And I can't, *won't*, stay on the Coast to prevent them.

So, instead of drawing that line in sand, I'm going to have to carve it into concrete.

CHAPTER
Twenty-Two

Rory

"My name is Rory Carter and I do bad things."

The words have barely left my lips before the wind snatches them up and carries them over the choppy sea. I say them in nothing more than a whisper; hyper-aware of the crowd just a few feet behind me.

All Saints Day. The first Sunday in November, dedicated to celebrating the loved ones that have passed. I already said a little prayer for my mom, and now, I'm among a sea of Viscontis, who've traveled far and wide to gather around the joint grave of Angelo's parents.

It's going to rain. The clouds are low and charcoal-colored, and there's a familiar mix of moisture and static in the air. Just as I look up at a crow flying overhead, a fat, wet droplet lands on my cheek.

It's followed by a heavy hand clamping down on my shoulder, and the way I flinch in response makes my ribs ache again. This morning, Greta gave me a handful of painkillers along with a side of I *told you so*, but they did little to numb the pain. She was right. She *had* told me not to wear my hair curly to the engagement party, but I didn't listen. And apparently, that small act of defiance warranted Alberto pushing me down the stairs once we arrived back at the mansion.

Now, he's standing beside me, his fingers clawing at my collarbone. "Get over here," he growls in my ear. The anger in his tone is last night's leftovers. It sends a shiver of disgust down my spine, and as more ice-cold droplets begin to fall, I close my eyes.

My name is Rory Carter and I might do a very, very bad thing.

But as always, I bite my tongue. Slip on that perfect smile. Alberto slides an umbrella over my head and a fat arm around my waist and guides me back to the crowd of mourners, stopping in front of the grave. It's beautiful; carved from marble and covered in dozens of fresh red roses.

Behind it, the priest smooths down his robes and glances awkwardly to his side, where a woman I've never met is already crying. Sobbing behind her lace veil, choking into a silk handkerchief.

"*Dio mio,*" Alberto mutters under his breath. "Not again." Then his hand slips off my waist and he presses the umbrella into my fist. "I'll try to shut her up," he grunts, ducking out into the rain and transforming into a gentleman. He pulls her into his arms and rubs her back.

Always has to be the center of attention.

Warmth kisses my knuckles as somebody slips the umbrella handle out of my fingers and into their own. My eyes land on the hand that now holds the umbrella over the both of us, and immediately, my heart stills.

It always does in Angelo's presence.

"She pulled the same stunt at the funeral."

Without looking up, I clench my fists against my chest. "Who is she?"

"No idea. My aunt's cousin's step-mom twice-removed, probably."

Despite the pain in my chest and the butterflies in my stomach, I bite back a laugh.

His gaze heats my cheek. "It's a rainy day in November. What's with the sunglasses?"

Heart thumping, I push them up my nose and keep looking down at the muddy grass under my stilettos. Before Alberto shoved me down the stairs, he attempted to swing for my face, but being so drunk, he missed, and only the faceted surface of his ring managed to scrape my cheek.

It's a small mark, but it's the kind of mark that people ask about, even with an inch-thick layer of foundation on.

I'm trying my hardest not to look at Angelo, because doing so is always a dangerous game. He has a magnetic pull I can only resist for so long. I peer up over the rim of my shades and allow myself to drink him in. *Goose*, his strong profile will never cease to punch me in the gut. He's standing tall under the black fabric of the umbrella, donning a crisp black blazer not unlike the one he slipped over my shoulders last night, and a soft turtleneck of the same color poking out from underneath. His jaw is tense, his cheekbone casting a shadow above it, and he's staring straight ahead.

Although, I can't tell what he's staring at.

"You're wearing sunglasses too," I snap back, jerking my chin up to his mirrored Aviators. "What's your excuse?"

"How else am I meant to check out your ass without getting caught?"

His retort comes quick and unexpected, and after the agreement we made last night, it gives me whiplash. Instinctively, my eyes shoot up and graze over the crowd from beneath the umbrella spikes, making sure nobody heard that.

But there's an old lady under an umbrella of her own to my right, and next to Angelo, Vittoria and Leonardo tap away on their phones, bored.

"Christ, Angelo," I mutter, pressing my lips together over my teeth to stop myself from smiling anyways. "What happened to the line in the sand?"

"Ask me for a sin."

The hairs on the back of my neck stand up.

"I—What?"

"A sin, Aurora. I know you're familiar with the term."

A cold cocktail of confusion pools in my stomach, peppered with a dash of annoyance. His tone is hard and the way he calls me by my formal name is even harder. I grit my teeth, staring at the priest's moving mouth, despite not being able to hear a word that comes out of it.

"Okay, tell me a sin, Angelo."

"I killed my father."

My blood turns to ice. I blink. Shake my head. But nothing thaws me from the shock.

"I thought he died from a bleed on the brain?"

"He did. I shot him in the head and then his brain bled."

"But *why*?" I hiss, emotion clawing at my throat.

"He was the one that ordered the hit on my mama. I found out a few days later that he had a whore from Devil's Dip on the sideline, and wanted our mom out of the picture." I steal a glance up at him, and the way he's so nonchalant sends a shiver down my spine. He tilts his head down to me, his expression impossible to reach from behind his glasses. "I killed her too. That's not my worst sin, though."

"It's not?" I choke out.

"No. Not telling my brothers is. They have no idea."

Air leaves my lungs in a puff of condensation. The rain brought a cold snap with it, and the icy chill coasts down the neck of my dress, taunting me. As if it's telling me that, although the cliff face is being battered by wind and rain, it's safer out there than it is under the umbrella with Angelo.

My gaze burns into the mud. "Why are you telling me this?"

Angelo pulls the umbrella down tighter around us, trapping me in his world of darkness and deceit. He leans closer, his hot breath grazing my cheek steals mine.

"Because you should know what type of family you're marrying into. Viscontis don't keep their promises, and the Cove Clan in particular?" He lets out a bitter scoff. "After they shake your hand you have to check your watch is still on your wrist." My pulse flutters even though it shouldn't. And when his soft lips brush against my cold cheek, everything I thought I knew about right and wrong evaporates from my brain. "You're disposable to Alberto," he growls, his tone even darker than before. "He'll fuck you and then do what he wants anyway. They are made men, Aurora. Cheats and liars."

"And you? You're a cheat and a liar, too?" I turn to face him so quickly, that my bottom lip swipes against his, sending a jolt of electricity to my lower stomach. I'd forgotten he was so close. I jerk back, like I've been shocked.

Angelo stills. I stare at the distorted version of myself in the reflection of his sunglasses, wishing I could see his eyes.

He swallows. "Like father like son, Aurora. I've cheated on every girlfriend I've ever had, lied to everyone I've ever known." Then he uncoils to his full height and turns back to the priest. Anger rolls off him in waves. "You were right to want to draw a line in the sand. Because I'm no better than them."

I feel nauseous. Like I've been punched in the back of the head and concussion is setting in. My eyes throb, and even when I close my eyes, it does nothing to relieve the pain.

My stomach is sinking like an anchor, dragging my heart down with it. But this is good. It's *great*, right? If Angelo's just like the rest of them, then he's easier to hate. But I can't ignore the unease creeping under my skin, the hollowness in my chest.

Because I know the old adage: *from the deepest desire comes the deadliest hate.*

If Angelo stays on the Coast much longer, I'll hate him most of all.

CHAPTER
Twenty-Three

Angelo

WEDNESDAY. I SHOULD STOP looking so fucking forward to Wednesdays.

In the forty-minute journey between Devil's Cove and Devil's Dip, Rory and I have said less than five words to each other. All of them polite and professional. I said "no" when she silently offered me a Big Red, and she muttered "okay" when I told her to be back in an hour.

Now, as I watch her bounce across the road and disappear into the darkness between the trees, my car hums with unspoken words. The ones that aren't so polite and professional.

Christ. I have a Wasabi-flavored Kit-Kat melting in my glove box. It's left over from my trip to Tokyo a few weeks back, and when I found it tucked into the seam of my luggage, my first thought was her. I'd smiled to myself, *fucking smiled*, picturing the adorable expression on her face when she bit into it and recoiled at the heat. But that was before the engagement party, before we drew lines under *whatever the fuck this is*.

The first line, she drew. But it was shallow and, judging by the flush on her skin and the way her eyes still found my mouth every time I spoke, I knew she'd crumble like a cookie if I stepped across it.

I drew the second line after talking to Tor. I made sure to reinforce it with warning signs and a barbed-wire fence at the

All Saints service by telling her my darkest secret, plus a few lies about being a cheat just to seal the deal. Now, she won't be tempted to cross the line because I've made it clear that it's not greener on my side. It's cold, dark, and barren over here.

She's better off over *there*.

Fuck. I need to get off this Coast and back to my real life, away from Rory and the dark temptation she holds. While I wait for her to finish up with her father, I strengthen my resolve by answering business emails and scrolling through meeting notes: anything to help me connect with my life in London again.

It feels a lot further away than just the other side of the Atlantic.

When Aurora finally emerges from the woods, I get out of the car and lean against the bonnet. She watches me wearily as she approaches, slowing to a stop just a few feet away.

Her gaze thins. "I don't like it when you stare at me like that."

I bite back my retort, keep my expression indifferent. "I need you to make me a list of every degenerate you know of in Devil's Dip."

She cocks a brow. "Of people I think could have killed your mom?"

I nod.

"Okay."

As she sidesteps the car, I push off the bonnet and block her path. She stills, her eyes trailing up to meet mine. "You mean *now*?"

Another nod. "Right now. The quicker you can help me find him, the quicker I can get off the Coast."

Disappointment flickers in her irises but I pretend like I haven't seen it. Like it doesn't punch me in the fucking gut. It passes quickly, replaced by a hardened expression and a steeled spine. She fishes in her purse, and hands me a fistful of candy wrappers. Amusement rises inside of me. Then, she pulls out a brochure, dog-eared around the edges.

"I have a map of Devil's Dip, actually." She gives a wide berth as she steps around me and unfolds it, smoothing it out over the bonnet of my car.

"Why the fuck do you need a map? You forget where you've lived your entire life?"

"No," she hisses, rummaging around her bag for a pen. "You'll be surprised how many times I've come across lost tourists in the forest. Every now and again they stray too far from their five-star hotel in Devil's Cove, looking for a relaxing nature walk. They never seem to realize that it's not *that* type of park. I like to have a point of reference to help them out."

I stand over her shoulder, my chest brushing against her back. "Sounds like something a good girl would do."

Her back tenses; a bird-word comes out in a whisper. Then she leans over the map and starts scribbling over different parts with shaky penmanship.

When she stands back up, I'm directly behind her. Closer than she expected. Close enough to hear the gasp escape her lips as her ass grazes my groin. Close enough to her for my cock to twitch.

"Um," she breathes, brushing her fingers over the map. "I've marked a cross next to the address of everyone I know in Dip that matches the description of the man that killed your mom. None are actually *criminals*, but they aren't model citizens, either."

I'm barely listening. I'm too busy playing referee to an argument between my brain and my cock. My brain wins, and I take a step back. "Thanks," I grunt, folding up the map and slipping it in my blazer pocket.

I head toward the driver's seat, but something tugging on my lapel stops me from moving. Scowling, I look down and see Rory's small fist bunching my blazer. My gaze moves back up to her face.

"Something you want to say?" I ask icily.

There's a threat underpinning my tone but it doesn't make her flinch. Instead, she meets my glare with defiance. "I, uh. I think we should stay for a while."

Fuck. Why does her voice wrap around my cock like a vise? It's low and syrupy. Full of heat and ill intentions.

I harden my glare and grind my molars. "And I think we should get in the car and search for the man that killed my mother."

She rakes her teeth over her bottom lip, nodding slowly. "Or...we could stay a while."

Lust creeps up my throat, too thick and sweet to swallow. I know what she wants; it's written all over those perfect fucking features. Despite my brain's protests, my cock tingles for her to say it.

Her eyes land on the church. "Confessing is great and all, but uh... I thought that, while we're here...perhaps I could atone for my sins again."

"Perhaps you could. How do you plan on doing that?"

She matches my indifference. "With a little help from you."

Jesus Christ and all his fucking Disciples. My eyes damn near roll back in my head at her confidence. It's the hottest trait I've ever seen in a woman, especially when it's so unexpected.

I pin her with a blistering stare, trying to keep my eyes trained on hers, and not her tits as she arches her back and pushes them against her baggy hoodie. What I need to do is remind her that's crossing the line. You know, the one I reinforced yesterday with warning signs and barbed wire.

But I'm only a man, for fuck's sake.

I clear my throat. Run my tongue over my teeth. "I see. Well, what sins have you committed since Saturday?"

She stills, her eyes darting to the side. "Uh…"

"Like I thought," I drawl, amusement rising inside of me. "No sins, no spankings, Aurora." Sucking in a lungful of air, I feel my resolve finally shift into gear. *All I need to do is get this girl back in my car where she can't look at me like that.* "Good girls don't get spanked."

Her eyes glitter with something dark and dangerous. It's the same something I saw in her the night she touched herself for me. She pauses, then without warning pushes herself off the hood of the car and slides her hand into the pocket of my slacks.

My blood runs cold, because all the warmth in my body suddenly runs to my dick. *Holy shit.* Her fingers are hot, grazing a delicate trail down my thigh, before brushing over the length of my cock, which is now rock-hard. Her confidence falters for a second, and I only catch it because I can't take my eyes off her.

"Oops," she says, a coy grin playing on her lips. "That's not what I was looking for."

I bite my tongue, staying still and silent, like my heart isn't slamming against my rib cage, and I'm not fighting an animal instinct to grip her by the nape of her neck and wipe that smirk off her face.

When she removes her hand from my slacks, something silver glints in her hands. My eyes drop to her fist as she holds it up, triumphant.

My car key.

"You're right," she rasps. "No sin, no spanking. I suppose I better commit one then." Widening her eyes, she pulls a face that would get her fast-tracked to Heaven if God had a weak spot for doe-eyed blonds. "Just a little one."

I catch the tail end of her smirk as she slips between me and the hood of my car and walks to the passenger side door.

My eyes flick between the key in her hand and the matte black bodywork of my Aston Martin. For some reason, they are just mere inches from each other.

My gaze darkens. "You'd be out of your damn mind."

She bites her lip and looks up at me, expectantly. "This is a sin, though, right?" she whispers. "One that'd earn me a spanking?"

My jaw locks, and by my side, my fists curl so tight my knuckles pop. "I think you have me confused with someone who you can fuck around with, Aurora," I growl.

"Okay." She pauses. "I won't key your car, and you can spank me anyway. How about that?"

"I don't negotiate with terrorists."

"Well then. *Oops*," she says again. Only this time, her chirp is accompanied by a scraping sound. Heat rises to my brain and down the length of my dick, making the blood in both of my heads boil. Fuck, she's annoying. Fuck, she's hot.

I take a step toward her. She takes one back.

"Come here."

She shakes her head and her brows shoot up to her hairline.

"Make me ask again, Aurora. I dare you."

Before she can reply, I grab her by the wrist, pull her back to the hood of my car and slam her face-down on the bonnet. With an animalistic growl brewing inside my rib cage, I pin her legs against the bumper with my thighs and hook my thumbs into her waistband.

And then I pull.

She freezes. "What are you *doing*?!"

"Giving you what you wanted."

"W—what?" She twists her head around in protest, but I wind my fist into her curls and push her back down on the hood, so her cheek is laying flush against it. "I don't want it *here* Angelo—"

"Shut up," I snarl, roughly yanking her leggings and panties down to her knees. My molars grind at the sight of her perfect peach ass, her pink slit poking out from underneath it. *Christ.* The faint red marks from where I decorated her with my belt on Saturday are still showing.

"Someone will see," she squeals, her cold breath creating clouds of condensation against my paintwork. "I—"

Before she can finish her sentence, I yank the silk pocket square from my top pocket, ball it into a tight fist, and muffle the rest of her sentence by stuffing it into her mouth. She stills for a beat, before her panting starts again, heavier and hotter than before.

I lean over her, grazing my lips against her ear. Pressing the rock-hard bulge in my slacks against the crack of her ass. My fingers press into the side of her neck. Christ, such smooth, silky skin that begs to be bruised.

"You want to act like an animal, you'll be gagged like one."

Still pinning her to the car with my chest, I reach down and unbuckle my belt. Rip it out of the loops and coil it by my side.

She's breathing heavy and so am I. My skin is lit up like a live wire, burning with a dangerous cocktail made of equal parts of rage and lust. Adrenaline hums just under the surface, and I know that my viciousness, in all of its hot, itchy glory, is about to be released onto Rory's perfect ass.

This time, I can't promise I won't touch her. But what I *can* promise is that this time, I'll last a lot more than three strikes.

CHAPTER
Twenty-Four

Rory

My heart slams against the hood of the car, and a similar thumping sound beats in my ears, fueled by disbelief. *This can't be happening. Can it?* The November chill coasts over my bare backside, a reminder that I'm *not* imagining this. I really am naked from the waist down, bent over a car in the cold light of day with a makeshift gag in my mouth. *In public.*

Oh, and, I'm about to feel the leather wrath of Angelo Visconti.

Holy crow. What I'd do to rewind time just a few minutes and take my stupid act of defiance back. I was led by the heat in between my legs, not my logic. Logic would have told me to swallow my lust, slip on a smile, and get in the darn car.

Not to cross that stupid line.

Angelo's slacks brush against my bare thighs and I gasp. I didn't know it was possible to crave something you've never had, and yet, my body needs Angelo's touch like my lungs need oxygen. So much so that even something remotely resembling *touching* lights all of my nerve endings on fire. My head is messed up in more ways than one. Because ever since I found out he killed his own father with those hands, I find myself wondering even more what they'd feel like against my body.

"You're a silly little girl, Aurora. And now, you'll learn that you're not ready to play with a real man."

My pulse flutters between my thighs. I'm salivating at the thought of his belt kissing my skin as much as I'm dreading it.

The first *crack* comes down without warning or mercy, stinging my ass cheek. I freeze, my heart nearly stopping from the sudden pain.

"Gah," I garble, fighting against the silk on my tongue. It's instinctive to slip my hand up to rip it out, by Angelo catches my wrist and twists it behind my back.

"Now, now, little girl," he drawls, voice coated in danger. "Every time you fight it, you earn yourself another lash from my belt."

I clamp my teeth over the silk, bracing myself for another slap. This time, the leather snaps in the wind just right, whistling like a warning sign before it lands on my cheeks. This one feels like it has the full extent of his force behind it, lurching me so far the top of my head touches the windshield.

This time, the stinging morphs into a low and slow burn, which I feel deep in my core. A cold chill blows over the throbbing welts, but instead of cooling me down, it reminds me how hot and how exposed I am. We're on the main road that leads from Devil's Dip to Hollow and then Cove. Not many people frequent it in the middle of the day, but it's not unheard of. The worst part is, if they are coming from Devil's Dip, there's a high chance I'll know them.

I'm sick and twisted to be so turned on by the idea of being caught.

"Good girl," Angelo purrs, suddenly pinning me to the hood with the weight of his body. "You took that one well."

I groan, feeling his enormous erection pushing between my cheeks, even through the fabric of his pants. It makes me feel giddy that I can make him so hard—*me*, the silly girl with the silly sins and the sour attitude. I can't help pushing up against it, standing on my tip-toes to grind my bare ass against his bulge. I guess I'm not *technically* touching him. There's a thin strip of fabric in the way...

But Angelo's fist bundles the back of my hoodie and roughly pushes my hips flat against the car. "Who gave you permission to move?" Suddenly, he rips the handkerchief from my mouth, and I quickly suck in a lungful of fresh cool air. "You've just earned yourself another spanking. And this time, I'm going to make you scream so loud the whole town will hear you."

"Wha—"

But before the protest escapes my lips, Angelo delivers another blow, and then another in quick succession. I almost choke on the air as it leaves my lungs in a long, loud scream.

Behind me, Angelo chuckles darkly, then moves to stroking the top of my head instead of fisting it.

When his voice grazes the back of my neck, it's softer than before. "Fuck, Aurora. I love it when you scream for me. It makes me want to spread that perfect pussy and shove my cock inside you and give you something to really scream about."

His hot mouth carves a path from my nape to the shell of my ear, and I feel every second of it in my lower core. Somewhere in the very dark corners of my brain, there's a small voice saying this *crosses the line*. No, not the spanking. My sick logic allows me to justify that because I'm atoning for my sins; enjoying it beyond belief just happens to be a side effect. But his lips touching my skin in such an intimate place, I know that's wrong.

But I also know that, right now, I couldn't care less.

I extend my neck to expose more of it, to feel more of him against me, even if it'll earn me another spanking. His breath vibrates against the pulse in my throat. *Goose*, what I'd give to feel that heat on my pussy, and feel his heavy weight on top of me instead of just behind me.

"You'd like that, would you, Aurora? If I shoved my cock inside you."

My moan leaves my lips as thick as syrup, and it's followed by a short gasp when his teeth nip my earlobe. Yeah, that's *definitely* crossing the line. When I don't reply, he stretches the belt taught over my backside in a silent threat. Heart thumping even harder, I nod.

"Say it."

"Yes," I gasp. "I want you to shove your cock inside of me."

His tut comes low and throaty beside me. "You're a taken woman, Aurora," he growls, dragging the belt over the curve of my ass and between my thighs. "What would your soon-to-be husband do if he heard you wanted my cock inside you instead? Do you think you'd enjoy his belt against your backside as much as you do mine?"

I shake my head, but with a light warning spank of the belt against my clit, I darn near collapse against the car. "No," I cry.

"I'm the only one you want spanking you, aren't I?"

"Yes!"

"The only one you want to fuck you." He punctuates his sharp words with another spank against my clit, and this time, my legs threaten to give way.

"Yes, yes!" I moan, pressing my palms hard into the hood, as if it'll relieve any of the tension building between my legs. But I know the only way I'll find relief is if Angelo keeps doing *that right there*.

"And when your husband fucks you on your wedding night, all you'll be thinking about is me." Another hard, stinging slap. "Wishing it was my cock stretching your tight pussy open."

"Yes," I sob, "God, how I wish it'd be you. Please, Angelo, don't stop doing that. *Please.*"

Behind me, he stills. Goes so silent that I can only hear the blood thumping in my ears. "This?" he hisses with another spank with the belt.

"Yes," I whimper, opening my legs wider, inviting him to spank my pussy harder. My lips and clit sting deliciously, and I can feel my wetness trickling down the seam of my thigh.

"Bad girls don't get to come, Rory," he says in a tone that borders on malice.

"I'm begging you."

"I can't hear you."

"Please, Angelo. Please, I'm begging you to let me come."

He groans, "Fuck, baby."

Another slap lands on my clit, lurching me forward. The bundle of nerves down there aches with a mix of pain and pleasure, the tension brewing like a storm.

Another slap. "Yes," I gasp. "Please, don't stop."

I'm almost there. I'm cresting an orgasm, chasing the delicious high that only Angelo and his leather belt can give me.

He spanks me again, and then again. And then when my knees buckle and a million fireworks erupt in my lower stomach and send a wave of delirium over my entire body, he holds the belt there, offering me cold, hard friction to rub against.

I collapse against the bonnet, my nipples tingling and my bare ass and pussy on fire. I can only imagine the state of Angelo's view right now, how swollen and red my backside must look.

Once I catch my breath and my high settles around me like dust, I prop myself up on my elbows, my head dipping between my shoulders.

"We're going to hell, Angelo."

He doesn't say a word. After a few beats of silence, he slowly pulls my panties back up my thighs, being gentle when he reaches the sensitive welts on my ass. He does the same with my leggings, and then I feel something soft falling around my shoulders.

I glance down and realize he's slipped his jacket around me. His hands run down my shoulders to my forearms and linger there, warm, strong and comforting.

For a brief moment, I close my eyes and lean my back against his chest, basking in the feeling. In the distance, the waves crash against the rocks below, and the trees lining the entrance to the Preserve rustle in the wind.

His lips graze over my crown.

"I'm already in it."

Goosebumps rise to the surface of my skin, despite Angelo now keeping me warm. Without another word, he releases me and strolls over to the driver's side, his cock still straining against his pants.

"Get in, it's about to rain."

The second he turns on the ignition, it does. Big fat droplets land on the windshield, creating a sheet before being dragged away by the wipers. Angelo stabs a button on the dash, turning on the heated seat on my side only. I smile softly into the collar of his jacket, basking in his thick scent and warmth.

For a few minutes we drive in silence, Angelo steering with one hand as he moves his attention between the road and my map on his lap.

"Open the glove box. There's something in there for you."

Frowning, I do.

Then my smile stretches into a wide grin.

CHAPTER
Twenty-Five

Angelo

"THERE'S ROT IN THE basement, mold in the drawing room, and one of the pipes in the laundry room has burst, so no washer and dryer for the time being."

I glance from the paperwork in front of me up to Gabe, standing in the doorway of our father's old office. Despite it being November and pissing down with rain, my brother is shirtless and sweaty, looking like a damn Chippendale calendar.

"Good thing all my clothes are dry-clean only."

He rolls his eyes and pushes himself off the door frame. "Of course they are, princess," he grunts as he strides back down the hall.

I bite back amusement, turning my attention back to the contracts my PA, Elle, had air-mailed to me overnight. I've spent the entire morning pouring over them and setting up meetings with legal and finance for next week. Making plans back in London gives me a deadline. I'll find the fucker who killed my mama and get off the coast in under seven days, and definitely, most-fucking-certainly, before the wedding.

Outside, an engine struggles to start. Frowning, I get up and walk toward the window, looking down at the drive. Gabe's moved on from the damp and the rot, and now he's pissing about with my father's beloved Firebird, which has been left to decay in the garage for almost a decade. He doesn't give a flying fuck about the rain pouring down on his bare back. He's too busy crouched under the hood, with a flashlight in one hand and a dirty rag slung into the back pocket of his jeans.

Last week, Gabe just turned up and said he'll come help with renovating the house like I'd asked him to. He's been here every day since, busying himself with renovations and removals, and in the process, removing every last trace of our bastard father from our childhood home. I came over last night after dropping Rory off to see our father's cigar humidor upturned in the garbage, and this morning, a stack of Giorgio Morandi paintings sat lop-sided against the patio doors, the canvas's slashed.

Our father loved those fucking paintings.

I slip my hands in my pockets and watch him for a while. My mind bounces back to the cherry field in Connecticut, and Gabe's words rattle around my head.

I know what you did.

I don't know how Gabe knows I killed our father, or why he thanked me for it. But then, there's a lot I don't know about Gabe these days. Like why the hell he's obsessed with gutting our house and what else he would normally be doing instead. But this is the most I've seen of him in years, the happiest I've seen him too, so I'm sure as shit not going to ruin it.

I turn back around, running a cold eye over the study. It's the only room in the house Gabe hasn't torn down yet, and when I asked him why, his gaze darkened and he grunted, "You can fucking do it."

It looks exactly the same as it did a decade ago. The same mahogany desk and matching bookcase. The same photo frames filled with the same pictures. The only difference is the thick layer of dust covering the cabinets and the dark stain on the carpet behind the desk.

That's the spot my father had his unfortunate bleed on the brain.

Slowly, I amble around the room, rounding the desk and coming to a stop with my back to the door. From here, my gaze coasts over the desks and through the window, where the steep hill rolls downward and meets the town below.

This was all meant to be mine. Something I don't recognize flickers in the pit of my stomach, but before I can give it a name, a car rolls onto the front drive.

What the hell is Tor doing here?

Going to find out, I take the stairs and come out onto the front porch, just as Tor is hot-footing over the drive, using the stack of files in his hand as an umbrella. He slaps Gabe's shoulder as he passes, before coming to a stop under the roof.

"Fucking hell," he grunts, craning his neck to peer through the front door and into the foyer. "Well, ain't this a blast from the past. You trying to flip it?"

"Nah. We'll use it as a base when we come into town. I'm getting sick of having your brother as a neighbor at the Visconti Grand."

"Yeah. Bet Dante is sick of bumping into you in the elevator, too. Here." He presses a manila envelope into my chest. "Big Al wanted me to give you this."

I eye the envelope. "What is it?"

"Fuck knows. Ever since you popped off Max I've become his new associate. Got me delivering files to you and—"

A car door slams. We both look up to see Aurora getting out the passenger door.

"—babysitting his sugar baby."

My heart flips in my chest, and I run a subtle eye over the length of her. Christ. What the fuck is she doing in that tiny skirt? It barely covers her ass. Both possessiveness and lust brew under my skin, and I have to clench my jaw to keep my expression unbothered.

Tor looks up at me, and our gazes clash. His jaw ticks, but he doesn't say anything about what he saw at the engagement party.

"Where are you headed?" I ask, feigned nonchalance flecking my tone.

"I'm dropping her off at a dress fitting."

"Why, what grand event are the Cove Clan planning now?"

He flashes me an odd look. "Her wedding dress, you fucking idiot."

The lump in my throat thickens. To stop my hands from curling into fists, I rip open the envelope instead. Inside, there are two files, and as I scan them, my scowl deepens.

"What?" Tor cranes his neck to look at them. "Wait, is that—"

I cut him off by stuffing the papers back into the envelope and tucking it under my arm.

"None of your business, otherwise you'd already know."

His gaze hardens. "Don't piss me off, *cugino*. Was that a planning permission application for the Devil's Preserve?" Only the slightest bit of relief flickers within me. He didn't see the second document, at least. "Cause I thought you already told him and Dante to fuck off..."

"I did." My molars clamp together. "And that was before he convinced Aurora to marry him."

"Yeah? What's that gotta do with anything?"

"Aurora's marrying your father to stop him building on the Preserve." I drink in the confusion clouding his face and nod. "Right. You didn't know."

He pauses, then leans against the brickwork. "No, I didn't," he mutters to himself, running his thumb over his lip. "I just thought she was a gold-digger like the rest of them."

"Nope. Just a hippie."

He looks up at me, thinning his eyes. "Big Al doesn't own that land. You do."

"No shit, Sherlock."

"So why does she think otherwise?"

"Because your father is a cunty pervert who can't get girls within the age bracket he likes without lying and blackmailing."

His eyes thin, and I realize that slipped from my lips with more venom than needed.

"You gonna tell her?"

"No, because then he'll kill her."

"Right," he mutters. But I can tell this revelation unsettles him. He scans the yard and lets out a little grunt as his gaze lands on Gabe. "Is that Uncle Alonso's old Pontiac Firebird?"

"Yeah."

"Man, I need to get a better look at that. Never could appreciate it as a kid."

I do a sweep of the yard too, realizing I can't see Rory anywhere in the rain.

"Where's she gone?"

Tor pushes himself off the side of the house and trots down the steps toward Gabe. With a mischievous grin over his shoulder, he says, "She spotted the hangar on the way up." He jabs a finger at me, gaze darkening. "Don't do anything I'd have to chop your hand off for."

"Shut up, Tor."

The rain drowns at his cackle. I slip around the side of the house toward the hangar. I had my dad's old helicopter hanger upgraded when I extended our private airstrip to accommodate my jet. I flew it in a few weeks back and prefer having it here accessible rather than at the commercial field.

It takes me a couple seconds to spot Rory, because she's balancing on the fucking wing, peering into the cockpit.

"You got a death wish?" I growl, striding over. "Get down. Now."

She peers down at me, catching my eyes running up the length of her tanned legs to the curve of her ass just visible under her skirt. Christ, Alberto must be insane for letting her leave the house in that.

"Sure you want me to get down?" She chirps with a coy grin.

I bite my tongue. Shoot her a warning glare. When her grin only gets bigger, I push myself up onto the wing and grip her around the thighs. She gasps as I hitch her over my shoulder like a fireman, my thumb grazing over her panty line as I clamber back down to the ground.

Panting, she looks up at me shyly. I try not to let my eyes drop to the flush creeping out from under her blouse, but it's near impossible.

"Don't clamber around like a fucking monkey, Aurora."

"Why, worried I'll ruin your paintwork?" she chirps back, eyes glittering.

I chew on the inside of my lip, giving her a little shake of my head. Un-fucking-believable. This chick really believes she got one-up on me yesterday by keying my car and forcing me to rip her ass red raw.

"Nah. More like I'm worried you'll break a leg and won't be able to walk down the aisle on Saturday," I drawl, glaring at her.

A cute little line dents her brow, and the way her bottom lip sticks out makes me want to bite it.

"Screw you," she mutters, turning on her heel.

Before she can stalk back out into the rain, I grab her wrist and pull around so she's just a mere inch or so away from me. So close that she has to crane her neck to meet my gaze.

"Why are you creeping around my jet, anyway? It's a bit harder to steal than a necklace, Magpie."

She drops a hip, that flush darkening on her porcelain skin. "You know it's a myth right?"

"What?"

"That magpies steal shiny things? Truth is, magpies are really scared of anything that glitters or shines. Sure, they do *hoard*, but it tends to be twigs and little pebbles, anything they can build a nest with. I think the whole shiny thing comes from European folklore…" She trails off, narrowing her eyes at me. "Why are you looking at me like that?"

Only now do I realize there's a stupid grin on my face.

"Like what?"

"Like…" She swallows. Drops her eye line to my lips. "Like you want to kiss me."

Because all I fucking think about is claiming those lips, even when they spout geeky shit about birds I couldn't care less about.

Ignoring the heat prickling down the length of my cock, I jerk my chin toward the door of the jet. "Would you like to see inside?"

Her eyes light up. "Cluck yeah!"

"Christ, Rory. Have you ever said a curse word?"

"Not once in my life," she chirps back, hot on my heels as I lower the stairs.

I lean back on the railing and drag an eye over those legs again. "After you."

She's too excited to notice my leer, bounding up the stairs and letting me almost see the color of her ass.

Taking a deep breath and muttering an oath under my breath, I follow her in and lean against the cockpit door as she fusses over the flight deck.

"Holy crow, the radar display is *massive*."

"That's what all the girls say."

"Uh-huh, I bet," she murmurs, without looking up. "Oh—your VOR reader is *touch-screen*? That is unbelievably fancy." She spins around. "Is this the G700 or the G800?"

I cock a brow. "G800. How do you know so much about planes?"

She hitches a shoulder. "I'm not as stupid as you think I am."

"I don't think you're stupid at all," I murmur back, before I can stop myself.

We lock eyes for a second. Hers wide and expectant and mine hardening the moment I realize what I said was *almost* a compliment. "Does your father fly?"

"No. I had a place at pilot school."

"You're shitting me."

The scowl she tosses in my direction suggests she's not. She sinks down in the leather pilot's chair and tucks a strand of hair—straight today, unfortunately—behind her ear. "Nope. I took the preliminary credits at DCA, because obviously it's the only school around here that offers a class like that. I passed all the exams and got a conditional offer at Northwestern Aviation Academy."

That's a really good school. "And then?"

She shifts. Crosses one smooth leg over the other. "I didn't sit the final exam."

I frown. "Why not?" I know the course she means, because I took it too. Instead of going to Aviation college I took my place at Oxford Business School and racked up my hours on weekends. Got my recreational license first, then the private pilot license around five years ago. But I remember the exam she's talking about; it was piss-easy.

"Didn't feel like it."

"Aurora."

She huffs, briefly squeezing her eyes shut. "Please don't say my name like that. It's a darn sin in itself."

"Tell me why you didn't sit the exam."

"Because your old school was filled with jerks," she snaps back, leaping to her feet and turning back toward the flight deck.

I run my tongue over my teeth. Right, yeah. How could I forget—she'd fucked half the Academy, if those little shits at the poker game are to believed. Bitterness and rage hit me like a punch in the gut. As my breathing labors, I bite back the urge to ask for the names of everyone she's ever fucked. I'll add them to the list of boys I need to kill before I leave the Coast.

Instead, I suck in a lungful of air and study the rain through the window of the hangar. *It's none of my business.* And I really don't need another reason to be angry. In my peripheral vision, I see Rory reach over to check out the altitude indicator.

My gaze drops to the hemline of her skirt, which is now riding up her ass to reveal the purple and red lash marks on the curve of her cheeks. *Christ.* She's still super raw. She really took that like a champ. I nearly lost my mind when she begged me to spank her clit too, and I'm fucking desperate to see how swollen her pussy is after that.

Letting out a small groan, I grab the pen resting on the fly log and use the tip to lift her skirt up and reveal her panties.

She freezes. "What are you doing?"

My eyes flutter shut. *I wish I knew.* "You're wearing the same panties you were on Halloween." With my cock throbbing, I slide the pen under the thin, pink fabric and gently push it to the side. "You know, I think I have the matching bra somewhere," I say dryly.

"Uh, yeah. Can I, um, get it back?"

"No, it's a souvenir."

"Of what?" she whispers thickly.

"Of the time I almost fucked the hottest girl I've ever met."

I graze the tip of the pen between her pussy lips, gently parting them. She makes this irresistible little breathy sound that instantly speaks to my dick. Holy fuck, what I'd give to have that sound in my damn ear while I pounded her.

"Open your legs a little wider, Aurora," I mutter, my voice coated in lust.

Like a good girl, she does what she's told, her arms quivering as they prop her up on the flight deck. Despite the urge to rip those silly little panties aside and plunge into her, I can't ignore the little flicker of malice licking at the corner of my thoughts.

Seeing an opportunity to play with her, I still. Then slowly remove the pen from her.

"You know, I think this counts as touching."

"W-what? No, it's—"

"Yeah, actually I'm sure of it. Definitely touching."

She dips her head between her shoulder blades and moans. "Seriously?"

"Mmm. Unfortunately."

"But it's a pen!"

"Yeah, but I touched the pen before the pen touched you…" I trail off, biting my lip in amusement. "Not a good idea. You're soon to be a married woman, Aurora."

She spins around, smooths down her skirt and pins me with a blistering glare. "You're serious?"

"Deadly."

"And is this because I keyed your car?"

"Nope." *Yes.* "Just making sure I don't cross that line."

We glare at each other.

Bang, bang, bang. The sound of a fist slamming the side of the jet makes Rory jump.

"Can you two love birds hurry up?" Tor's voice booms up the stairs and into the cockpit. "I've got other shit to do today other than be my father's lackey."

Rory's mouth gapes open at Tor's comment, but I just smirk. He's such an ass. I lean in, drinking in her sweet perfume and the heat from her embarrassment.

"I'll go first to give you a moment to…*collect* yourself."

With a dark, satisfied chuckle, I trot down the stairs, using the manila folder to hide my rock-hard erection from my cousin. Rory comes down a few seconds later, and I'm impressed with how cool her demeanor suddenly is.

"I'm ready to go," she huffs, breezing past me without so much as a glance back.

"Good," Tor grunts. He strolls out the hangar, raising a lazy wave to me as he goes. "See you in a bit, *cugino.*"

"Later."

With a smile still playing on my lips, I stand in the doorway of the hangar and watch Tor's car disappear down the hill. Then, I run through what else I need to do today.

First and most importantly, I need to go and fuck my fist, because the sight of Rory's pink panties and wet pussy have put me in a spin. Then I'll get out into the town with Rory's map, paying visits to the kids we didn't get around to scoping out yesterday.

I take one step out into the rain, then realize I left my phone in the cockpit. Tucking the file under my arm, I take the stairs two at a time and scoop it up off the first officer's seat

Something catches the corner of my eye. It's pink and lacy, slung over the center stick. It takes me a few seconds to realize what it is.

Underneath, there's a note scribbled on the flight log in loopy, girly handwriting.

To add to your collection.

Shaking my head in disbelief, I fist Aurora's panties and bring them up to my lips. They are still warm and wet.

I inhale deeply, filling my soul with the scent of a girl that will never be mine.

CHAPTER
Twenty-Six

Rory

F RIDAY NIGHT, ANOTHER VISCONTI dinner.

It's a rare occasion that I'm in the dressing room without Greta buzzing around me like a bitter fly, but Dante has sent her into town to run a few errands. So, I take my time, showering in the en suite and gently rubbing lotion onto my sore backside.

Each time my hand grazes over my skin, or I sit down with too much force, a shock wave of pleasure ripples through my lower stomach. It's a constant reminder of Angelo and the dirty sin that we share. As I snowball toward the wedding, I find myself feeling more and more reckless; I'm unable to claw onto my decorum or morals every time Angelo lays that heavy, sea-green gaze on me. Yesterday, as I stood in the reception room of Donatello and Amelia's beachside mansion in the white wedding gown I'll be walking down the aisle in, something dawned on me.

Perhaps getting close to the day I marry Alberto is akin to the feeling people get when they know they are about to die, and there's nothing they can do about it. You hear stories of people's true colors coming out. Declaring their undying love in their last few breaths, or confessing their deepest, darkest secret that they don't want to take to the grave.

The wedding feels like the end. I'm hurling toward it, getting closer and closer and now, my true colors are showing.

I'm Rory Carter and I do bad things.
I *like* doing bad things.
I bite back a smile as I slip on my bra and panties, then wrap a silk robe around myself. I'm striding toward the closet in an attempt to choose something that doesn't make me look like a Grade-A whore before Greta comes back, when there's a *thump, thump, thump* on the door.
It stops me in my tracks. It's heavy and off-beat.
I clear my throat and call, "Hello?"
No response. Heart skittering in my chest, I'm crossing the room to see who's there when the door bursts open and Alberto tumbles into the room.
I jump back in shock, pushing myself against the mirrored wall.
"What are you doing?" I snap.
He stumbles into the middle of the room, swaying as he stretches to his full height. "Good evening, *Signora* Visconti," he murmurs, dragging a leering eye over my body.
My gaze narrows. "You're drunk."
Very drunk. I watch him cautiously as he folds himself into the armchair in the corner of the room and looks up at me. He's been out all day at the Devil's Cove Gentleman's Club at a bridge tournament. And even if he could stand upright without swaying, I'd be able to tell he's half-cut by the sour whiskey stench he's brought into the room with him.
"Come and sit on my lap, baby." With a weird little grunt, he slaps his fat hand against his even fatter thigh.
I sneer at him, disgusted. "Absolutely not. Ask someone to bring you a coffee and an Advil."
Bitterness burns the back of my throat, and I resist the urge to throw a damn lamp at his head. It's been almost a week since he shoved me down the stairs, and even though the pain in my ribs has settled down to a dull ache, the anger I feel when I see him still burns bright. I've managed to avoid him for the most part, but that doesn't mean my mind hasn't been constantly racing with ways to get my revenge.
Perhaps this time, it won't be so petty.
"Sit on my lap, Aurora," he growls again. "I want to feel that tight ass against my cock." He lowers his tone, licking his already-wet lips. "I can't wait to feel what that tight pussy feels like, too."
A shiver runs down my spine and settles in a pool of disgust. Heat burning my cheeks, I try to ignore him. Ignore bullies and they'll eventually get bored, right? Hopefully, that playground

advice can be applied to overweight mafia men with a God complex.

But as I sit in front of the vanity and start applying my makeup, I can see him still leering at me in the reflection of the mirror.

"I can't believe in one week and one day, I'm going to be fucking a virgin." He rearranges the fabric at the front of his slacks, chuckling darkly. "At my ripe old age. Tell me, Aurora. Is that ass unclaimed, too?"

Heat flames my cheeks, but I still don't reply. Instead, I dab on my foundation with a sponge, going over the faint cut on my eye socket a few more times. Now, it's barely visible under a thick layer of makeup.

"Hmm. You know..." The armchair creaks as he shifts his weight forward. "I could fuck you in the ass and you'd still be a virgin, right?" I freeze for a second, my eyes widening at my own reflection. "Perhaps I'll do that tonight to give you a little taster of what married life is like."

"Get stuffed," I hiss. The venom pours out of my mouth before I can stop it. I cringe at how loud my words are, but for once, I don't wish I could take them back. I'm too angry. My temples are thumping and my skin is blistering. "If you come near me, I'll kick you so hard in the groin that your kids won't be able to have kids."

The silence is deafening. I suck in a shaky breath and force myself to hold my ground. Not brave enough to look at Alberto in the mirror, I drop my gaze to my makeup bag and clench my fists over the silk of my robe.

But I'm not done. I've opened the floodgates and more venom decides to pour through.

"Anyway, maybe I won't hang around to find out what married life is like. I overheard you talking to the lawyer about changing our contract. What are you planning, Alberto? Because if you're going to play me regardless of what I give you, I'm not marrying you, and I'm *certainly* not going to have sex with you."

Now, I dare myself to look at him. Despite his unsteady gaze, he's glaring back at me. With one loud *huff*, he heaves himself off the armchair and crosses the room. *Christ.* He's quicker than I thought he'd be, and when he clamps his hand around the nape of my neck and jerks my chin up to face him, I realize I'd forgotten how strong he is.

Even for a drunk, old man.

"You've been snooping," he leers, his grip forcing me to arch my back and meet his gaze. "You'll do well to learn to mind your fucking business, Aurora. Otherwise, this marriage is going to be a lot more painful for you than you can even imagine."

"Tell me," I rasp, feeling the skin around my throat stretch.

"You really want to know?" he spits.

I manage a nod.

A sinister, lop-sided smile stretches across his wrinkled lips. From my upside down view, it's demonic. "I've added a clause to your contract that states our agreement is null and void the moment you aren't a virgin anymore."

I blink. A heavy thump beats in my chest. "But if I have sex with you, I'll no longer be a virgin..."

The realization trails off, lingering in the thick air between us. His laugh is slow and syrupy, and I feel it churn in my stomach.

"Now you get it," he purrs.

Fueled by rage, I attempt to rip myself away from his grasp, but he yanks me backward and I go flying over the back of the chair and come crashing down on the floor. The dressing room spins in shades of white, and then suddenly, Alberto is on top of me, his heavy stomach pressing against mine.

Oh, swan. Now I'm in trouble. I open my mouth to scream, hoping that even if Vittoria or Leonardo hear me, then at least *someone* might come and help. But his hot, sweaty hand clamps over my jaw before I can utter a sound.

"You really think that contract meant jack shit, anyway? The Devil's Preserve isn't even my land, you stupid bitch."

Feeling my body still underneath him, a sly, satisfied grin crosses his face. "It's Devil's Dip. Angelo's territory."

An awful feeling swirls in the pit of my stomach, making me want to throw up. *How could I have missed this?* The forest is Devil's Dip territory. Of course, I had no idea Alberto didn't have authority in Devil's Dip, because I didn't know Angelo existed. And even when I did, I didn't piece it together because the first thing I learned about him was that he'd gone straight. He barely *visits* the town, let alone has authority over it.

"I thought he handed it over to you," I whisper, not even caring how desperate my tone sounds.

"Even though he's not currently the capo, it's still his territory." He squeezes his thumbs against my jaw. "You have a lot to learn about the Cosa Nostra, silly bitch."

I can't draw a deep breath, and not just because Alberto's gut is crushing me. "And he gave you permission to build on it?"

"No," he huffs. "I asked him for planning permission, but he said no. I'm working on that."

"When?" I pant, a fresh wave of unease washing over me. "When did you ask?"

His eyes glitter with glee, and I can tell he can't wait to answer this question. "Two days before you signed the contract."

"So you knew," I rasp, fighting against his weight. "You already knew you weren't able to build on the land, and yet, you made me sign that darn contract anyway!"

And Angelo knew. He *knew* that I was marrying his disgusting uncle to stop him building on the land, and yet, he sat back and did nothing. My eyes sting; for some reason, Angelo's betrayal cuts deeper.

"Stop moving," Alberto hisses in my ear, lowering himself to pin my arms above my head. "What do you not understand? The contract means *nothing*. I'm Alberto Visconti, I don't need a fucking contract to claim you. Besides, I have a feeling Angelo is going to agree to hand over the Preserve to me very soon."

He has a feeling? What the hell does that mean?

"So you don't need me then," I spit, "If you're just going to mow it down anyway."

My heart splits in two at the thought of my poor father. *All of this, and I still couldn't save him.*

"No, I don't need you," he says simply. "But I want you, and that's all that matters." As I buck underneath him, he presses his hands harder against my wrists, my bones threatening to snap. "And if you try anything stupid, I'll kill you and your father anyway. And that," he adds, with a grin, "is about the only promise I'll keep."

My heart slams against my chest, and rage runs through me like an uncontrollable disease. My throat burns, bubbling with the need to scream. To say something I never thought I would. Never in this lifetime—

"*Go fuck yourself*," I hiss, tasting each drop of venom as it passes my teeth.

Alberto stills for a moment. And then, without warning, hot, searing pain shoots through my head, and white stars cloud my vision.

He punched me in the face.

Oh my god. He *punched* me.

My head spins, my lip gushing hot and red as my blood dribbles down my cheek. My ears are ringing so loudly, I barely hear the door creek open.

Alberto looks up from me and grunts. "What?"

Greta's tone is calm yet stern. "My apologies, *signore*. But I need to get *signorina* ready for dinner, if she's to be ready on time."

He pins me with one last hazy stare, then paws on the wall in an attempt to get himself upright. As he staggers out of the room, he treads on my hair, and even though my scalp screams, I barely feel it.

I barely feel Greta pulling me to my feet, or pushing me down in front of the vanity. Every part of my body, even my busted lip, feels numb.

She makes no move to break the silence hanging thick in the air. Instead, she picks up my makeup bag and rummages through it. When she finds what she's looking for, she holds it up so I can see it in the reflection of the mirror.

It's a lipstick.

"I think this shade will hide the cut nicely."

The air hangs still and stagnant over the dining table, and everything underneath it points to it being an excruciatingly long night. The pianist plays hauntingly slow classics. Cocktails are long and whiskey glasses remain untouched. Even the ocean, just a stone's throw beyond the French doors, is deathly silent.

I've been promoted again, back to the top of the table. Back to being within the wingspan of the dirty old crook I'm marrying, and in the firing line of his eldest son's sneer.

I ignore them both in favor of glaring at the gilded wallpaper behind Dante's head and sipping a Long Island Iced Tea through a straw. My lip throbs with its own pulse, but the shade of lipstick Greta chose for me matches the cut perfectly.

I suppose that solves the problem, then.

Dante whips a napkin off the table like it's done something to offend him.

"Where are Don and Amelia tonight?" His gaze shifts over the empty sits. "And everyone else, for that matter?"

Alberto's fist hits the table, narrowly missing an appetizer plate. "Hiding," he slurs, raising his whiskey to nobody in particular.

"Because nobody in this fucking family wants to spend time with their father."

Dante stills, narrowing his eyes on his father. "Are you—"

The swinging doors crash open, interrupting him.

"Sorry I'm late," Tor drawls, sauntering over to take his seat next to Dante. "I didn't get held up, I just didn't want to come." Dropping to his seat, he cocks a brow at the empty room. "Clearly, I wasn't the only one."

I'd smile at his crappy joke if it wouldn't make my lip bleed.

Dante smooths down his tie, still scowling at his father. "Should we wait?"

"And that's why you'll never make a good capo, son. You still rely on Daddy to answer all your questions," Alberto mutters darkly, taking a slug of whiskey.

Tor lets out a low whistle, but before Dante can bite back, the swing doors open again, carrying in a whole different flavor of tension.

"Am I interrupting something?" Angelo's voice brushes over my skin like a fever chill. I briefly close my eyes and wish that when I open them, I'll be anywhere but here.

"No, you're just in time to watch Dante get schooled by Big Al," Tor says, raising his glass over my head then sinking the liquor in one.

"There he is," Alberto booms. "My favorite nephew. You always show up, don't you kiddo? You'd never let me down."

Behind me, Angelo's footsteps come to a stop. I glance up at Alberto and realize he's staring up at Angelo, desperately trying to convey something to him with unsteady eyes.

Dante's gaze shifts between the two of them and darkens. "You're shitting me right? Angelo's never let you down? He literally turned his back on the Outfit. Left Devil's Dip completely uncovered. What the fuck do you mean he's never let you down?"

"Angelo sticks to his word, son. He said he was going straight, and he did it. You know what else? He doesn't ask my fucking permission for every little thing. He saw that kid, Max, was a snitch, and he handled it. Isn't that right, kiddo?"

Angelo remains deathly silent, like a predator assessing his prey. He pulls out the chair to my left, but Alberto holds his hand up.

"No. You'll sit right here tonight, Angelo." He thumps Dante's place setting. "It should have been you, Vicious," he grunts into the bottom of his glass. "It should have always been you."

"What's that supposed to mean?" Dante growls, rising to his feet.

"Dante—"

"Shut up, Tor. I want to hear what Father has to say."

All eyes fall on Alberto expectantly. Except mine. I focus on the table cloth and beg the ground to open and swallow me up.

"He should have been my underboss. And if he'd stuck around, that's exactly what I'd have offered him."

"I'm nobody's underboss," Angelo cuts in. His voice is so calm that it instantly chills the room.

Alberto pauses. Shifts his gaze to him. "You're right. You were born to be a leader. We'd have made a great team, you and me. We'd have created an even more powerful outfit." His lids droop, but he quickly catches himself and snaps them open again. "Never too late, kiddo. Especially if you think about my offer..."

"What offer?" Dante growls. When he doesn't get an answer, he rises to his feet. "Are you two making deals behind my back?" He turns to Tor. "Did you fucking know about this?"

"Don't ask me, I'm no better than a lackey these days," he mutters, yanking a cigarette carton out of his top pocket and strolling toward the patio. The glass windows rattle under the force of his slam.

The room falls quiet, the only noise coming from the piano. Dante's glare scorches the length of the table, before it lands back on his father.

"You're drunk," he sneers. "And I'm not sitting here listening to you spout shit all night. I've got better things to do, like run the entire organization while you drown yourself in liquor and women young enough to be your granddaughter."

As I slurp from my straw, my busted lip causes dribble to run down my chin. I catch it with the back of my hand. Dante's gaze falls to me, disgusted.

"Good luck, Aurora. The only thing worse than being born into this family is marrying into it."

With that, he storms out into the lobby, and a few seconds later, the front door slams.

Tor pokes his head in, flicking a cigarette butt in the direction of the beach. "And then there were four."

Great. I drain the rest of my cocktail and sweep the room for a server, but even they are hiding tonight. Despite Alberto's insistence that he take Dante's seat, Angelo drops into the chair next to me.

"Are you okay?" His cold knuckles graze over my thigh, instantly warming my lower core. But I force myself to ignore the feeling, ignore *him*, and hone in on the wallpaper. His gaze rests heavy on my cheek, but he doesn't say another word.

Out come the appetizers. Lemon garlic scallops served with tiny forks. We watch in silence as Alberto crams one into his mouth with his bare hands, and drops another on the floor. Angelo grabs the wrist of a passing server and pulls him low enough to mutter in his ear.

"Cut him off."

"But—"

"Cut him off, or I'll cut your fucking hand off."

"I'll see to it immediately, *signore*."

Tor flashes me an amused grin and settles into his seat, like he's getting ready for a show. I can feel what he feels, the tension brewing in the air, and it's going to spill over any moment. Although, while he wants a front row ticket for when it does, I want to run and hide.

Without warning, Alberto's heavy hand clamps down on my thigh, making me jolt. On the other side of me, Angelo stills, then releases a sharp hiss.

"Let's make a toast," Alberto booms. He's so drunk, he doesn't realize he's now sipping air from an empty glass. "To my soon-to-be-wife."

With a sarcastic smirk, Tor raises his glass. "To Aurora," he murmurs quietly. "The only chick stupid enough to marry a gross, old, drunkard to save a few acres of land."

I blink. *He knows?* How the hell does he know? I thought Dante was the only member of the Cove Clan who knew I wasn't marrying him for his money. Before I can think about asking, Alberto thumps his fist against the table again.

"Hurry up with the main course," he bellows in the direction of the kitchen. "I want to go and fuck my soon-to-be wife!"

My blood runs cold, but heat blisters in my cheeks. *Here we go.* I knew it was only a matter of time before Alberto turned his attention back to me. I close my eyes, bracing myself for the onslaught of humiliation.

"Go to bed, Alberto."

The menacing tone in Angelo's voice makes me pop a lid.

"What was that, kiddo?"

"Angelo, don't—"

But he's already rising to his feet, my tiny protest falling on deaf ears.

"Go to sleep." His knuckles crack in my ear. "Or I'll put you to sleep myself."

My fingers clench around the hemline of my dress. The tension is palpable now; thick and bitter, and I worry if I take a breath I'll choke on it.

I need to get out of here.

Slipping out of my chair, I make a beeline for the French doors. My name rings faintly in my ears, but I'm not sure who says it, nor do I care. I burst out onto the patio and turn left, breaking into a run down the beach. Somewhere along the way I lose my heels to the sand, but I don't stop. Not until I reach the wall of rocks that marks the end of the Cove.

Lungs on fire, I slump against them and close my eyes. The gentle waves lapping the rocks serve as a backdrop to my heavy breathing, and after a few long minutes, my breath matches the steady rhythm.

I can't do this. How can I paint a smile on my bruised, bloodied lips and continue with the plan to marry the man I despise most in the world, knowing it's all in vain? Knowing that all this time, he held no real power over me? Except of life and death, of course. Not just mine, but my father's.

What hurts more than knowing the contract never meant a thing is knowing Angelo knew it too. We shared secrets. Dark and twisted ones. I thought...

I dig my fingernails into my palms.

I thought he was different.

Betrayal beats in my chest. When I open my eyes, there's a large, dark silhouette walking down the shoreline toward me.

Great. I'd rather walk into the Pacific with bricks tied to my ankles than talk to Angelo Visconti right now. I gather up the hem of my dress and stomp back toward the house, giving him a wide berth. But as I pass, his hand shoots out and grabs my wrist.

"Stop, Rory."

"Get off me," I hiss. "The last person I want to see tonight is you."

Under the moonlight, his gaze flashes. "Yeah?"

"Yeah."

I try to yank my arm back, but his grip only tightens.

"You're not a very good liar." My aching bottom lip starts to tremble, worsening when Angelo slips his fingers under my chin. "Look at me." While his voice is firm, when I meet his gaze, his eyes are soft. They search mine under knitted brows.

"Tell me what's wrong."

"Why do you care?" I snap back, looking away.

He yanks me closer by my wrist, until my nose brushes against his hard chest. "Of course I care," he growls, "I think I've made that very fucking clear."

"Yeah, right. If you cared, you'd have told me you owned the Devil's Preserve when I told you it was the only reason I was marrying your disgusting uncle. But you've never cared. Not when you thought I was going to jump off that cliff, and not now, even when you know I'll be marrying him for no damn reason."

He stills. Silent rage oozing out of his pores. "You really think I didn't tell you because I don't care?"

"You saw me as nothing but a plaything, something to amuse you while you were back on the Coast. I bet it was exciting to you, knowing you could have your uncle's fiancee at the snap of your damn fingers."

"You're insane," he murmurs, gripping my jaw. "If you think I'm anything but crazy about you, Rory, then you're fucking insane."

"Then why didn't you tell me!" I cry.

His jaw locks. "What would you have done if I'd told you?"

I open my mouth to shoot out another bitter retort, but nothing comes. I pause for thought.

"I'd have left him."

"And then you and your father would have been killed." His strong forearm snakes around my waist, pulling me closer. The urge to drop my head against his chest and breathe in his warm scent is overwhelming, but the desire to punch him in the jaw is just as strong. "It's the Cosa Nostra, Rory. They play by their own rules. Alberto wanted you, so he took you. Any deal you struck with him was an illusion. Men like Alberto don't give, they only take, and whoever doesn't comply gets killed."

"You could stop him."

"I have. I rejected his planning permission request before I met you. He asked again yesterday, but I'll reject that too." His thumb brushes over my cheek and his voice softens. "I'll never give him the Preserve, you have my word."

"That's not what I meant."

The thickness in my voice makes Angelo still. We stare at each other for a few heavy beats, until the realization settles on the hard plans of his face.

"Stay," I croak.

By the exhale that escapes his lips, I know what he's going to say. My bones cringe at the mere thought of hearing it, and I know I can't face the pitying look he'll give me when he shoots me down.

It'll be a gentle rejection, delivered softly in a patronizing tone. I'd rather claw my eyeballs out than stay here while he tells me *no*.

Eyes stinging and my cheeks blistering from embarrassment, I twist out of his grasp and storm toward the house. *Christ*, it was a stupid idea. I shouldn't have even alluded to it. As if he'd give up his life in London and move back to a tiny town that haunts him so much, all because of me.

"Rory, wait—"

But I take off running, my feet pounding the sand as I head back to the Cove mansion. Nothing good waits for me there, but I'll take anything, *anything*, over being out here on the beach with Angelo.

Wheezing, I burst through the patio doors and into the dining room, where Tor sits alone, swirling whiskey round a glass. He looks tired as he glances up at me with dark eyes.

"Your keeper is looking for you."

On cue, Alberto's booming voice floats through the swinging doors, wrapped around my name.

"Rather you than me," Tor mutters, taking a swig.

Behind me, heavy footsteps sound against the patio. Without looking back, I push through the doors and into the foyer. Two worried-looking servers linger at the bottom of the stairs, staring up to the first-floor landing.

"Maybe we should sedate him," one mutters.

"Or hope he falls down the stairs and breaks his neck," the other sniggers back.

When they spot me, they freeze, then scurry into the shadows, whispering between themselves.

Still panting from my run, I force myself to look up the stairs and spot Alberto at the top of them. Naked. All of his glory covered only by his enormous gut swooping down to the top of his thighs.

"There you are," he leers, beckoning me up the stairs with a curled finger "My bedroom. *Now*."

My heart comes to a skidding stop. Okay, this was a *really* bad idea. I spin around to head back into the dining room, but Angelo darkens the doorway.

He glares at me, hands tucked into his pockets. "Stop running from me, Rory."

"I—"

"Aurora!" Alberto's voice is louder this time, laced with impatience. "Don't keep me waiting."

Confused, Angelo looks up to the top of the stairs, his stare turning knife-like as his naked uncle staggers across the landing and into his bedroom. "Don't move."

I tilt my head up in defiance. "You don't get to tell me what to do."

His nostrils flare. "I'm not playing games. You're not going up there."

"I don't have a choice."

"Because I'm not giving you one."

My breathing shakes, but I'm determined to hold my ground. I glance up the stairs, at Alberto's closed door. I know once I cross the threshold, it won't be long until his fat, sweaty body is writhing on top of me.

My fingernails carve half-moons into my palms. "Are you staying?"

"Rory—"

"Are you staying?" I repeat, louder this time. "Are you going to stay on the Coast, take over Devil's Dip and protect me, my father, and the Preserve from your uncle? Or are you going to leave me to fight this on my own?"

His silence is deafening. As I look up at him, he runs his tongue over his teeth, breathing heavy.

"Use your words, Angelo," I spit at him, mimicking what he often says to me.

"You know I can't."

My eyes flutter shut and I feel like I've been punched in the gut. But I don't break down. I'm too bitter and spiteful for that. Instead, the urge for revenge licks at the walls of my stomach, and I want him to feel even just a fraction of the pain I'm feeling.

I take one step up the stairs. "Before dinner, he told me he wanted to do anal tonight. I guess that's what's waiting for me on the other side of that door." I take another step. "I'll let him claim my ass, and even my pussy, if that's what it takes." Another step. "I'll moan his name, just like I moaned yours. But unlike you, he'll get to put his hands all over my body. *Wherever he wants.*" The thought makes the backs of my eyes prickle with tears, but I blink hard, and keep ascending the stairs slowly.

"Aurora."

The pure, unfiltered anger in Angelo's voice stops me in my tracks. I spin around to face him. He's standing on the bottom step, glaring at me, hands clenched at his sides.

"So help me God, if you take another step, I will not be responsible for what I'll do."

"You're not a made man, anymore. Remember?" I spit. "You're just dressed like one."

His gaze blisters my back as I walk up the stairs and slip into the bedroom. Plunged into darkness, I press my back against the cold door and breathe.

He let me go.

Of course he did. He's no better than them—he told me that himself at his parents' memorial service. I'm as disposable to him as I am to his uncle.

Angelo Visconti isn't a knight in shining armor, and I was foolish to think otherwise.

Steadying my breathing, I drag my gaze upward and squint through the darkness. Thanks to the sliver of moonlight peeking through the curtains, I can just about make out Alberto's enormous silhouette on the bed. His breathing is heavy and even, and despite the sickness swirling in my stomach, I immediately feel lighter.

He got so drunk he passed out. *Thank god.* The only thing that would make this night any worse is having to follow through with—

Suddenly, the walls of the bedroom light up white and orange. A loud explosion follows a split-second later, violently shaking the window panes and threatening to burst my eardrums. It's instinctive to duck. I drop to the floor and wrap my arms over my head, but after a few deafening beats of silence, nothing else comes.

What on earth?

Shaking, I clamber to my feet and glance over at Alberto. Christ, he's so drunk he didn't even flinch at the explosion, and for a moment I wonder if he's actually dead. But then the snoring starts again, and I turn my attention back to the window. Behind the curtain, the sliver of moonlight has been replaced with a flickering orange glow.

A sickly feeling settles on my skin. I cross the room and pull back the curtain.

My eyes fall to the front drive below.

There's fire. Lots of it. Charred gravel and black, billowing smoke, too. I blink, my eyes adjusting to figure out what I'm looking at, and when I realize, my heart stops.

Alberto's Rolls Royce is on fire. Angry flames escape from the windows and windshield, licking the doors and roof. And just a few feet away, a dark figure looms.

Angelo. He's looking up at me, expressionless.

I swallow the thick lump in my throat, not daring to breathe. Angelo Visconti isn't a knight in shining armor, he's a monster in an Armani suit.

CHAPTER
Twenty-Seven

Rory

THE GRANDFATHER CLOCK STRIKES twelve, its chimes momentarily interrupting the silence of the suite.

Amelia sits in the armchair opposite me, spine rigid and staring out to the terrace with a blank expression. I know she's not watching anyone on the other side of the glass except her husband.

"If it was up to me, we'd be on the next flight to Colorado."

I stop picking at the stitching of the cushion on my lap. "What's in Colorado?"

"It's what's *not* in Colorado that matters." Her gaze shifts unwillingly to me. "Aurora, I sleep with a gun under my pillow every night. If Donatello is more than five minutes late to anything, I start to panic." Her fingers gently brush over her stomach. "All this constant stress—it's not good for me."

I stare at her stomach but say nothing. Instead, I twist around and look out onto the terrace. The Cove brothers stand in a tight circle, each with a stern expression on his face. Dante's talking, his lip curled as he spits venom. Next to him, Donatello is solemn, stroking his chin and occasionally nodding his head in agreement. Tor looks bored, like he'd rather be anywhere than a private suite at the top of the Visconti Grand Hotel with his family.

"Do you know what the worst part about all of this is?" Amelia asks. I turn back round to face her. "It's that this family has so many enemies, it'll be near-impossible to tell who did it."

Yeah, and the last place they'll look is their own family tree.

I grit my teeth and nod, before going back to picking at the cushion.

I'm tired. My lip hurts and my brain aches from not enough sleep and too much overthinking. Last night, I stood at the window in shock, until a whole host of guards burst into the bedroom and insisted on taking us to the Visconti Grand via an armored van. We've been here ever since, holed up in the Viscontis' version of a safe house—a suite with a hidden entrance and bullet-proof windows—while men in suits scurry about, piecing the puzzle together.

Alberto is in one of the bedrooms, sleeping off his hangover. My eyes keep darting nervously between the guards flanked outside his door and to Tor on the terrace. Perhaps Alberto would have been too drunk to remember the way Angelo spoke to him, but Tor wasn't. Surely, he'd know that Angelo is the only logical culprit—the mansion security is iron-clad; nobody is getting in or out of the grounds without the guards noticing. It would have to have been an inside job.

Anxiety jitters inside of me, even though I keep telling myself I don't care. Why should I? Angelo Visconti doesn't care about me, so I shouldn't care about him.

The sound of the terrace door sliding open makes me jump. I peek up over the back of the sofa, trying to keep my expression neutral.

Amelia leaps to her feet and comes to a stop beside Donatello. He wraps an arm around her and kisses the top of her head.

"Well?" she snaps. "Did the guards see anything?"

Donatello glances at me. Swallows. "There was only one guard working the gate, and the perpetrator shot him dead on the way out."

Amelia stills. "And on the way in? Did the security cameras pick up anything on the way in?"

He shakes his head. "Uh, whoever did it ripped out the fuse box attached to the side of the house. It shut down the entire estate's electricity supply, including the cameras. It also means we can't recover any footage."

"Christ," she mutters, sinking down on the arm of the couch. "That means whoever it was knew the layout of the house."

"It was Angelo."

My heart comes to a skidding stop. Dante's words slice through the suite like a steak knife, and everyone turns to face him. He's glaring right at me, and I feel my pulse tick, tick, ticking in my throat.

Oh, swan. Here we go.

"Angelo?" Amelia cries. "Why on earth would Angelo do something like this?"

"He was the only other person at the house last night. He and father were being very secretive about a new business deal. I reckon, after I left, negotiations went sour and the old Vicious Visconti came out of the woodwork." He pops his knuckles, gaze darkening on me. "Once an asshole, always an asshole. No matter how much tax you pay."

"Shut up, Dante." Tor turns and pins him with an annoyed glare. "We've been over this. It wasn't Angelo, because we left the house and went into town together."

The shells of my ears burn. *Why is Tor covering for him?*

"Any proof of that?"

Tor steps forward, jutting his jaw. "Are you saying I'm lying?"

"I'm saying you'd cover for him to stay on his brother's good side." His glare morphs into a sneer. "You're so far up Rafe's ass you can see his fucking tonsils."

"If you don't believe me, ask Aurora. She came with us."

I blink. *What?*

Everyone's eyes turn to me, and my face blushes under all the attention.

"Well?" Dante growls. "Did you?"

I'm frozen to the couch, my gaze shifting between Dante's glower and Tor's piercing stare. I have no reason to lie for Angelo anymore, but my answer slips through my mouth like a natural instinct.

"Yes."

"See," Tor snaps, without missing a beat. "It seems like you want everyone to believe it's Angelo to stop everyone pointing the finger at you."

Thick tension stretches out between them. It's Donatello who punctures it. "What's that supposed to mean?"

"Last night, father told Dante he's a shit underboss. Said he'd rather work with Angelo, and of course Dante, being the little bitch that he is, stormed out of the house. Less than an hour later, Father's Rolls was on fire. You do the math," Tor spits.

All eyes fall on Dante.

Donatello's gaze darkens. "Is that true?"

"If you think for a second—"

Dante's protest is cut short by a small cough by the front door. Everyone turns to look at the guard hovering in the entryway, hands clasped in front of him.

"My apologies for interrupting, but Raphael and Angelo are here."

My blood turns to ice. *What the hell is he doing here?* After last night, I thought he'd be on the next flight back to London, or at least have the common sense to lie low for a little while. But he doesn't. Instead, he strolls into the suite with his brother by his side, indifference carved onto his features.

He comes to a stop behind the sofa, casting a dark shadow over me. The hairs on the back of my neck stand up and my skin crackles with electricity, like it always does when he's near.

I grit my teeth and stare at the cushion on my lap, trying my best to ignore the butterflies in my stomach.

"Well, isn't this the most delightful family gathering," Rafe drawls, perching on the sofa armrest. "I'm a little offended that I didn't get an invite."

"I thought you were back in Vegas?" Tor says.

The diamonds in Rafe's watch glitter in my peripheral vision as he stretches out his arms. "The wonders of modern air travel, *cugino*."

"What are you doing here?" Dante growls. Behind me, I feel Angelo shift, the atmosphere shifting with him.

"Now, now, Dante. You might want to adjust your tone, especially since I know who carried out that little act of vandalism last night."

My breathing shallows.

Amelia whips around to face Rafe. "You do?"

"Someone called the hotline to confess. I traced the call back to your pool cleaner. I don't know what Big Al did to offend him, but if I had to sift his pubic hair out of the pool every other day, I'd probably blow up his Rolls too."

Silence.

"Emilio did this?" Suspicion laces Dante's voice.

"Apparently so."

"I want to hear the call."

"Nice try, *cugino*. Hell will freeze over before I give you access to Sinners Anonymous."

My heart is beating wildly, and with every heavy pause in the conversation, I panic that everyone can hear it slamming against my chest.

"Donatello, Tor. I need to speak with both of you outside."

I glance up just in time to catch Dante's blistering glare, before the Cove Clan brothers slink back out onto the terrace.

"Amelia, be a doll and make us some coffee."

Amelia glances up at Rafe uncomfortably, but she rises from the sofa and disappears into the kitchen without another word.

I feel Rafe's gaze scorch my cheek. When I force myself to look up at him, he pins me with a dazzling smile, one that doesn't match the dark storm in his eyes.

"You're proving to be trouble, girl."

His voice is equal parts calm and sinister and sends a shiver down my spine. It's a threat, one delivered with a smile, and it makes me realize that underneath the charm and the heart-breaker good looks, Raphael Visconti is *terrifying*.

"Shut up, Rafe." Angelo's hands clamp down on my shoulders. They are warm and strong and immediately, my eyes flutter shut under his touch. *Damn it.* "Rory, we're leaving."

I pop a lid and twist around to look up at Angelo. I wish I hadn't. The same fire from last night rages in his eyes; a cocktail of turbulent rage. For a moment, my heart flutters at his words. "We are?"

"It's Saturday. I'm taking you to see your father."

I blink. Then with a new-found annoyance, I wrestle out of his grip and rise to my feet. "I'm not going anywhere with you," I spit. "You could have killed me last night." *And you told me what I didn't want to hear.*

"I *wanted* to kill you last night," he growls back, without missing a beat. "I want to fucking kill you today, too." The way his eyes drop to my lips belies the venom of his words. "Get your coat. Don't make me tell you twice."

My gaze flicks to Rafe, who's watching the exchange in amusement.

"I can't just *leave.*" I gesture to the terrace, where Dante, Tor, and Donatello are in a heated conversation. "Don't you think you've done enough damage for one weekend?"

"Then don't make me do any more. We're leaving. *Now.*"

We glare at each other. I'm torn between standing my ground or picking up my coat off the back of the sofa. I wish I could say it's just because I want to see my father, but I know, deep down, it's because I'm fearful of what Angelo will do. I can see it in his eyes—he's crazed, dishing out revenge like it's candy, and I can't give Alberto any more reasons to be angry at me.

Jutting out my jaw, I snatch up my coat and spin around, coming face-to-face with Amelia. She hovers in the kitchen doorway, clutching four mugs of coffee in her hands.

"I'm going to see my father," I say breathlessly, avoiding her suspicious stare. "Please relay that to Alberto when he wakes up." I ignore Rafe's smirk and stomp toward the front door, Angelo hot on my heels.

We ride the elevator in blistering silence, and by the time I slide into the passenger seat of his car, I can feel hot, angry tears prickling the backs of my eyelids. They won't fall because I refuse to let them. I *never* let them. Angelo doesn't get to have this hold on me—not if he's not going to help. Not if he won't stay and fight for me.

"I stopped you from having to fuck him." The rage blisters off Angelo like a furnace. His knuckles are white around the steering wheel and he's driving his Aston Martin like he stole it.

"What does it matter, I'll have to eventually."

He slams his fist against the dashboard, making me flinch. "Sure, I guess it doesn't matter then. Wouldn't be the first fucking time you whored yourself out, anyway."

My blood runs cold, and for a moment, my heart forgets to beat. "What?"

"You heard me," he growls, eyes trained on the road ahead. We cross into Devil's Dip and he picks up speed, weaving in and out of traffic to the tune of angry car horns. "You think I don't know you fucked half the guys at Devil's Coast Academy? I didn't believe it at first, but now seeing how quickly you went up those stairs last night, I don't doubt it for a second."

Squeezing my eyes shut, I draw in a shaky breath. "What should I have done instead, Angelo? Left with you?"

"Yes."

"For what? To bare my ass to you? Treat you to a show of me touching myself?" I thump my head against the window and grit my teeth. "And then what? Go back to Alberto and face an even bigger beating?"

The car skids to a sudden halt, the tires screeching against the slick road. I lurch forward, the seat belt cutting into my neck. When I whip around to ask Angelo what the hell he's playing at, he's pinning me with a dangerous glare.

"Say that again."

The ice in his tone forms a lump in my throat. "What?"

His fists clench on his lap. "An even bigger beating. What does that mean?" His glare is molten, so hot I cower again the door to get away from him. "What does Alberto do to you, Rory?" He speaks slowly, like he doesn't trust himself to say the words. "Tell me what he does to you."

My face grows hot. A few tense seconds pass, before I lick my thumb and run it over the tender spot under my eye. The thick layers of concealer feel greasy against my thumb pad. Then, I carefully wipe the back of my hand over my mouth, smearing my bottom lip. The action tugs on my wound, making me wince.

His gaze travels over my features, grazing over my black eye, and then landing on my busted lip. His silence is deafening. Suddenly, he lunges for the door and jumps out, and through the windshield, I watch him with bated breath as he storms down the road and stops. He interlocks his fingers at the back of his head and tilts his face up to the gray sky. By the way his shoulders move up and down I can tell he's breathing heavy.

Before I can think it through, I get out of the car and head toward him. As I approach, his voice slices through the wind, thick and gravely. "Get back in the car, Rory."

"Angelo—"

"Get back in the fucking car."

When I put a hand on his arm, he spins around and grabs my wrist. His eyes are burning with rage, and the intensity of his anger makes me want to spin on my heels and run. If I wasn't so frightened, I'd be annoyed.

Angelo Visconti doesn't have the right to be so angry.

His gaze falls to my mouth again, and suddenly, it softens. With his other hand, he runs a gentle thumb over my bottom lip, and I feel it in the bundle of nerve endings between my thighs.

"He did this to you," he murmurs, more to himself than me. "Why didn't you tell me, Rory?"

"Would it have made a difference?" I whisper. "Would it have made you stay?"

He clenches his jaw and turns his gaze upward. When it lands back on me, there's resolve in his eyes. "You're coming home with me."

My heart stutters. "Home?"

"To London. You and your father."

I shake my head, feeling breathless. "I can't."

"To wherever you want then. Anywhere but this fucking coast. New York? You seem like the kind of girl that likes New York."

"We can't leave the Coast, Angelo."

A venomous hiss escapes his lips as he slides his hand around the nape of my neck and grips me there. "All right, so you like nature. Christ, Rory. There's nature everywhere. I'll buy you land. I'll buy you a whole fucking island, if you want."

"You don't understand I can't leave the Preserve—"

"What's so special about Devil's Preserve?" he growls, angrier than I've ever seen him. "And don't you *dare* tell me it's the fucking eagles."

I close my eyes, blocking out Angelo's demanding stare. I suck in a deep breath and open them again. "Come, I'll show you."

CHAPTER
Twenty-Eight

Angelo

WE CROSS INTO THE mouth of Devil's Preserve in silence, but inside my head is chaos. Fury licks every inch of my skin, and it takes every ounce of willpower I have not to get back in the car, race back to Devil's Dip and put a bullet in Alberto's head, just like I did my father.

But I have to restrain myself, because my ruthless actions will have consequences. Now more than ever, I need to think less like Vicious Visconti and more like my brothers. Their rage burns slow like a candle, whereas mine is like a firework. My fuse has been lit but I can't explode, not yet.

Not without a plan.

The only reason I agreed to go into the forest with Rory is because I hope it'll cool me off a bit, just enough to form coherent thoughts. But I can't stop staring at her; stealing glances at that purple smudge underlining her eye, and the bloodied cut on her lip.

It makes me want to burn the entire fucking coast down.

"Stop!" Rory's dainty fist grips the front of my jacket.

I frown at her. "What?"

She's looking at me like I'm insane. "Seriously? You're about to walk straight into quicksand."

I'm distracted, and it takes me a few beats to realize what she's saying and follow her gaze. In front of me, there's a murky puddle of mud. It looks bad enough to destroy my shoes, but that's about it. "Huh?"

"Christ, did you not study geology at school? Quicksand. The mud is waterlogged, so if you step into it, it'll drag you under. There's a lake in the middle of the forest, and when you get closer to it, there's quite a few patches of quicksand. Be careful."

The way she's staring up at me so worried is fucking adorable. She lets go of my jacket and brushes her fingers over my clenched fist. Her hand is warm and delicate, and immediately, I open my hand and slide hers inside. Fuck the "no touching" rule. That went out the window the moment I saw her busted lip.

"All right, David Attenborough," I grumble, biting back a smirk. "Lead the way, then."

She does, snaking through the muddy trail, not caring that her bright white sneakers are now shit-brown, or that her jeans are filthy. I don't care either; all I can focus on is how good it feels to have her hand in mine. I haven't exactly stuck to the "no touching" rule, but to finally fucking touch her with intention, even if it's in the most juvenile way possible, feels incredible.

Christ. This girl has turned me into a twelve-year-old virgin.

Soon, the trees thin and we reach a lake. I rake my eyes over the water. "Whatever rare bird or fish or fucking insect you want to show me won't be enough to convince me to let you stay here."

"That's not why we're here," she says quietly. She tugs her hand back and reluctantly I let it go. She fishes her cell out of her purse and fires off a text.

I study her. "You're nervous."

Her eyes meet mine from under her thick lashes. "I've never brought a guy to meet my father before."

I suck in a lungful of air and release it as a small hiss. "Rory, I—"

"Please," she whispers. Annoyance flickers like a flame in my chest as she twists that fucking ring off her finger and slips it into her pocket. "Just wait."

Putting my hands in my slacks, I lean against a tree, looking out onto the lake. A few moments pass before Rory's cell buzzes. She checks the screen, lets out a shaky breath, and nods. "Let's go."

She leads the way to a dock halfway around the lake. There's a small hut on the end of it, and inside, I can make out two figures moving. As we draw nearer, a woman emerges from it and walks down the gangway to meet us. When she spots me, she slows to a stop and her face pales.

"*Signor* Visconti," she says slowly, eyes darting to Rory. "I wasn't expecting..."

"It's fine, Melissa. He's with me." Rory's tone is clipped. She brushes past her and adds, "Would you mind waiting here today?" Melissa's mouth opens and closes just as quick. She manages a nod.

I follow to the dock, falling in step with her. "Who's that?"

"One of my father's caregivers. She's nice enough and my dad loves her, but she was hired by Alberto so..."

Her sentence trails off and I nod. She doesn't need to explain anymore. But still, I didn't realize her father needed a caregiver.

At the door of the hut, she holds out her hand, stopping me from entering. Her eyes check the sky and she takes a deep breath, before plastering a dazzling smile on her face. She knocks on a wooden panel and says, "Hi, Dad!"

There's a grunt from inside the hut, then a man steps out. He's short and wearing cargo pants and a heavy lumber jacket. A pair of binoculars swings around his neck. He stretches his arms wide and brings Rory in for a big hug.

I hover, trying not to stare at him. He's...not what I expected. He's no spring chicken but he definitely doesn't look old enough to need an attendant. And physically, he seems fine. He spins to face me, his eyes thinning. "And who's this?"

"Dad, this is—"

"David," I say, sticking out my hand to shake his.

I can feel Rory's gaze boring into my cheek, but I ignore it. Her father is old enough to have lived under my father's reign over Devil's Dip, and he'll definitely know who I am. For some reason, I don't want to be tarnished with the same brush as the rest of the Viscontis.

For some reason, I feel the need to make a good impression. Which is why I turn on the charm and pretend I'm not a monster.

He drags his eyes over my tailored suit and Italian wool jacket and scowls. "You're way too old to be my daughter's boyfriend."

I laugh. *Yeah, if you think I'm old, you should see her real fucking boyfriend.*

"Dad!" Rory splutters, face turning an adorable shade of pink. "We're just friends. He's...in town visiting."

"Ah. A college friend?"

"Yes. David...uh, is in my aviation course."

I keep my smile frozen on my face but shift my gaze to Rory. *Her father thinks she's still studying to be a pilot?* Something cracks in my chest, something too foreign to put a name to.

Now, Rory's father brightens up. "Another pilot! Delightful! Well, I'm Chester, and it's a pleasure to meet you David. Welcome to the Devil's Preserve. Come," he directs as he strolls past me toward the edge of the dock, where a small boat bobs lazily in the water. "Let's go for a ride."

I get in first, helping Rory and her father into the boat after me. Chester goes to pick up the oars, but I take them from him. "I insist," I say.

He glances at his daughter and raises his eyebrows. "Quite the gentleman, isn't he?" Another fleeting look over my shoulders and chest. "But you're a very large man, I hope you don't sink the boat."

"Dad!" Rory laughs. She catches my eye and shakes her head, a sheepish grin on her face.

I row into the middle of the lake and slip the oars back into the oarlocks.

"Right, then," Chester murmurs, patting the large number of pockets dotted all over his jacket. "Where in the flamingo did I put the candy?"

I laugh. "You bird-curse too."

He grins, scooping out a fistful of boiled candies from his pocket and offering the pile to me. I take one, just to be polite. "Before my wife and I had Rory, I had an awful potty mouth. Swore like a sailor. Once she was born, my wife would clip me around the ear every time I cursed, and I soon learned to adapt my language to be more…child friendly." He nudges Rory with his elbow and shoots her a mischievous wink. "Educational, too."

Rory rests her head on his shoulder and slips her hand in his. "I think my first word was a bird-word."

"It was," Chester chuckles, kissing the top of her curls. "I told you it was bedtime, and you told me to "finch off.""

Rory meets my gaze, smiling shyly. I can't help but smile back at her like a stupid fool, something warm and soft snuffing the rage in my chest. I can't keep my eyes off her as she laughs and jokes with her father. As she rocks the boat in her haste to point out fish swimming past, and as she snatches her father's binoculars to get a better look at birds soaring overhead.

It's like she comes alive around her father. Like the woodland lights a spark deep within her. But the feeling in my chest is marred by something bitter, something I have no right to feel.

I wish I made her come alive like that.

I swallow the thought with my fourth boiled candy. It seems like bird puns and nature aren't the only things Rory inherited from her father, and if I eat one more peppermint humbug my teeth are gonna fall out of my head.

When it's time to row back to shore, I notice Rory grows quiet. It's me and her father doing all the talking now, while she curls up on his arm and stares through me. I help her out of the boat and whisper in her ear, "Are you okay?"

She nods, but doesn't look at me.

At the end of the dock, Melissa hovers awkwardly, still stealing sideways glances at me. I wonder what the fuck she's doing here and why Uncle Al hired her. She doesn't seem to be a nurse or whatever, and she's definitely not the other type of *caregiver* the Cosa Nostra tends to hire. If she was, she'd be a man with a radio in his ear and a Glock in his waistband, not a mousy woman in a beanie hat.

When we reach her, Chester glances up at the sky and claps his hands. "Looks like it's going to rain. Back to the cabin for tea and cookies?"

Something in the air shifts; I can feel it. Next to me, Rory stills, and she and Melissa exchange a look.

"Rory has lots of schoolwork to catch up on, Chester," Melissa says in a patronizing tone. "Maybe next time—"

"Tea and cookies would be great, Dad." Rory's voice is small but firm.

Melissa's eyebrows shoot up. "Uh, are you sure?"

Rory nods.

"Marvelous, then." Chester turns on his heel and stabs a finger through the trees. "To the cabin we go!"

Soggy leaves squelch underfoot. Up ahead, Chester whistles an old sea-shanty, and next to me, thick puffs of condensation leave Rory's lips to a labored beat.

"What's wrong?" I murmur, bending down so my lips meet her ear.

She shakes her head. "You'll see."

I brush my knuckles against hers, then, remembering I don't give a fuck about the *no touching* rule anymore, I grip her hand, hard. It's cold and shaky and I wish I could get her the fuck out of here and away from whatever she's afraid of.

After a few minutes of walking, the muddy path opens up to a stone driveway. At the bottom of it, a large log cabin spills out over the clearing, its sloped roof dusted in moss, and the windows letting out a warm amber glow. It's the type of joint Airbnb would list as "rustic" and "charming", and the three shiny cars parked out front look out of place.

Chester stands under the awning and rummages about for his keys. "I don't know why I bother locking up," he mutters, patting his pockets, "it's not like I have anything to steal."

Before he can find them, the door swings open and a woman appears in the entryway. There's another woman behind her too, both wearing nurse scrubs and friendly smiles.

"Why didn't you just knock, Chester? You know we're always here," the one at the front chimes. Her eyes then land on Rory and she falters.

"Rory," she says softly, stealing a glance at Melissa. "You came to the house."

"Of course she did," Chester says, strolling into the foyer. The other nurse helps him take off his jacket, then he sits on the bottom step and starts unlacing his boots. "It's Rory's house too, Lizzy! She's lived here her whole life. Born here, in fact. Right in front of the fireplace in the living room! Isn't that right, sweetheart?"

Rory's still standing under the awning, shuffling her weight from foot to foot. "Yes, Dad," she all but whispers.

Chester kicks off a boot and looks up at her. His smile morphs into a scowl.

"Are you lost?"

Instinctively, I look over my shoulder, the harshness in his tone making me reach for a gun I'm not carrying. There's no one there. When I turn back around, I realize he's talking to Rory.

Melissa steps between them. "Chester, it's Rory. Your daughter." She puts a hand on the banister and crouches down. "She's come to visit, remember?"

Chester's eyes dart between all of us, frantic and scared. "I don't have a daughter." He struggles to his feet, a frailness to him I didn't see in the woods. "Get out! Leave!" Melissa reaches for his shoulder but he bats her off. "I'll call the police!" he yells, voice getting louder and more strained. "Go away!"

Melissa looks up with sorrow in her eyes. "Rory, you should probably—"

But before Melissa can finish her sentence, Rory spins on her heel and takes off running, slipping out of my reach. She disappears between the trees and without hesitating, I break into a run too, following after her. I catch up within seconds but fall back to a light jog, giving her space to calm down. By the time she bursts out onto the road by the church, she's wheezing.

I rake a hand through my hair. *Fuck*. I don't know what I was expecting, but it wasn't that. She doubles over to catch her breath, but her breathing is only getting more labored.

"Rory, look at me." I grip her chin and tilt her face to mine. "Breathe."

"I-I can't—"

"You can." I run my thumb pad over her red cheek. "Just look at me and breathe."

Her watery gaze meets mine, working its way to my chest. She takes a deep breath, letting it out in a shaky exhale.

"Good girl," I murmur, stroking her face before curling my fingers around the base of her neck. "You're okay."

Her hand finds my wrist, and she wraps it over my watch strap and leans her face into my palm, her eyes fluttering shut. *Fuck*. I hate how such a simple movement floods my stomach with warmth, but at the same time, I'd give my left nut to have her do that again.

Once her breathing slows, she looks up at me through wet lashes.

"Environmental dementia. It's when a patient's long-term memory only functions in certain familiar environments. For my father, it's this forest. Walking around the woods or being on the lake, he's just my dad. But..." I feel her throat bob against my palm as she swallows. "The moment he leaves the Preserve, or even goes inside our own house, his long-term memory goes."

Her jaw grinds and she catches a sob before it forms.

"He doesn't recognize me outside of the forest, Angelo. That's why it can't be knocked down, and that's why we can't leave. What my father and I have, it doesn't exist outside of it."

CHAPTER
Twenty-Nine

Rory

An old-timey Christmas song trickles out of the car radio, even though it's only mid-November. Heat blasts from the vents on the dash, and the condensation on the window does little to cool my burning skin when I press up against it.

The tension in the car could be chipped at with an ice pick, and it feels like a survival instinct to breathe as shallowly as possible to stop myself choking on it. Angelo says nothing. Does nothing, except drive too fast and breathe too heavy.

I wonder if he can hear my heart slamming against my chest, or the nervous chatter of my teeth. I wonder if he cares. Because while I'm uncomfortable in the most maddening of ways, having been stripped naked and my vulnerability carved onto every inch of my flesh for all to see, he has said *nothing*.

Not when I told him the truth. Not when the tears finally came. Not when I insisted on going back to Devil's Cove. When I walked back to the car on unsteady legs, I expected to feel his tight grip on my wrist, pulling me back, but it never came. And now, my stomach is growing heavy with every mile closer we get to Alberto's house.

As the gates of the mansion come into view, I squeeze my eyes shut. I pop them open again when there's a loud screech, and the safety belt cuts deep into my neck.

"What the hell?" I choke out, palming the dashboard.

Angelo is silent, a thousand-yard stare on his face. Thick tension rolls off him, sucking what's left of the air in the small space. His fists tighten on the steering wheel, then he releases it and drags a knuckle over his beard.

"You're not going back there." His tone is matter-of-fact, a stark contrast to the rage blistering off him like freshly stoked flames. "Not a chance in hell."

The smallest, most hopeful part of my heart collapses in relief. *Thank god.*

But then I take a deep breath and glance up at the mansion behind the gates. A colonial cage in all of its sick, twisted glory. It's a prison, but if I don't willingly walk through the door today and lock myself behind its bars, I'll only make it worse for myself and my father. "Angelo I—"

"Not another word." The sharpness of his tone slices my protest in half. One-handed, he spins the wheel into a full-lock, the car roughly mounting the verge, until we're facing the way we came.

"Stop, Angelo." My hand shoots out to grip his bicep, and I feel it flex under my touch. "*Please.*" Now, it's my voice that's the most vulnerable part of me. "You're being selfish."

His jaw tightens. A small shake of his head. When his gaze clashes with mine, my breathing staggers from its violence. "If you think I'm letting you go back there and be man-handled by that drunken cunt, you must be smoking crack."

His glare burns against my cut lip, and instinctively, I clamp my top lip over it. Irritation sparks in my chest. I'm suddenly reminded that Angelo Visconti doesn't *get* to be demanding. Not if he's going to whip up a storm and leave me here in the debris. I tilt my chin up. "Are you going to stay?"

His eyes flash. A beat passes. "I'm going to get you out of this."

"That's not what I asked."

His tongue runs over his perfect teeth, each silent second another bullet wound in my pride. With a bitter huff of embarrassment, I reach for the door handle. This time, his tight grip comes. Iron-like and unrelenting, a handcuff around my wrist.

"You heard what I said. You're not going back there."

My skin burns as I twist my wrist in his grip. "Let me *go*. You're only going to make it worse for me." He doesn't move. I shoot a glare at him, baring my teeth. "You're not thinking straight."

"Yeah, you seem to have that effect on me."

My eyes flutter shut, but I refuse to buckle under the weight of his half-assed compliment. "If I don't go back there, what do you think Alberto will do to me then?" I raise an eyebrow and wait for an answer. All I get is a snarl and a nostril flare. "You're thinking like a thug, not caring about the consequences."

His shoulders lower a fraction and I know I have him.

"I need a plan," he mutters darkly, eyes darting out of the windshield. "I need to bide my time."

It seems like he's talking more to himself than me, but I answer anyway. "Exactly," I whisper back. "Letting me go will bide your time." His eyes narrow on me, but before he can shoot me down, I say, "Think like a businessman, not a thug."

He falls silent. Swallows. Then gives the tiniest shake of his head, before rolling his eyes up to the roof of the car. "I must be mad," he sighs. "Utterly fucking mad." When his gaze shifts back to me, something dark and determined swirls among the emerald green. "Open the glove box."

With shaky hands, I open it and a silver gun glints back up at me. Angelo lunges over and grabs it, placing it between us on the central console.

"Come here."

I look back at him, confused. The car is tiny and there's nowhere else to go. Impatience flickers over his features, and with a barely audible hiss, he unclips my seat belt and tugs me onto his lap in one, swift motion. The movement is like silk, but it grates over my skin, rough as sandpaper, making me feel raw and *alive*. My heartbeat stops, and instead, I can only feel his thumping against my spine. He's hard and warm and the way his masculinity surrounds me like a death hug makes me feel delirious.

His fingers graze my hip, lighting my nerve endings on fire. His breath skitters over my throat. A few beats pass before he picks up the gun again and lets the magazine land on the passenger seat with a dull thud.

"If I can't protect you, I'll teach you to protect yourself," he rasps. With his chin resting heavy on my shoulder, he wraps my right hand around the gun, pressing my fingers into the ridges. "Dominant hand first," he says, lips brushing my neck. His palm grazes my thigh as he reaches for my other hand and lifts it to hold the butt of the gun. "Support the weight of it with the other."

His hands leave mine and trail a gentle path up my arms and land just beneath my breasts. My nipples tighten, and I fight the urge to grab his hand and slip it inside my bra cup. Instead, I white-knuckle the grip of the gun and fall back until I'm leaning flush against him, my head against his chest, my ass pressing against his crotch.

His heartbeat thumps a little louder. Something stirs in his slacks. *Christ.* Nothing but heavy breathing and tension fill the car and although I feel like I might die, I've never been more alive. His hands tighten around my ribs. Lips brush against my neck. "How does it feel?"

I don't know whether he's talking about the gun or his cock, now straining to slip between my ass cheeks.

I swallow. "Big."

He huffs out a laugh against the nape of my neck, raising goosebumps on my skin. Dropping his hands a few inches until they meet my hips, he pulls me closer to his body, rubbing me slowly up the length of him. The friction sparks like a live wire. "What about now?" he murmurs, voice dropping an octave.

I respond by arching my back and grinding against him. His moan is guttural and the way it vibrates against my neck sends my head spinning. I drop the gun into my lap and close my eyes, drinking in every last drop of this delicious moment.

I feel safe, warm. *Excited.*

Until the realization hits me with the speed of a freight train: *It should have been you.*

It should have been Angelo's door I ran to when I heard the Devil's Preserve was going to be knocked down. I should have sunk to my knees on his doorstep; should have signed my name in blood at the bottom of his contract. But some twisted turn of fate meant he was an ocean away, and I was left to make an empty deal with a man who makes my blood curdle.

It should have been *him.* Sure, it would have been a twisted start to our story, but I know, simply by the way he makes my body sing, it would have had a happy ending.

I pop a lid and draw a deep, shaky breath. Nausea flips my stomach. Behind me, Angelo stills. "Not too late, Magpie," he murmurs darkly. "I can take you back to Devil's Dip right now." His teeth scrape the shell of my ear. "You'd look good in my bed."

My moan leaves my mouth like melted butter. *In another life.* But I'm living in this one, and in this one, I need to save myself and my father. Grinding my teeth together like it'll help me think straight, I pick up the gun and balance it in my hands. "Why did you give me this?"

"If he so much as touches a hair on your head, you shoot him. You run. And then you call me. Understood?"

I nod.

"I'll put my number in your cell." When I don't answer, he strokes his thumb over my stomach and says softly, "Rory."

Something in the way he says my name pulls me to look at him. I twist around, meeting his dark gaze. It flickers with something I don't recognize.

"I will get you out of this. I just need to have a plan in place. Do you trust me?"

I chew on my wounded lip. With every second of silence that passes, anger brews behind his eyes. They study me intently, and it feels like the tiniest spark would make all of the tension between us explode.

But I'm not thinking about whether I trust him or not. I'm wondering why I'm so sure that I do.

I trust him. He has all of my sins and not a single one of them has slipped through his lips. But trusting him to get me out of this doomed deal with Alberto is akin to me jumping off the edge of the cliff and believing he'll be at the bottom to catch me.

When really, I know it'd be safer not to jump at all.

I offer a small nod.

"No. Use your words. I need to hear you say it."

My gaze falls to his mouth. Hope inflates my chest, and I pray to God that it's not false. "I trust you," I whisper.

His eyes flutter shut but if I'd blinked, I'd have missed it. "Rory?" His thumb pad carves a trail over my jawline. It stops at the corner of my mouth, but I turn my head to catch it between my lips. He lets out a soft moan, watching me, eyes half-lidded with lust, as I slowly lick it.

"Yes?"

Danger sparking in his eyes, he pushes his thumb further into my mouth, and with wetness pooling between my thighs, I open my mouth wider to take him all in.

"Out of all my sins, you're my favorite."

CHAPTER
Thirty

Rory

THE WHITE SUN IS low in the sky, scorching through the bedroom window and burning my retinas through my eyelids. It wakes me up. I throw the duvet over my head and stretch out all my limbs.

It's amazing how soundly I slept with a loaded gun under my pillow. Or, perhaps my good night's sleep was because it was the first time in *months* that I haven't had Alberto's fat, sweaty body pinning me in.

When I arrived back at the mansion last night, Angelo's gun buried under the candy wrappers in my purse, Alberto was waiting for me in the hallway. Every muscle in my back tensed, but to my surprise, he wasn't angry. He was *sheepish*. The great mafia don, flushed with embarrassment, twisting his hands.

"You're a temptress, Aurora," he said. "It'd be best if you slept in the guest wing until the wedding day to help me avoid temptation, especially with all the shit I'm dealing with right now."

By "shit," he meant his poor Rolls Royce having its windows blown out. I'd bit my broken lip to suppress my relief. Thank *god*, because I didn't know if I'd be able to go another night staring at his gilded ceiling without putting a bullet in his head.

The chimes of the grandfather clock float under the doorway, and when I count eleven of them, I shoot upright in surprise. I've *slept until eleven a.m.?* Christ, I can't remember the last time I slept in, and it definitely wasn't in this house.

I jump up and head straight for the shower, a nervous energy bubbling in my gut. I have less than an hour until Sunday lunch; less than an hour until I get to see Angelo. I can't wait to hear what plan he came up with to get me out of here. It feels like the end is so close, I can taste it.

Late last night, I picked up a bunch of clothes from my dressing room so I didn't have to get changed in there with Greta today. I haven't seen her since she walked in on Alberto pinning me to the ground and did nothing except find me a shade of lipstick to match the damage he'd done.

I don't know what my revenge will be yet, but I do know that it won't be petty.

I let my hair dry naturally and pick up a velvet, green shift dress slung over the back of an armchair. Winter is coming, and I feel like it goes well with the frost on the windows and the fog hovering low over the grounds.

As I descend the stairs, I hear my name being called from the family room. Ice threads through my veins when I realize it's Amelia. There's *no way* she didn't hear mine and Angelo's argument from the kitchen of the suite yesterday. She's nice, but she's still a Visconti. I can't trust her to keep her mouth shut.

Heartbeat jumping, I poke my head around the door. I'm too surprised to force a fake smile, because she's sitting on the rug in front of the fireplace, a mountain of catalogs and mood boards fanned around her. The moment she looks up and greets me with a dazzling smile, I know I'm in the clear.

"Hi! Come in, I want to show you something."

I stroll over and sink to my knees beside her. She double-taps one of the mood boards with her long red fingernail. "What do you think?"

"It depends, what am I looking at?"

Her laugh tinkles. "This is what we're thinking for *Le Salon Prive* on Saturday."

My blank stare is met by a fleeting scowl. "The wedding reception, Aurora. It'll be at our French restaurant on the beach, remember? It's a beautiful space but I've been working with the wedding planner to make it *just* right." Her eyes dart to me. "You know, since you seem to miss every appointment we have with her." She points to the top corner. "White lilies and sweet peas for a pop of color?" Before I can answer, she lunges over and picks up another board. Rows of models with beautiful, flowing hair beam up at me. "Oh, and I've collected some hair and make-up ideas for us to think about. I love the gold eyeshadow, don't you? And what about the flower crown?"

The heat of the fire brushes up against my back. Amelia stares at me, wide-eyed and happy. But there's a flicker of desperation in her eyes, and suddenly, I realize I was wrong about her. She's not the innocent outsider that believes I'm marrying Alberto for true love. No, she's willfully ignorant. She knows exactly what's going on, and yet, she'd rather sit still and let me drown than get up and rock the boat.

My makeup isn't even that thick today; the ghost of my black eye is visible, and there's no way she can't see the wound on my naked lip. But she hasn't asked about the cuts and bruises, because she already knows how I got them.

She's no better than Greta.

She cocks her head. Raises a brow. My fingers twitch with the desire to *do bad things*. But instead, I choke down my bitterness and rise to my feet.

"Aurora?"

"Another time."

Without looking back, I stride out of the living room. I don't *care*. I don't care whether I've offended her, or whether she'll relay my lack of enthusiasm to Alberto.

I don't care and it's freeing.

I won't be here for much longer, anyway.

I breeze into the dining room feeling lighter. Today, the room is as winter-inspired as my dress. Frosted champagne flutes, sparkling silverware, and a runner with an embossed glitter trim grace the long table. The mood is surprisingly jovial; laughter carries through the room to a backdrop of plucky piano music, and servers weave between full seats to top off glasses. It's a stark contrast to the sinister hollowness of Friday night.

Immediately, I scan the dining room for Angelo, but he's not here yet. Well, that's fine, because neither is Tor or Amelia—she's too busy planning my non-existent wedding in the family room. Alberto's in his usual spot at the head of the table, holding a glass of whiskey and boring Donatello with an anecdote. Everyone seems to have forgotten about the explosion. I try to become one with the wallpaper and creep around to the far end of the dining room without Alberto spotting me, but I can't escape Dante's glare. It scorches the side of my cheek, following me like a laser as I take a seat next to Vittoria.

She looks up at me lazily. "What happened to your lip?"

"Your father beat the ever-living crap out of me. Thanks for noticing."

It slips off my tongue with ease. The truth tastes good. Her eyebrows shoot up and I raise a champagne flute to toast to her, before sinking it back in one. As the bubbles hit the back of my throat, I feel a familiar rush of adrenaline coast down my spine.

"Jesus, my father is *the worst*," she mutters to herself, before plucking out her cell and tapping out a text at breakneck speed. She's right, he is the worst, even to her. Being a side character in the Visconti family saga means I'm often left in dark corners of rooms, forgotten about. I've overheard several conversations that don't concern me, including that Alberto has struck a deal with his daughter, too. She was allowed to forgo attending the Devil's Dip Academy in favor of a public school, but only on the condition she...*entertains* potential future suitors of his choice. As his only daughter, it's important that she marries well, and he's starting the search young.

I sink a second glass of champagne. The buzz in my blood is pleasant, and it takes the sharp edge off the memories I have in this dining hall. It'd almost be a shame, *almost*, to never see the inside of it again.

Tor breezes in, a face like thunder, and for once, no giggling girl on his arm. Amelia follows in not long after, throwing me a wary glare before slipping into the seat next to her husband, who's grateful for the interruption. But I'm not looking at Amelia or Tor or even my obnoxious fiance at the top of the table. I'm looking at the empty seat right next to him.

My ears begin to burn, but I swallow the freshly formed panic. *Calm down, Rory. He's coming. Of course he's coming. It's still early and—*

Ding, ding, ding. Silver against crystal makes the pianist stop playing. My gaze shifts to Alberto, who's now on his feet, a champagne flute in one hand, a steak knife in the other. "What a wonderful turn out!" He booms, a plastic smile stretching his withered lips. "It brings me great joy when I can get most of the family in the room together. Now, let's eat!"

The pianist strikes a few cheery chords. I glance back toward Angelo's seat, as if, by some miracle, I've managed to miss his imposing frame the first time I looked.

"Wait." I blurt it out before I can stop myself. Halfway between sitting and standing, Alberto's eyes dart up to me. I swallow. "Uh, shouldn't we wait until all the guests are here?"

Silence. The kind that's so thick you can taste it. Someone coughs. Next to me, Vittoria sighs.

"He's not coming."

I look left. Tor. He's glaring at the wallpaper above Amelia's head. His nose stud glints as he tilts his chin up to drain the last of his whiskey.

My heart fissures but my face doesn't show it. "Who's not coming?" I say, as nonchalantly as the ache under my ribs will allow me to.

His gaze shifts to me. "Angelo. He's left town."

My ears ring. The fissures turn into fractures, threatening to crack my heart into pieces. I drop my gaze back to the empty plate in front of me before anyone can see how winded his words have made me. A syrupy chuckle comes from Alberto's direction. "That kid always comes and goes as he pleases. I'm sure he'll make another appearance around Christmas."

An icy hand claws at my throat, threatening to cut off my air supply. I'm itchy to find out how Tor knows, and *if it's true.*

He wouldn't leave me here. He promised. It can't be true.

Can it?

Wednesday. I'm being prodded and poked, like a cow, in the family room, and beyond the bay window, the sky is darker than my mood. The fire crackles. The wind roars. And my soul screams for Angelo's car to roll onto the circle drive on the other side of the glass.

Sunday evening I was numb but in denial. Monday, I was itchy. By Tuesday, I'd curled up in the bathroom, my back against the door, my finger hovering over the 'call' button on my burner cell. It took me forty-five minutes to work up the courage to press it, because the only thing worse than not knowing is finding out the truth.

Well, the truth came in the form of an automated voice on the other end of the line: *The number you have reached has been disconnected.*

Now it's Wednesday, and I'm angry. Bitter, burning rage floods through my veins, making my skin spark like a live wire. Making me grit my darn teeth every time the dressmaker pokes me with her needle, or when Greta pokes her head in to sneer at the sight of me in a wedding dress. It's the final fitting, and I want nothing more than to rip all the silk and lace off my body and throw it in the fire.

The door opens, and Tor appears. He casts an indifferent eye over my dress and leans against the frame. "You ready?"

I stare at him blankly. If there weren't five other people in this room fussing over me, I'd tell him to go to hell.

"As I'll ever be," I bite out through gritted teeth.

He frowns. "Not for the wedding, idiot. To see your father."

My heart hitches. "What? Now?"

He yawns. Checks his watch. "It's Wednesday. Won't be able to see him on Saturday, will you?"

Without another word, I step off the box and stagger across the room, kicking over the dressmaker's haberdashery box as I pass. "Yes," I breathe. "I'm ready, I'm ready."

I have enough wits to stay in the room long enough to be helped out of the dress. Then I bound up the stairs and throw on a hoodie, leggings, and sneakers. I hesitate for a moment, before reaching under my pillow and slipping the gun into my purse. I have a half-baked plan forming in my head, and my heart is beating in my throat at the mere thought of it. By the time I run out onto the drive, I'm out of breath.

Tor looks up at me with a mixture of amusement and disgust. Without a word, he opens the passenger door and rounds the car to slip into the driver's seat.

"Did Angelo ask you to take me?"

The engine purrs under my thighs. A beat passes.

"No."

I sink into the leather seat and let out an exasperated sigh. The tiny space in my heart reserved for hope is getting smaller and smaller by the second. It had inflated, just a fraction, when Tor appeared in the family room. Last time Angelo was away, he'd asked Tor to take me to my father's instead, and I thought maybe, *just maybe*, he'd done it again.

He eyes me sideways as the gates open. "I was just being nice."

I clench my jaw shut and glare out of the windshield. Of course, I'm happy I get to see my father, and I feel guilty that I'm so disappointed. The silence is heavy, punctuated only by Tor's fingers drumming on the steering wheel.

We slow to meet a red and he glances over at me again. "Ain't you got any candy for me today?"

I shake my head.

"Aw, come on. You always have something in that purse." He reaches over to the tote on my lap, and immediately, I snatch it out of his grasp. He scowls, then his gaze thins. "What's the matter, getting cold feet already?"

I don't reply.

"He's gone, Aurora. Forget about him."

"How do you know?"

"He told me so himself."

Unease trickles under the surface of my skin. No. I don't want to believe it. He wouldn't leave the Coast without telling me. But then again, his cell phone has been disconnected...

I need to see for myself.

"Take me to Angelo's house in Devil's Dip."

"Hell no," he snaps. The car speeds up and annoyance rolls off him in waves. "I already covered for him being gooey-eyed over you. I'm not getting involved in more of this mess. This is going to start a war."

"I'm asking you nicely."

"You can ask in all the ways you want, girl. Not going to happen. This isn't a normal family, Aurora. When a family member betrays you, it's not a case of crossing them off your Christmas card list, it's life or death. Loyalty is everything." His jaw flexes and he rakes a hand through his hair. "You have to choose a side and stick to it."

It doesn't feel like my hand that reaches into my purse and pulls out the gun. Doesn't feel like my thumb that flips off the safety catch, or my fingers that press the barrel against his temple. Doesn't sound like my voice either, when I choke out, "I *said*, take me to Devil's Dip." Desperation. It's crawling around my body like a nasty virus, making me do the unthinkable. A handful of days ago, I'd never even held a gun before, and now I'm using it as a threat. Maybe I *am* a bad girl.

It takes him a moment to realize what's happening. But it's clear from the dizzying speed with which the car mounts the pavement and he grabs the gun from my hand and presses it against my own head that it's not the first time he's been on the wrong end of a weapon.

His growl is guttural. His fist slams against the dash. I squeeze my eyes shut, the weight of my stupid actions settling around me like dust. "Are you fucking *crazy*?" he hisses. The barrel knocks against my temple. "I should fucking kill you for that. Where did you even get this thing?"

My bottom lip trembles. It doesn't go unnoticed, because Tor's barks melt into a mutter. "Don't think you're getting out of this by pulling that girly shit on me."

A few heavy moments pass, before he lets out a deep grunt and tosses the gun in the central console. "You're crazy," he mutters, before kicking the car into drive with a small shake of his head.

I breathe out all the stale air in my lungs. It takes me at least five minutes to work up the courage to interrupt the silence. "You already chose a side."

"What?"

"On Friday night. You knew it was Angelo and you covered for him. That means you chose a side."

His jaw works. Fingers start strumming on the steering wheel again, like he didn't have a gun against his head just a few minutes ago. "Everyone has moments of madness. I chose to sweep it under the carpet before this all blew up to something bigger."

"But Alberto's your father."

Darkness crosses his features. "Yeah, well. Big Al dragged me up. Angelo raised me. He's only a few years older than me, but he always had his shit together." He pauses. "Dante taught me how to shoot a pistol. How to beat up a man within an inch of his life but keep him lucid enough to talk. Made men shit. But Angelo? He taught me just *man* shit. How to tie a tie. How to sweet-talk girls." He smirks. "Drilled it into me not to fuck chicks without wrapping it up first."

Heat prickles my cheeks. Even now, in the middle of his disappearance and the ever-growing rage I have toward him, the thought of Angelo being a know-it-all on picking up women irks me. My fists wind into my sleeves, and I focus on the rain that's just started to fall on the windshield. "Has he really gone?" I whisper.

He swallows, avoiding my gaze. Nods.

"I need to see for myself."

With a heavy sigh, he slows the car. Rolls his head on his shoulders and then shakes it. "Fine," he mutters. "But if you hold a damn gun to my head ever again, I'll snap every single one of your fingers."

"Deal."

We drive in blistering silence; the only sounds are my heart thumping against my rib cage and the rain growing increasingly heavier on the windshield. I twist my ring around and around my finger, until the skin underneath it feels raw.

He promised.
I trust him.
He'll be there.

My breathing shallows as the house comes into view at the top of the hill. The sky is a smudge of gray behind it, and in front of it, building supplies lie littered on the forecourt. Tarpaulin sheets flap violently in the wind, and work trucks are parked haphazardly, their doors still open.

I strain against the seat belt and squint through the windshield to get a better look. Trucks aside, there are no cars. No Aston Martin, no Bugatti. Logic tells me Angelo wouldn't park his super cars outside in the pouring rain anyways, but the hope in my chest is shrinking.

As Tor kills the engine, I notice the garage door is open, and inside, I can make out the silhouette of a male working underneath the hood of a car. My pulse flutters, but it's fleeting. As he steps to the side and cranes his neck at us, I realize it's his brother, Gabe. Despite the freezing weather, he's shirtless. He pulls out an earphone and glares in our direction.

"He's not here, Aurora. Just go ahead with the wedding and we can forget any of this happened." Tor's voice is the softest I've ever heard it, and for some reason, it makes me even more angry. There's something I need to see, something that'll make me know for sure. Without another word, I leap out of the car, running through the icy rain around the side of the house. Droplets slither down my neck, and my curls turn slimy and stick to my forehead.

When I reach the hangar, my knees threaten to buckle underneath me.

It's empty.

His plane has gone.

He's gone.

My heart shatters into a thousand tiny pieces. My vision blurs behind the tears I've been holding back for so long, but now, I let them fall. Hot and fat, they roll down my cheeks in a mix of frustration and heartache, and I know, *I just know*, that now I've started, I won't be able to stop.

I'm as mad myself as I am at him. *I can't stay, Rory.* He'd warned me, more than once, that he'd leave. That he had no plans on being my knight-and-shining armor. But when someone is desperate and hopeful, they'll cling onto the things they want to hear. Like him promising he'll get me out of this. Like him asking me to trust him.

I guess he was right. Viscontis are cheaters and liars and I'd be foolish to believe anything they say.

Heavy footsteps come up behind me.

"He's isn't here." Gabe's gruff words physically hurt me.

"Well, where is he then?"

"No idea, probably London. He didn't say he was leaving."

I spin around, angry. "Your own brother didn't say goodbye?"

He huffs. "We're not exactly that type of family."

There's a hollow, dull ache under my breastbone, but there's something warmer in the pit of my stomach. It feels like an old friend, one that's dark, bitter, dangerous. The spark morphs into a flame, then spreads through my veins like wildfire.

I steel my jaw. Carve half-moons into my palms with my fingernails. Turning on my heel, I move to stomp back out into the rain, but Gabe sidesteps to stop me.

A tinge of fear colors my expression; he's as big and as imposing as his brothers, but doesn't have the same charm to take the edge off. And then there's that angry scar that carves a path down his face...

I swallow and wait, expectantly.

Water droplets roll down his muscular chest. He palms them away from his torso with a large paw.

"Our hotline is for sins committed, not sins you're thinking about committing."

His voice is dry, indifferent, but his words immediately make my cheeks flame.

"I-I don't understand?"

"You do." He takes a step forward, and instinctively, I take one back. My eyes dart over his shoulder for any sign of Tor, but he's nowhere to be seen.

I suck in a shaky breath. "You've been listening to my...?"

He taps the AirPod in his ear. "I listen to every single sin that comes through."

Oh, swan. We stare at each other, the insinuation hanging in the air like a storm cloud. He knows. Gabriel Visconti knows my deepest, darkest sin, and I'm all alone with him in an empty hangar.

I should beg him not to tell anyone, but I can't seem to make myself care. I don't have the energy. Instead, I drag the back of my hand over my wet cheeks and shrug.

"Okay."

This time, he lets me pass without stopping me, but then his hand shoots out, grabs my wrist, and spins me around.

His eyes are dark and dangerous, smoldering like a sea-green sun. "If Angelo doesn't come back, I expect another call."

My temples thump. *What?* How sick and twisted can this man be?

Behind me, Tor blasts his horn. Gabe looks over my shoulder, irritation crossing his features.

"And this time, I hope your sin won't be hypothetical."

With a lingering glare, he brushes past me and storms back into the rain. I watch him until he disappears around the side of the house. *Holy crow.* Nausea rolls in my stomach, and for a brief moment, I wonder if that short exchange was a fever dream.

Tor blasts his horn again, longer this time. With another glance back to the empty hangar, I swallow the lump in my throat, and run out into the rain.

CHAPTER
Thirty-One

Rory

FRIDAY NIGHT. TWO FLOORS below me, the basement hums with a good time. But up here, in the guest suite, it's silent. Deathly so.

I wrap my hands around the mug of hot cocoa and squeeze myself onto the windowsill. Rain streaks the glass, and on the other side of it, yellow headlamps come and go in a smeary blur as guests I've never met arrive at my bachelorette party.

This night was meticulously planned out on my five-year vision board, the one I made when I was eighteen and had yet to be corrupted. I'd cut out a gorgeous red satin dress from the pages of Vogue; stuck on Polaroids of all my friends I'd invite. But that's the thing about plans: they change.

I rest my forehead against the window as another car rolls onto the drive. Immediately, I recognize the obnoxiously loud voice escaping from it: Alberto. But I can hear that he's not alone. Using the sleeve of my robe to wipe away the condensation, I squint down at the driveway. He emerges from the car, two women around my age dangling off either arm. I run my tongue over my teeth and immediately sour. His bachelor party was at a strip club in Devil's Cove, and no doubt, he's picked up some *employees* to bring back to the after-party. Which also happens to be his fiancé's bachelorette party. I couldn't care less about him groping other girls—rather them than me—but it's the blatant disrespect that irks me.

A bitter laugh escapes my lips, and I take another sip of lukewarm cocoa.

Yes, plans change because life throws you constant curveballs. That's why I had several of them. The first was simple; marry Alberto to stop him building in the Preserve, thus forcing my dementia-ridden father out into a world he no longer recognizes. That changed when I found out Alberto didn't even own the darn land, but planned on tying me to him anyway.

The second plan, to rely on Angelo, was a naive and stupid one. One fueled by lust and adrenaline, built on false promises and fluttering heartbeats. The only plan I know I can rely on is the one that involves only myself. That's why I'm back to one of my original plans. The one I concocted on the very edge of the cliff in Devil's Dip.

It'll be the ultimate sin. A steep upgrade from spitting in mouthwashes and keying car doors and perhaps when I first thought of it, up there on the cliff, it was nothing but a sick fantasy. But I'm different now. I'm hardened by betrayal and humiliation, and *I am ready.*

I set the mug on the dresser, cross the room, and double-lock the door. Then, I slip my robe off and slide between the sheets. The party rages on underneath me, but in my mind, it's quiet. I've found peace, knowing that when I fall, I don't need Angelo to catch me.

I'll plunge right into the dark abyss, and it'll welcome me with open arms.

CHAPTER
Thirty-Two

Rory

"RISE AND SHINE, BLUSHING bride!"

I pop an eyelid at the sound of Amelia's cheery voice. She's standing at the end of the bed, a champagne flute in her hand and a grin on her face. "It's finally your big day!"

For flamingo's sake. I want to roll over and bury my head between the pillows, but unfortunately, that's not on the agenda for today. Instead, I grit my molars and roll out of bed, blistering rage already consuming me. As I pass Amelia to head toward the bathroom, I snatch the flute out of her hand and sink it in one. I'm going to need the liquid courage today.

Her footsteps creak over the floorboards, so I quickly lock the bathroom door behind me.

"Hey, where did you go last night?" she calls through the keyhole. "You disappeared at like, nine p.m."

Instead of feigning a crappy excuse, I step in the shower and let the hot water burn my body. I crank the dial up a few more degrees and scrunch my eyes, trying not to wince as it scalds my skin.

I wonder if this is what hell is going to feel like?

By the time I dry off and slip on a fresh pair of silk pajamas, I fully expect Amelia to have gotten the hint and left. Alas, she hasn't. She's still hovering by the door, only now, her smile is frozen to her face.

"We're due at the Visconti Grand at twelve."

No reply.

"Aurora—"

She reaches for my wrist as I pass her, but I'm quick to snatch it out of her reach. It's a sharp movement, one that makes her flinch.

"Leave me alone," I snap. "You tell me what to do, and I'll do it. But I'm not going to pretend like this is the happiest day of my life, so I'd prefer if you'd cut the crap and stop pretending like it is too."

She stares at me in shock. My brows shoot up. "Got it?" I hiss. A nod. "Good. Now, where do you want me?"

A few beats pass. "Hair and makeup are set up in the family room."

I grab my purse and storm out of the bedroom without another word.

Downstairs is chaos. Deliveries come and go, orders are barked rather than spoken, and everyone who crosses the foyer does so in a frantic jog, rather than a walk. I pause at the top of the stairs, shifting my weight from one foot to the other. My plan relies on opportunity, so I need to keep an eye out for one. While the door is wide open, there's a cluster of suited men standing on the porch, and when one of them turns, his earpiece glints under the harsh winter sunlight.

Not yet, Rory. Not yet.

I suck in a lungful of air, pad down the stairs, and burst into the family room. A wave of applause ripples through it, a chorus of whoops and whistles by a group of women I barely know. There's the makeup artist, the hairstylist, and the dressmaker, all of whom have had more conversations with Amelia than they have me. And then there are the *cousins*. Tanned women with silky black hair and judgmental stares. They turned up at the first fitting, where they did nothing but mutter in Italian behind their perfectly manicured hands.

I'm poked and prodded like a cow being prepared for the auction block. My hair screams as it's braided; my face stings as inch-thick makeup is plastered onto it. Then I'm sewn into a corset, then my dress, and then everyone chuckles and hollers as the dressmaker slides a lace garter up my thigh.

I clamp my jaw shut and sweep the room with my stare. They are all accomplices, and I want nothing more than to chuck a grenade in here and run.

The dressmaker stops fussing with my hemline and sits bolt upright. "All finished! You look beautiful," she coos, clasping her hands together. "Look."

With gentle hands on my shoulders, she spins me around to face the full-length mirror before I can protest. My eyes clash with my reflection and I feel like I've been shot in the stomach. I *do* look beautiful. Any outsider would think I'm a virginal bride about to walk down the aisle and find the love of her life waiting for her at the end of it. My hair is fashioned into a long French braid, diamonds adorning it. The dress is voluminous; a bardot neckline framed with puffy lace sleeves and a skirt big enough to hide a bomb underneath.

I look beautiful, but I don't look like *me*.

Heat prickles my skin under the scratchy fabric, spreading across my collarbone like a rash. *It should have been him. Him at the end of the aisle, him who weighed down my finger with a rock.*

I bite back the emotion rising up my throat. *No, it shouldn't have.* But for some pathetic reason, I wish it was. Despite the fact he used me, spat me out, and broke his promise, if it was Angelo waiting at the end of the aisle, I wouldn't be looking for my opportunity to escape.

Like it's a touch of fate, my opportunity comes the moment I open my eyes. My gaze shifts from my reflection out the window to the front porch. It's empty.

Calmness engulfs me. Feigning a smile, I smooth down the dress and step off the box. "Thank you, everybody. I just need to use the bathroom."

"I'll come with you—"

I shoot Amelia a death glare. "I'll manage," I bite back icily.

Snatching up my purse from an armchair, I leave the room lingering in a state of confusion, and with my heart thumping in my chest, I take a sharp right toward the door. The late-fall wind works against me, attempting to blow me back into the house, but I grip the fabric of my dress, put my head down, and break into a run.

Gravel blurs under my heels, blood pounds in my temples. *This is happening. It's really happening.* But my twisted excitement is cut short when a pair of shiny men's dress shoes come into view.

I freeze. Bite back my panic, and look up to see who owns them.

Tor. He's leaning against the side of his car, cutting a sharp figure in a tux. A lit cigarette is halfway up to his lips, but he pauses to rake a suspicious eye over me.

We stare at each other for three painstakingly long beats. He flicks his tongue between his teeth. Draws in a deep breath and shoots a dark look in the direction of the house. Then he pushes off his car, flicks the cigarette, and drops something at my feet.

"Oops," he drawls indifferently, without looking at me. "I think I just dropped my car keys." His shoulder brushes against mine as he passes. I feel his hot breath in my ear. "Hopefully they aren't found by a runaway bride."

He leaves me there, panting and bewildered. In the distorted reflection of the car door, I see him stroll into the house without so much of a glance back.

My eyes drop to the silver glinting in the gravel. *Thank you, thank you, thank you.* A cocktail of disbelief and adrenaline coasts through my veins. I snatch them up and slide behind the wheel, tossing my purse and heels onto the passenger seat.

I've never driven anything other than my father's beat-up Land Rover and a golf buggy, both of which are nowhere near as sleek or as powerful as this. As my bare foot slams against the accelerator, the engine roars in protest, and I lurch forward. *Holy crow.* My eyes cut to all three mirrors, making sure I haven't attracted any unwanted attention, and then I try again, slower this time. I need to just drive normally until I get out of the grounds, and then it's a race to get to the cliff.

Another stroke of fate; the gates are wedged open, probably because of all the deliveries coming in today. The guards are so focused on looking at what's coming in, they don't bat an eyelash at Tor's car driving out.

Okay, I've got this. Relief dissolves some of the tension in my shoulders as I turn onto the coastal highway and Devil's Cove becomes a speck in the rear-view mirror. The journey passes in a numb haze, because I'm too focused on the destination. I don't drive anywhere near as fast as Angelo, yet, it seems like I'm pulling up under the willow tree next to the graveyard within a matter of minutes.

This is it. The plan I never thought I'd have to resort to. I fill the car with a bitter laugh, remembering when this moment was nothing more than a sick fantasy. So sick that I called Sinners Anonymous to confess that I was merely *thinking* about it.

I thought it'd feel different, though. I thought my legs would be shaking as I made my way to the edge of the cliff. I thought I'd be scared. But as I stand on the edge, my heels sinking into the mud and pebbles scattering under my toes, I *feel alive.*

"My name is Rory Carter and I do bad things."

As always, the wind snatches the words from my lips, carrying them away from the cliff edge and over the choppy sea. I always say it here, just to see how the truth tastes, and today, it tastes delicious.

Another step closer to the edge. The fabric of my dress billows, a gust of wind finding its way up my skirt.

The first time I stood on this cliff, I called it. *It was always going to come to this.* Me, standing on the edge of the Devil's Dip's highest cliff and thinking bad thoughts.

I tried doing a good thing, but good doesn't seem to ever cancel out the bad.

Balling my fists around the lace of my dress, I close my eyes. I lift my toe and inch it further to the edge, until there's nothing underneath my foot but air.

Adrenaline zaps down my spine. *I'm ready.* I pop a lid, but before I can look around for my purse, I'm thrown backward by a force so strong that it knocks the wind out of me me.

What the hell?

Hot hands scorch my rib cage, strong and warm. A familiar scent—one I associate with danger—assaults my senses.

"I swear to God, Rory. You better know how to fly, because if you fall, I'm coming with you."

Panic punches me in the gut, but it's quickly replaced with a relief so strong I feel breathless. *Angelo.* I slam my head against his chest, curl my hands over his, and gasp. Big, desperate gulps of salty air. The buttons of his shirt are cold against my spine, but his labored breaths are warm against my neck.

"What are you doing here?" I gasp.

My feet leave the mud as he grips me by the hips and pulls me even further away from the edge. Even if I wanted to jump, his body is wrapped around me so tightly, I'd never be able to escape him.

"Making sure you don't do something stupid," he growls in my ear. The venom rolls off his tongue in waves.

He gives me just enough room to twist around in his arms and face him. I look up at him and take a moment to drink in the planes of his handsome face. The dark rage that masks it. *Holy crow.* Every fiber of my body is buzzing with the urge to kiss him. With *hope.*

His gaze is stormy but conflicted, but when it falls to my lips, it softens just enough to let me in. "Fucking hell, Rory." He squeezes the back of my neck as his nose brushes against mine. "Are you trying to give me a heart attack?"

"Ask me for a sin."

He stills. Eyes dart to the raging sea behind me, then he gives a small shake of his head. "I don't want it." His hand moves to the nape of my neck possessively. "Not here."

I suck in a lungful of air and give it to him anyway.

"The day you saw me up here, I wasn't going to jump." I swallow. "I was *never* going to jump. Not then, not today."

His eyes thin. He doesn't believe me.

"I was trying to see if it was high enough. Because I need it to be high enough so that if I push Alberto off it, he'll definitely die."

My sin sits heavy between us. His hardened expression gives nothing away. "You're going to kill Alberto." It's strange, hearing it aloud. Coming from someone else's lips. I nod. An emotion I can't name coasts over his features, but he doesn't say anything. Instead, he pins me with his intense stare and waits.

"I think, deep down, I always knew his contract was bogus. So, if the marriage wasn't going to keep my father safe, I needed a back-up plan." I twist around, glancing at the rolling tide on the horizon. "I was going to call him to come get me. I know he'd come himself, because he'd be mortified if anyone else knew he had a runaway bride. And then..." I swallow, turning back around to Angelo. "I'd do it. I'd *push him.*"

Silence. Angelo rakes his teeth over his bottom lip. "I was your backup plan," he bites, running a hard thumb over my cheekbone. "I told you I'd get you out of it. You said you trusted me."

"I did, and then you disappeared!"

"Because I was working on a plan, Rory, like I told you I would. This shit doesn't happen overnight."

"Tor told me you weren't coming back!"

"Tor?" I nod and his expression hardens. "*Bastard.* I told him to keep you safe while I was gone, so what the fuck was he playing at?" Before I can reply, he palms the back of his neck, his nostrils flaring. "Fuck, baby. Do you know what it feels like to kill a man?"

"A man like Alberto? Probably pretty good."

Despite his fury, dark amusement tugs at his lips. He gives a small shake of his head. Disbelief. "My bad girl."

Fireworks spark in my stomach. I can't believe he came back to me. *For* me. I tilt my chin upward. "So, what's the plan?"

His grip tightens around my nape. "Remember how you told me to think like a businessman, not a thug?"

I nod. His jaw muscles flex as his eyes drop to my hand pressed flat against his chest. His slips his over mine, fingering the ring on my finger. Then he tugs it off, rough and fast.

"What are you—?"

The diamond glints against the gloomy sky as he hurls it, hard, over the edge of the cliff. When he looks back at me, his gaze clashes with mine, the word *vicious* flashing across his eyes like a warning sign.

"Sorry, Magpie. I'm a thug through and through."

Before I can respond, he scoops me up and slings me over his shoulder, roughly gripping the fabric of my dress. His hands are warm and possessive as they find my thigh. He snaps the garter against my skin, *hard,* and lets out an animalistic growl. "I'm going to burn this fucking dress when we get home."

Home. The word alone makes my pulse flutter.

"What's going on?!" I gasp, dizzy from the sudden movement and the feeling of him *touching* me.

"I'm taking what's mine"

"Yours?"

He drops me onto the passenger seat of his car and leans against the door frame. "Yeah. A capo needs a wife. Guess I choose you."

Heat rips through my veins, and I can feel my heart sewing itself back together.

"You guess?" I whisper, looking up at him through my lashes.

He grips my chin. Runs a soft line over my bottom lip. "I *know.* I've always fucking known."

The pleats of my dress get caught in the car door as he slams it shut, but I couldn't care less. My heart is beating to a different rhythm, now that it's been stitched back together and it's heavy with hope. *I'm not marrying Alberto.*

As Angelo's warmth brushes up against me from the driver's seat, a million questions fight for space in my throat. One of them being, *am I really marrying you instead?*

But I don't say it. Instead, I watch as he pulls out a gun from his waistband, another from the breast pocket of his suit jacket, and sets them carefully on the central console.

"Are you really coming back?"

"Yes."

"For good?"

His hand finds my thigh, heavy and reassuring. "For good."

He kicks the car into drive and races through country lanes, until his house appears on the horizon. I can't take my eyes off him; I'm worried that if I do, I'll wake up in the guest suite of the Cove mansion and realize this was all a fever dream.

"Why didn't you call?" I whisper. "I wouldn't have believed Tor if you'd *just called.*"

His gaze flickers sideways and he looks disgruntled. "I gave you *my* number to call in an emergency. I don't even have yours."

"I called your number and it was out of service."

He considers this. "Fuck, you're right, baby. I disconnected it in preparation of becoming Capo. I need an untraceable line. I didn't even think, I was just so fucking busy." He swallows and squeezes my thigh. "I'm so sorry."

"And you couldn't have come back a few days ago? You know, before the actual wedding day?"

"Do you know how much shit I had to do in a week, Rory?"

"Like?"

"Like, appoint a new CEO for my business, sell my London apartment. Completely upend my life and move to Devil's Dip." His jaw flexes. "Also, I took a detour to San Fran. I had...unfinished business there."

I nod, slowly taking it all in. "But you hate Devil's Dip."

His eyes harden on the windshield. "But I don't hate you."

My pulse beats like a drum, and I lean against the cold window in an attempt to cool myself down. As we wind our way around the hill, I bask in the all-too-familiar scent of the car; a cocktail of aftershave and leather, it's unapologetically *him*. I inhale it, all of it, getting high like it's a drug.

We reach the top of the hill, and I'm surprised to see the house is as busy as the Cove mansion, and there's definitely no wedding being planned here today.

Is there?

Despite the unknown crackling in the air like static, the hope in my heart flickers. But when I glance over at Angelo, he nods to the burly men pouring out of the house.

"Gabe's men. They'll be here for a while, at least until we figure things out. Okay?"

"Okay."

"Gabe's going to keep you safe. I'm going to need you to do everything he says until I get back."

I whip round. "Get back? Where are you going?"

His expression darkens. "To tell Alberto not to expect you to walk down the aisle today."

Dread trickles into my chest. "No," I murmur, putting my hand over his. "Stay with me. At least for today? He'll figure it out soon enough."

His smirk is cold, calculated. *Vicious*. The darkest part of me wants to clamp my mouth over it and breathe it all in. "It's not the only thing I need to tell him, baby."

The thought of Angelo walking into the Cove mansion and announcing he's *stolen* me and he's reclaiming Devil's Dip makes me sick to my stomach.

"Shouldn't you take Gabe with you? Just in case?"

Annoyance coats his features. "In case *what*? You think I can't handle it?"

I *know* he can handle it. Angelo might have been on a straight and narrow path for the last nine years, but I've never met a man scarier than him. He reigns a quiet terror; it hums off him like a sonic signal when he walks into a room, and it makes the air immediately shift.

He was raised to be a made man, but he was destined to be a king.

"Kiss me."

Instinctively, his eyes drop to my lips. "What?"

"I've always wondered what it'd feel like to kiss you, ever since you turned up to that first Friday night dinner. So kiss me before you go, because if anything happens to you, then at least I'll know." I swallow. Shift in my seat. "I'll know what it feels like to kiss Angelo Visconti."

The silence is heavy, and it lasts for a few achy seconds.

With one hand still resting on the steering wheel, he leans in. Drugs me with a more concentrated version of his scent. My heart stills as his lips brush over mine; as his stubble grazes my chin.

But then he pauses.

"If I kiss you, it means I'm not sure if I'll make it back to you." He nips on my bottom lip, provoking a pathetic moan from me. "And I'm very fucking sure I'll make it back, Magpie."

He watches me intently as I reluctantly get out of the car. Gabe strides over the gravel and comes to a stop next to me.

Angelo greets his brother with a stern expression. "Look after my girl for me."

"Yes, *boss*."

His gaze shifts to mine. "Come here."

Swallowing, I take a step toward the car and wrap my hands over the window frame. He rakes a hand through his hair.

"When I come back, you better have taken that fucking dress off, or I'm going to rip it off with my teeth."

Breathless from the venom threaded through his tone, I only have enough wits to nod foolishly.

His voice and expression soften. "Good girl."

Gabe and I stand shoulder to shoulder as we watch Angelo's Aston Martin disappear down the hill, taking a piece of me with it.

Beside me, he shifts. "Shame."

I turn. "What is?"

"I was looking forward to listening to your call. I never *could* stand uncle Alberto."

CHAPTER
Thirty-Three

Angelo

I'VE GOT THE MANILA envelope in the glove box, gun tucked into my waistband, and a freshly lit fire under my ass.

That *fucking* wedding dress. I wanted to tear it off her body and stuff it down Big Al's throat until he choked on it. The sight of her in it feels like reason enough to start a war, but of course, that'd be petty.

Capos can't be petty. They can't be impulsive, either, which is why it took me a whole week to get my shit in order.

I breathe out fire as I pass through the Cove mansion gates. It'll be the last time they are left open for me, that's for damn sure.

Pulling up at the edge of the driveway, I kill the engine and stare up at the house. I've played hide and seek in its darkest corners; swum a million laps in its pool. The people inside it are family, and I'm about to sever the tie with the sharpest pair of scissors.

Who thought it'd ever be like this? Not me. I always thought, *if* I came back to Devil's Dip, I'd announce it over cigars and whiskey; drop it into casual conversation with a smirk and a halfhearted shrug. Everyone would cheer, raise a toast to me. Welcome back Vicious Visconti with open arms.

But it's not going to be like that. Instead, they are about to find out how vicious I can really be.

Puffing out my chest, I stroll over the gravel and take the steps up to the house two at a time. A storm is stirring just over the threshold, a buzz of panicked activity. Amelia grabs my arm as she passes. "Have you seen Aurora? We've lost her!" Our eyes clash, and she immediately recoils at my expression.

I stride into the dining room. Alberto leaps to his feet, but doesn't hide his disappointment when he realizes it's me. Next to him, Tor feigns indifference, but the way his Adam's apple bobs in his throat betrays him. *Bastard.* I want to put a fucking bullet in his head, but surprisingly, the rage I feel toward toward him dwindles quickly. On the drive over, I'd realized why he'd told Rory I'd skipped town. He didn't want to choose between me and his father, and thought Rory would just go through with the wedding if she thought I wasn't coming back, and everything would return to normal. But the fact he gave her his car and told me so as soon as I turned up at the house means he'd had a change of heart.

I'm still going to kick his ass, but I'm not going to kill him.

"The stupid little bitch has done a runner," Alberto growls, smoothing down the front of his waistcoat. "Do you know how fucking embarrassing this is for me?"

My fingers twitch with the urge to grip his throat. Christ, I can't believe Rory was planning on pushing him off the Devil's Dip cliff this whole time, but I can't say I can blame her.

"Alberto. You, Tor and Dante need to meet me in your office." I'm met with a blank stare. "*Now.*"

Without waiting for an answer, because I didn't ask a fucking question, I turn on my heel and stroll into the foyer and to Alberto's office. A few seconds later, Alberto comes in, Tor just behind him.

He stretches his arms out. "What the fuck, kiddo? This better be important, because we've got a lot of shit to deal with right now."

I glance over his shoulder to Dante in the doorway. He spots me and freezes, his eyes turning pitch black. "I should have known."

"Known what?" Alberto growls, "Somebody fill me in, now!"

The door opens again, revealing Donatello, a panicked Amelia tugging on his arm. "Think of the baby!" she hisses.

When the door swings open again, I wedge it with my foot. "Donatello, I'll be honest with you. You're a straight-laced guy, you have a beautiful wife and by the sound of it, a baby on the way." Amelia cowers, placing a protective hand on her stomach. "I'd rather not have to put a bullet in your head. There will be no wedding today, and if you stay out of the way, we'll remain on good terms." I lower my voice. "And trust me, you'll want to stay on good terms with me."

Before he can respond, I slam the door shut. Lock it. When I turn around, I find myself staring down the barrel of Dante's gun.

"I fucking knew it," he hisses. "I saw how you looked at her. You're really going to start a family war over a piece of pussy, Angelo?"

Behind him, Alberto groans. Sinks into his desk chair and rubs a fat hand over his face. "You've got to be kidding me," he mutters into his palm. "Angelo, tell me this isn't true."

My glare doesn't leave Dante's, and my silence tells my uncle everything he needs to know. "*Gesù Cristo*. You're my nephew. More like a son. You'd never do something like this."

"Always the ones you least expect, isn't it?" I drawl, side-stepping Dante's gun and striding over to the desk. I place my palms on the surface and tower over him.

"We can do this the easy way or the hard way. I'm taking over Devil's Dip. The Devil's Preserve is my territory, and Aurora is now my girl. Accept that, and I'll allow you to keep running shit through my port, and I'll walk out of here." I shift my focus to Dante, who still has his gun trained on me. "Hell, I'll even shake your hand if you're lucky."

Alberto thumps the desk with his fist and scowls up at me, venom and betrayal swirling in his eyes. "I can't fucking believe it."

Behind me, a safety catch releases.

"I choose the hard way."

I lazily turn to face my cousin, but while his gun is pointing at me, his gaze isn't. He's too busy glaring at Tor, who sits quietly in the shadows. "Are you not going to get out your fucking gun, too?"

He doesn't move an inch.

"Hard way works for me, too." I slide the manila envelope out of my breast pocket and hold it up, like I'm presenting evidence in a courtroom.

All the air leaves Alberto's lungs, and when I glance at him, he's flustered. Vulnerable like I've never seen him. "No," he mutters, rising to his feet. "No, no, no. *Basta*, please. Take her, take the girl—"

"I'm not asking for your permission," I growl, sparks of irritation flashing inside of me. I turn back to Dante, to the confusion softening his scowl.

"What's going on?"

"Your father has been quite persistent in his pursuit of getting planning permission for the Preserve. So much so that his last-ditch attempt included a little bribe." I flick the envelope. "An adjustment of his will."

Dante pales. "Is this true?" No response. His gun shifts from me to his father. "Have you—?"

"Written you out of his will, yes," I drawl, feigning boredom. "All of you. When Big Al dies, the entire Cove empire is passed on to me."

A snarl escapes his lips. From the corner, Tor says nothing. "Father, is this true?"

Alberto's body tenses in defense, but then his shoulders sink. "It's just business. M-my lawyer told me it'd work. I was going to write you straight back into it after I got the park..."

But Dante isn't buying it. Not after his father's drunken outburst at last Friday night's dinner. Fury and humiliation flicker behind the windows of his eyes as they dart between me and Alberto.

He steels his jaw. "What's your point, Angelo? It's not worth the scrap of paper it's written on, not while my father is alive."

I suppose it's the perfect time to change that, then. I whip out my gun and fire one shot. Shit, after all this time, my aim is still as sharp as a razor, because the bullet goes straight through Alberto's temple. He doesn't see it coming, and I remember my father didn't either. I guess you never expect a bullet in your head from a family member.

"What about now?"

Indifference flecks my voice, but inside, I feel *alive*. My nerve endings buzz with satisfaction, because *shit*, I've been itching to do that ever since I saw the bruise lining under Rory's eye.

Now, Tor leaps out of the armchair and draws his gun. "What the fuck, Angelo?" Dante stares at me for a beat too long, frozen in shock. And it's in this exact moment that I know Alberto was right: this cunt will never make a good capo. I could have put a bullet in his head by now, too.

I take an easy step back, just in case.

"You just killed my father," Dante eventually rasps. His stare grazes over the lifeless body slumped over the desk. The smashed paperweight on the floor, and the blood *drip, drip, dripping* onto the rug. It smells like iron and danger in here, and I love every fucking second of it.

"Yeah, think so."

He raises his gun to me again, newfound determination on his face as he takes a deep breath. "*So what's stopping me from killing you?*" he roars, spittle flying from the corners of his mouth. "I'll put a fucking bullet in your head, and then I'll find that stupid whore and put one in hers, too!"

"Mmm. See, this is where being a businessman comes in useful. If I die, Rafe and Gabe become beneficiaries of *my* will. Which now," I hold up the envelope again, "Includes every bar, restaurant, casino, and hotel in Devil's Cove." I take a step forward, my gun-hand lax at my side. "Are you going to go up against both of them, too? Doesn't sound like a good idea to me, especially when it looks like Tor is also about to jump ship."

Dante scowls at his brother, who's still staring at Alberto's lifeless body. His expression is impossible to read.

"Take the deal, Dante."

The silence is long and heavy, stretching out between us. It feels endless, and my jaw is aching from grinding it by the time he gives me a reluctant nod.

It's so small, I'd have missed it if I'd blinked.

I nod too, sliding the envelope back into my pocket. Back away in the direction of the door.

I stop in the doorway and pin Dante with a smirk. "Congratulations on finally becoming Capo. Maybe we can swap tips some time."

The lobby is bright and silent, filled with frozen servants and distant relatives who all heard the gunshot. I ignore every single set of eyes on me and make a beeline for my car.

Driving back to Devil's Dip, I feel *tired.* Detached from my body, following what just happened in Alberto's office. His blood is splattered on my white shirt, and the gunshot still rings in my ears.

As I pull into the driveway, the front door flies open, and Rory runs out from under the awning. *Fuck.* My chest tightens at the sight of her, barefoot and swamped by one of the sweaters I left here. *No fucking wedding dress, thank god.* We stare at each other through the windshield and I make a silent oath to myself: Nothing and nobody will ever fucking hurt her again. Not Alberto, not Dante. Not me.

I couldn't save my mama from the Viscontis, but I sure as shit will save Rory.

Her chest rises and falls, her perfect mouth slack as she watches me get out of the car and walk past her. She follows me into the kitchen, where Gabe's men are littered around. Some play cards on the breakfast counter, others take private phone calls in the shadows.

I head to the liquor cabinet and pour out a large whiskey. She stands on the other side of the counter, bunching the sleeves of my sweater in her fists.

"Is it over?"

It's far from fucking over; in fact, it's only just begun. But I'd give my left nut to wipe the panic off her pretty little features.

I give a small nod.

She breathes out all the pent-up tension in her lungs and palms the counter. Her head dips between her shoulder blades, and she looks up at me from under her thick lashes. "Now what?" she whispers.

Our gazes clash. Static crackles over the counter. I set my tumbler on the island. Loosen my tie.

"Everybody has five seconds to get the fuck out of my house."

CHAPTER
Thirty-Four

Rory

HIS COMMAND LEAVES ME breathless. The kitchen clears, and in the sudden silence I realize I'm not just leaning against the counter, I'm using it to brace myself. My palms are sweaty, frictionless against the marble.

Angelo glances at me.

"So, now you're stuck with another old man."

"I guess I am."

His gaze flashes. "I'm old enough to be your father. How does that make you feel?"

Heart thumping, I feign boredom. Look up at him through my lashes. "Does that mean I can call you daddy now?"

Dark amusement graces his features. He gives a small shake of his head. "Come here."

Oh, swan.

I feel like we're back in the dark hallway of Alberto's mansion, on the night he pulled Vittoria's pearl necklace from my bra. I had an awful impulse to run away from him then, and I feel that same instinct now, even under the bright kitchen lights. Even though he's rescued me from the worst fate possible. Even though he's seen me naked and vulnerable already, in every way possible.

With my heart struggling to find a natural rhythm, I round the island and step into the lion's den. As soon as I'm within arm's-length, his hand shoots out and snakes around the back of my neck; his thick fingers twisting into my braid. He buries his face into my throat and makes a delicious, animalistic noise I feel wholeheartedly between my thighs. *Touching. Real, darn, touching.* I melt into him, my breasts grazing against his shirt. My nipples tighten in anticipation, and I'm practically delirious at the thought of him *touching skin.*

He runs the bridge of his nose down the side of my neck, as though breathing in my scent. His groan vibrates against my pulse. "Fuck, baby. I've waited too fucking long for this."

With one hand around my throat, he wraps the other around my waist and hoists me onto the counter. The backs of my bare thighs brush against the cold marble, sending a lightning bolt down my spine. It's a stark contrast to the warmth of his hips as he pushes himself between them.

I'm coming apart like a cheap suit; every time he presses his warm mouth to my throat feels like he's unpicking another stitch. I tilt my head to give him more access, because the desire to have those lips on every inch of my body is maddening.

His hands are rough and desperate as they run down my ribs to my hips and come back up underneath my sweater, trailing a scorching path against my bare skin. Under *his* sweater, one that I found in a laundry basket in the basement. For a whole tense hour, I thought the ghost of his scent on the collar would be the last time I got to smell him, and yet here I am, drinking his masculine scent right from the source.

I grip the sides of the counter and buck my hips, my body begging to get closer to him. His erection presses on the inside of my thigh, making my eyelids flutter. It's *oh-so-close,* but not close enough. I'm sick of the teasing; that's all I've ever known with him. The graze of leather against my backside; his hot breath deliriously close to my clit. Never touching, never feeling. Not really. So I shift forward an inch, until his bulge is right where I need it, pressing against the damp spot on my panties. Suddenly, his hands grip me tighter around my waist, holding me in place. We lock eyes, his flashing dark with irritation, and it's at this moment I realize he wants it his way. *Me,* his way.

His gaze drops to my breasts, making me shiver.

"Take it off."

"You take it off," I bite back, for the sheer sake of being petty. Despite everything he's done for me, a part of me is still bitter about him leaving without a word. He can't just storm back into my life and demand I get naked for him.

His gaze thins. I flinch when he takes a step back. My fingers twitch to hook onto his belt loop and drag him back to me. But he yanks open a drawer and returns with kitchen scissors and a crazed look in his eyes.

Before a gasp can even escape my lips, he pulls the fabric and runs the scissors up the middle of the sweater, from the hem to the neckline. It falls off around my shoulders and pools on the island behind me.

I stare at him in shock, a new, frantic pulse thumping in my clit. "I liked that sweater."

"You can have all my sweaters."

His stare is intense, electrifying my stomach and cleavage as it rakes every inch of my exposed flesh. I'm in nothing but a white thong and a matching bra, and without thinking, I unhook it and let it fall to the floor.

His face remains indifferent, but the way his hands curl into fists gives me a tiny insight into what he's thinking. He licks his lips, reaches for his whiskey. Takes a long, slow sip, still eyeing my body over the rim.

I feel drunk on his attention, and it's the most exciting thrill I've ever experienced. Better than any sin I've ever committed, better than standing on the edge of the cliff.

He takes a step forward, grips my jaw and tilts my face to his. "Open your legs for me." His command is callous and rough, grating up my spine like sandpaper.

But I've learned what happens when I don't comply.

I spread my thighs and his hands run a rugged path up to my seam, where the lace of my gusset meets my inner leg. He grips me there, *hard*, his fingertips disappearing into my flesh. *Oh, swan.* The tension is palpable, and I drop back on my elbows to bask under its rays. His rough thumb pad finds my clit through the lace, and he brushes over it, sending static crackling through my veins. My moan melts into a whisper as his hot mouth clamps over my nipple, his tongue hard and wet as it flicks over the nub.

Holy crow. I've never felt so hot, so darn alive. So *free.* I don't care that the noises escaping my throat are embarrassingly guttural, I don't care about anything but feeling him on me. With a low growl, he hooks my thong and yanks it down my thigh, like the sight of it pisses him off. I spread my legs further, cold air grazing over my lips, reminding me how wet I am.

He breathes long and heavy breaths. When he swears, it comes out in a thick, strangled rasp that hits me deep in the pit of my stomach. Hands back on my thighs, he yanks me closer, and sinks to his knees. My heart stills in anticipation, but I don't have long to wait until his hot, hard tongue meets my clit. I shudder, adrenaline rolling through me like a wave. My muscles clench with every slow, soft lick he gives from my entrance to my clit.

"Good girl," he growls into my lips as I grasp his hair.

Good girl. What he's doing to me now is a stark contrast to the sharp whip of his belt; a reward, rather than a punishment. But if this is what *good girls* get, then maybe I won't be bad anymore.

A hard, angry slap against my pussy dissolves that thought immediately. *Holy crow.* The sting fizzes in my blood like shaken-up champagne. *Maybe I can be both.*

Christ, I'll be whatever Angelo Visconti wants me to be.

A finger slips inside of me, thick and rough. I've wondered how it'd feel inside of me ever since I imagined him fingering me in the sea, and my imagination did not come close to reality. I rock against him, desperate for more length and girth, but his grip on my hip is vise-like. I'm clamped to the marble counter, and I have no choice but to lie back at his mercy.

He takes his time, driving his finger in and out of me. Then he slips another in and sucks on my clit. The feeling of his beard grazing me down there makes me feel like I might explode. Pressure builds and builds in my lower core until I'm a whimpering, shivering mess. Fire to his ice, crazed to his calm. So much pressure, so much electricity. It feels dangerous, and a strange part of me feels panicked, overwhelmed, like I need to press pause and catch my breath.

But when pressure explodes in my clit like a raging inferno, all of my hesitation dissipates into clouds of smoke and dust.

I melt into the counter like warmed butter, struggling to catch my breath. Between my thighs, Angelo slowly pulls his finger from inside me and carves a wet, sloppy trail down my seam with his finger, and then kisses along the same path.

Even though I feel exposed and vulnerable—I'm spread on the kitchen counter stark naked, while he didn't even shed his tie, for flamingo's sake—the silence filling the air is comfortable. It feels calm, like the peace that rolls in after a big storm.

Angelo rises from his knees and places a hand on either side of me. He stares down with something like admiration settled comfortably on his face. The blade of his silk tie dips between my breasts.

"You taste even better than I imagined," he murmurs in fascination, brushing a stray curl away from my cheek. He cocks his head, a smirk dancing on his lips. "Starting a war with my family was worth that alone."

His gaze drops to my heaving chest, rising and falls. He shakes his head in disbelief, mutters a curse under his breath, and then strides out of the kitchen.

I sit up and curl my arms around myself, feeling awkward. Where has he gone? He is coming back? And are there, uh, still men lurking around the house? The thought makes me panic, and my eyes dart to my panties on the floor. Just as I hop off the island to tug them back to claw back at least *some* shred of modesty, Angelo comes back into the kitchen, a bath towel in hand.

He holds it out. "Come here."

I walk toward him and he catches me in it, wrapping me up in the soft fabric and pulling me into his warmth. "I'm running you a bath," he murmurs into my crown.

I freeze. "Why?"

A hot huff fans my scalp. "Would you prefer a shower?"

"N-no, I just..."

"Shut up then," he growls, low and sultry, punctuating it with a nip on the shell of my ear.

He leads me to the bathroom and leans against the doorway, staring at me in mild amusement as I take it in. Bubbles spill out over the roll-top tub, and candles cast flickering orange shadows up the walls.

Emotion clogs my throat, and I clench my jaw to stop it from spilling from my lips. Instead, I suck in air and steady myself against the bathtub.

"Thank you, Angelo."

"Mhmm."

"Are you going to join me?"

He rakes his teeth over his bottom lip, then his gaze darts toward the window. "Wish I could, Magpie. I've got to some shit to do." He jerks his chin toward the towel wrapped around me. "I'll watch you get in, though."

I huff out a laugh, my cheeks flaming. But the weight of his lustful gaze feels so delicious against my skin that I drop my towel with hesitation, making a show of bending over as I get into the bath.

A guttural moan escapes him. He smooths down his tie. "I stick by what I said," he mutters.

"And what was that?" I rasp back, sinking into the warmth of the bath.

"You're worth starting a war for."

With a wink that shoots me between the thighs like a bullet, he clicks the door shut, and I hear his footsteps disappear on the other side. I sigh, roll my shoulders back, and melt under the bubbles.

Holy crow. It's crazy how quickly life changes. Only this morning I was hell-bent on vengeance, ready to throw Alberto off the side of a cliff in desperation. My heart beats double-time for a moment—I wonder what he's doing now? What Angelo said, or did, to get him to let me go so easily? He was gone less than an hour, and came back without so much as a scratch on him.

He's either the smoothest talker, or the scariest man alive.

I submerge myself completely, unable to stop the dark smile from forming on my lips.

I like the idea of the latter. It excites me.

Fumbling around in the half-lit bathroom, I find shower gel and shampoo, both marketed to men who know nothing about skincare. I laugh, lathering myself up with Angelo's scent. When I get out of the bath, I wrap the towel around myself and absentmindedly peer out the window. It looks out onto the backyard, and at the far corner of it, a raging fire reaches high against the navy sky. Squinting, I realize the dark figure next to it is Angelo, and the lump of charred white poking out of the flames is my wedding dress.

Something warm and satisfying pools in my lower stomach. I lean against the window and watch him for a moment. He's glaring into the flames, sipping from a whiskey tumbler.

Christ, I think I love him.

I shake the thought off as quickly as it comes, because it's utterly ridiculous. I've never been in love, but even I know, it's way too early to have the word so close to the tip of my tongue. Despite everything that's happened, I've only known Angelo a handful of weeks, and for a good chunk of them, he hated my guts. I'd like to say we hated each other, but really, I know I only disliked him because he held the key to all of my secrets and sins. Now though, I know I'd give them all to him willingly, without hesitation.

Scanning the room for something to put on, I realize there's a small pile of clothes set on a dresser. A pair of Nike sweatpants and a hoodie, both of which have the ghost of Angelo's laundry detergent woven into the fabric. Even though they are comically big on me, I slip them on and pad out to the hall and down the stairs. Angelo is waiting for me at the bottom of them.

"Nice bath?"

I nod. "Nice view."

He laughs, the type of laugh that'll turn me into an addict. As I reach the bottom step, something over his shoulder catches my eye. A shadow, distorted by the frosted glass in the door.

And then the doorbell rings.

The cry that leaves my lips reflects the sheer panic I feel in my chest. Angelo's eyes flash with concern, then anger, and he pulls me into his chest. "Relax," he soothes, stroking my hair. "It's pizza. Just pizza."

When he comes back into the foyer holding a stack of pizza boxes, I'm still getting my breath back. Raking a cautious gaze over me, he balances the pizzas on his forearm and grips my hand possessively, pulling me into a room I haven't been in yet. A living room. Like the rest of the house it's crisp and minimal, like a blank canvas. The walls still smell faintly of paint.

Angelo drops the boxes on the coffee table and sinks onto the sofa. "Come here," he rasps, patting his lap.

I don't hesitate crawling onto him. He wraps a strong hand around my waist and sets the other on my thigh. "Look at me, Rory."

I do, meeting the storm raging in his green irises. "No one is going to come for you, and if they do, they'll have to get through a whole fucking army, and then through me. Alberto's gone." He smooths his tie. "I killed him." He says this so matter-of-factly, it's hard to believe he was ever anything but a capo. Studying my features carefully, he grips my waist a little tighter and waits for my reaction.

His words throb at my temples for a moment, but then a weight lifts off my shoulders.

I swallow. Palm his chest. There are a million questions bubbling on my tongue, like *how*, how did you do it? Did he beg you for mercy, did he put up a fight? Was it slow, painful, or did he not even see it coming? And what about the rest of the family? I can't imagine Dante taking it lying down. And it's at this moment, I know he lied to me when he walked through that front door.

It's not over.

But none of that emerges from my throat. Instead, I muster two simple words.

"Thank you."

Amusement tugs the corners of his lips. "You're welcome. Now, you need to eat." He drags his gaze from mine and nods to the coffee table. "I don't know what you like yet, so I just got everything."

I laugh into his chest; he smells like bonfire smoke and warm whiskey. "Ham and pineapple, please."

He wrinkles his nose. "Fucking hell. Is it too late to give you back?" Despite his disdain, he flips open a few pizza boxes until he finds the Hawaiian.

"Way too late. You stole me, remember?"

His smirk is dark and delicious. "And so I did." He picks up a slice and brings it to my lips. "Eat." I pause for a moment, then reach up for the slice, but he pulls it out of my reach. *He wants to feed me?* Heat rises in my cheeks, but also between my thighs. It's only pizza, for goodness sake, but something about him feeding me feels so...*intimate*.

I take a bite, eyes never leaving his. Underneath me, his cock stirs in his slacks, and it's instinctive to roll my thighs against it.

"Bad girl," he growls. "Eat first. You'll need your energy for later."

My pulse quickens, and although it sounds more like a threat than a promise, I find that I can't wait for whatever *later* is. I take another big bite, wanting to get through the pizza and to this enigmatic *later*.

"So, uh. What exactly does stealing me entail?"

Angelo's mouth twitches. "I'm not too sure. I'm kinda new to this whole capo thing."

"Oh. So I'm your first captive, then?"

"Mhmm," he murmurs, watching me with dark amusement.

I squirm again, this time, rolling along the length of his erection. The way his jaw ticks and his eyes shut briefly makes me feel like I have all the power in the world. His hand clamps down harder on my hip, and he lets out a small hiss.

"I don't think you're meant to be so gentle with your captives."

He clamps his tongue between his teeth. "No?"

I take another bite. "No," I mumble through chunks of crust. "Don't think so."

He watches me finish off the slice and feeds me another in crackling silence. When I finished that, his eyes trail the length of me, his jaw ticking in thought.

"You know, I think you're right."

"About?"

"The whole being too gentle thing." He grabs the waistband of my sweatpants and lifts me up. The pizza box overturns onto the floor as he flings me over his shoulder and storms out of the living room. "What are you doing?!" I squeal, playfully beating my fists against his back.

"Chaining you to my bed," he snarls, giving my ass a hard slap. "That seems more appropriate, right?"

White hot delirium rushes through me. The threat of *later* now sounds like a dark promise, and I can almost taste it. He bursts into a room on the top floor and throws me onto a bed. A quick glance at the suitcase in the corner of the room is all I get before Angelo consumes me, pinning me to the bed with his weight.

An animalistic growl in his chest vibrates against mine, making my nipples tighten. "You look so hot in my clothes it pisses me off," he barks in frustration, tugging at the hoodie. "Maybe I won't buy you a new wardrobe, I'll just force you to wear my shit all the time."

I laugh into the planes of his shoulder, but it melts into a moan when he forces my thighs apart and flicks my clit, *hard*. "I'm going to fuck you so hard you won't be able to walk straight for a week."

My muscles tense. I'm surprised with how in tune he is with me already, because he stills too. Props himself up on his hands and pins me with a blistering glare. "What?" he snaps. My mouth opens, closes again. His expression hardens. "Say it."

Nerves skittering under the surface of my skin, I realize the time has come to tell Angelo my final sin.

My mouth is dry, but I swallow anyway. "I, uh. I've only done this once."

He scowls. Tugs at my waistband. "Yeah, right."

I slam my hand against his chest and reluctantly he stops. He looks up, irritated.

"I'm being serious, Angelo. I didn't have sex with those guys...it's just a rumor."

He sits up and stares at me. There's something in my expression he doesn't like. I know because his eyes soften, and he reaches for a pillow to prop my head up. "Talk to me."

"I had to study for the final aviation exam at the Devil's Coast Academy. It was an after-school thing, once a week. I dreaded every class I had, because it was just five guys and all of them were such *creeps*." Even after all this time, anger heats my blood up a few degrees at the mere thought of them. Christ, they were the reasons all of my sins started. "Always slapping my ass, or trying to take pictures up my skirt."

Angelo hisses bitterly, his chest tensing under my hand.

"The class before the exam, something felt different. It was like there was a big joke going on and I wasn't part of it. So, once the professor had left, I tried to leave too, but one of the boys locked the door." I shift my attention to the ceiling, uncomfortable with the slow-burning fury that's starting to seep from Angelo's pores. But I've started, and I need to get it off my chest. It's the only thing about me he doesn't know, and I want him to have the entire puzzle.

"It was the ringleader, Spencer. He and his crew were like the gods of the school—they could do no wrong. He informed me that they'd been talking, and they all wanted to know what a Devil's Dip girl looked like naked..." I trail off, the insinuation dangling in the air. But still, it's not enough, I need to *say* it. "They tried to rape me," I announce, with as steady of a voice as I can muster. "They tried to pin me to a desk and rape me."

The silence is blistering. I steal a look at Angelo, and the indifferent expression on his face scares me. I flinch when he suddenly jumps to his feet and grabs his cell and car keys off the bedside table.

I bolt upright. "Where are you going?"

"Give. Me. Names."

"Angelo—"

"Names, Rory." His voice is rough and strangled, like he's trying—and failing—to suppress his rage. "And addresses. *Now.*"

Rolling onto my knees, I tug the back of his jacket and he stills, hard and tense, at my touch. "Please," I beg.

He pauses, then drops to his haunches next to me and grabs my nape. "I have killed every man on this coast that has touched you inappropriately. From Max to my own fucking uncle. These kids are next, and if anybody besides me puts so much of a finger on you from now on, they'll be killed too."

A shiver runs down my spine, loaded with equal parts fear and excitement. But the thought of having him leave me here again makes me sick to my stomach. "Tomorrow," I whisper, trailing my hand down his hard chest. It's crazy that I *still* haven't seen what's under there. "But tonight, I just want to spend it with you. *Please.*"

His stomach softens and I know I have him. In one swift motion, he pulls me onto his lap and grips my jaw. "Tomorrow, first thing. Write me a list right now."

"Thank you," I whisper, nuzzling into the crook of his neck. "If it makes you feel any better—"

"Nothing you say is going to make me feel better about this, Rory."

"Well, uh. I bit one guy's ear off." He stills. "So, he should be quite easy to find."

A few beats pass, then a dark chuckle rolls over the top of my head. "Yeah?"

"Uh-huh. And one of the other guys, I pressed my thumbs so hard into his eyes that he's now blind in one of them."

His strong, warm hand rubs my back. "How'd it feel?"

I smile into his neck. "Exhilarating."

He pushes me away and looks down at me. Only now, do I realize my words have done nothing to calm his fire, despite his chuckle. "You said you've fucked once before. I want his name, too."

Shaking my head, I say, "No. He's got nothing to do with anything. He was a nice guy, just some kid from school."

Angelo's jaw ticks. "I don't like that answer. Did you love him?"

"No! Truth is, after that incident, I just wanted to get the deed done and over with. I hated the idea that I had something men wanted, and that they could take it from me so easily."

"Like Alberto thought he could."

"Exactly."

His nostrils flare, but he gives me a curt nod. "No sex," he suddenly announces. "Not tonight."

"What—?"

He pushes me onto the bed and gets up, disappearing into the closet. Disappointment beats in my chest, but when he comes back with a large bag, my curiosity is piqued. "I've got something better than sex."

"I doubt it," I mutter.

Laughing, he tips the bag and a mountain of candy falls onto the bed.

I rake it through my fingers, picking up different bars and boxes, confused. There's nothing I recognize. "What's all this?"

"British candy. Picked it up for you when I was tying up my loose ends in London. Thought you might like to try some things you can't find in the local Walmart."

He slides himself behind me, wraps an arm around my waist, and pulls me back so I'm flush against his chest. "Have you tried Wine Gums?" He lunges over and picks up a red roll. "Don't know why they are called that, they've got no alcohol in them, but they are fucking great."

Without warning, he pops one in my mouth and runs a possessive hand over my stomach.

"Do you like it?"

Numb, I nod in agreement, but I'm not thinking about the darn candy, I'm thinking about him. Us. *This*.

Bad things happen to bad people. So how the hell did I end up getting so lucky?

CHAPTER Thirty-Five

Angelo

Sitting back in my father's old chair, I roll my neck, but it does jack shit to release the tension pinching my shoulders. Restlessness crawls under my skin like an itch, and it's only when I realize I've spent more time glancing toward the study door than poring over the port's traffic logs on the desk, do I realize Rory is the source of it.

Christ, if I could spend all day watching her sleep, I would. Skin warm and mouth parted, her golden curls tangled on the pillow. I want to watch over her, protect her like a fucking rabid guard dog. But unfortunately, I can't protect her simply by watching her.

Grunting in frustration, I grip the back of my neck and force myself to stare at the logs again. I've spent nine years chairing an investment company for fuck's sake. I'm used to working with spreadsheets populated with numbers a hundred times bigger than this, yet I can't seem to make sense of them.

My obsession with her is *maddening*.

Just as I'm starting to settle, floorboards at the end of the hall creak, making my abs tighten.

She appears in the doorway, a mix of sleep and confusion smeared over her perfect features. I lean back and rake an unapologetic gaze over her body. Okay, I definitely need to get her clothes and *fast*, because her prancing around, wearing my sweaters and shirts as dresses, is going to drive me insane.

"Why didn't you wake me?"

"To do what?" Amusement prickles my lips at her frown. "Come here."

She rounds the desk and the moment she's within arm's reach, I tug her onto my lap and cave to my addiction. Breathe in her warm scent and run my hands up her bare thighs. Fuck, she's so small and delicate. So breakable. The thought makes my chest tighten, and I wrap my arms tighter around her waist, as if someone's going to burst into the office at any moment and try to take her from me.

I've spent nine years carving out a new life for myself, one as far away from Devil's Dip as possible. And yet, in just a fistful of weeks, I've given it all up. Moved back to the town I hate, started a civil war with my own fucking family, all for *her*. A girl that curses in bird puns, eats enough sugar to be pre-diabetic, and is addicted to petty revenge.

Oh, not to mention she's almost young enough to be my daughter. Sometimes, I think I must be fucked in the head. I was up at the crack of dawn like a crazed man, and dedicated my morning to making her feel as comfortable and as protected as possible. Her father's caregivers are now on my payroll, and the cunts who dared to touch her are chilling at the bottom of the Pacific with the help of a couple of bricks tied to their ankles. Suddenly, I realize I've gone from killing one man a month as part of our Sinners Anonymous tradition, to averaging one hit a week, and all of them trace back to her.

Her breath skitters over my neck, and the way it makes my dick tingle pisses me off. I *hate* her hold over me; it makes me feel weak and pathetic. I slap her thigh and nip on the shell of her ear.

"You need to wear more clothes around the house, baby. If I catch one of Gabe's men so much as glancing in your direction, I'll carve their eyeballs out."

Her chuckle is sleepy and content against my chest. "Okay."

I rake my fingers through her hair. Christ, she has so fucking much of it, it's all-consuming. "I'll send a personal shopper over this afternoon." I pause. "Do they have them here?"

Another laugh, followed by a playful slap on my chest. I grab her hand and graze my mouth over her knuckles. "It's Devil's Dip, not New York. I'll just go into town."

I still, and I know she feels it, because she looks up at me from under those thick lashes. "You're not leaving this house until it's safe, Rory."

She bolts upright. "Why isn't it safe?"

"It's not your problem to worry about, baby. I'll make sure you have everything you need."

She pushes against my chest, pinning me with an angry glare. " No. I want you to tell me, I want to be kept in the loop. I'm sick of not knowing—I didn't know Alberto didn't have the power to tear down the Devil's Preserve, and I didn't know what you were up to when you disappeared for a whole week. Don't keep me in the dark!" Frustration flecks her tone, and even though it's adorable when she gets angry, a hot urge to bend her over my desk and spank her for her insolent tone crawls under my skin. But I don't have time for that right now, so I push it down and stroke her cheek with my knuckle.

"I'm not going to tell you everything Rory." She opens her mouth to protest, but I grip her jaw and growl, "And that's non-negotiable. But, I'll tell you what I think you need to know. Deal?"

By the annoyance smeared on her face, I know it's not good enough. Reluctantly, she nods.

"I killed Alberto, and now Dante is the new capo of Devil's Cove. It's not going to be clear sailing, and if I know him, the revenge will come cold and calculated. He already has a pre-established army, and he's always had his sights set on Dip."

When panic crosses her features, I tighten my grip on her jaw and tilt her face up to meet mine. "There's nothing to worry about, baby. I've got Gabe, who's building out an army twice the size of Dante's as we speak. And then there's Rafe, who's everything Dante wishes he was."

She plays with the blade of my tie, chewing on her bottom lip. "Is there going to be a war?"

It's instinctive to tell her no, but when she looks up at me with those big, whiskey-colored eyes, I know I can't fucking lie to her. "Yes," I say simply. "I don't know when it's coming, but it'll come. I'll be working long hours, and I won't make it home to you every night."

I study her for a while, tense as I wait for her reaction. I'm surprised when a shy grin spreads across her face. "It's kind of exciting."

Shaking my head in disbelief, I flick her button nose and pull her tighter into me. Her dark streak is small and innocent, but it's one of the sexiest things about her.

"Not for you. You'll be holed up here surrounded by security for a little while."

Something flickers across her features. Something between disappointment and regret.

"Rory, look at me." I don't give her a choice, threading my fingers into her hair and clamping my palms against her cheeks. "I am not Alberto. You're not really my captive, but you are *mine*. I need to keep you safe, but I'll do my best to give you the world." I run a thumb over her pillowy bottom lip. "As long as the world fits inside the walls of this house. Okay?"

She nods. Pulls out of my grip and grazes her lips over the curve of my throat. I groan into her hair, fisting it at her nape. "Don't tease me, baby girl. I don't have time."

She stills at my collar. "Why? Where are you going?"

"I've got a meeting with Gabe and Rafe."

"Oh. Can I...?"

"Spit it out, Rory."

She brushes a curl away from her face and looks up at me nervously. "Can I have a friend over?"

My gaze darkens. "What friend?"

"Just Tayce."

"The tattoo girl?"

She nods, and I chew this over for a second. "Give Gabe a list of friends, and he'll have them vetted, and then they can come and go as they please. But yes, she can come round."

"Thank you," she breathes, lighting up in a way that makes me want to give her everything she's ever fucking asks for. I know I will, anyway. "Can I uh, use your cell?"

My eyes thin. "Where's yours?"

"I just have the burner Alberto gave me."

Of course. I'd forgotten what a tight fucking leash Big Al kept her on. I fish it out of my pocket and toss it onto the desk. "I'll get you your own cell, and anything else you need. Write a list."

She smiles, curling her hand around my iPhone. "Lists, lists, lists. You really are a businessman, aren't you?"

I let out a hiss of breath and twist the fabric of her sweater. Her eyes widen as I suddenly rise to my feet, spin her round and pin her between my thighs and the desk, before winding my hand in her hair and bending her over.

Fuck it, I'll make time.

My belt leaves my slacks with a loud *thwap*. "I'll show you exactly what type of man I am, baby."

Seek hope where the air is salty and the cliffs are steep.

That's what the fortune cookie said. The one I brought from the chick in San Francisco's Chinatown. It held the exact same fortune that convinced my mom to move here all those years ago.

Sure, they are all made in the same factories; a coincidence rather than fate. But it led me to Rory, and I like to think my mom had something to do with that.

I'm standing on the edge of the cliff, toying with the cigarette packet in my slacks. It suddenly dawns on me that I haven't smoked since I brought Rory home. I guess I haven't felt as stressed, now that I know she's safe.

Charcoal-colored clouds hang low in the sky, the air crackling in anticipation underneath them. The wind carries over a familiar purr of a sport's car, and a few moments later, Rafe's shoulder is grazing mine.

The *click-clack* of tossed dice in his hands accompanies his words. "All yours now, brother."

I huff out a laugh, following his gaze to the town below. "Nah. I'll deal with the port. Everything else is all yours."

"You don't know how long I've been waiting for you to say that."

But I do. Despite being one of the most powerful men on the West Coast, with the whole of Vegas at his fingertips, Rafe's always had a strange obsession with Devil's Dip, in all of its moody glory. He's big on family, big on *home*. I've always known he'd move back to the coast in a heartbeat. And weirdly enough, there's a dark excitement bubbling under my rib cage. For once, I'm looking down at Devil's Dip and don't have the urge to burn it to the fucking ground.

Maybe Rafe's enthusiasm is rubbing off on me, or maybe it's because the town now has something—*someone*—that I need. It feels like a new beginning, the start of a new era.

But I can't start it with secrets.

I glance back at the road, and when I see Gabe's Harley still hasn't pulled up, I walk the three steps to our parent's grave. Rafe joins me.

"I need to tell you something."

"No, you don't."

"Nah, I do—"

"No." Rafe's voice is as sharp and cold as an icicle, forcing me to look at him. His eyes are trained on the grave. "I already know. I know Mama was killed, and I know you killed Dad."

A sinking feeling settles in my stomach. "How?"

"'Cause the night you killed him, you called Sinners Anonymous."

I frown, gazing up at the church, trying to rack my brain for details of that night. Of course, I remember my father's lifeless body so clearly, remember the tangy iron smell and the dark satisfaction that sparked in my veins. What I don't remember is what happened after I sat at his desk and sank a bottle of Smugglers Club.

"You didn't say anything."

Silence stretches between us. He thumbs his mouth, his diamond cuff link glinting. "You called the hotline because you wanted us to know, not because you wanted us to react to it. I knew you'd tell us in your own time."

"You're not pissed at me."

His gaze darkens, and I'm suddenly reminded of what a good asset Rafe is to have on your side. "After hearing what he did to Mama, I'm glad you killed the cunt. And the kid?"

An icy hand grips my heart. I give a quick shake of my head. "Working on it."

He nods.

We stand in contented silence for a few moments, until Gabe's motorcycle rumbles into view. Rafe's hand slaps my back. A dark chuckle melts from his lips.

"The Angels of Devil's Dip, back together again. Fuck man, this is all I've ever wanted."

CHAPTER Thirty-Six

Rory

"Fucking hell, Rory. You're living a Gothic fairy tale."

I've just finished telling Tayce everything, right from the moment I signed Alberto's contract, all the way up to the candy Angelo brought back from London for me. Of course, I've left out some of the *darker* stuff, like getting spanked in a church and the fact I seriously considered pushing Alberto off a cliff. I guess I like having some sins that only Angelo and I share.

She sits on the sofa opposite me, curled up under a blanket and a pile of British candy in her lap. Her mouth is slack in disbelief. "I can't believe Angelo Visconti is in love with you."

My ears grow hot at the mere sound of the word. "He's *not*."

"Shut up, Rory. He left his entire life in England and came back to Devil's Dip for you. He's so in love with you that it makes me sick."

"She's right, I am."

We both jump at the sound of Angelo's voice. My eyes dart up and land on him, leaning against the doorway, humor carved into his features.

My face blisters with embarrassment. But also—*did you just say you love me?* We lock eyes, and I swallow. The air shifts and Tayce can feel it, because she rises to her feet, stuffs a handful of candy in her purse, and flashes me a knowing grin. "I...should probably get going."

"I'll have someone escort you home, Tayce."

She scoffs at him. "No need. I can look after myself."

Without taking his eyes off me, Angelo gives a small shake of his head. "It's non-negotiable."

Tayce huffs, then rolls her eyes at me. "See? This is why you should have come to me before willingly shacking up with a made man. I'd have told you how crazy they are!" As she passes Angelo, she slaps him on the shoulder and adds, "But in all seriousness, thanks for saving my best friend from that big fat creep."

His lips twitch. "Anytime."

"And if I hear anything in the shop, I'll let you guys know."

Angelo's gaze turns serious. "I'd appreciate that."

"Oh, and if you ever want Rory's name tattooed in a love heart on your chest, I'm your girl. I'll even let you skip the waiting list."

"Uh-huh. Sounds like an offer I can't refuse."

We say our goodbyes, and she disappears through the front door, one of Gabe's burly men in her shadow.

Our gazes clash, and suddenly, I'm overcome with shyness.

"Come here."

I shake my head.

His eyes spark with dark amusement. "Dare you to say no to me again."

Feigning a sigh, I rise to my feet and take the short journey over to the door, my heart beating faster with every step. His eyes narrow on me, but he doesn't take his hands out of his pockets. Instead, he waits, like he's expecting me to do something.

"Did you mean it?" I can't bring myself to say it, but I don't need to, the insinuation hangs heavy in the air between us.

He rakes his teeth over his bottom lip and nods. Such a small movement, but one that melts all of my insides into nothing more than a slush pile.

I didn't know it was possible to crave something and be so frightened of it at the same time. I want nothing more in this world than to be loved by him, yet the same thought makes me want to leap out of the nearest window.

My heart slams against my chest, my fingers burn with the need to touch him.

"But we haven't even kissed," I whisper. It sounds pathetic, even to me, because deep down I know that wouldn't change a thing.

"Kiss me then."

The challenge swirls like an eye of a storm in his gaze.

I pause. "Okay."

"Okay."

Swallowing, I bring my hand up to his neck and hold him at his thick nape. He waits, still and silent, eyes thinning on me. Burning with anticipation, I stand on my tip-toes, but still have to crane my neck to even get near his mouth. I hover there for a while, so close that I can't tell whose heavy, labored breaths belong to who. A little closer, and my mouth brushes against his. So soft and warm. For a moment, I think he's not going to react, but then he parts his lips, and I press mine against them and slide my tongue inside his mouth. His groan is guttural, triggering hot, electric sparks between my thighs. I palm his chest and attempt to pull back, just to say something snarky, but I have just enough time to meet his molten gaze, before he fists my hair and brings me back into him.

His kiss is deep and wet and messy. *Desperate.* Like an arid desert in need of a good storm. His hands roam all over my body, stopping at my ass to grip my cheeks, snaking up to my hips to pull me against his erection. He's rough and unrelenting, and I wouldn't have it any other way. Even when he scrapes his teeth on my lower lip, smacks my ass, and hisses in my ear with strangled venom.

"You have ten seconds to get on my bed before I lose my shit."

A stolen glance at his burning expression, then I turn on my heel and scurry into the foyer and up the stairs. Before I can reach his bedroom, he catches up behind me, snaking his arms around my waist and throwing me onto the bed.

I'm breathless, drunk on the excitement of the unknown. He flips me over onto my back, nudges my thighs apart and looms over me, in all of his masculine glory. His gaze rakes over his clothes on my body, and he rubs his jaw, like he's trying to control his urge.

"Fuck. I knew you'd look good on my bed," he bites out.

I decide to make it harder for him, because I'm addicted to the way he stares at me. With one swoop, I tug off my sweater and buck my hips to slide down the pants. Before I can bask in his leering gaze, he drops onto his elbows on top of me, yanks down the cups of my bra, and latches onto a breast. Desire shoots through my core like a lightning bolt, settling between my thighs in a restless beat. I pull his hair, *hard,* as he switches breasts and reaches down to shove his hand into the front of my thong.

His hand is rough and needy, cupping my sex with a desperation that makes all of the goosebumps on my body stand to attention. His fingers curl up, dragging through my slick lips, before he flicks his forefinger against my clit. I yelp, which makes him chuckle into my breasts.

"You're so wet baby." He slides his hand back down and plunges a finger into my hole, and then another, stretching my canal and filling me with the most delicious burn. "I want to taste every last drop." He kisses a hungry trail down my stomach, until his mouth reaches the waistband of my thong. Snarling, he clamps his teeth onto the lace, as if he's going to tear them off like a darn animal ripping apart his prey.

"Stop," I breathe, although every part of my body is screaming in disagreement.

He stills, his gaze sparking. "What?"

Panting, I force myself up on my elbows. "I..."

As the rest of my sentence burns up between us, he growls and flicks my clit again in annoyance. "Spit it out, baby."

"You've seen and touched every part of me, but uh, I haven't seen *you*." I swallow, heart hitching in my throat. "I want to see you."

He pauses for a moment, his gaze thinning, and then pitch-black mischief dances across his features. Without a word, he sits back on his heels and pushes himself off the bed. It's that he knows every curve and contour of my body, as well as all of the sins that lay within it, and yet I have no idea what lies beneath the Italian suits and the cashmere sweaters.

Without breaking eye contact, he loosens his tie, tosses it aside. The shirt goes next, revealing a tanned, toned stomach, and bulging biceps, both carved from marble. "Holy crow," I mutter, more to myself than him, but it raises a small, breathy laugh from his lips anyway.

He slides off his belt, then slips his slacks off. A flustered rash creeps across my chest at the sight of his black Calvin Kleins, his erection straining against them.

The unknown is scary and enticing, and I'm practically salivating to know what's underneath that fabric.

He raises his arm and drags a hand through his hair, eyes glittering with ill intentions. "Come and see me, then."

First the kiss, now *this*. It's a stark contrast to the way he dominates me with his belt. But suddenly, I realize it's because now he knows of my inexperience, he wants it to be on my terms, not his. *I'm* in control. But by the way he clenches and unclenches his fists, I can tell it's a struggle.

Breathing heavily, I work my way out of my bra and panties and toss them onto his pile of clothes. Then I scoot to the end of the bed, roll onto my knees, and carve a delicate path down the length of his stomach with just one finger. Tension rolls off him in waves, and when I swoop my finger over the horizon of his waistband, his eyes flutter shut and his jaw tightens. I stay there for a moment, grazing over the dark hair there, but then he growls and grips my wrist.

"Don't fucking play games," he rasps "*Touch it.*"

Gasping at the venom in his voice, I slide my hand under the waistband and grip his girth.

He lets out a sharp hiss and throws his head back, all of his abs clenching at my eye level.

Oh, swan. The moment I wrap my fingers around it, I know I'm in over my head. I feel the length of it, its heat and thickness, and my morbid curiosity wonders how the *hell* it's going to fit inside of me.

Biting in frustration, Angelo pushes me back onto the bed and clambers on top of me, pulling out his erection. He fists it at the base and nudges my thighs apart with his knees, settling like a heavy weight on top of me. One hand slips around the back of my neck, the other presses his tip against my entrance.

"Ask me for a sin, Rory," he growls in my ear, nipping at my lobe.

"Tell me a sin," I groan, tilting my hips in desperation, but he pushes me back down into the bed.

"The thought of fucking you has been so dominant all day, I had a raging hard on in the car ride home."

I moan, feeling the length of him open me up as he inches himself slowly inside of me. It's smooth and lazy, a stark contrast to the grit in his voice.

I clamp my hand over his jaw, stopping him from pushing in any farther, and press my lips against his. My lower core burns, a cocktail of pain and pleasure coursing through my veins like a drug. "Tell me another," I beg.

He thrusts a little deeper, filling more of me as he nuzzles my neck. "Those little panties you left in my plane, I've fucked them so many times I've lost count."

"Yeah?"

"Yeah," he grunts. Another inch. "And that stupid fucking matching bra."

I groan under the weight of him, and with every dirty sin he whispers in my ear, he fills me with him. *All* of him. His hips grind against mine, spreading white, heat from my clit up to my core.

"I killed Max because I hated the way he touched you."

"I've never had a girlfriend, let alone cheated on one. I just needed you to hate me."

"On Halloween, I had to pull over and fuck my fist in my car at the thought of you because I couldn't wait to get home."

Fireworks fizzle and pop, lighting every nerve ending on fire. I'm torn, stuck in a desperate limbo between wanting this feeling never to end, and frantically chasing the release. Eventually, the latter wins, and my orgasm explodes from the inside out, sending an uncontrollable shudder through every muscle and every limb. Angelo freezes, cock jerking inside me, watching me in fascination as his name rolls off my tongue in panicked waves.

"Fuck," he groans into my mouth, slowing his thrusts. "That was the hottest thing I've ever seen." A nip on my bottom lip. "*You* are the hottest thing I've ever seen."

With his hot, sticky cum pooling between my thighs, he rolls me over so I'm lying against his chest. His heartbeat is heavy and fast, matching his labored breaths.

"I love you too."

Underneath me, he stills. Stops tracing circles on the small of my back. I'm in such a haze, that the words slipped from my mouth like chocolate on a warm day. My heart beats once, twice. But then I realize I don't want to take the words back at all.

"Say it again."

My lips curve into a smile. "I *love* you."

His chest rises, then falls as he releases a long hiss. "I'm a bad man, Magpie."

"And I'm a bad girl. What's your point?"

He chuckles, then slides my hand into his and rubs the bare flesh on my ring finger with his thumb. He stares at it, thoughtfully. "When I say you're mine, I mean you're mine *forever*. No ifs, no buts. No changing your mind. Sure you want that?"

I prop myself up on my elbow and glare at him. A few heavy beats pass, but his gaze doesn't let up, and neither does mine. "Are you giving me a choice?"

"No." His eyes narrow. "Unless you want the choice?"

My grin returns as I entwine my fingers into his. Thick to my slim, rough to my soft. They are hands I craved on my body for what feels like *forever*. It still doesn't feel real that I get to touch him now whenever I want.

"I thought capos take what they want."

He grunts, irritation crossing the planes of his face. "What I *want*, is for you to be happy." I'm about to let out a snarky retort, but he cuts me off by fisting my hair and clamping his lips against mine. "Not just regular happy. I mean *really* fucking happy," he growls into my mouth, palming my ass to pull me on top of him. "Can't stop fucking smiling, don't want to go to sleep because reality is better than your dreams kind of happy. I want to make you so damn happy that you shit sunshine and piss rainbows and people think you're as high as a kite when you walk into a room." He nips my lower lip in mild frustration, and his fingers dig deep into the back of my thighs as he slides me up to his groin. "If you *want* to be mine, I'll make you that happy, Rory."

Pleasure floats down my spine like a ghost as his cock swells between my lips. "And if I don't?"

He pauses, lifts his hand to grip my chin and forces me to meet his molten gaze. "I'll get on my knees and beg you until you get so sick of me you agree to be mine anyway."

The amusement in his eyes tells me he's half-joking, but the intensity in his voice suggests that he's deadly serious. I bite my lip and rock against his erection.

"Hmm. Angelo Visconti on his knees." I pretend to consider this. "What does that look like?"

His eyes thin. A shake of his head. A huff of disbelief from his lips. Then his hands find my waist and drag me off his lap like I weigh nothing. Before I can ask him what he's doing, he spins me around until I'm sitting on the edge of the bed. With a raw roughness, he pushes my thighs apart and sinks between them onto the carpet.

I choke out a moan at the mere sight. He glares at my pussy like it's done something to piss him off. Then he looks up at me, eyes thick with lust and something darker.

"I'll show you what it looks like. Now, be a good girl and moan my name while I worship you."

And then all the sass I have left evaporates from my body as his mouth settles into a hungry rhythm between my thighs.

CHAPTER
Thirty-Seven

Rory

THE NEXT MORNING, I wake up to an empty bed and a loud drilling noise outside of the window. Despite the satisfying ache between my thighs and the fullness in my heart, irritation flickers at the walls of my contentment.

I swing my legs over the side of the bed and stride toward the window. Under the low-hanging sky, Gabe is hunched over a woodworking table in the garden, the offending tool in his hand. A glance at the screen of my new cell tells me it's barely dawn.

Grunting to myself, I throw on Angelo's sweater and pad downstairs in search of him. I find him sitting on a sofa in the living room, earphones on and MacBook on his lap.

Sharp suit, coffee in hand. He looks every inch the businessman he pretended to be for nine years.

I come to a stop behind him, lift up one earphone and bring my lips to his ear. He doesn't even flinch, like he could sense I was there all along.

"Your brother's renovation obsession woke me up and now I'm in the mood to do *bad things*."

Even being so close to his cheek, I can see his smile. He shifts his face slightly toward me, so that his lips brush the corner of mine. Barely a touch, but the way my knees buckle would make you think he'd just slid himself inside of me.

"You don't have to do bad things anymore, baby girl. I'll do them for you."

I round the sofa and come to a stop in front of him. He slides off his earphones and closes his laptop lid, then tosses both on the coffee table. I put my hand on my hips and wait for a few beats, enjoying the way he settles back into his seat and rakes his gaze down the length of my body. It's like I'm his favorite stripper at his favorite strip joint, and he's been waiting all week to see me dance.

"I appreciate the sentiment, but I *like* doing bad things. Makes me feel good."

He tilts his head, his eyes sparkling with amusement as they finally meet mine. "What do you have in mind?"

"I'm going to tie the shoelaces of his work boots into a constrictor knot. It's impossible to untie." I hitch a shoulder and bat my lashes. "It'll only be a minor inconvenience. I don't want to piss him off *too* much, he will be my brother-in-law, after all."

Angelo says nothing. Instead, he stares up at me with pride licking the walls of his irises. It's an expression that reads, *that's my girl.*

His hand reaches out and runs up the back of my thigh, leaving a blazing trail of anticipation in its wake. *Will I ever get used to his touch?* I can't ever imagine taking it for granted. I stand between his legs, watching him, waiting to see what he wants. Because I've already decided that whatever it is, I'll do. There's so much I haven't done with *any* man, and I want nothing more than to give him all of my firsts.

When his fingertips graze the hem of my panties, he lets out a low grunt.

"What did I tell you about putting on clothes when there are other men in the house?" Before I can reply, he wraps his forearm around the backs of my knees and pulls me onto his lap.

Now I'm just a mere few inches from him, burning under all of his attention. My clothes are soft and baggy to his sharp and tailored. My heavy breathing a contrast to his ice-like stillness.

His nose grazes against mine, then finds the crook of my neck. He breathes in my morning scent, groaning. The way his chest caves under my palm makes me feel powerful.

"You still sure about what we discussed last night, baby?" He rasps in my ear. "Because I can take you to the doctor right this second."

I swallow, my eyelids fluttering at the feeling of his hot breath on my skin. It was only after the third time we made love last night that Angelo realized we hadn't been safe. Immediately, I'd felt foolish; I'd been so all-consumed by *him* that using a condom hadn't even crossed my mind. But the feeling was fleeting, soon replaced with a warmth in the pit of my stomach that I'd never felt before.

Satisfaction to the point of delirium. Contentment so heavy it'll keep me full for the rest of my life. I may be young, dumb, and twenty-one, but I know what I want. I want Angelo and everything that comes with him, including marriage and babies and the constant threat of war. I want all of his sins and secrets. I want to know every one of his memories and make a million more together.

When I'd told him this, he kissed me so hard I thought my jaw would break.

"I'm sure."

I catch the relief on his face before he winds his hand into the base of my hair and pulls me into his chest.

"I've got a busy day today, baby."

"Then I'll leave you to it," I murmur into his white shirt, with no intention of moving.

His fingers trace the length of my spine, coming to a stop at the small of my back. He brushes over the waistband of my panties and snaps it.

"Not until I fuck you senseless. Only *then* will you be free to leave me to it."

I palm his chest and pull away, just enough to meet his gaze.

"I'm sore," I say shyly.

"Then I'll kiss it better," he deadpans, without missing a beat.

I say nothing. His gaze blisters against my reddening face as I fiddle with the buttons on his shirt. With an impatient huff, he puts two fingers under my chin and tilts my eyes to his.

"I don't just want you because you're a tight fuck, Magpie. You wanna lay on my chest and watch a movie while I feed you gumballs like you're a modern-day Cleopatra? Because we can do that instead."

I can't hide my smile. "No, it's not that."

His gaze darkens. "Well, what is it, then?"

My trembling hands slide down his shirt and his abs harden under my touch. I grip his belt buckle and flick my eyes back to his. *Gulp.*

"I want to, uh..."

He stills, then a lazy smirk softens his face. "You want to *what*, Rory? Use your words."

Grinding my back molars, I steel my jaw and swallow. "I want to suck your cock, but I haven't done it before. Okay?" A cocktail of frustration and embarrassment bites my tone

"You've never given a blowjob?" Angelo lets out a laugh, the type that makes my bones cringe. The type that screams my innocence at full volume for the world to hear.

The shells of my ears grow hot. "Forget it," I snap.

I try to push myself off of his lap, but he grabs my waist and holds me against his groin.

"I will *not* forget it," he rasps, all traces of humor suddenly evaporating. It's replaced by a dark lust that burns hot in the back of his throat as he speaks. "Are you being serious?"

"I told you. I've only been with one guy, and it was—"

He clamps a large hand over my mouth, cutting me off. "Mention that other guy again and I'll drop him in the Pacific with a couple of bricks attached to his ankles."

The threat rolls so smoothly off his tongue that I don't doubt he'd go through with it. The dominance in his tone hangs like a weight between my thighs, thumping hot and heavy. His expression softens as he removes his hand and runs a thumb over my bottom lip.

"You going to suck my cock, baby?" he whispers, studying my features. "Or are you going to sit there like a deer caught in headlights all day?"

I bat his hand away. "I don't know how," I mutter.

His lips twitch. "As long as it's in your mouth, I'm sure I'll be a happy man." We stare at each other for a moment, his gaze dancing with amusement, mine hot enough to burn a hole into his face. He clears his throat. "Here." His hand comes back to my mouth again. This time, instead of clamping over it, he slips a thick finger into my parted lips. "Suck," he demands.

Without breaking eye contact, I run my tongue from his knuckle to his fingertip, then suck. His eyes flash like a warning sign, and he mutters a curse word I don't quite catch under his breath.

"See? You're a natural," he says, strangled.

He bucks his hips so his erection grinds harder against my clit. Despite the indifference coating his features, I can tell he's growing impatient by the balled fist at his side.

Taking a deep breath, I slide to my knees in front of him. He quickly slips his cell from his pocket and brings it up to his ear. Three rings. Then, the faint drilling in the distance stops.

"Tell your men the living room is off-limits until I say otherwise."

He doesn't wait for a response. Instead, he drops the cell to the couch and glares at me. "I don't have all day, Magpie."

Making a sound that's somewhere between a tut and a whimper, I turn my attention to his pants and the bulge straining against them. The belt unbuckles with the smoothness of melted butter; the zipper opens like silk. Another glance up at Angelo. He's tense, I can see it in the hard lines of his shoulders and the angle of his jaw, but he offers me a tight nod of encouragement.

My hands shake as I pull down his Calvin's and palm his erection. *Holy crow.* We've had sex more than a handful of times, but this is the closest I've been to his *thing*. It's bigger in the cold light of day. Smooth and thick and *intimidating.*

I swallow the little lump of panic clotting my throat. Watching a movie and eating gumballs doesn't sound too bad—

"*Suck. It.*"

I flinch at the cocktail of venom and desperation in Angelo's voice. He's not a man who likes to be teased. He spreads his thighs wider and throws an arm over the back of the sofa. Stares at me expectantly.

Come on, Rory. It's just like his finger. So I treat it as such, sticking out my tongue to lick it from the base to the tip. Once I get to the head, his abs tense, and a small, almost inaudible hiss escapes his lips. The sound feels good against my skin, raising the hairs on the back of my neck, so I do it again. This time, I harden my tongue and flick the tip, which elicits a small groan.

"Yes, like that," he mutters, clenching and unclenching his fist. "Now, show me how much you can fit in your mouth."

I sit back on my heels, wipe my wet mouth with the back of my hand and stare at his dick warily. It looks like a choking hazard. Planting my hands on his thighs for support, I suck it all into my mouth, stopping about two-thirds of the way down when his head hits the back of my throat.

His groan is guttural, sparking fireworks of pleasure in my lower core.

"Relax," he breathes. He winds his hand into my hair and gently pushes my head down. "You can take more than that." I resist, but his grip only tightens. My gaze flickers up to his. "I thought you were a bad girl?" he says with a dangerous smirk playing on his lips.

Two words with enough power to tune the pulse in my clit to a new rhythm. One that's frantic and desperate to reach the crescendo. So, I relax my throat and take in a few more inches. My eyes are watering and my jaw aches, but the hot heat swelling between my thighs overshadows any other sensation. Keeping my jaw slack, I let Angelo control my rhythm with his hand wound tightly into my hair. Up, down. Up, down. His breathing grows more and more labored, his eyes darkening every time his cock hits the back of my throat.

"Fuck, baby," he says roughly, throwing his head back against the couch. "You're going to make me a five-minute man."

I have no idea what that means, not until a strangled moan escapes his lips and a shudder rolls through his body, one that ends in his shaft. Hot, salty ropes fill my mouth, which, to my shame, I greedily swallow. He holds my head against him with one hand and fists the base of his cock with the other, as if squeezing out every last drop of pleasure.

We pant to the same rhythm for a few moments, my cheek resting on the inside of his thigh as he strokes my hair.

Suddenly he stops. The couch groans as he sits up straight. "Did you swallow?"

I flash him a coy look. "Yes."

He licks his lips. Gives a small shake of his head. "You're incredible. Come here."

I crawl up onto the couch and curl up beside him. *Ba-dum. Ba-dum. Ba-dum.* His heartbeat thumps hard against my ear, and I feel delirious knowing *that was all my doing.*

"I suppose I should let you get on with your work," I sigh, reluctantly dragging myself out of the crook of his arm.

"Actually, I think you've earned the right to help," he says throatily.

Before I can ask what he means, he picks up the earphones from the coffee table and slips them on my head. Then, he opens his laptop and taps a few keys.

A familiar voice fills my ears.

You have reached Sinners Anonymous. Please leave your sin after the tone.

My blood runs to ice and I bolt upright. "Is this...?"

"Yes," Angelo says, with a smirk playing on his lips. "A playlist of all the sins the hotline received this month. I want you to choose your top three for our monthly meeting." He runs a thumb down my cheekbone, then leans in to nip my bottom lip. "I want the *darkest*, most *depraved* ones you can find," he growls, each word like a spike in my lower core. "You think you can do that for me, baby?"

Adrenaline coasts down my spine. *Darkness. Depravity.* I can taste them on my tongue, feel them humming in my veins. I manage a nod, before settling down into the crack of Angelo's arm. He types out emails one-handed, answers calls that I can't hear. All while I let sins that aren't mine fill my soul.

CHAPTER Thirty-Eight

Rory

THE NEXT WEEK PASSES in a blur of sex and sin. Sometimes he screws me slow and sensual, and I savor every thrust, lick and suck, committing them to memory. Sometimes he screws me hard and frantic, his belt or his hand, or both, leaving its mark on my ass and my throat. Afterward, he's gentle, giving me baths and rubbing lotion on the rawest parts of me, which I love almost as much as the spankings themselves.

I'm allowed to go and see my dad whenever I want, as long as Gabe's men escort me. There's no hourly time limit, and thankfully, Melissa and the rest of the care team have seamlessly transitioned to Angelo's payroll. When Angelo's working, sometimes Tayce will come over and we'll watch a movie, or pore over Architectural Digest magazine in search of design inspiration for the renovated house. He's adamant I can do what I want with the place, and I'm not sure if it's because he wants to keep me busy and distracted, or if he wants to rid every inch of the house of his father. It's still a blank, white canvas, but it doesn't feel suffocating like the Cove mansion did. It feels like a home instead of a prison, with a closet full of my own clothes and no bitter Greta forcing me into sizes that are too small. No formal dinners, just pizzas or pastas, curled up on the sofa; it's pure bliss.

When Friday evening rolls around, I'm sitting crossed-legged on the bed, creating a vision board for the games room, when Angelo slips through the door. My heart beats on the double, like it always does when he gets home. It's a mix of relief that he's back in one piece, and excitement of getting to feel his warmth against mine.

He loosens his tie and settles in behind me, leaning over my shoulder to admire my work. "When are you going to stop sticking and cutting and start actually ordering some furniture?"

"When you sign off my ideas!"

His chuckle is deep and throaty. "I already told you, baby. Whatever you want to do, I'll love it."

"Mhmm." I twist in his arms and plant a soft kiss on his lips. "Good day?"

"It's not over yet."

My heart sinks a few inches, but I thread nonchalance through my tone. "No?"

"Nah. Got a meeting with the harbormaster at the Rusty Anchor."

"Oh."

"Wanna come?"

My disappointment is immediately upgraded to excitement. "For real?"

"Yeah, you're friends with the girl that works there, right? It's Dip territory, and my men will be there."

"Woohoo!" I scramble to my feet, kicking the stack of magazines out of the way.

Angelo leans back on the pillows, watching me in amusement. "Fucking hell, you'd think I was taking you to a ball."

"No more balls, *please*," I moan, dipping into the closet and tugging a pair of jeans off the rack. "I never want to see a ball gown again."

"Deal," he drawls, rising to his feet and smacking my ass on his way to the door. "Meet me downstairs in five."

Five minutes later, he's waiting at the bottom of the stairs for me, a flask in one hand, a bundle of clothes in the other. "Take," he demands, giving me the flask. "It's hot cocoa."

I bring it to my chest. "You made it for me?"

"Yeah," he mutters darkly. "But I'm not a fucking chef. We need to get some help around here, a few maids and an assistant will do. Scarf." He wraps it around my neck and pulls tight. "Hat, gloves, coat."

"Jesus, Angelo. We're going to a bar, not going skiing."

He slips the coat over my shoulders and tugs on the lapel, bringing me in for a deep kiss. "It's cold outside."

"Who knew a Cosa Nostra don could be so sweet?"

He dips down to cup my ass cheek, and squeezes, *hard*. "Use that smart mouth again, and I'll remind you that I'm not," he growls with a twinkle in his eye.

The car has already been warmed up, and as I slide inside, I check the glove box expectantly. Sure enough, Angelo's refilled it with some of the British Wine Gums I like so much. His hand is heavy and possessive on my thigh as we drive the short distance, flanked by two cars with Gabe's men inside. Pulling up to the Rusty Anchor, excitement prickles in my chest; it feels *almost* like being normal again. Not spending a Friday night around a stuffy table with people who hate me as much as I hate them, but at a dive bar, catching up with my friends.

Only this time, I have a made man watching my every move.

The warmth from the fire brushes my face as soon as we step inside. Angelo's hand is clamped around mine, but I tug away the moment I recognize a familiar face.

"Bill!"

I run over and throw my arms around Dad's best friend. He smells like cigars and leather, and I'm hit with childhood nostalgia. I haven't seen him in ages. He still visits my father at the Preserve almost daily, but always different times from me.

"My little Rory! My goodness, how have you been?" he says, giving me a squeeze.

As I turn around, Angelo's gaze is narrowed as he watches us from the doorway. "Angelo, meet Bill. He's my dad's best friend."

His lips twitch. He takes a step forward and sticks out his hand for Bill to shake. "Dad's best friend and harbormaster. Devil's Dip really is a small place."

I spin around, wide-eyed. "You're the port master now, Bill?"

He grins. "Sure am."

Pinning Angelo with a scowl, I say, "Well, then. You better be extra nice to him." With a wiggle of my finger, I walk toward the bar. "I'm watching you."

He shakes his head in disbelief, probably not used to being undermined by his girlfriend at the start of a meeting. Before I can cause any more trouble, I slide onto one of the seats by the bar and ring the bell. A few moments pass before Wren strolls out of the back. She freezes in surprise, then her face melts into a big grin.

"Rory Carter. We have *so* much to catch up on."

I let out a chirpy laugh. "Yeah, you can say that again. But for now, can you just pour me my usual white wine spritzer and we can pretend like everything's how it used to be?"

"Sure thing." She slams the glass on the bar and points up to the sign above her head. It's yellowing and curling at the edges, but everyone knows what it says, because it's been here for as long as Wren's worked here:

More than two drinks will require handing over your car keys to a member of staff.

"That includes your scary man now, too." She palms the bar and peers over at him. "Unless he owns the place. Does he? Is he my boss now?"

"Honestly? I have no idea. But don't worry, he's a puppy, really." *Lie.*

I look over and, even though he's in deep conversation with Bill, his gaze shifts to mine. He winks, and fireworks ignite in my chest. Trying to conceal my smile, I take a sip of wine and turn back to Wren. "So, what have I missed over in Dip?" She strums her fingers against the bar and thinks. "Come on, you know everything!"

It's true. Not just because she works at the Rusty Anchor, but because she's always in Devil's Cove, too. She's fondly known as the Good Samaritan around these parts, because after her shift, she gets on the bus to Devil's Cove and stays on the main strip until all the bars and clubs close, handing out flip-flops and water to drunk tourists and hailing cabs for those who need it. Rinse and repeat, every single night.

"Ah, yes!" she says, blue eyes suddenly lighting up. "Remember Spencer Gravelty and his crew?"

I force my face to remain indifferent. I know she's heard the rumors, but she's too respectful to ever bring them up. "Uh-huh."

"Well, they've all gone missing. All five of them!"

My ears grow hot, and I steal another glance at Angelo. *He did it.* Wren carries on, talking about their last sighting and a potential camping trip gone wrong, but I'm barely listening. *Angelo Visconti killed them for me like it was nothing.*

Holy crow, I'm so in love with this man it makes my teeth ache. Not just because he's handsome and protective and loving, but because he's *bad.* Real darn bad, and it appeals to the darkness inside of me, too. Spencer and his crew might have been the reason I committed my first sin, but I think they just brought my darkness to the surface. It's Angelo who stokes the fire. The desire to be bad *with him* burns under my skin like a flame.

The door to the bar swings open, letting in an icy chill. A man strolls through it, uneven footsteps echoing around the shipping container.

Immediately, unease consumes me.

"Oh no. Not this guy again."

Out of the corner of my eye, I see Angelo stop talking and glare at him. I drag my gaze to Wren. "What?"

She gives a small shake of her head, twisting a rag inside a beer glass. "Almost every day this week, he's come into here, talking about how it's good to be back home."

"He's a local? I don't recognize him."

"Me either."

Angelo's still staring at the man. He's rugged, weather-worn, wearing a running jacket and jeans, a combination not suitable for the late-fall chill. He looms at the end of the bar, swaying unsteadily on his feet. As he clicks to get Wren's attention, Angelo rises.

"He just stands there, drinking a pale ale and giving me a chemistry lesson. So weird. I really hope he's *not* a local and that he's just passing through."

The man turns to look at Angelo, revealing a dark, angry scar on the side of his face. My blood turns to ice, and before I can think about it, I slide off the stall and make my way to Angelo. Gabe's men come out of the shadows, but I reach Angelo first, putting a hand against his chest. His eyes are crazed, but he won't look at me. *Can't* look at me. Too focused on the man.

"Angelo—"

"Move."

The venom in his voice snatches the air from my lungs and I stumble back. He fills the bar with his imposing silhouette and all of the fury rolling off it. He turns, just enough to nod in the direction of the burly man coming up behind the guy.

"Angelo," I hiss, eyes darting frantically to Bill, who's standing now too. "Not in here. *Please.*"

His chest tenses under my palm. He pauses. Gives a hurt nod. "Get him outside." He turns to me, eyes an uncontrollable fire. "You stay here."

"Wait—"

He whips back around, gripping my wrist. "Don't fuck with me, Rory. *Stay. Here.*"

"No!" My voice comes out shaky and pathetic, but I ball my fists and hold my ground. "No. I'm coming with you. I *need* to." Angelo snarls, but as he turns to walk out again, I grip his jacket. "You got rid of my demons, I want to help you get rid of yours."

His gaze studies mine, fury and annoyance ghosting through it, but then, finally, he gives me a sharp nod.

My heart threatening to beat out of my throat, I scurry out of the bar with Angelo, breaking into a run just to keep up with his fast strides. "Get him in the trunk," he growls, glaring at the man. He's too drunk to put up more than a mild protest, but Angelo's men don't argue, folding him up and putting him in the back of one of their cars.

In his Aston Martin, the rage blisters off him at a dangerous temperature. I let him fester, too scared to utter a word. A handful of minutes roll past until I realize where we're headed.

I sit up a little straighter. Swallow the thick lump in my throat. "Are you sure it's him?" I whisper.

Nothing but a small nod.

I've never been on the cliff at night. It feels even more dangerous, the elements harsher and the drop to the raging waters below even steeper. Angelo pulls up to the curb and kills the engine. The headlights from the car behind dazzle me in the mirrors.

"You're staying in the car."

"No. I want to watch." With a new-found surge of confidence, I tilt my chin up and add, "I want to watch you kill the man who killed your mother."

His knuckles whiten on the steering wheel. Then he growls, making me flinch. But when he gets out, I get out too, and to my surprise, he doesn't shout at me to get back in the car.

His men bring the guy out to the cliff. He's slurring his words but the panic is there now, caught in his screams and ever-present in his flailing limbs. I fall into step next to Angelo as he strides toward the edge of the cliff. His profile is sharper than ever, cutting an ominous shadow. He's calm in the scariest of ways, taking his time to reload his gun and polish the barrel with his sleeve.

"Line him up."

My pulse skitters.

Two suited figures take an arm each and drag him across the mud, until he's standing with his back to the starless sky. Below, the sea rages hard and fast, breaking against the rocks. It sounds like a warning sign, a reminder that you should never get too close to the edge.

To my surprise, Angelo turns to me, and even in the darkness, I can see the sardonic smirk splitting his beautiful face.

"What do you reckon, Magpie?"

"W-what?"

"Will he fall, or fly?"

My breath dances between us in a puff of condensation. It's labored and heavy, fueled by a morbid buzz of adrenaline that swirls in my lungs. *Holy crow*. My body is buzzing with the thrill, the *danger* of it all.

"Fall," I choke out. "Fall all the way to hell."

He nods. "Let's hope," he grinds out.

With one swift motion, he spins me around so I'm facing the church behind us. The old, withered building that the man I love learned to be bad in. The gunshot is louder than I expected, and a white flash of light coats the cobbled walls of the church for a split second, before plunging us back into darkness.

No scream, no thud. Just the allure of gunpowder and the sound of ringing in my ears.

When Angelo breathes out a long hiss, I snake my arms under his coat and hold him, tight. Despite being still and silent, the way his heart hammers so violently gives his true feelings away.

"I love you," I breathe into the placket of his shirt. "I love you so much."

It suddenly occurs to me: it's ironic that Angelo calls me "Magpie." Because I'm not attracted to the shiny things, I'm attracted to the darkness. And now, I can feel his darkness radiating against mine, a gentle hum under the surface of his tanned skin. A few moments pass, and then his hand finds the back of my skull, winding itself into my hair and tilting my face to him.

"I love you too, baby."

He kisses me, desperate and ruthless, grazing his teeth over my lip. It's the kiss of a killer, one that's just scored the biggest revenge of his life.

As he pulls away, his features are a fraction softer. He strokes a rough thumb over my cheek, his gaze slotting in perfectly with mine.

"You know, my mom always said the good always canceled out the bad." He swallows, the Adam's apple bobbing in the trunk of his throat. "But what happens if you're both bad? Both the same side of the coin?"

I graze my nose against his, smiling.

"Magic happens, baby."

ONE MONTH
Later

Angelo

RORY'S LAUGHTER FLOATS FROM underneath the door, making me stop in my tracks. Instead of knocking, I press my forehead against it and smile, my heart full of *her*. Over the last month, that girl has managed to fill every inch of my soul, my mind, and my home. Fuck, I find pieces of her in every corner; her long blond curls stuck to the seat of my car, the ghost of her perfume when I walk into a room hours after she does.

I know war is coming, but with her, all I know is peace.

As much as I'd like to stay out here all day, I've got shit to get on with. So I knock, smirking as her laugh turns into a squeal. Tayce pokes her head through the crack and scowls.

"You can't be here! It's bad luck."

I cock a brow and wedge my foot between the door and the frame. "Well, is she dressed yet?"

Her gaze narrows, dropping to my shoe. "No. Is it urgent?"

"Wouldn't be wasting my time talking to you if it wasn't."

With a dramatic sigh, she yells over her shoulder, and Rory comes bounding up to the door.

Our eyes clash and my throat tightens. Fuck, I don't know how I'm going to do this. She's not even in her wedding dress yet, but just her hair and makeup alone are making me want to put my fist through a wall, because I can't figure out how else to deal with all the emotion brewing inside my rib cage.

I lick my lips. Shake my head in disbelief. "Sometimes I think I conjured you from a wet dream."

She laughs, a delicious, throaty noise that I've quickly become addicted to. "You know you're not allowed to see me before the ceremony. It's not traditional."

"We're not exactly a traditional couple, baby."

Her grin is all-knowing, our own little web of sin and secrets swirling silently around us. She knows I'm right. From stealing her off my uncle to spanking her for her sins, we've never been normal. Hell, even the way I proposed wasn't normal. It was in bed, after a particularly long night of fucking, and the urge to chain this girl to me forever became all-consuming. I didn't ask her to marry me, I fucking *begged*, and then let her choose her own ring. All I wanted to do was give her the biggest diamond I could source, a loud-and-proud warning sign that she was *mine*, but I knew she'd hate that. She wanted simple, something that blended in with her running pants and oversized hoodies.

"Are you going to tell me what you want or are you going to stare at me all day?" she asks, eyes glinting under her false lashes.

I grind my jaw, letting her insolence slide, because I have more important things to give her than a spanking today. "Come. I want to show you something."

"But—"

"It'll be quick, I promise."

With a glance over her shoulder, she steps out of the room and slides her hand in mine, allowing me to lead her across the hall and down the stairs. The house is slowly turning into a home, *our* home, each corner punctuated with touches of Rory. We reach the back door and I wrap her up in my big parka and lead her out into the mid-December chill.

"Holy crow," she grunts, wrapping her arms around her body. "I wish I chose a dress with sleeves now. Remind me why we didn't wait for a summer wedding, again?"

In response, I pick her up, wrap her in my arms and carry her to the back of the garden. "I wasn't waiting another week to marry you, let alone a whole fucking season. Close your eyes," I mutter against the crown of her hair. We pass the pond she insisted on building, and the little bird-watching hut that looks over it. When we reach our destination, a small, alcove covered in shrubbery right at the bottom of the garden, I gently lower her to the ground and spin her around.

"Okay, you can open them now."

She pops her lids. Gasps. Immediately, my heart flutters at the feeling of her back tensing against my chest.

"Is it really...?"

"Yes," I smirk, rubbing my palms down the length of her arms. "It's the phone booth from the cliff."

"But...*how*?!"

"Don't worry yourself about the details. Look." I open the door and pull her inside. Our warm bodies and breath immediately steam up the paneled windows. Without a word, I lift the receiver and put it to her ear, watching her face melt into pure elation as she hears the automated voicemail message on the other end of the line. "It's not connected to the real hotline, it's a replica with a private connection, just for you."

She laughs, choking back emotion. "I don't know what to say."

"Makes a change," I bite back, flicking her perfect button nose.

I know how much she misses confessing her petty little sins, but from now on, that's all they'll ever be—petty. Because any real sin she wants to commit, I'll do it for her. I've managed to somewhat fill the void by letting her listen to the sins that come in to the hotline, which she finds fascinating. Once a week, we curl up on the sofa after dinner and press play, with the promise she'll get to choose the sins I'll put forward to my brothers on the last Sunday of every month.

She hitches herself on her tip toes and grazes her mouth over mine. I grip the back of her hair and deepen the kiss, stealing all the labored breaths slipping out from her lungs; like everything else about her, they belong to me now. It's insane how something so simple as a kiss from her makes my cock rock hard. I groan into her mouth and reluctantly push her off.

"I need to get changed."

She looks up at me, a shy expression on her face. "And I probably need to redo my lipstick. Thank you," she adds with a quick peck, before slipping out the door. "I'll see you at the altar!"

An hour later, I'm by the lake at the Devil's Preserve. We knew immediately that this was the only logical place to get married; not only because the park means so much to Rory, but because her father can walk her down the aisle and actually remember the day. The wedding doesn't start for another hour, but I'm here to check the security is tight and everything is going to run smoothly.

Gabe's men are everywhere, barking orders through earpieces and doing constant laps of the perimeter. Gabe himself strides past with a stern expression on his face, an AK-47 slung over his arm. Amusement prickles at my chest. *Christ.* I don't know why I ever bothered to be worried about the Cove clan's retaliation to me killing Alberto. My brother is a true psychopath and completely in his element heading up an army; not even Dante would be stupid enough to go up against him.

I whistle over to him. He scowls and strides over, raking a stern eye over my tuxedo. "We need to call the wedding off."

My turn to scowl. "Not a chance in hell. What makes you say that?"

His gaze shifts around the rows of white chairs, the rose-covered arbor at the end of the dock, and the dozens of lit candles floating on the lake. "I have a bad feeling about it."

I suck in a lungful of air and give a shake of my head. "Fucking hell. We haven't heard a peep out of the Cove clan since I left Alberto dead in his office. I know it isn't over, but the chances of anything happening today are low."

His jaw ticks in thought. I clamp a hand on his tense shoulder. "Can you switch out of killer mode for just an hour, and, you know, be my best man?"

A few heavy seconds pass, conflict coasting the planes of his face. Eventually, he nods, bringing his cell to his ear. "One hour, that's all."

I watch him leave, in disbelief, before sinking in one of the guest chairs and studying the chaos that goes into creating a perfect wedding. Servers haul in last-minute deliveries, cleaners do a final swipe, and at the far end of the lake, I spot Rafe on the phone, talking animatedly at whoever is on the other side of the line. Despite him agreeing to handle the entire entertainment side of the wedding, I've barely seen him over the last month. He's been too busy making plans to build an exclusive casino and club in the cave network underneath Devil's Dip. Initially, I'd agreed to give the space to the Hollow clan, but they were more than happy to back out of the deal, once they learned of the feud between us and the Cove brothers. Ever the businessman, Cas was firm and fair with his reasoning: They wanted to be Switzerland—completely neutral—and to stay out of it.

I can respect that.

I sit there until the guests start arriving. No fucking distant cousins from Sicily, just people Rory and I actually give a fuck about. The Hollow clan turn up, Benny and Nico throwing me cheesy thumbs-ups across the rows. They are followed in by the harbormaster, Bill, and some other familiar faces from the port. As Rafe makes a beeline toward me, texting as he walks, I rise to my feet to greet him. Suddenly, he looks up and stops, an unreadable expression on his face. Heart quickening, I turn to follow his gaze.

Tor.

He's alone, cutting a sharp figure in a navy three-piece suit, that nose ring glinting under the early moonlight. We lock eyes and stare at each other for a few beats.

He nods. I nod back, and when I turn back to Rafe, he has a shark-like grin stretching his face.

"He chose us."

"Dante might have sent him. Radio Gabe, I want him checked out."

Rafe's face flickers with annoyance. "Tor wouldn't do that to us."

"Do it."

With my harsh command hanging heavy in the air, I turn on my heel and storm toward the bar area. I hope to god he's chosen us, but nothing or nobody is going to ruin this fucking night for Rory. I take a deep breath in the hope it'll extinguish some of the unease in my lungs. Slowing to a stop, I absentmindedly watch the row of servers loading up champagne flutes onto trays for incoming guests.

The girl at the end of the bar catches my eye, because it's immediately obvious she's never poured a glass of champagne in her life. She's not even tipping the flute, and then she curses loudly when the bubbles spill out over the rim. Gaze darkening, I make a beeline for her. The Cove Clan aren't going to ruin this wedding, and I sure as hell won't let a shitty server ruin it, either.

As she shakily picks up the tray, crystal clinking dangerously, I step in front of her. "You're fired," I growl. "Put it down and go home."

The venom in my voice makes her flinch, and the glasses tumble like a house of cards. Another loud curse word escapes her lips, and then she scowls up at me.

"For *fuck's* sake, where do you get off scaring people like that?!"

My heart comes to a crashing stop as our eyes lock.

"You."

She stills. Her gaze thins. "Do I know you?"

Big blue eyes. Wild red hair. Freckles that pool together when she scrunches her nose at me.

I'd recognize this girl anywhere. Under the heavy silence, her expression softens, morphing from annoyance into poorly disguised panic. A beat passes. Then without a word, she drops the tray, turns on her heel, and runs. She doesn't get very far, because Rafe steps out of the shadows and she crashes into his chest. His hand shoots out, grabs her arm, and he drags her back to me.

"Get off me!" she hisses, trying to wriggle out of his grip.

"Are you scaring my servers, Angelo?" he drawls. "I know it's your wedding, but gee, try not to make a scene before the ceremony even starts."

"You hired the chick?" I growl.

He frowns at the rage threading through my tone. I'm barely able to contain it, and if it was a man standing in front of me, my hand would already be around his throat.

"Why? Have you fucked her?"

"No, it's her. The girl who sold me the fortune cookie in San Francisco," I bite out, shaking my head in disbelief. There's no doubt in my mind that it's her. But back then, she was wide-eyed and scared, desperate for whatever dimes she could scrape together by selling broken fortune cookies in China Town. Got into my fucking pockets with a sob story about needing to eat.

Rafe stills, narrowing his gaze on the girl. "Is this true?"

She goes for another fruitless tug to get her arm back, but Rafe's knuckles only whiten on her sleeve. "I don't know, I've had loads of jobs. Now get *off* me!"

He yanks her closer, spitting venom in her ear. Around us, guests and servers alike are staring at the scene. "Did you, or did you not, sell fortune cookies in San Fran? Simple question, girl. Don't make me break your fingers to get an answer."

"Yes!" she yelps.

"So what the fuck are you doing here?" he grinds out. "Who are you working for?"

"What? I just moved here! Got a job at an events agency and they put me on this wedding! Jesus," she spits, face flushing red. "You never heard of a coincidence?"

"What's a coincidence is that I have a lying little brat on my hands and only one bullet left in my chamber." Rafe looks up and gives me a stern nod. "I'll handle it."

"What does that mean?" she breathes, eyes darting between me and my brother. "Please, just let me go, I'll—"

"Let her go, Rafe."

He stills. Pins me with a glare that suggests I'm crazy.

I huff out a bitter laugh, my eyes flicking to the navy sky. "Mama always believed in fate. It was a fortune cookie that brought her to the Coast in the first place, and the exact same fucking fortune brought me back here, too. I thought it was to find the cunt that killed her, but now, I realize it wasn't. It was to lead me to Rory. This is Mama's way of telling me she's here today."

They both stare up at me like I've lost the plot. I bite back a smirk, nod to the girl. "Let her *go*, Rafe."

Reluctantly, he releases his grip on her arm. She smooths down her uniform and takes a few shaky steps away from my brother. He glares at her, still unconvinced that it's a coincidence. "Leave the Preserve. Hell, if you had any common sense, girl, you'd leave Devil's Dip."

"What, do you like, own it, or something?" she snaps back.

A demonic smile creeps across his lips. "Or something."

His words make her recoil. With one last cursory glance in my direction, she turns on her heel and takes off running, disappearing into the thickness of the trees.

Rafe turns to me. Shakes his head. "You've gone soft, my brother."

Rory

"They'll be calling you *Signora* Aurora Visconti soon."

A delirious laugh escapes my lips, forming a cloud of steam against the dark sky. It's crazy to think that just a handful of months ago, the thought of being called that made my stomach curdle. Now, it sparks little fireworks of joy in my chest. I slip my arm into my father's and plant a kiss on his cold cheek.

"I'll always be a Carter at heart, dad."

He grins, eyes shimmering. "Always."

Tayce comes up behind me, adjusting the train of my dress. It's only a small one, and it's simple, like the rest of my outfit. A sleek, satin gown that hugs the curves of my body without being too revealing. Of course, I'm also wearing a white padded jacket, because it turns out weddings in December are incredibly cold. As I turn around to thank her, something behind the trees catches my eye.

My breathing shallows. "*Amelia?*" She steps out from the shadows, eyes darting nervously through the clearing. In front of the dock, guests are beginning to take their seats, and the officiant is under the arbor, going over his speech. "Excuse me for a moment," I say to my father and Tayce, slipping away to meet her.

She breathes hard and grabs my forearm. "Oh, Aurora, you look beautiful," she murmurs. I rake a gaze over the length of her; wearing a big puffer jacket and jeans, she's definitely not dressed for a wedding. Not that she was invited—none of the Cove clan were. In fact, I haven't seen her since I was wearing a *very* different wedding dress.

"What are you doing here?"

"Don't worry, I'm not staying. Here." She thrusts a beautifully wrapped present into my hands. "From me and Donnie. I just stopped by to say congratulations, and that I'm sorry."

My jaw works. "For what?" I bite out.

"For turning a blind eye to what was happening to you. Deep down, I knew there's no way you were marrying Alberto for love. But I've seen so many horrors while being a member of that family that I'll cling onto any sliver of hope I can." She swallows. Wipes a tear from her cheek. "You deserved better."

I'm silent for a few moments, weighing my emotions. I come to the conclusion that I don't hate Amelia, and I never have. She's just another victim of the Cove clan. In a room full of people who despised me, she was always the beacon of light. I bring her in for a hug. "Thank you. You deserve better too, Amelia."

As she pulls away, she gives me a firm nod. "You're right. Donatello thinks so too, and we'll finally be leaving the Coast!" With a small grin, she rubs her stomach and adds, "Me, Donnie, and the baby. Starting a new life in Colorado!"

"Congratulations!"

"Thanks, Aurora. Oh, and he also wants me to thank Angelo for him."

"For what?"

Her gaze darkens. "Killing Alberto. He's never wanted to be a made man, and now this is his out."

I grin, my heart soaring with happiness. "Now the villain is dead, I hope you get your happy ending."

Her laugh is drowned out by the sound of the orchestra coming to life in the distance, marking the start of the ceremony. "And you're about to get yours." With one last squeeze of my arm, she flashes me a small smile and starts walking back into the woods. "Enjoy it, you're perfect for each other."

I watch her disappear and turn back around to the lake.

Yes. Yes, *we are.*

"Maybe wearing heels on a damp December evening wasn't the smartest idea," Angelo mutters, picking me up again to carry me over another muddy patch.

"What else was I going to wear?"

"Your sneakers? Those stupid Wellington boots with the fluffy socks?"

"On our wedding day?"

"Your dress is long enough, nobody would know."

I laugh as he gently drops me onto firmer ground and slides his large hand over mine. Behind us, the jovial hum of the wedding party grows quieter as we make our way through the forest and back onto the main road.

"Now I'm married to the head of the Devil's Dip mafia, I suppose I'll have to wear dresses and heels all the time."

"Nah. Your sweats and sneakers will do."

"Yeah?"

"Yeah." Angelo's lips meet my crown, his voice growing darker. "But if you ever want to wear that leather dress to bed you wore on Halloween, I wouldn't complain."

Hot, spiky lust spreads between my thighs, warming my skin despite the chill in the air. At the road, we cross over to the church and snake through the graveyard, until we're standing right on the edge of the cliff. Closing my eyes, I rest my head against his chest, and bask in the medley of his heartbeat and the crashing waves below. The wedding reception is great, but having a few stolen moments with my husband, exactly where we first met, is even better.

The sound of a Zippo lighter sparking. The taste of smoke on my tongue. I pop a lid and crane my neck up, just in time to see Angelo slip a lit cigarette between his lips.

"I can't remember the last time I saw you smoke."

"For old time's sake," he purrs, slipping it between my lips and holding it there. He watches me in fascination as I take a long, slow drag. When I exhale, he captures the smoke in his mouth. My breath and his breath, his heart and mine, they are interchangeable now.

His gaze darts up to the sky. "That'll be you, soon."

I follow his eye line to the plane soaring overhead. A grin splits my face in two, excitement buzzing in my veins. A few days ago, Angelo surprised me with a letter. It was from the Northwestern Academy of Aviation, letting me know that my place at the school was still valid, on the condition that I passed the final exam I never got to sit. I don't know how many people my husband had to bribe or intimidate to wrangle that, but the dark side of me doesn't care.

Above my head, Angelo takes a final drag and flicks the butt into the sea below.

"You know, that's not very good for the environment."

"And you're not very good for *me*," he growls, nipping at my ear. He spins me around and palms my ass, pulling my hips flush against his.

"You're hard," I smirk, grinding against his erection.

"See? Not good for me. Ever since I met you I walk around with a permanent hard-on." He grazes his lips against mine, wrapping me in tobacco, leather, and warm whiskey. "I've got a question for you."

"Another one? I already said yes."

He chuckles into my mouth, parting my lips with a swipe of his tongue.

"You hoping to fall, or fly?"

I pull away from him and gaze over the edge. His grip tightens on my waist, as if he's worried a strong gust of wind will blow me over it.

"Fly," I announce.

I turn back to him, loving how his eyes twinkle under the moonlight. "Yeah?"

"Uh-huh. I've already fallen." I pause for dramatic effect. "Fallen in love with you."

He stills, then shakes his head in disbelief. "Fucking hell, I think that's the cheesiest thing you've ever said."

Laughing, I press my lips against his again, pulling his nape to deepen the kiss. A lustful growl vibrates in his chest, and I press my hand against his ribs to feel it better.

Suddenly, the inside of my eyelids flash white. A deafening explosion follows a split-second later.

Angelo violently tugs me away from the edge of the cliff and steps in front of me.

"What the...?"

But my question trails off as my eyes land on the port below. Angry orange flames lick the harbor, hazy smoke tendrils rising up and melting into the black sky. My heart thumps hard in my throat, the realization of what we're looking at settling on my skin. "Someone blew up the port," I whisper.

Angelo's still and silent, a stark contrast to the screams floating up from the town below. Tension locks his shoulders, and when he slowly turns around, the look on his face steals my breath away.

It's dark and dangerous. *Vicious.* The reflection of the flames licks the walls of his irises.

"You ready to go to war, baby?"

A cocktail of lust and adrenaline trickles down my spine.

"Ready as I'll ever be."

ALSO BY
Somme

SINNERS ANONYMOUS
Sinners Condemned
Sinners Atone

EAST COAST DEVILS
The Devil's Keepsake
The Devil's Deal
The Devil's Obsession

CONNECT WITH *Me*

Sign up to my newsletter for teasers & excerpts for upcoming books.
Join "Somme Sketcher's Sin Room" on Facebook to chat all things Somme. Alternatively, like my author page on Facebook!
You'll also find me on Instagram and TikTok at @authorsommesketcher
Or if you'd prefer to slide into my inbox, you can reach me at: somme@authorsommesketcher.com

Printed in Great Britain
by Amazon